THE BOOK OF ADVENTURES

GREGORY BOUTHIETTE

CB555-02: The Book of Adventures
ISBN: 978-0-9962768-3-2

Carrion Blue 555
Chicopee MA / Lambertville NJ
carrionblue555@gmail.com

Cover art copyright ©2015 by Matthew Revert.
www.matthewrevert.com
Carrion Blue 555 logo designed by Brent Carpentier.

"This is Heaven alright, but there's a man outside with a gun."
—Cardiacs, "What Paradise is Like"

TABLE OF CONTENTS

THE HERO'S JOURNEY
An Introduction by Joseph Bouthiette Jr.

When Josh Myers and I decided to get into the publishing gig on our own, we immediately had two projects we knew we wanted to start with:

1) the massive anthology project that would eventually become *555 Vol. 1*
2) the book currently in your hands

I'd like to immediately dispel what I feel has become an elephant in the room while talking about this project: Gregory Bouthiette, the author of this book, is a young man with autism. In the vast majority of circumstances, this is not something that needs to be said. But the fact that it occurs to me to do so probably means I should. All together now, with feeling!
Gregory Bouthiette has autism.
My generalized views of how people will react to this are as follows: some subset of people will automatically dismiss this work for that fact alone. I don't know anyone like this, and I don't care to, but they probably exist, and if you just so happen to be reading this book and have a problem with the author's mental state, there are millions of other books you can read to fill the voids where your heart and brain should be.
The vast majority of cases actually play out quite differently: tell a friend or coworker or family member or your mailman that your autistic younger brother is publishing a book, and the typical response is, "Oh wow, that's so great! Good for him! Who would've thought?" In my particular case, tell them

that you, his brother, are also his publisher, his editor, his co-conspirator, and it goes even further: "Man, that's *so nice* of you. Good for you for working with him like that."

It's this particular reaction that becomes tiring because of how *fake* it seems. Greg has written a *damn fine* book, and it deserves to be judged by those merits alone. I fully accept that it gives an excellent peek into the inner workings of the autistic creative mind, but only because Greg and I have put countless hours into making this into a product we both feel truly represents Greg's image. And really, this is all any author wants.

It's a weird, occasionally awkward dichotomy: we could simply let the work speak for itself. No one needs to have any idea who Gregory Bouthiette is to find something to like in *The Book of Adventures*. But I do believe a work of art can only be strengthened with context, so we say that this book was written through an autistic lens. At the same time, we don't want to belittle the accomplishment: this isn't just a stream of words and symbols without purpose. It's a book Josh and I felt should have been published. It was never an embarrassment, and it wasn't for pity. I hope you, the reader, can gain the full range of entertainment I have from this collection of stories.

To further expand on the aforementioned *context* of the work, I'll be continuing with some various notes on the text that I feel will enhance the reader's experience. This will be full of spoilers, so if you wish to go into the text spoiler-free, I suggest quitting this intro now. You can come back and read this part later. Otherwise, here are some bits and pieces I hope you keep in the back of your mind as you're reading the collection proper.

In the course of full disclosure, these three stories use the *Sly Cooper* video game series as a foundation and frame. Anyone familiar with the games will see the same plotlines, some of the same names, and most of the same dialogue. But Greg manages to transform these three games into completely different entities.

On the surface, name changes are simple changes that are easy to point out: instead of the titular Sly Cooper, Gregory himself has taken the lead for these adventures. And instead of Sly's inseparable best friends, Bentley and Murray, we see names that Greg has used for imaginary friends for years: Sneaky Hermit and Anti Gregory. Sly's love interest Carmelita has kept her name, but instead of being an antagonistic force, Gregory the author has completely rewritten her as an additional friend to Gregory the character. This creates interesting moments where Carmelita continues performing antagonistic actions while justifying them as either "friendly" or "fun" or simply not providing reasoning at all. For example, there are numerous times Carmelita explains she must "chase" Gregory, which harkens to the game sequences where Carmelita is chasing Sly Cooper while shooting huge balls of electricity at him from a comically over-sized gun. In this world, people are morally aligned however Gregory wishes them to be, rather than how they were in the source material. Video game Carmelita is essentially a good-guy cop character, but since the main cast are a band of master thieves, they obviously clash quite often. Greg has declared that he and his crew are a band of *heroes* instead of thieves, which should liken Inspector Carmelita to their side. And when logic fails, Greg simply says *screw it, Carmelita is a friend*. This is fiction, after all.

A major thing worth noting, for those who haven't read ahead into the main text, is these stories are written strictly in dialogue. All semblance of plot and action must be obtained from characters communicating with each other. Unlike most scripts, there aren't any notes on visual cues for character action:

GREGORY
Roger is holding up in his temple, got any idea how to get
him out of hiding?

SNEAKY HERMIT
I heard from the radio that there is a jet inside this truck
that I can use to break that dam.

GREGORY
Awesome. Now be careful, Sneaky Hermit: Roger may have
other jets up there. They may stop you from breaking that
dam.

ROGER
[on intercom]
All jets, go stop that other jet from breaking the dam.

SNEAKY HERMIT
I'd better be careful, Roger just called those jets in to stop
me.

GREGORY
Nice shooting, Sneaky Hermit. That dam is out of the
picture.

In this particular example, numerous notes can
be made: everything is dialogue, but communication
isn't always face-to-face. Much of it is over walkie-
talkies or some form of long-distance transmissions.
This is true for all three stories. So Gregory and Sneaky
Hermit could very well be on opposite sides of a city in
this instant, or in any other instance in the book.

The use of the phrase *[on intercom]* is an
editorial touch I added to not completely bewilder the
reader, but comes up sparingly. Expect all other
dialogue to be either face-to-face or personally linked
via technology.

The last line is from Gregory: "Nice shooting,
Sneaky Hermit. That dam is out of the picture." This is
all the evidence we get that Sneaky Hermit has actually
infiltrated the jet he just spoke of, managed to get

airborne, avoided the enemy jets, and actually succeeded in his mission to destroy the dam. This is a side effect of using video game dialogue: so much is seen on screen that simply what the characters say often isn't deliberate enough to create a clear concept of the action occurring. Some imagination is required.

At the same time, ellipses "..." are common, and signify breaks in speech of various lengths. They may simply represent a trailing thought, or pauses during which "off screen" action is occurring, before and after which the same character is speaking:

SNEAKY HERMIT

So far, so good. I bet if you stay still inside the barrel, the guard won't be able to see you, even if he shines his flashlight on you... Gregory, do you see that machine wheel? If I think about this... I think you might be able to make the wheel move, and you might go up on that platform up there. And you will make your way to that door up there.

There is clearly a jump in action between Sneaky Hermit's advice to stay still inside the barrel, and his scheming with the machine wheel. This sort of disconnect is most common in the first story: dialogue and character interaction improved as the video game series went on, and thus, in the stories as well.

A final note on the connection between the games and the text: the *Sly Cooper* series is a family-friendly franchise. Its cartoon antics and lack of truly violent content speak to this end. However, Greg transposing the story into his own work yielded some cruel and creepy things sneaking in. I won't take the time to list any here, since I personally perceive this entire book to be full of unremitting nightmares, but it is worth noting that the source material from which these stories are based is not rife with crippling amounts of horror... unless you play the game series through Gregory's eyes, where his fear of snakes and spiders hinders his ability to get through levels, and is even present where applicable here (along with his fear of heights).

From here, I'll let the stories speak for themselves.

We humbly thank you for your time.

Joseph Bouthiette Jr.
Spring 2015

I want to thank mom and dad for being supportive of me and my work. I also want to thank Joejoe and Josh for helping me make my book a reality.

This book is dedicated to me, Gregory Bouthiette, for showing myself I can do it.

GREGORY BOUTHIETTE AND THE BOOK OF ADVENTURES

SNEAKY HERMIT
Gregory, come in. Gregory, do you read me?

GREGORY
Yeah, I read you loud and clear, Sneaky Hermit.

SNEAKY HERMIT
Okay, good. Are you in position?

GREGORY
Yes, I am, Sneaky Hermit. And don't worry, you are safe in the car. I'm the hero here, Sneaky Hermit. I just have to borrow Carmelita's book that's all about me.

SNEAKY HERMIT
Okay, Gregory, you can count on me to be your eyes and ears. That wall is kind of too tough to scale. There is another way to go through: try that air vent.

GREGORY
Alright, Sneaky Hermit. I'm going in.

ANTI GREGORY
And don't forget that you got me at the wheel, Gregory. All you have to do is borrow that book of Carmelita's, then get back to the team car. We'll do the rest.

GREGORY
Just keep the car running, Anti Gregory. I'll be down in no time... Hey, Sneaky Hermit, I think I'm seeing things. It must be new or something. Can you see those lights?

SNEAKY HERMIT
I do, Gregory. And I think I have seen those lights before: it must mean you have light powers now. All you gotta do is to go near them and walk on the wall, and you will do a new move.

GREGORY BOUTHIETTE

GREGORY
Go near the wall and walk on the lights. I'm on it.

SNEAKY HERMIT
Be very careful here, Gregory. If you go through those lasers, you will set off the alarm. And don't worry, you will only get burned if you touch them... Nice job! You are in. Carmelita's office will be behind the red door... Way to go, Gregory! I know that this is your first vault to open, but I think you can do it. I've already found the code to the vault: try putting in 9, 3, 6.

ANTI GREGORY
Nice job, you got it! If you come down through the window and head through the parking lot, we will be waiting in the team car.

CARMELITA
Freeze, Bouthiette. I'm just playing around, Gregory. I know it's you, buddy.

GREGORY
Hey, Carmelita. It's been two days since I've seen you.

CARMELITA
I want to help you out everywhere you go with your friends.

GREGORY
You know I really like when you come along on adventures with me and my friends.

CARMELITA
You know I will be with you on the journey, Gregory. I will not let anything happen to you, buddy.

GREGORY
Are you ready to go to the team car now, Carmelita?

CARMELITA
You know I am ready to go with you, Gregory.

GREGORY
Hey, let's get a move on now, Carmelita. I don't want to
keep my friends waiting.

CARMELITA
I'll be right behind you, Gregory.

SNEAKY HERMIT
That was nice work back there at the police station,
Gregory. Just come see me if you want to talk to me
about something, or if you want, you can see your
movies. I got all of them right here on my computer.

GREGORY
Okay, Sneaky Hermit.

***

GREGORY BOUTHIETTE

ANTI GREGORY
Okay, Gregory, who is the first person that we are
going to take down?

GREGORY
Well, I'm glad you asked, Anti Gregory. The first
person that we are going to take down is none other
than Rob the Frog.

ANTI GREGORY
Rob the Frog?

GREGORY
You heard me, Anti Gregory. Rob is the first person to
go down for what he did to my family.

SNEAKY HERMIT
I'm with you, Gregory. I want you to take him down so
bad for us.

CARMELITA
Gregory, I'm going to arrest Rob when you are done
with him.

GREGORY
You got it, Carmelita.

ANTI GREGORY
I really want you to beat him so bad, Gregory.

GREGORY
Don't worry, Anti Gregory. I will beat Rob as fast as I
can, buddy.

SNEAKY HERMIT
Anti Gregory, there's the stop.

ANTI GREGORY
I see it, Sneaky Hermit.

SNEAKY HERMIT
Good luck out there, Gregory.

GREGORY
Thanks, Sneaky Hermit. I will be waiting for you to call me.

SNEAKY HERMIT
Hey, Gregory, I just spotted something that is going to stop us from doing your mission: see that bad-looking gate? It blocks the only road leading into Rob's hideout.

GREGORY
No problem, I'll just use my climb move.

SNEAKY HERMIT
Okay, but remember, Gregory, you can only climb on certain objects. Like pipes and ropes...

GREGORY
Yeah, sure, and like that ladder there.

SNEAKY HERMIT
That is right, but do not forget, Gregory, you have to get close...

GREGORY
I just need to get up close to the ladder, and just climb onto it. Yeah yeah yeah, relax, Sneaky Hermit. I live for this stuff.

SNEAKY HERMIT
I know, Gregory. And that's what I like to hear... Hold on, Gregory, see those searchlights? One step on them and you will get burned.

GREGORY
Thanks for the help, Sneaky Hermit. Now let's go.

SNEAKY HERMIT
I'm just trying to keep you alive, buddy. And there is
good news for you: I just put these cameras everywhere
in Rob's hideout. Just get close to one and I will check
on your position.

GREGORY
Nice, Sneaky Hermit.

SNEAKY HERMIT
There's Rob's hideout, Gregory. And it looks like his
hideout is a big blimp. That is where you will be able to
find Rob.

GREGORY
You know, Sneaky Hermit, that blimp looks more like a
machine than a hideout.

SNEAKY HERMIT
Hey, you're right, Gregory: that is a storm machine! It's
the reason why it never stops raining around here.

GREGORY
And that explains all the wrecked ships.

SNEAKY HERMIT
But why would Rob want bad weather in his own
hideout?

GREGORY
Beats me. Rain or shine, I'm gonna get my book back.
And if Rob gets in my way, it's on.

SNEAKY HERMIT
Nice job so far, Gregory. To get over the next gate, you
need to grab onto this hook.

GREGORY
Got it, just jump up and grab onto the hook... That

blimp is a good location to hide. If Rob is really as smart as I was thinking, that's where I'll find him.

SNEAKY HERMIT
Wonderful idea, but your plan is a little bad.

GREGORY
Why is it a bad plan, Sneaky Hermit?

SNEAKY HERMIT
Because it's going to be hard to get near him. To get inside Rob's blimp, you will have to sneak inside through that power tube. To do that without getting hurt, you have to break that power box. And to do that, you still need two more of Rob's keys, which are locked away safe.

GREGORY
Okay, so when are you going to give me some more details?

SNEAKY HERMIT
I will give some more details soon, but I had to warn you, Gregory. I marked where you need to hide from the guards. Just get there when you need to hide.

GREGORY
Thanks for the help, Sneaky Hermit.

SNEAKY HERMIT
No problem, Gregory. I just want to help you out... You better close those fire doors. Just jump up and close them with your hands. That will make them stay closed forever... Oh my goodness! You are in the engine room! If I'm right about this, you can go all the way down through here, then you will be able to find Rob's key, and break his machine while you are at it... Remember, Gregory, you have to go near the wall and walk up on the lights to perform a new hero move.

GREGORY
Those rats got killed.

SNEAKY HERMIT
Rob has put a lot of traps around this place.

GREGORY
I think I might like it.

SNEAKY HERMIT
Wait a minute, Gregory! If you step on that, forget
about becoming a hero: you will become a dart board.

GREGORY
Hey, wait a second, Sneaky Hermit. What if I jump in
this barrel for a little help?

SNEAKY HERMIT
I don't know, Gregory, it looks really bad to use it. And
I think it won't work for you.

GREGORY
Well, we have to see, Sneaky Hermit.

SNEAKY HERMIT
So far, so good. I bet if you stay still inside the barrel,
the guard won't be able to see you, even if he shines his
flashlight on you... Gregory, do you see that machine
wheel? If I think about this... I think you might be able
to make the wheel move, and you might go up on that
platform up there. And you will make your way to that
door up there.

GREGORY
Okay, Sneaky Hermit, I will give it a try right now.

SNEAKY HERMIT
I think you can do it right now, Gregory. Just try your
best... You better close those doors again, Gregory...

Hey, I can see another wheel over there. But I can see some hooks above that wheel. If you can run on that wheel, you might be able to jump on those hooks as well.

GREGORY

Okay, Sneaky Hermit. I'll give it a try right now.

SNEAKY HERMIT

Jackpot, Gregory! Look at all this stuff! It must be worth millions. And you know what that means: tighter security. You are going to have to be extra sneaky to get the key here... Good job, Gregory! I can't believe that you really broke that power box.

GREGORY

I've never been good at math like you, Sneaky Hermit.

SNEAKY HERMIT

Well, here's a real test for you, Gregory: I have found a way up to Rob's hideout, but I do have some bad news as well. I think it might make you scared.

GREGORY

You're not going to tell me that I have to shoot myself out of that cannon.

SNEAKY HERMIT

I'm afraid that's the only way, Gregory.

GREGORY

Now you are talking, buddy.

SNEAKY HERMIT

You are really scaring me, buddy... Anyway, to get inside that thing, you are going to have to steal all seven of Rob's keys.

GREGORY BOUTHIETTE

GREGORY
Okay, so what are we waiting for? Let's go find those keys.

SNEAKY HERMIT
And you might need to do everything on your own as well, Gregory.

GREGORY
Yeah yeah, I know. I will do whatever it takes to get shot out of that cannon and steal back those pages from my book.

ROB
[on intercom]
Ahoy, you guards. I just got word that there is a 17 year old boy that is trying to get the keys that I hid down there. It seems that he thinks he is a hero. I want all of you to keep those keys safe down there, so that he doesn't get his hands on them. If any of you do let him get his hands on any keys, then I will fire all of you forever.

SNEAKY HERMIT
Okay, Gregory, you need to do some shooting underwater, and a lot of moving around as well! You have to shoot a lot of treasure chests, and you cannot let any crabs get any of the treasures. You need to get thirty treasures before a crab takes any to its tube... Good job, Gregory, you did it! You got all the treasures. Now grab that key and get out of there.

ROB
How wonderful! We have a guest. The only thing is... I hate having guests!

GREGORY
Listen, Rob: wipe out some of my family and steal what's mine, you better be happy to have a guest.

ROB

Oh, I am so sorry, but you do know that I will never be happy about having guests. Once I'm done talking to you, I will take you right down.

GREGORY

Bring it on, Rob.

ROB

Blast it, you beat me! Well, gloat all you want, Gregory Bouthiette. You are no match for Matthew, my best friend. He is too tough for anyone who gets in his way. He is hiding in Mesa, and it's so guarded that a snake couldn't get in without setting off the alarms.

GREGORY

Psst, Carmelita, I'm on my way down now.

CARMELITA

Okay, Gregory, I'm on my way there right now. Just stay where you are! I will go to you.

GREGORY

Okay, Carmelita. I'll just wait for you right here.

SNEAKY HERMIT

Good job beating Rob, Gregory.

GREGORY

Thanks, Sneaky Hermit. I did my best beating him.

CARMELITA

Gregory, is that you over there?

GREGORY

It is me, Carmelita. I'm fine.

CARMELITA

Come on, Gregory. Let's get back to the team car.

GREGORY
You got it, Carmelita.

ANTI GREGORY
Gregory! You are back safe and sound.

GREGORY
Okay, Anti Gregory, thanks for the hug. Now let's go
already.

SNEAKY HERMIT
Anti Gregory, start driving, buddy.

ANTI GREGORY
You got it, Sneaky Hermit.

***

CARMELITA
Okay, Gregory, who is the second guy now?

GREGORY
I'm glad that you asked, Carmelita. The second guy is
Matthew.

ANTI GREGORY
Wait a minute, Gregory, Matthew is the second guy?

GREGORY
Yes, Anti Gregory.

SNEAKY HERMIT
Okay, so where is Matthew hiding, Gregory?

GREGORY
Matthew is hiding in Mesa City, Sneaky Hermit, and I
think that town is in the state we live in.

SNEAKY HERMIT
It is, Gregory. Mesa is in the state that we live in.

CARMELITA
And how are we going to find him, Sneaky Hermit?
Matthew might be hiding anywhere in Mesa.

SNEAKY HERMIT
We just have to look hard, Carmelita. And we can't go
with Gregory at all, because Gregory is the only one
who can do this.

GREGORY
Yeah, Sneaky Hermit is right, you guys. I will find
Matthew in Mesa.

ANTI GREGORY
And speaking of Mesa, we are already here, guys.

SNEAKY HERMIT
Good luck out there, Gregory.

GREGORY
Thanks, Sneaky Hermit. I will be waiting for you to call
me again.

ANTI GREGORY
I'm hoping he'll be okay out there.

CARMELITA
He will be okay out there, Anti Gregory. Just look at
this magazine for diapers, buddy.

ANTI GREGORY
Thank you, Carmelita.

CARMELITA
No problem, Anti Gregory.

SNEAKY HERMIT
Hey, Gregory, I thought you said that Mesa is going to
be loud and busy. This is more like a ghost town.

GREGORY
Something happened. Where is everyone?

SNEAKY HERMIT
I don't know, but it's starting to scare me. What do you
say we take off...

GREGORY
And miss all the fun? Besides, I want to try out that
new move that I got from the first page of my book.
That page we got from Rob.

SNEAKY HERMIT
You mean your new jumping move?

GREGORY
Yeah. Do me a favor and read it to me again.

SNEAKY HERMIT
Okay, do you see those little dots? You can jump and
land on them as well.

GREGORY
Okay, so I just need to jump and land on those blue
dots.

SNEAKY HERMIT
That's the plan, Gregory.

GREGORY
What's with those flashing lights?

SNEAKY HERMIT
They said that those lights are some kind of secret. If
you step on them they will go off, and you are a goner.

GREGORY
Nice one, Sneaky Hermit.

SNEAKY HERMIT
They are safe to walk on while flashing, but that also
means that they are about to switch from spot to spot...
This Matthew is not really shy. Okay, so we know that
he is here somewhere, but how are we going to find
him? Mesa is a big place.

GREGORY
Since he looks like a bulldog, it seems that he may
choose to live in that giant fire hydrant.

SNEAKY HERMIT
That is a good idea, Gregory. Now you just need to find
a way to break into the building's base.

GREGORY
Oh, don't worry, Sneaky Hermit; I'm sure I'll think of
something.

SNEAKY HERMIT
Anti Gregory is ready to go, and all set to get that key
up there.

GREGORY
Okay, Sneaky Hermit, so what am I going to do here?

SNEAKY HERMIT
The only thing that you need to do is to help him, and
save him all the time.

GREGORY
Okay, Sneaky Hermit. I'll give it a try right now.

ANTI GREGORY
Time to move, Gregory... I'm almost there... I'm really
close... I did it! Thanks for the help, Gregory.

GREGORY
No problem, Anti Gregory. I'll see you back at the team
car.

SNEAKY HERMIT
Nice job getting in, but look out for those guards:
Matthew's got those machine gun-toting dogs hunting
like a pack... Gregory, this wheel is going too fast for
going in the other way, I think you have to go to the left
to get the key.

GREGORY
Anti Gregory, what's going on down there?

ANTI GREGORY
Well, I drove to this hot dog stand for a quick snack,
and the next thing I know I'm being challenged to a

race by these gangster dogs.

GREGORY
Is there a key for the winner?

ANTI GREGORY
Yeah, there is key for the winner, but I have to do this race three times around the track to get the key.

GREGORY
It's all you, buddy. Just keep on driving and you will be able to get the key. Now go get them!

ANTI GREGORY
I'm on it, Gregory.

GREGORY
Way to go, Anti Gregory... Would you look at that big head!

SNEAKY HERMIT
I am, and I find it really nice.

GREGORY
And what do you mean by that, Sneaky Hermit?

SNEAKY ISLAND
I mean that there is an elevator to Matthew's penthouse, and it is in that giant head.

GREGORY
Okay, so how do I get in?

SNEAKY HERMIT
Behind this locked wall, there's a lever that is for the elevator. But you need all seven of Matthew's keys to open it up.

GREGORY
I'm on it.

SNEAKY HERMIT
Man, these rooftops are dirty. Well, they are the only way to get to the key since my head tells me that it's in a safe place, somewhere near Matthew's penthouse.

CARMELITA
Well well, look who it is. Gregory Bouthiette, I'm happy to see you again, buddy.

GREGORY
Hey, Carmelita, it's good to see you out of the team car, I see.

CARMELITA
Sneaky Hermit told me to help you out in this place to get to the key, and I will put Matthew in jail.

GREGORY
Yeah, I do know that you will put him in jail... When I'm done beating the crap out of him.

CARMELITA
But just to warn you, Gregory, I will be coming after you a lot as well.

GREGORY
And that's okay with me, Carmelita. I really like it when you come after me, and you know that I will run away from you as well.

CARMELITA
Yes, I know that, Gregory. And I really like it when you do run away from me a lot... I'm gonna see you later, Gregory. Just stay safe for me.

GREGORY
Okay, Carmelita. I'll see you back at the team car.

SNEAKY HERMIT
Forget it, you're never going to break that glass with
your hands, Gregory. But I think I see a wrecking ball
up there that you can use... Hey, Gregory, do you see
those light beams? I think you can climb on them as
well. Go ahead and give it a try.

MATTHEW
I got a feeling that there's a hero who's running around
everywhere, getting all of my keys... You are dead, kid!
If I get my hands on you, I will kick your butt a lot of
times, you hear me? You're lunch meat, kid. What, my
boys have been yapping about some little hero kid who
is running around, cracking skulls, and this is it? You
are the monkey wrench in my operation? It's just some
kind of boy with glasses! Hey, wait a second, I've seen
those glasses before...

GREGORY
Well, maybe you have seen me and my dad knock your
block off with me wearing these glasses, Matthew.

MATTHEW
Your father? Wow! You are a Bouthiette? You know,
that storybook that you had has got a lot of nice
pictures, but way too many big words.

GREGORY
Well, maybe you won't mind just handing them over to
me, Matthew.

MATTHEW
What, are you kidding? You break into my place, steal
my stuff, trash the guards... I feel very mad when I see
you. Let's rock... My guns are not working anymore!
Good thing I got some spares upstairs... This is

impossible... A little hero like you, beating a big strong guy like me? It's not right. You want all of that dumb picture book? You gotta go cross paths with Beckey. And believe me, Bouthiette, you won't want to be you.

CARMELITA
Gregory, where are you?

GREGORY
Carmelita, I'm up here.

CARMELITA
How did you got up there, Gregory?

GREGORY
I used that thing over there.

CARMELITA
Don't worry, Gregory. I'll get you down, just stay there. I'm on my way up.

GREGORY
I don't really have a choice, Carmelita. I'm scared of heights.

CARMELITA
I know, Gregory, and I will get you down, buddy.

GREGORY
Thanks for the help, Carmelita.

CARMELITA
No problem, Gregory. I'm happy to help you out a lot, buddy.

GREGORY
Let's head back to the team car.

CARMELITA
Okay, Gregory, let's get a move on right now.

ANTI GREGORY
Gregory, you're back!

GREGORY
Okay, Anti Gregory, you can stop hugging me now.

ANTI GREGORY
Oh, I'm sorry, Gregory. I'm just happy to see that you
are still alive.

SNEAKY HERMIT
Okay, Anti Gregory, I think you should look at more
diapers in your magazines.

ANTI GREGORY
Okay, Sneaky Hermit. I'll look at diapers.

SNEAKY HERMIT
Okay, Gregory, who is the third person now, and where
is he hidden?

GREGORY
Well, the other person is Beckey, and she is in the
swamp.

CARMELITA
The swamp? But are there spiders there, Gregory.

GREGORY
Yes, Carmelita, there are spiders there, and I don't like
spiders. If I step close to a spider, I will run away from
it.

SNEAKY HERMIT
Don't worry, Gregory: I'm gonna be with you the whole
time in the swamp, and I will never leave you out there

alone.

GREGORY
Thanks, Sneaky Hermit. I knew I could count on you, buddy.

SNEAKY HERMIT
Hey, Anti Gregory, it's time to go now.

ANTI GREGORY
You got it, Sneaky Hermit. Where do we need to go now?

SNEAKY HERMIT
We have to go to Beckey's place. And that is the swamp.

ANTI GREGORY
The swamp? Oh man, why do we need to go to the swamp, Sneaky Hermit? I don't like the swamp. That place scares me a lot.

GREGORY
Don't worry, Anti Gregory, I'm scared of spiders. But Sneaky Hermit will be with us the whole time in the swamp.

SNEAKY HERMIT
That's right, Anti Gregory. I'm gonna be with Gregory the whole time in the swamp.

ANTI GREGORY
Okay, Sneaky Hermit, but what are Carmelita and I going to do while you two are out there doing stuffs?

CARMELITA
Hey, don't worry, Anti Gregory: you and me are going to play some games that I brought from Gregory's house.

ANTI GREGORY
Okay, Carmelita, we can play while those two are out doing stuffs in the swamp.

SNEAKY HERMIT
Okay, Anti Gregory. Stop talking and keep on driving.

ANTI GREGORY
Okay, Sneaky Hermit, I'll keep on driving... Hey, look at that. We are already here.

***

GREGORY BOUTHIETTE

SNEAKY HERMIT
Gregory, let's go, buddy.

GREGORY
Okay, Sneaky Hermit. I'm on my way.

SNEAKY HERMIT
Okay, Gregory. This swamp is an okay little place.

GREGORY
I don't really like this place at all, Sneaky Hermit.

SNEAKY HERMIT
Don't worry, Gregory. I'm gonna be with you the whole
time in this place, and this is perfect for you to do your
moves from the pages you got from Matthew.

GREGORY
Okay, Sneaky Hermit, I'll give it a try. But how are you
going to get on those branches?

SNEAKY HERMIT
Don't worry, Gregory, I'll find a way to walk on them.
There's always a way for me to walk on stuffs as well.

GREGORY
Wow, Sneaky Hermit. I like it when you get so happy a
lot.

SNEAKY HERMIT
That's my way, Gregory. Now let's get a move on.

GREGORY
Okay, Sneaky Hermit.

SNEAKY HERMIT
There's Beckey's gate, Gregory. It looks like it will not
open until we break that bad mojo over there.

GREGORY
Okay, Sneaky Hermit. Let's go and break that bad mojo.

SNEAKY HERMIT
Hold on a minute, Gregory: there are some flashlight guards down there that are walking around. If we go down there, we will get caught.

GREGORY
Okay, so let's just go down there and try to sneak around those guards.

SNEAKY HERMIT
That might work, Gregory, let's give it a try... There's Beckey's hideout. I think we have to get more keys to get to the top of that dragon head up there.

GREGORY
Okay, Sneaky Hermit. So where should we go first?

SNEAKY HERMIT
I think we should go where the beast lives.

GREGORY
Uh, Sneaky Hermit, did you just say, "the beast"?

SNEAKY HERMIT
Yes, I did say the beast, Gregory. Why?

GREGORY
Uh... Nothing. Let's just get a move on now.

SNEAKY HERMIT
Okay, Gregory, let's go... This is one big gate right in front of us. I think Beckey is trying to keep something out.

GREGORY
Or maybe she's trying to keep something in.

SNEAKY HERMIT
I don't like the look of this, Gregory. Whoa! Did you just see those leaves move in the water? There's something big down there. We gotta move fast right now, Gregory.

GREGORY
Okay, Sneaky Hermit. I'm moving as fast as I can.

SNEAKY HERMIT
Well, you better move faster than that, Gregory.

GREGORY
I'm trying to move faster, buddy, but I can try to move really fast.

SNEAKY HERMIT
Just give it a try, Gregory... Gregory, we have got to be on our toes in this place. I think this place is really scary here... Hey, Gregory, you did it! I think these gravestones are kind of a thing where ghosts come out. If we can break all of these gravestones, then the ghosts will stop coming... Gregory, the only way to open that gate over there is for us to light up all twenty-five tiki torches with the flamethrower down there. Oh, and one more thing: we need fuel for the flamethrower, but the only way to get fuel is from those piranhas that we see swimming down there. And we need to hurry, Gregory: we've only got two minutes to light up the tiki torches... It looks like a big voodoo egg-beater to stir up that mess there.

GREGORY
If we can unlock that egg-beater, you will be able to throw me up to Beckey's place, Sneaky Hermit.

SNEAKY HERMIT
Okay, Gregory. It looks like we got a plan, buddy. We need to move into the shadows made by the egg-beater so that the guards don't see us. Oh man, Gregory, that big green water under us has some bad-looking ooze. I'm telling you, Gregory, we might be in big trouble.

BECKEY
[on intercom]
Hey there, Gregory and Sneaky Hermit. Yeah, that's right, I know that you guys are here. I do know what's going on. I will take you guys down one by one if I have to. But just to remind you guys, I will be watching you...

SNEAKY HERMIT
Hey, Gregory, there's a lot of secrets here. We had better be careful so that we don't get spotted... This vehicle is really helpful for us to fire at everything in this place. And remember, Gregory, we need to shoot in one place at all times... I think we need to be careful here, Gregory: that thing is some kind of power for the guards in this place. I think it is time for us to work together in this spot... With all that hay down there, it is really cool and all, but we don't have time to spend here. That ghost up there called me when we were coming in, and we made a deal. If we need to get that key, we need to whack all fifty chickens here. I'm guessing the ghost wants to make some kind of gumbo, but he won't come down because of the bomb roosters. Do you think we can do it as a team?

GREGORY
Okay, Sneaky Hermit. Let's do this.

SNEAKY HERMIT
Okay, Gregory. Get up into my hands and I'll throw you on that thing.

GREGORY
Okay, Sneaky Hermit, thanks for the help in this
swamp. I think you should head back to the team car
now.

SNEAKY HERMIT
Okay, Gregory, I'll see you back at the team car.

BECKEY
Mmm, I could feel that Bouthiette coming. Must be the
bad juju.

GREGORY
Yeah, well, you give me the creeps, too, lady. Cooking
up an army of ghosts is just not a good thing to do with
your time.

BECKEY
Oh, Gregory, I can see your mouth moving, but all I
hear is "blah blah blah." Well, if jaws need to flap, then
let them flap. See you in the next world, Gregory
Bouthiette.

GREGORY
Come back here, you can't run away forever.

BECKEY
Quite true, quite true. Why don't I have my servant
Chuckles bring you over here?

GREGORY
Alright, what's the catch?

BECKEY
Oh, not much... Just a little game I like to play with all
of my annoying guests. I want to see how well you pay
attention.

GREGORY
What do you mean?

BECKEY
Well, I'll release my Mighty Mojo Magic upon you: if you repeat what I do, you will dodge it just fine; if not, you will get zapped.

GREGORY
A little voodoo Simon Says, huh? Sounds easy enough.

BECKEY
You really got some moves, Bouthiette, but it will never help you enough to go after The Panda. He's tough with a capital T. You go poking around his stronghold in China, you will get poked back.

GREGORY
Yeah, well, if he's anything like the rest of you guys, I think I can handle him.

CARMELITA
Hey, Gregory, are you up there?

GREGORY
Yes, I am, Carmelita. But I don't think I can get back down.

CARMELITA
Don't worry, Gregory. I'll be up there soon.

GREGORY
Okay, Carmelita, just get up here fast, please.

CARMELITA
Okay, Gregory, I'll be up there. Just don't move.

GREGORY
Oh, don't worry, Carmelita. I won't be moving from

this spot.

CARMELITA
Okay, Gregory, I'm here. Let's get out of here.

GREGORY
Okay, Carmelita. I'm right behind you.

CARMELITA
Okay, Gregory, just stay behind me the whole time.

GREGORY
Oh, don't worry, Carmelita. I will stay behind you the
whole time.

***

ANTI GREGORY
Hey, Gregory, you're back!

GREGORY
Whoa, hey, calm down, Anti Gregory. I know that you are happy to see me, but I need to talk to Sneaky Hermit.

ANTI GREGORY
Okay, Gregory. I'm sorry about that, buddy.

GREGORY
It's okay, Anti Gregory. Now just get ready to drive, buddy.

ANTI GREGORY
Okay, Gregory, I'll do that.

SNEAKY HERMIT
Okay, Gregory, who is the next person to go after now?

GREGORY
Okay, Sneaky Hermit, the next guy to go find now is The Panda. And he is hiding in China.

CARMELITA
So we need to go to China now, and The Panda is the next guy. Great, he's going to be fun to mess with.

GREGORY
Yeah, it is going to be fun messing with The Panda, Carmelita, but we need to do it. And I only need two more pages back for my book.

SNEAKY HERMIT
Okay, enough messing around, Gregory. We need to get to China right now. Anti Gregory, start driving now, buddy.

ANTI GREGORY
You got it, Sneaky Hermit. Let's head to China right now. You better hold on, you guys, because this going to be fast.

SNEAKY HERMIT
Okay, Anti Gregory, we will hold on tight, buddy.

CARMELITA
How is Anti Gregory going to get us to China, Sneaky Hermit? He doesn't know how to get there, and we have never been to China before.

SNEAKY HERMIT
Don't worry, Carmelita. Anti Gregory will find a way to get to China. And he will get us there fast, too.

CARMELITA
Well, I hope that you are right about that, Sneaky Hermit.

GREGORY
Hey, Carmelita, I think you might be shooting at me again like at Matthew's place. How cool would that be?

CARMELITA
I think it will be cool, Gregory, but we are not at China yet.

ANTI GREGORY
Hey, guys, speaking of China... We are already here.

SNEAKY HERMIT
Gregory, I think you are going alone into this place.

GREGORY
You are right, Sneaky Hermit. I will be going on my own from here in this place.

ANTI GREGORY
Good luck out there, Gregory. I'll be waiting for you to come back, buddy.

GREGORY
Uh, okay, Anti Gregory. I will be coming back safe and sound, my friend.

SNEAKY HERMIT
Hey, Anti Gregory, maybe you should look at diapers again.

ANTI GREGORY
Okay, Sneaky Hermit, I'll look at diapers again.

SNEAKY HERMIT
Would you look at that, a firework show! Oh my goodness, that's not good: that poor town just got buried in that big pile of snow from that firework!

GREGORY
I think that firework came from that statue; I need to get to it before another rocket hits another town.

SNEAKY HERMIT
That gate there is kind of locked, Gregory.

GREGORY
Okay, Sneaky Hermit, there has to be a key somewhere around here.

SNEAKY HERMIT
Yep, you are right, Gregory: there is a key, but it's over there. And there are guards down there as well. Just sneak around and you will get the key.

GREGORY
Okay, Sneaky Hermit. One key coming up.

SNEAKY HERMIT
Nice job breaking into The Panda's hideout. I think there is a way to get on top to that giant statue, but it's kind of locked down tight.

GREGORY
No problem, there seems to be a fair amount of firework powder here. I just need to find more keys to get at it.

SNEAKY HERMIT
Anti Gregory is ready to make a run for it to that key.

GREGORY
Okay, Sneaky Hermit. I'll keep him safe while doing some firing with this gun here.

SNEAKY HERMIT
That's good, Gregory. I did tell you how to do this in Matthew's place. I'm sorry I didn't know.

GREGORY
It's okay, Sneaky Hermit, you just didn't know.

ANTI GREGORY
I'm going in, Gregory... I'm almost there... Alright, thanks for the help, Gregory! I'll see you back at the team car.

GREGORY
Okay, Anti Gregory, I'll see you back at the team car.

SNEAKY HERMIT
I think this place is really tricky for you, Gregory, and it must be a battleground here. Just stay on your toes in this one... This looks like a good place to try out your new invisibility move: just stop and turn invisible. While invisible, nothing will be able to see you: not lasers, not spotlights, and not guards; only if the

guards have already seen you will the invisible move not work on them... Gregory, this place is almost like the same one back in Chicopee, and it might be a little tricky. Just try your best on this one... I looked at those rockets, and I'm 99% sure you'll be able to ride them to the top of that statue before they explode.

GREGORY
Hmm, what about that other 1%?

SNEAKY HERMIT
Well, in that case, Gregory, you'll be blown to bits. But these rockets won't blow up, so you will be okay.

GREGORY
Okay, that's good, Sneaky Hermit.

SNEAKY HERMIT
Now, to unlock these rockets, you are going to need all seven of The Panda's keys.

GREGORY
Right on, I'll steal them in no time.

CARMELITA
Freeze, Gregory.

GREGORY
How can I freeze when my heart is so warm with you around, Carmelita?

CARMELITA
I'm just kidding, Gregory. I'm here to help you again, and I need to shoot you again.

GREGORY
You know what I always say to that. I'm happy that you and I can help each other a lot.

CARMELITA
I will be waiting for you to beat The Panda, and I will put him in jail once you are done with him, Gregory. Now let's get a move on... I'll see you back at the team car, Gregory. And I'll be waiting to put The Panda in jail.

SNEAKY HERMIT
This place is almost identical to the one you found in Beckey's lair. I know that you already know how to do this; you know, I think you may be able to shoot down that door with that gun there.

PANDA
[on intercom]
Attention, all you guards: I heard that there is a little hero in my hideout. I need you all to stop him as soon as possible. Thank you. That is all.

GREGORY
Anti Gregory, what are you doing down there?

ANTI GREGORY
Well, I'm minding my post, when I see this snow cone stand and I think to myself, "Hey, Anti Gregory, you have to keep your energy up," and so I hurry over here, when all of a sudden monkeys are everywhere, bugging me to race them three times around this track for a key.

GREGORY
We could use the key... Think you can take them?

ANTI GREGORY
Come on, Gregory, they are pack of monkeys; how can I lose?

GREGORY
Alright, just remember what I said at Matthew's place. And keep clear of the icy road, buddy.

ANTI GREGORY
Thanks for the advice, Gregory, but trust me, I got this
under control.

GREGORY
Nice driving, Anti Gregory. Now go get that key.

PANDA
I see you with your powers from your Bouthiette
history. Have you come here for revenge? To steal back
the pages of your book?

GREGORY
That was my plan at first, but now I'm more interested
in putting a stop to your firework show.

PANDA
Why should you care if I bury a few towns in snow?
You are a hero, just like me.

GREGORY
No, that's only half right: I am a hero from a long line
of great heroes. While you... You are just a firework
king covering towns with snow.

PANDA
Oh really? Bouthiette, you shall pay for your
disrespect... Still, to honor your Bouthiette ancestry, I
will send you to your doom with the beauty of my new
firework move: Flame Fu... Your skill with your powers
is really good.

SNEAKY HERMIT
Gregory, I found out about that really big noise, and it
can only be found in one place: it's in Russia! That's got
to be where we will find the last guy. So get what you
came for and let's get out of here.

GREGORY BOUTHIETTE

CARMELITA
Hey, Gregory, are you up there?

GREGORY
Yes, I am, Carmelita, but I can't get down there.

CARMELITA
Hang in there, buddy, I'll be there soon.

GREGORY
Okay, Carmelita. I'll just wait here for you.

CARMELITA
Okay, Gregory, I'm here, buddy.

GREGORY
Oh, good. Thank you, Carmelita. Let's get out here.

CARMELITA
Okay, Gregory, let's get out of here.

ANTI GREGORY
Gregory, you're back!

GREGORY
Whoa, okay now, Anti Gregory. You can get off of me
now, buddy.

SNEAKY HERMIT
Hey, Gregory, I just built this gun for you.

GREGORY
Uh, okay, thanks, Sneaky Hermit. What did you build a
gun for anyway?

SNEAKY HERMIT
I built it because we are going to Russia, and the guy
that you are going to fight is there, and he has the last
page of your book.

GREGORY
Oh yeah, right, I forgot about that. Thanks for reminding me about it, Sneaky Hermit. Now let's get a move on. Anti Gregory, it's time to go, buddy.

ANTI GREGORY
You got it, Gregory, let's go to Russia.

GREGORY
I think I should get on the gun now, Sneaky Hermit.

SNEAKY HERMIT
Yeah, I would get on that gun right now.

CARMELITA
Good luck on that gun, Gregory. I'm going to be watching you.

GREGORY
Thanks, Carmelita. I'll do this for you.

CARMELITA
He's going to do it for me, Sneaky Hermit.

SNEAKY HERMIT
Yes, I heard, Carmelita. I hope that he will do it for you as well.

ANTI GREGORY
Sneaky Hermit...

***

GREGORY BOUTHIETTE

ANTI GREGORY
...We are here.

SNEAKY HERMIT
Okay, Anti Gregory, but I think that gate is locked, buddy. We have to wait until Gregory shoots it off for you.

CARMELITA
Well, just call Gregory and tell him about the lock.

ANTI GREGORY
Hey, Gregory, the road to King Carrion's hideout is blocked. Do me a favor and shoot off that lock for me, would you, pal? Whoa, check out all of those mines. Think you can blow them away to clear a safe path for us?

SNEAKY HERMIT
That tower is really big. I think King Carrion is up there.

ANTI GREGORY
Hey, Gregory, there are some robo-birds flying around us.

SNEAKY HERMIT
That's no tower, it's a giant death ray! Gregory, take out those rocks or we are in trouble.

ANTI GREGORY
Heads up, the robo-birds are back... We are getting swarmed... Nice work, Gregory! The robo-birds are gone.

GREGORY
Uh, Anti Gregory, I don't think that the gun is going to make it all the way through.

SNEAKY HERMIT
We have got to get through that gate to the other side.
The only way to unlock it is to run over sixty of those
hanging computers.

GREGORY
It would be easier to get at if Anti Gregory hadn't
trashed our new gun.

SNEAKY HERMIT
It won't be a problem. I can type in the code so that
they will fall to the ground, then Anti Gregory will have
to run over them with the car.

GREGORY
Okay. And Anti Gregory, remember to use the new
battering ram if anyone tries to stop you from getting
to those computers.

SNEAKY HERMIT
Anti Gregory, there are only a 119 computers up there,
but these fire slugs are really fast and trying to get to
them before us. The first one to get sixty computers
wins... Good work, Anti Gregory! Now that we have
enough computers to open the gate, I think it's time to
do some hero stuffs. What do you think, Gregory?
Careful, this place is a booby trap! You better get out of
there.

GREGORY
Hold on, that's Carmelita! She looks trapped.

SNEAKY HERMIT
I thought that she was still with us! I didn't know that
she got kidnapped.

GREGORY
It's just a misunderstanding. We've got to free her.

GREGORY BOUTHIETTE

SNEAKY HERMIT
Are you crazy, Gregory? King Carrion probably stuck
her there to trap you.

GREGORY
But if I don't do anything, Carmelita is doomed.
Besides, fighting just won't be fun without her.

SNEAKY HERMIT
Gregory, you are so crazy. I think I have found a way to
help you with this: that barrel will really help, but I
have no idea how you are going to get up there.

GREGORY
Sneaky Hermit, there's a jump here, and a slide there.
I've done this a million times.

CARMELITA
Gregory, oh thank goodness. I know that you will come
save me.

GREGORY
Thanks, Carmelita. I'll save you soon.

KING CARRION
HAHAHA, YOU LITTLE PUNK. NO ONE WILL EVER GET OUT OF HERE,
BECAUSE I WAS THE ONE WHO MADE THIS TRAP.

SNEAKY HERMIT
I knew that this was a trap. It looks like I need to find a
way to turn off that gas before Gregory's brain is turned
to cheese... This code is going well, but a little hard as
well... Uh oh, I need to be careful here: that bad thing is
from King Carrion. If that thing hits me, it's game
over... I am the best! No code can stand before me.

CARMELITA
Gregory, you did your best to save me. Now I need you
to break this cage so that we can get out of here

together... I know you can do it, Gregory. Now it's time to work together again. Now we need to help each other, and try to stop these villains. What do you say, Gregory?

GREGORY

Hmm. Carmelita, we have been working together for a long time, and you know I will never say no to you. Now that that big evil robot owl is trying to kill us and gas us to death, that guy is on my list.

CARMELITA

I see your point, Gregory. Okay, I think we can do this together. If you can listen to me and hear what I say to you, we may be able to defeat King Carrion.

GREGORY

Okay, Carmelita, let's do this together and forever... Oh wait, I need those glasses. They have been with me for a long time. I can't see without them.

CARMELITA

Don't worry, Gregory, I'll cover you while you get them back. If you can make your way to the top of the death ray, I left my jet-pack there before King Carrion kidnapped me.

GREGORY

Now that we are working together again, Carmelita, I don't want to leave you here alone.

CARMELITA

Don't worry about me, Gregory. I will be right behind you. And once we beat King Carrion, I'll be coming to see you with Sneaky Hermit, and Anti Gregory as well.

GREGORY

Okay, Carmelita, I think you can do this by yourself. I will be waiting for you.

GREGORY BOUTHIETTE

CARMELITA
Okay, Gregory, enough wasting time. You have to get
your glasses back right now, my friend... Nice job,
Gregory! I'll see you at the death ray.

SNEAKY HERMIT
There's Carmelita's jet-pack, right where she said it
would be. I heard that King Carrion made this big
death ray that was going to kill you, and was going to
make it run off your powers. You better hurry: this
whole thing is about to fall apart.

GREGORY
I'm on it, Sneaky Hermit.

SNEAKY HERMIT
It's sinking fast; climb, Gregory, climb! Okay, that jet-
pack is easy to fly. Just do whatever you can do, and try
to fire its rockets as well... Gregory, behind you!

KING CARRION
GREGORY BOUTHIETTE, YOU HAVE ESCAPED MY CHAMBER AND BROKEN
MY DEATH RAY. WHEREVER I GO, YOUR BOUTHIETTE FAMILY ALWAYS
FINDS A WAY TO IRRITATE ME.

GREGORY
Always. So that was you in the back in all of those old
pictures from my book. How old are you?

KING CARRION
I HAVE NO AGE.

GREGORY
What are you, immortal?

KING CARRION
REVENGE IS HOW I SPEND MY TIME, AND HOW I'VE KEPT MYSELF ALIVE
FOR HUNDREDS OF YEARS. YOUR PLANET EARTH WILL NEVER BE THE
SAME.

CARMELITA

Gregory, my rockets don't hurt him too much, but I can shoot him from here. When I give you the sign, just shoot him when I'm done.

SNEAKY HERMIT

Nice shooting, Gregory! You got him! Wow, that is one tough owl.

GREGORY

I don't get it. You are so angry at me. You must have known my mom and my dad have two sons: if you hated the Bouthiettes so much, why did you let us live when you stole my book?

KING CARRION

BECAUSE I WANTED TO SHOW THE WORLD THAT WITHOUT YOUR FAVORITE BOOK, THE BOUTHIETTE FAMILY IS NOTHING.

GREGORY

Uh, well, there's where you are wrong. My book didn't create the Bouthiette heroes: it took the great Bouthiette heroes to create the book.

KING CARRION

ENOUGH, GREGORY BOUTHIETTE. IT ENDS NOW. THE BOUTHIETTE FAMILY WILL BOW TO ME. THE REAL HERO WILL BE KING CARRION.

SNEAKY HERMIT

Now is your only chance, Gregory! You have got to get to his head and break it before his power kicks in.

KING CARRION

BOUTHIETTE, YOU WILL NEVER BEAT ME. KING CARRION IS ALL-POWERFUL.

ANTI GREGORY

Gregory, you did it! King Carrion is done now.

GREGORY
Whoa, hey, okay, Anti Gregory. Thanks for the hug.

SNEAKY HERMIT
Good job, Gregory. You defeated King Carrion.

GREGORY
Thanks, Sneaky Hermit. I couldn't have done it without
you helping me out along the way.

SNEAKY HERMIT
Well, I'm happy you are doing the things that I tell you
to do.

CARMELITA
Hey, Gregory! You did good, buddy.

GREGORY
Hey, thanks, Carmelita. I couldn't have done it without
you as well. And I love it that you are with us.

CARMELITA
Uh, thanks, Gregory. Now I think it's time for me to
count from 10 to 1, Gregory, if you know what I mean.

GREGORY
Yes, I do know what you mean, Carmelita. And when
you are done counting, I will give you a little kiss.

CARMELITA
You got it, Gregory. Now let's do this: 10, 9, 8, 7, 6, 5, 4,
3, 2, 1... Now, Gregory!

GREGORY
You got it, Carmelita.

CARMELITA
Thanks for the kiss, Gregory. I really loved it so much.

GREGORY
And thanks for letting me kiss you, Carmelita. I really liked it, too. Now let's go.

CARMELITA
You heard Gregory, guys. Let's get a move on.

ANTI GREGORY
Okay, Gregory. I'll drive us home right now.

SNEAKY HERMIT
It's time for us to go home.

GREGORY
Now that King Carrion is out of the picture, we are going home and planning our new missions, you guys.

SNEAKY HERMIT
You got that right, Gregory: we will be planning our new missions when we get home.

ANTI GREGORY
So, what are we going to plan for our missions, Sneaky Hermit?

SNEAKY HERMIT
I don't know, Anti Gregory. We just have to wait until we get home and find out.

GREGORY
This is going to be fun.

THE BOOK OF ADVENTURES 2: BAND OF HEROES

SNEAKY HERMIT
Gregory, can you read me?

GREGORY
I read you, Sneaky Hermit.

SNEAKY HERMIT
Okay, good. Are you in position?

GREGORY
Yes, I am, Sneaky Hermit. I'm ready to get the King
Carrion parts, but do you know how to get to them?

SNEAKY HERMIT
Yes, I do know how to get to the King Carrion parts,
Gregory. But I'm kind of stuck in the basement. I can
get to that computer if you can open the basement
door.

GREGORY
Hang on, Sneaky Hermit. It might take some time, but
I'll find a way to get up there.

SNEAKY HERMIT
Okay, I'm coming upstairs right now. Ouch! Hold on,
here I come... Okay, let me at the computer... The
spotlights are offline... There go the lasers... I'm
working on the gate right now... Okay, Gregory, all
clear.

GREGORY
Thanks, Sneaky Hermit. Hey, did you tell Anti Gregory
to meet me at the building where we need to meet up?

SNEAKY HERMIT
Yes, I did tell him to meet you at that building. I'll stay
here and keep working on this computer while you go
ahead... Okay, Gregory, I heard that the King Carrion
parts are being held up there. You need to meet with

GREGORY BOUTHIETTE

Anti Gregory up there, but there is no way for you to get there.

GREGORY
No problem, I'll just take the shortcut.

SNEAKY HERMIT
If you can remember how, you can still walk on ropes. Go ahead and give it a try... Anti Gregory must have gotten lost along the way. Just go on ahead without him.

ANTI GREGORY
Psst, Gregory, look out! Hey, Gregory. I didn't scare you, did I?

GREGORY
No, Anti Gregory, you didn't scare me.

ANTI GREGORY
Okay, good. I'm here to help you carry out the King Carrion parts.

GREGORY
Yeah, can you open that gate?

ANTI GREGORY
No problem, I'll open that gate like it's my job... Okay, Gregory. All clear.

GREGORY
Thanks, Anti Gregory.

ANTI GREGORY
Another gate stands before you! No worry, I shall break it like the truth.

GREGORY
Great work, Anti Gregory. You are really in the zone.

ANTI GREGORY

I can't walk on this small rope. You go on ahead and
unlock the doors from the inside. I'll be waiting in the
hallway to help you carry out the King Carrion parts.

SNEAKY HERMIT

I don't get it, Greg. The King Carrion parts should be
here... This is all wrong. We need to pull the plug on
the operation right now!

CARMELITA

Hey, Gregory. It's good to see you.

GREGORY

Hey, Carmelita, nice to see you again. You still look
pretty as always.

CARMELITA

Thanks, Gregory. You know I always look pretty.

GREGORY

Hey, Carmelita, do you know what happened to the
King Carrion parts?

CARMELITA

There were some people here last night, and they made
out with all the King Carrion parts.

GREGORY

What? Someone already stole the parts?

CARMELITA

Yeah, I know, right? People coming here at night and
stealing the King Carrion parts... But I didn't see who it
was.

NEYLA

Well, we know that it wasn't him, Carmelita. I do know
that those people that were here last night were called

the Bandit Thief Gang.

GREGORY
Wait, the Bandit Thief Gang?

CARMELITA
Neyla, please. I need you to stay out of this for once. I really don't need any help.

NEYLA
Oh, I think you might. Just let me help, please!

CARMELITA
Okay, you can help out, Neyla. But you have to do what I tell you.

NEYLA
Okay, no problem. I'll do whatever you say.

GREGORY
Hey, uh, ladies, if you are done talking, can we get a move on?

CARMELITA
Oh, okay. Sorry, Gregory.

ANTI GREGORY
Hey, Gregory! Wait up.

GREGORY
Shake a leg, Anti Gregory. It's time to go.

SNEAKY HERMIT
This wasn't part of the plan!

GREGORY
Yeah, well, this is where things get fun.

CARMELITA
Sneaky Hermit, Anti Gregory, you guys go on ahead.
Gregory and I will keep on going from here.

GREGORY
Yeah, you guys heard Carmelita. You just go ahead. I'll
keep going with Carmelita. Just pick me up where I tell
you guys to.

SNEAKY HERMIT
Okay, Gregory. Just tell us where to pick you up.

CARMELITA
Gregory, follow me. I know a shortcut.

GREGORY
Okay, Carmelita, I'm coming. Wait for me... Hey, uh,
Carmelita, can I ask you something?

CARMELITA
Yeah. What's up, Gregory?

GREGORY
Uh, who was that girl who was with you?

CARMELITA
Oh, that girl who was with me back there? Her name is
Neyla. She's kind of like my partner.

GREGORY
Oh, okay. I was just wondering who she was. Does she
help you a lot?

CARMELITA
Yeah, she kind of helps me put bad guys in jail.

GREGORY
Oh, okay. So do you guys always help each other a lot?

CARMELITA
Yes, we do help each other a lot.

ANTI GREGORY
We are heading to your position. Jump down fast so
that we can get out of here.

GREGORY
No problem, Anti Gregory, we are coming now. Are you
ready to jump, Carmelita?

CARMELITA
I'm always ready to jump, Gregory.

GREGORY
Okay, let's do it... Let's get out of here, guys.

***

SNEAKY HERMIT
Okay, Carmelita, who is the first Bandit Thief Gang member we need to get King Carrion parts from?

CARMELITA
The first King Carrion part that we need to get is from Demetrie.

GREGORY
Okay, so what King Carrion part does Demetrie have, Carmelita?

CARMELITA
Demetrie has the King Carrion tail feathers, and he is using them as money-printing plates.

ANTI GREGORY
Why does Demetrie want to use the King Carrion tail feathers as money-printing plates, Carmelita?

CARMELITA
It's a long story, Anti Gregory. But Demetrie is an owner of a nightclub, and his hideout is under the nightclub.

GREGORY
Okay, so Demetrie owns a nightclub, but his hideout is under the nightclub... How do we get inside the nightclub?

CARMELITA
I have no idea, Gregory. But we need to get the King Carrion tail feathers from him.

SNEAKY HERMIT
Don't worry, Carmelita. I have a plan to help us get inside the nightclub. But before we do that, we have to do some missions on the outside first.

GREGORY BOUTHIETTE

GREGORY
Okay, so let's get to it. I'm ready to get out there to do
my mission right now.

SNEAKY HERMIT
Okay, Gregory, just go on top of the hideout's roof.

GREGORY
I tell you, Sneaky Hermit, it's going to be a real blast
getting the King Carrion tail feathers back from
Demetrie.

SNEAKY HERMIT
I'm happy to hear that, Gregory. But before we hit the
inside, we need to do some missions outside first.

GREGORY
What do you have in mind?

SNEAKY HERMIT
I hooked up this radio antenna on the safe house's roof
and we can hear whatever Demetrie is saying.

GREGORY
Nice. So I need to get the radio rays from Demetrie's
antenna?

SNEAKY HERMIT
Well, I need you to go to this position, and I will give
you the rundown.

GREGORY
A good place to start. I'm on it.

SNEAKY HERMIT
Okay, Gregory, I need you to hit the code on that
machine and make the rays hit our safe house antenna.

GREGORY
So I just need to climb up, put the code in, and make the ray hit the safe house antenna?

SNEAKY HERMIT
Yeah, that's right. And you are in luck: there is a pipe over there that you can climb, on top of the water tower.

GREGORY
Alright, let's do this thing.

SNEAKY HERMIT
Nice job, that's one done. Just look for the other two, and stick to the roofs. I don't want you to get caught by the guards.

GREGORY
I'll keep that in mind.

SNEAKY HERMIT
Good work. There's just one more left. Look around for it. And remember, the safest place is the rooftop.

GREGORY
I hear you, Sneaky Hermit.

SNEAKY HERMIT
Great work, Gregory. All the rays are hitting the safe house antenna.

GREGORY
Thanks, Sneaky Hermit. So, where do we go from here?

SNEAKY HERMIT
I just heard that you can go find the King Carrion parts in the basement.

GREGORY
Okay, I'll head for the basement.

ANTI GREGORY
Good to see you, Gregory. I think the path through the
basement is guarded by those guards. Sneaky Hermit
thought that you might need some help taking them
out.

GREGORY
Sounds like fun, you and me back-to-back.

ANTI GREGORY
Oh yeah, outnumbered, fighting five guards together.
It's perfect.

GREGORY
Okay, Anti Gregory. Let's get to it.

ANTI GREGORY
Hold on, Gregory, let me lower those bars for you... It
looks like you are on your own from here.

GREGORY
Hey, I'm used to it. Thanks for the help.

ANTI GREGORY
Any time, Gregory.

SNEAKY HERMIT
Gregory, I think you can crawl under that table to go
through the lasers.

GREGORY
Why do you want me to crawl under the table, Sneaky
Hermit?

SNEAKY HERMIT
I know that crawling is not your thing, Gregory, but I

just want you to do it for this mission. Just for a while.

GREGORY
Okay, Sneaky Hermit. I'll crawl under the tables.

SNEAKY HERMIT
Watch out, Gregory: there are flashlight guards up ahead, and if they hear you, they will get you. Crawl under the table to get to the other side.

GREGORY
Okay, Sneaky Hermit. I think I got this now.

SNEAKY HERMIT
Aha! There's an air vent. It looks like it will lead you to the side of the nightclub. Go ahead and crawl under the air vent, and take a look.

GREGORY
Okay, Sneaky Hermit. I'll give it a try.

SNEAKY HERMIT
It looks like there's a guard in your way, and there are some lasers, too. Just take that guard out and the lasers will turn off.

GREGORY
Okay, Sneaky Hermit. I'll do it right now.

SNEAKY HERMIT
That move will only work if the guard hasn't seen you. Just sneak up behind that guard, and let him have it.

GREGORY
Got it, Sneaky Hermit. I'll do my best.

SNEAKY HERMIT
If you get into a fight with those rats, the sneak attack won't work on them.

GREGORY
Okay, Sneaky Hermit. So I just need to fight them all by not using the sneak attack on them.

SNEAKY HERMIT
Yeah, that's a good idea, Gregory. Just do your normal attack on the rats for now... Aha! Another air vent. I think it will take you right to Demetrie.

GREGORY
Yeah, I think you are right about that, Sneaky Hermit. I think I should take a look.

SNEAKY HERMIT
It looks like I was right, Gregory. Now go near one of the windows and take some pictures.

GREGORY
Okay, Sneaky Hermit. I'll get on it right now.

SNEAKY HERMIT
That machine keeps the power going down here... The King Carrion tail feathers are being used as money-printing plates... There's our target: Demetrie, the owner of the nightclub and the evil behind all of this... That should do it, Gregory. Head back to the safe house and we'll cook up a plan of attack... The photos are good to show what our target, Demetrie, is up to: spotlights and guards the whole way through. It is gonna be really hard to get to the King Carrion tail feathers, so I came up with some missions for us to do: first, replace one of the paintings in his office with a bugged one I made so we can hear what he's up to. Second, if you see the boss, tail him: we might be able to find out what he's up to for the operation, and learn some of his movements. Now, once we got some stuffs figured out for the operation, those King Carrion tail feathers are as good as ours.

GREGORY
Okay, Sneaky Hermit. I'm on my way back right now.

CARMELITA
Okay, Sneaky Hermit. What's the plan to get the King
Carrion tail feathers back?

SNEAKY HERMIT
I want to wait until Gregory comes back, Carmelita.

CARMELITA
Okay, I can wait. I'll be over there.

SNEAKY HERMIT
Okay, Carmelita. I'll keep my eye out for Gregory.

ANTI GREGORY
I really want to do a mission, Sneaky Hermit.

SNEAKY HERMIT
Don't worry, Anti Gregory, you will get to do a mission
right after one of Gregory's missions. Then you get to
do your mission. But until then, just wait, okay?

ANTI GREGORY
Okay, Sneaky Hermit. I'll wait right now.

GREGORY
Okay, guys. I'm back.

SNEAKY HERMIT
Okay, good! Now, there are some problems getting to
the King Carrion tail feathers.

ANTI GREGORY
What kind of problems, Sneaky Hermit?

SNEAKY HERMIT
I knew you would ask that, Anti Gregory; the problem

is that Demetrie has a lot of guards everywhere, and he also has a lot of spotlights as well.

CARMELITA
So, how are we going to get inside the nightclub, Sneaky Hermit?

SNEAKY HERMIT
I haven't figure that out yet, Carmelita, but I think we can replace that painting in his office with this bugged painting. And if you guys see the boss himself, tail him: we need to find out he's up to. Now let's get this over with.

GREGORY
I'm going out there first, Sneaky Hermit. I will get all my missions over with, and let Anti Gregory do his mission after I'm done.

SNEAKY HERMIT
Okay, Gregory. Just go to your position, and I will tell you where to go from there.

GREGORY
I know where to go, Sneaky Hermit. You don't have to tell me.

ANTI GREGORY
Please, go and do your missions, Gregory. I really want to do my mission after yours.

GREGORY
Don't worry, Anti Gregory. I'll try to be fast.

SNEAKY HERMIT
Okay, Gregory, I need you to carry that bug and put it in Demetrie's office.

GREGORY
Okay, Sneaky Hermit. I'll give it a try.

SNEAKY HERMIT
Just stay away from the guards: if you take any hits, the painting will break.

GREGORY
I'll keep that in mind.

SNEAKY HERMIT
Okay, Gregory, the door to Demetrie's office is locked: you won't be able to get in.

GREGORY
No problem, Sneaky Hermit, I wasn't really thinking about using the door. But I think I can see an air vent up there.

SNEAKY HERMIT
That's a good idea, Gregory. Go through that air vent and it will bring you to Demetrie's office... Good job, Gregory! If you can bring that original painting back to the safe house, I will sell it for a lot of money. Just be careful getting that painting back to the safe house, and stay away from the flashlight guards. And remember, the safest place is the rooftop.

GREGORY
I hear you, Sneaky Hermit... Okay, Sneaky Hermit. I'm back.

SNEAKY HERMIT
Okay, Gregory. Are you going to do your other mission right now?

GREGORY
Yes, I am, Sneaky Hermit. I'm gonna go do my other mission right now.

GREGORY BOUTHIETTE

ANTI GREGORY
Hey, Gregory, when you are done with your mission,
just call me.

SNEAKY HERMIT
Don't worry, Anti Gregory, I'll let you know when you
can go and do your mission.

ANTI GREGORY
Okay, Sneaky Hermit. Just tell me when I'm up.

SNEAKY HERMIT
Relax, Anti Gregory. Just look at this paper for some
diapers you might want to buy.

ANTI GREGORY
Okay, Sneaky Hermit. I'll look for some diapers in this
paper while on the couch with Carmelita.

CARMELITA
Why did you let him look at a paper for diapers, Sneaky
Hermit?

SNEAKY HERMIT
Because, Carmelita, I just want Anti Gregory to do his
mission well.

CARMELITA
Oh, okay. Forget I asked.

SNEAKY HERMIT
Okay, Gregory. Demetrie told one of his guards to ring
the bell when the coast is clear.

GREGORY
Coast is clear for what?

SNEAKY HERMIT
Well, that I'm not sure. Just ring the bell and follow

him without being seen.

DEMETRIE
Oh, smooth. Keep it smooth, baby... Walk tall, stand
tall...

SNEAKY HERMIT
Be careful, Gregory. Just stay on top of the roof.

GREGORY
I hear you, Sneaky Hermit.

DEMETRIE
Juice! Who's got the juice? I got to keep it smooth...

SNEAKY HERMIT
You will not be able to see Demetrie enter the code
from up there. Just go down there without being seen.

GREGORY
No problem, Sneaky Hermit. I'll do my best on it.

SNEAKY HERMIT
Good job tailing him, Gregory. He had no idea that you
were watching him when he punched that code in...
Hold on, that door leads to his water tank... Hmmm,
this might be useful for the heist... Okay, Gregory, head
back to the safe house. Anti Gregory is ready to go.

GREGORY
I'm on my way back right now, Sneaky Hermit... Okay,
Sneaky Hermit, I'm back.

SNEAKY HERMIT
Okay, Gregory. Anti Gregory, you are up, buddy.

ANTI GREGORY
Okay, Sneaky Hermit. I'm going there right now.

CARMELITA
It looks like Anti Gregory is happy to do his mission.

SNEAKY HERMIT
Yes, he's always ready to do his missions, Carmelita.

CARMELITA
I can see that, Sneaky Hermit.

GREGORY
Anti Gregory is going to do his mission right now,
Sneaky Hermit.

SNEAKY HERMIT
Okay, Gregory. He just needs to put the code in and he
is in... Okay, Anti Gregory, you need to get through
those lasers, but there is a box for you to break.

ANTI GREGORY
How am I going to break that box, Sneaky Hermit?

SNEAKY HERMIT
Don't worry, Anti Gregory, there's an ice cube right
next to you: if you can pick up that ice cube, then the
lasers will turn off.

ANTI GREGORY
Okay, I'll try breaking that box with this ice cube.

SNEAKY HERMIT
Anti Gregory, if you pick up that ice cube, you should
be able to knock out that guard up there. Then you can
throw that guard into those lasers... I think you can
pick up those guards and throw them in that thing, and
the water tank will break... Good job, Anti Gregory. The
water tank is out of the picture. Now Demetrie won't be
able to work in this place any more. Those punks! They
are walking right under us... Okay, guys, I have come
up with a plan to get to the King Carrion tail feathers.

But before we can get to that, we need to do some other missions first. To start, I need Gregory to go and pick the pockets of some guards in the theater so that we can have access to the spotlight control center; once that's done, we will be able to turn off the security around the printing press. We may need your help, Anti Gregory, to take out all of the alarms around the nightclub: we don't want anything to alert the guards while we pull off the big job. And finally, we'll need to get into the discotheque to drop this huge disco ball. Trust me, it's all part of the plan.

GREGORY
Okay, Sneaky Hermit. I'll go do my mission right now.

NEYLA
Hold it, Bouthiette.

GREGORY
Neyla... Another police woman on my tail.

NEYLA
Please, I led you here.

GREGORY
So that Bandit Thief Gang slip was a clue? Why are you helping me out?

NEYLA
I'm not as black-and-white as Carmelita, and I really want to help you out.

GREGORY
So, what? It takes a cop to help a hero?

NEYLA
Something like that. Now, if I'm going to trust you on this, I need to see if you can keep up with me.

GREGORY
Really? You want me to keep up with you? Okay, I can
try.

NEYLA
Okay, Gregory. Just try not to fall behind.

SNEAKY HERMIT
Gregory, you need to stay behind Neyla at all times.
And stay on top of the roof.

GREGORY
I hear you, Sneaky Hermit.

NEYLA
Well done, Gregory. I think I can trust you now, and we
can really work together.

GREGORY
I just needed to keep up, like you said.

NEYLA
Now, I can't really enter in the back of Demetrie's
nightclub, but I think one of your friends can do this
mission.

GREGORY
Oh, we are really going to work together, Neyla.

SNEAKY HERMIT
I think that mission is for me. I'm ready to do my
mission right now. Just head back to the safe house,
Gregory.

GREGORY
I'm on my way back right now, Sneaky Hermit... Okay,
Sneaky Hermit, I'm back.

SNEAKY HERMIT
Okay, good. I'm ready to go out there now.

ANTI GREGORY
Good luck, Sneaky Hermit. I'll be waiting for you.

SNEAKY HERMIT
Thanks, Anti Gregory. I'll do my best coming back
alive.

CARMELITA
It sounds like you are worried about Sneaky Hermit,
Anti Gregory.

ANTI GREGORY
I am worried, Carmelita. Me and Sneaky Hermit and
Gregory have been friends forever, since we were little
kids.

CARMELITA
I can see that, Anti Gregory. You guys have been
friends for like, forever.

GREGORY
Yeah, we have, Carmelita. I will never be without my
two best friends on my side.

CARMELITA
And I'm still on your side as well, Gregory.
GREGORY
I know that, Carmelita. I'm sorry.

ANTI GREGORY
It's okay, Gregory, you didn't forget about Carmelita.

CARMELITA
Yeah, Gregory, you didn't forget about me. Nobody can
ever forget about me.

ANTI GREGORY
It looks like Sneaky Hermit is on his way inside now,
Gregory.

GREGORY
Yep, I see him, Anti Gregory... Okay, Sneaky Hermit,
you need to use your Hermit Nippers to turn off those
lasers... Good job. Now do the same thing on that
guard right there. Now there's more lasers in your way:
just use your Hermit Nippers on them... Hey, Sneaky
Hermit, how are you doing in there?

SNEAKY HERMIT
I'm doing fine, Gregory. I'm just fine.

GREGORY
How are you going to break that disco ball up there?

SNEAKY HERMIT
I can use my Hermit Nippers on the wall parts where
they hold down the disco ball.

GREGORY
Wow, Sneaky Hermit, we felt that all the way from the
safe house. And you were right: the nightclub's sign did
crack a little bit... Good job, Sneaky Hermit. Now come
back to the safe house. Anti Gregory is ready to do his
mission now.

SNEAKY HERMIT
I'm on my way back right now, Gregory... Okay, Anti
Gregory, you can go do your mission now.

ANTI GREGORY
Okay, Sneaky Hermit. I'm gonna go out there right
now.

SNEAKY HERMIT
Okay, Anti Gregory, you need to break the alarm boxes;

there are three of them out here. If you can break them, Demetrie won't be able to find out what we are up to.

ANTI GREGORY
I don't know if I can do this, Sneaky Hermit. What if the guards get me before I break those alarm boxes?

SNEAKY HERMIT
Don't worry about it, Anti Gregory; you can throw the guards at the alarm boxes as well.

ANTI GREGORY
Okay, Sneaky Hermit. I'll give it a try.

SNEAKY HERMIT
Good job, Anti Gregory. There are just two more left. Just look around for them, and stay away from the guards.

ANTI GREGORY
I got it, Sneaky Hermit.

SNEAKY HERMIT
Nice one, Anti Gregory. Now there's just one more. Look around for it, and stay on the rooftop.

ANTI GREGORY
I hear you, Sneaky Hermit.

SNEAKY HERMIT
Great job, Anti Gregory. The alarm boxes are all done now. Come back to the safe house.

ANTI GREGORY
I'm on my way back right now, Sneaky Hermit... Okay, Sneaky Hermit. I'm back.

SNEAKY HERMIT
Okay, good, Anti Gregory. Now I can tell you guys

about the operation. First, Anti Gregory: you have to help me break into the water tower nearby, and I will turn off the water in the water fountain. Then Anti Gregory and I will meet up with Carmelita at the repair truck, and she will drive us to Gregory on top of the nightclub sign. And then Gregory will go down to get the King Carrion tail feathers, and we are out of here.

ANTI GREGORY
Come on, Sneaky Hermit, let's get you to that water tower... Jump into my arms, I'll throw you up there.

SNEAKY HERMIT
I need to turn the water pipes one at a time to change the water through the tube. I should turn it to the left... Yes, I knew it! I am really good at these things... Gregory, the water from the fountain should be turning off right now.

GREGORY
It's off, alright. They are already sending out the repair guy to fix it up.

SNEAKY HERMIT
Pickpocket the keys to his repair truck without being seen... Good work. Now head back to the water fountain to make the switch.

GREGORY
It's all you.

ANTI GREGORY
Let's head out to the repair truck.

SNEAKY HERMIT
Carmelita, are you in position?

CARMELITA
I'm at the truck right now.

SNEAKY HERMIT
Okay, we're on our way right now.

CARMELITA
I'll take the wheel. I know how to drive a truck.

GREGORY
I'm in position.

CARMELITA
Great, we are just driving up right now. Get ready to
grab the hook.

GREGORY
The hook is on, pull away.

SNEAKY HERMIT
Gregory, the guards are on to us! Protect the truck...
The secret door to Demetrie's nightclub!

GREGORY
That was really funny, Sneaky Hermit.

SNEAKY HERMIT
Okay. Just get in, grab the King Carrion tail feathers,
and we are out of here.

DEMETRIE
Uh, so Bouthiette, let's do this. You're like, bringing me
up and bringing my house down. So very uncool. Why
can't you let birds and bees be, bro?

GREGORY
Listen, Demetrie, you have no idea what you are
playing with. It will bring more than just your house
down.

DEMETRIE
Look, bro, I think you are a tough cowboy, and you are

looking to take everything I have away from me. Look at me! Look! See the money! You like the money? You can take all you want.

GREGORY

No deal. You and the rest of the Bandit Thief Gang have to be stopped. King Carrion will never see the light of day. Just hand over the tail feathers and we can...

DEMETRIE

What is this with King Carrion, bro? Have you heard anything? Are you hearing what I'm saying to you? You think you can swing the bat? Show your bling and let me shine you!

GREGORY

I have no idea what you're talking about, but your suit sucks.

DEMETRIE

What? Okay, let's dance... You took the King Carrion feathers, which is very uncool to do when you are a hero.

GREGORY

I'm doing you a favor. What kind of a thief prints money? There's no honor in that.

DEMETRIE

You crackerbox.

GREGORY

Okay, guys: I got the King Carrion tail feathers.

SNEAKY HERMIT

Okay, good, Gregory. Now let's get out of here right now.

ANTI GREGORY
Hey, uh, Sneaky Hermit? If we have time for a break, I
really want to get some diapers, please.

SNEAKY HERMIT
Okay, Anti Gregory. If we have time for a break, you
can get some diapers.

ANTI GREGORY
Okay. Thanks, Sneaky Hermit.

SNEAKY HERMIT
No problem, Anti Gregory. Anything for you, buddy.

***

GREGORY BOUTHIETTE

GREGORY
Okay, Carmelita, what is the next King Carrion part we need to get now?

CARMELITA
The next King Carrion part we need to get is the King Carrion wings, and the guy who has the wings is Roger. He is in India.

SNEAKY HERMIT
Why does Roger have the King Carrion wings, Carmelita?

CARMELITA
I don't know why, Sneaky Hermit, but we need to find out why he has the King Carrion wings.

ANTI GREGORY
And why is he in India? I think it's just dumb that he is in India.

CARMELITA
It may be dumb, Anti Gregory, but we need to get going right now, you guys.

SNEAKY HERMIT
You heard Carmelita, guys. Let's get a move on right now.

GREGORY
I'm already up ahead, Sneaky Hermit; you guys need to catch up.

ANTI GREGORY
Hey, wait up, you guys!

SNEAKY HERMIT
We're almost there, guys.

CARMELITA

Just to remind you guys, I'm going undercover when
we get to the safe house.

SNEAKY HERMIT

Okay, Carmelita. Speaking of undercover, I may need
Gregory to go undercover as well.

CARMELITA

You hear that, Gregory? You and I are going
undercover together.

GREGORY

Yeah, I heard that, Carmelita. I don't mind going
undercover with you, Carmelita.

SNEAKY HERMIT

Well, that's good, because you are going to have to
dance with Carmelita at Roger's party.

CARMELITA

Well, that's a good plan, Sneaky Hermit. I really like it
a lot.

SNEAKY HERMIT

I knew that you would say that, Carmelita. But before I
have Gregory dance with you, I may need him to dance
with someone that you may know, Carmelita.

CARMELITA

I think I know who you're talking about, Sneaky
Hermit, and you are right about it, too; she is
undercover as well.

SNEAKY HERMIT

I knew that she would be undercover as well,
Carmelita.

GREGORY BOUTHIETTE

ANTI GREGORY
While you guys are doing that, I'm just going to look at some more diapers. I'll just be sitting on the couch if you need me.

GREGORY
That sounds like a plan. Good luck, Carmelita, and remember to be happy when we dance together.

CARMELITA
Don't worry, Gregory, I'll make sure to be happy when I dance with you during your mission... Well, I'm off now. I'll see you guys later.

SNEAKY HERMIT
Okay, Carmelita, see you later. Okay, Gregory, you have to do your mission right now.

GREGORY
Okay, Sneaky Hermit, I'm going out there right now.

SNEAKY HERMIT
Gregory, scope out the palace, and then try to break into the ballroom. Let's find out who's at this party... Careful, Gregory, that's a snake hole right there. I don't think you are going to make it to the palace.

GREGORY
Don't worry, Sneaky Hermit, I'll just go around the snake hole.

SNEAKY HERMIT
That's a great idea, Gregory: there is another path for you to take. And make sure to stay on the rooftop when you get to the palace.

GREGORY
Don't worry, Sneaky Hermit. I will do everything that you tell me.

SNEAKY HERMIT
Nice job getting to the palace. Now, there's a window for you to get inside and see where the King Carrion wings are, but there's no way for you to get up there.

GREGORY
No problem, I'll just take a shortcut on those tree branches.

SNEAKY HERMIT
Nice job getting in, but don't stay on that rug where the guards are. The best place for you to be is by the doorway. Now take those pictures... Those wings are being held on that statue... They look heavy... Getting the King Carrion wings out of here will be a real challenge... There's the man himself: Roger, the host of this party, and mastermind behind all this... Maybe you should take pictures of the guests... That's Jean, he owns all of the trains in Canada... That's Cammy, she's kind of a nice cop at this party. She must be working undercover to see what Roger is up to... Look at that, it's Carmelita! She must be working with Cammy to help bust Roger... It's Neyla! Another officer undercover... Watch yourself, Gregory, this party is crawling with cops... Another Bandit Thief Gang member, Andy, is a smart bird that makes a lot of stuffs out of metal... That should do it, Gregory. Now head back to the safe house, and we'll start making a game plan... Stealing the King Carrion wings in the middle of a crowd in a ballroom is going to take some serious misdirection, especially when three undercover cops are only going to make things harder, although we might be able to use them for one of our missions. But no matter what we do with the ballroom, sooner or later, we may need to deal with Roger's security chopper. Anti Gregory can take it out with some local guards, but he won't be able to get inside the palace unless Gregory lowers the drawbridge for him... Gregory: Anti Gregory and I can't get into the palace

unless you bring down the drawbridge for us.

GREGORY
I'd love to, Sneaky Hermit, but the bridge is locked
down tight. Got any ideas to find the keys?

SNEAKY HERMIT
The guards that are carrying the keys are everywhere;
you can pickpocket their pockets to get the keys.

GREGORY
Alright, let's do this thing.

SNEAKY HERMIT
You can use some noise to lure the guard away. Just
ring that bell, sneak up behind the guard, and then
pickpocket him... Nice work, Gregory. Now go unlock
the drawbridge... Good work, Gregory. Now Anti
Gregory and I can go to the palace.

GREGORY
Hello, I'm here for the dance.

DOORMAN
Uh, sorry, sir. We have a dress code. Get a tuxedo.

GREGORY
Oh no.

DOORMAN
Sorry, pal. No tux, no entry.

SNEAKY HERMIT
Sorry, Gregory. Somehow, I forgot to look for formal
wear. That guy is not gonna let you in without a tuxedo.

GREGORY
Don't beat yourself up, Sneaky Hermit. In a party this
good, there has to be another tuxedo somewhere.

SNEAKY HERMIT
Try the guesthouse, someone may have overpacked.

GREGORY
Okay, Sneaky Hermit, I'm in the guesthouse. How do I find a tuxedo in this place?

SNEAKY HERMIT
Well, I just figured you should try to find parts of the tuxedo in every room.

GREGORY
And how do I do that, Sneaky Hermit?

SNEAKY HERMIT
I was thinking that you should ransack this place until you find every part of the tuxedo.

GREGORY
Making a mess in this place is a good idea for me, so l can dance with one of my cop friends.

ROGER
[on intercom]
Attention, guards: this is Roger. The party here is doing well. All the guests are now in the ballroom. Please, try to keep my guest house clean when this party is over; I don't want anything messy in there when this party is done.

SNEAKY HERMIT
You can use your sneak attack in this room to take out those guards. Just sneak up behind them and let them have it... Good job, Gregory. That doorman will let you in now......Nice job, Gregory. Now head back to the door guy and let him know that you got a tuxedo.

GREGORY
I hear you, Sneaky Hermit.

GREGORY BOUTHIETTE

DOORMAN
You got your tuxedo now, sir?

GREGORY
Yes, I do, sir. I'm here to dance.

DOORMAN
Then come on in.

SNEAKY HERMIT
Your tuxedo really looks nice on you. Now you need to dance with Carmelita to keep the crowd happy. She knows about the plan already, so you need to dance with someone else first.

GREGORY
Alright. I know just the girl for the job... Neyla, I want to dance with you.

NEYLA
I'm sorry, do I know you?

GREGORY
I used to follow you back in Paris.

NEYLA
Paris? Gregory Bouthiette, you clearly don't mind turning yourself in. Carmelita will see you here.

GREGORY
Don't worry, Neyla, Carmelita knows that I'm here. She was with me in my safe house. But do you want to dance with me?

NEYLA
Okay, Gregory. I'll dance with you for Carmelita to see... Try to remember the steps... Now your turn... Are you using me to dance with Carmelita?

GREGORY
Yes, I am. Do you mind?

NEYLA
Not at all.

ROGER
That boy is a really good dancer.

JEAN
If only you moved Spice shipments as well.

ROGER
Shut up.

NEYLA
Thank you. That was nice dancing.

GREGORY
Thank you, Neyla. Now I know that Carmelita will really like our dance as well.

NEYLA
Well, I hope that she will like dancing with you, Gregory.

CARMELITA
Neyla, you and Gregory really know how to dance together.

NEYLA
I tried to make him a great dancer.

CARMELITA
Please, Neyla. I would like you to see our dance in the operation that Sneaky Hermit will have us do later.

GREGORY
I can't wait to dance with you, Carmelita.

CARMELITA
I can't wait as well, Gregory. I'll see you later in the
operation. And nice dancing with Neyla.

SNEAKY HERMIT
Nice job dancing, Gregory. Now come back to the safe
house! Anti Gregory is ready to do his mission.

GREGORY
I'm on my way back right now, Sneaky Hermit... Okay,
Anti Gregory, you can do your mission now.

ANTI GREGORY
Okay, Gregory. I'm going out there right now.

SNEAKY HERMIT
Okay, Anti Gregory, you have to take down that
chopper so it can't be a problem in our operation. So
you need to take it out with that gun.

ANTI GREGORY
This is cool. I've never had a gun. I think if I can do
good with this gun I will use any gun in any place that
we go.

SNEAKY HERMIT
Nice job, Anti Gregory. Now that the chopper is out of
the picture, we can go on with the operation... Good
work, Anti Gregory. Now come back to the safe house.
I'm ready to do my mission now.

ANTI GREGORY
I'm on my way back right now, Sneaky Hermit... Okay,
Sneaky Hermit, you can go now.

SNEAKY HERMIT
Okay, thanks, Anti Gregory. I'm gonna go do my
mission right now.

ANTI GREGORY
Good luck, Sneaky Hermit.

SNEAKY HERMIT
Thanks, Anti Gregory. I'll be okay out there, you don't
have to worry about me. And you are with Gregory,
buddy.

GREGORY
Sneaky Hermit, what's your status?

SNEAKY HERMIT
I'm in position, and the truck should be coming any
time now.

GREGORY
Great. Do you know how to use your Hermit Nippers
on the truck?

SNEAKY HERMIT
I will know when I fire at the truck as it's coming out.

GREGORY
Just make sure that you take it down as fast as you can,
Sneaky Hermit.

SNEAKY HERMIT
The truck is on the move.

GREGORY
Okay, Sneaky Hermit, just aim at the truck with your
claws. If you lose track of the truck, I'll make an arrow
for you to find it... It's shooting at you, Sneaky Hermit!
Try to dodge it... Nice job, Sneaky Hermit. That means
everything's all clear for the operation.

SNEAKY HERMIT
Okay, Gregory. You can go and do your mission now,
buddy.

GREGORY
Thanks, Sneaky Hermit. I'll try to open the door for
you guys when I get in.

SNEAKY HERMIT
Okay, Gregory. I need you to check under every table to
see if you can find the code to open the door for me and
Anti Gregory.

GREGORY
Okay, Sneaky Hermit. How do I find the code?

SNEAKY HERMIT
The only way for you to find the code is to crawl under
every table.

GREGORY
Okay, I'll give it a try... There's no code here.

SNEAKY HERMIT
Keep on checking under other tables. It's sure to be
there.

GREGORY
No code here... No code under this one... I have found
the code, Sneaky Hermit.

SNEAKY HERMIT
Nice job finding the code, Gregory. Now find the door
and open it for us. And watch out for the snakes: I
don't want you to be scared right now.

GREGORY
I'll keep that in mind.

SNEAKY HERMIT
Nice work opening the door, Gregory. Now that we're
all together for this mission, we have to work as a team.

ANTI GREGORY
But what are Gregory and I here for, Sneaky Hermit?

SNEAKY HERMIT
You guys are here because I need to hack these computers and I'm sure that there are going to be guards coming to stop me. So I need the two of you to work together to watch my back.

GREGORY
You and me, Anti Gregory. Side by side.

ANTI GREGORY
Oh yeah, I'm ready, Gregory. Let's do this.

SNEAKY HERMIT
Okay, I'm in the computer now... I'm almost there... Yes, moving on to level 3 right now... Almost there... I got it. Now I'm moving back to level 2... I'm so close... I got it! Now I'm moving back to level 1... I'm almost done... I got it, yes.... Nice job working together, guys. Now we can get the King Carrion wings.

GREGORY
Okay, that's good. Now let's get out of here, guys.

ANTI GREGORY
Yeah, I agree with Gregory, Sneaky Hermit. I want to get out of here now.

SNEAKY HERMIT
Okay, guys. Let's get out of here right now.

GREGORY
Okay, Sneaky Hermit, what is the operation this time?

SNEAKY HERMIT
I'm glad that you asked, Gregory. This operation is going to be pretty easy. I have to start the operation

again: I have to start by taking down the bridge. Then Roger has to tell his guards to go and check it out. And then Anti Gregory has to hook up, go down and grab the King Carrion wings. Then Gregory has to dance with Carmelita, and keep the crowd and Roger distracted while Anti Gregory climbs back up to make his way back to the team car. And I will save him with my Hermit Nippers. Then we will all get our butts out of here.

GREGORY

Okay, Sneaky Hermit. Anti Gregory and I are moving into position. You still think that you can take the bridge down?

SNEAKY HERMIT

Trust me, Gregory, I think I can take this bridge down with my claws. I'll start at the bottom of the bridge to take it down first. Once it starts, the whole thing will come down.

GREGORY

Just make sure that you watch out for the falling rocks that come down. We need that brain of yours in one piece.

SNEAKY HERMIT

That's one down. Uh oh, it looks like the bridge is coming down now. I better not let any rocks hit my head... That's it for this one, now I can do the upper one... Just three more left... One more left and this bridge is coming down... Okay, Gregory! The bridge is done now. I'm going to my other part of the operation. Just let Anti Gregory know that he is good to go now. Good luck.

ROGER

What? The bridge is down? Take a look at it and try to fix it.

GREGORY
Anti Gregory, are you in position?

ANTI GREGORY
I'm in position right now, Gregory.

GREGORY
It looks like Sneaky Hermit's plan is working. I'm
gonna dance with Carmelita now, you just start
working on getting the King Carrion wings free...
Carmelita, I think that you owe me a dance.

CARMELITA
Is it the operation now, Gregory?

GREGORY
Yes, it is the operation now, Carmelita. Would you like
to dance with me, my lady?

CARMELITA
I would love to dance with you, my good man... You are
a great dancer, Gregory.

GREGORY
And you are a great dancer, too, Carmelita.

CARMELITA
Thank you, Gregory... Thanks for the dance, Gregory.
You did well.

GREGORY
Well, thank you, Carmelita. I love dancing with you.

CARMELITA
I would love to dance with you all the time.

ROGER
The wings! What happened to the King Carrion wings?

GREGORY BOUTHIETTE

CARMELITA

Sorry, Roger, but I'm here to crash your party! Let's get to the team car, Gregory.

GREGORY

Okay, Carmelita. Let's get out of here.

SNEAKY HERMIT

Anti Gregory, I'm gonna help you with my Hermit Nippers. Let me worry about the guards, you just keep moving.

ANTI GREGORY

These things are heavy... I'm not that far now... Keep on using your Hermit Nippers, Sneaky Hermit... I'm almost there... Punch it!

SNEAKY HERMIT

Good work, Anti Gregory. Now we need to get out of here right now.

GREGORY

I'm ready to get out of here now.

CARMELITA

I'm ready as well.

SNEAKY HERMIT

Uh, Carmelita, did Roger leave his own party?

CARMELITA

Yes, he did, Sneaky Hermit. But I just found out that Roger is somewhere deep in the jungle! And he has the King Carrion heart.

ANTI GREGORY

What? Roger has the King Carrion heart now? Man, how many parts does Roger have?

CARMELITA
It's just two parts, Anti Gregory; don't worry, he won't have them too long, because tonight it comes home with us.

GREGORY
I love hearing you say that, Carmelita.

CARMELITA
I knew that you would say that, Gregory, but it's not going to be easy for us to get the King Carrion heart. Roger will be carrying one half of the King Carrion heart on his stick.

ANTI GREGORY
Oh man, do we have to go into the jungle, Carmelita?

SNEAKY HERMIT
It's okay, Anti Gregory, we will get the King Carrion heart from Roger.

GREGORY
Sneaky Hermit's right, Anti Gregory. We will get the King Carrion heart from Roger.

ANTI GREGORY
I hope you guys are right, because I think we have to walk on foot to get the King Carrion heart.

CARMELITA
Anti Gregory's right, guys. We have to walk on foot for this one.

SNEAKY HERMIT
I don't mind walking in the jungle.

GREGORY
I like to walk a lot, but sometimes my feet get tired from walking a lot.

CARMELITA

Don't worry, Gregory, we will get there as fast as we can.

SNEAKY HERMIT

Carmelita's right, Gregory: we will get there as fast as we can. And no matter what happens, we will be there.

GREGORY

Well, I hope that you are right about that, Sneaky Hermit, because there are snakes in the jungle as well. And I'm scared of snakes.

SNEAKY HERMIT

We are not going to let you go near any snakes, Gregory. Not on my watch.

ANTI GREGORY

I'm not letting Gregory go near any snakes as well, Sneaky Hermit.

CARMELITA

If there are going to be snakes near my friend Gregory, I will shoot those snakes with one shot.

GREGORY

Okay, guys, let's get a move on now.

SNEAKY HERMIT

We're almost there, you guys.

CARMELITA

Sneaky Hermit's right, guys, we're almost there! Just need to get to the safe house, and then Gregory has to find out what Roger is doing with the King Carrion heart.

SNEAKY HERMIT

You are right about that, Carmelita, and I'm going to

tell him what to do out in the field.

GREGORY
I like it when you tell me what to do, Sneaky Hermit.

ANTI GREGORY
I also like it when you tell me what to do, Sneaky
Hermit.

SNEAKY HERMIT
Thanks, guys, I like being with you guys. I don't want
to be a bad guy again.

GREGORY
Well, it's a good thing that you are not going to be a
bad guy any time soon, Sneaky Hermit.

SNEAKY HERMIT
Thanks, Gregory. But now you have to stop talking
because we are at our safe house, and you have to go do
your mission now.

GREGORY
You got it, Sneaky Hermit. I'll go do my mission right
now.

ANTI GREGORY
Good luck out there, Gregory. I'll be waiting for you to
come back.

GREGORY
Thanks, Anti Gregory, but you don't have to worry
about me. I'm going to come back. Just look after him,
Sneaky Hermit.

SNEAKY HERMIT
Don't worry, Gregory, I'll make sure that he does not
worry about you. I'm gonna have him look at more
diapers, and have him help me come up with some

more missions.

CARMELITA
Why is he always worried about Gregory getting into
trouble, Sneaky Hermit?

SNEAKY HERMIT
It's just how Anti Gregory is, Carmelita. It's his thing to
be worried; sometimes I get worried a lot, too.

ANTI GREGORY
It's true, Carmelita. I always get worried about my
friends getting into trouble.

CARMELITA
I love it when you guys help each other. I always work
by myself.

SNEAKY HERMIT
Thanks for that, Carmelita, but I need to tell Gregory
what to do now... Okay, Gregory, you have to get inside
Roger's hideout and see what he's doing with the King
Carrion heart.

GREGORY
Okay, Sneaky Hermit, I'll let you know what Roger is
doing with the King Carrion heart when I get inside.

SNEAKY HERMIT
Okay, Gregory, you need to get inside that cave, but
there's no way for you to get up there.

GREGORY
Don't worry, Sneaky Hermit. There's always a shortcut
for me to take.

SNEAKY HERMIT
It looks like there are snakes in this place; just stay
away from the snakes, Gregory... Looks like you have to

stay on the side you are on now. Just take some pictures, and then come back to the safe house... It looks like that Roger has half of the King Carrion heart on his stick... The other half of the King Carrion heart is being held on that hook... Good job, Gregory. Now come back to the safe house and we will start planning on our attack.

GREGORY

I hear you, Sneaky Hermit... Okay, Sneaky Hermit, I'm back now.

SNEAKY HERMIT

Okay, good, Gregory. Now I need you to do your other mission now. And then Anti Gregory will do his mission after yours.

GREGORY

Okay, Sneaky Hermit, I'll go do my other mission right now. I'll be right back, Anti Gregory, and then you can do your mission.

ANTI GREGORY

Okay, Gregory, you just go do your mission now, and I'll just stay on this couch and keep on looking at diapers.

GREGORY

Okay, Anti Gregory, I'll be right back. Then you can do your mission.

SNEAKY HERMIT

Okay, Gregory, you have to take that ray down. But the problem is that there's an animal running it.

GREGORY

Okay, so how do I take this ray down, Sneaky Hermit?

SNEAKY HERMIT
There are a lot of Spice plants that are not good for animals. And people, too.

GREGORY
Keep that stuff away from Anti Gregory... Oh wait, wait! I think if I get six Spice plants from the top of the trees and bring them back to the animal, and if he eats the Spice plants, that animal will go on a rampage.

SNEAKY HERMIT
That is a great idea, Gregory! Go ahead and give a try right now... Good job, Gregory. Now bring all those Spice plants you got and bring them to the animal's basket.

GREGORY
Goodbye, radio ray.

SNEAKY HERMIT
Good job, Gregory. Now come back to the safe house. I'm ready to do my mission now.

GREGORY
I hear you, Sneaky Hermit... Okay, Sneaky Hermit. You're up, my friend.

SNEAKY HERMIT
Okay, good. Thanks, Gregory. I'll be right back, Anti Gregory.

ANTI GREGORY
Okay, Sneaky Hermit. I'll just stay here on this couch with Gregory, my good friend, and look at some diapers.

GREGORY
Uh, no thanks, Anti Gregory. I don't really want to look at diapers with you right now, buddy. Need to wait for

Sneaky Hermit to get to his mission. Then he is going to talk to me.

ANTI GREGORY
Okay, Gregory, I'll just look at some diapers by myself then.

SNEAKY HERMIT
I know Roger is getting ready to go on his walk with half of the King Carrion heart, and I'm going to get it from him.

GREGORY
Too bad that he just doesn't have the other King Carrion heart half on him, you could just grab the whole King Carrion heart and we could all just go home.

SNEAKY HERMIT
That's not a good idea; if we do that, he could find out what happened to the King Carrion heart.

GREGORY
So how are you going to get the first half of the King Carrion heart then?

SNEAKY HERMIT
I heard that Roger can follow loud sounds: he can be led to that watermelon over there and he will eat it. I already put special pills in it to make him fall asleep. Once he's asleep, I'll sneak up behind him and steal his blueprints...

ROGER
The blueprints, they're gone! What happened to the blueprints?

GREGORY
Nice job, Sneaky Hermit, you took the blueprints. He

has no idea that you took them from him... Okay,
Sneaky Hermit, come back to the safe house. Anti
Gregory really wants to be with you.

SNEAKY HERMIT
I'm on my way back right now, Gregory... Okay, you
guys, I'm back. But I've got some bad news.

ANTI GREGORY
What's the bad news, Sneaky Hermit?

SNEAKY HERMIT
I had a feeling you would ask that, Anti Gregory. Roger
has gone into hiding somewhere in his temple.

GREGORY
So how are we going to get him out of hiding, Sneaky
Hermit?

SNEAKY HERMIT
I don't know how we're gonna do it, Gregory, but all
four of us have to work together to get him out of
hiding.

CARMELITA
What do you want me to do, Sneaky Hermit?

SNEAKY HERMIT
I'm glad that you asked, Carmelita. I may need you to
help Gregory to get past the snakes if he goes near
them.

CARMELITA
Okay, no problem, Sneaky Hermit. I'll do my best
helping my friend out there! I don't want him to be
scared when I shoot those snakes away.

GREGORY
Are you sure that you want to help me out, Carmelita?

Because those snakes really scare me.

CARMELITA
I'm sure, Gregory. I won't let anything happen to you, because if anything does happen to you, I will kick some butts.

GREGORY
Thanks, Carmelita. I'm glad that you got my back.

SNEAKY HERMIT
Okay, stop it, guys. Gregory, you have to do your mission right now.

GREGORY
Okay, Sneaky Hermit, I'll go do it right now. I'll see you guys later.

ANTI GREGORY
I hope that Gregory will be careful out there, Sneaky Hermit.

SNEAKY HERMIT
Don't worry, Anti Gregory, Gregory will be careful out there. Just look at some diapers until you do your mission.

ANTI GREGORY
Okay, Sneaky Hermit. I'll keep on looking at some diapers while I wait for my next mission.

NEYLA
Bouthiette, we meet again.

GREGORY
Neyla, thanks for helping me out back at the ball.

NEYLA
I should be thanking you: when Carmelita found out

that you were a good dancer, I told her everything that happened when I left the ball.

GREGORY
I know that. She's still with me in my gang, Neyla.

NEYLA
I'm glad that she is still with you in your gang, Gregory, but I need you to keep up with me.

GREGORY
Don't worry, Neyla. I won't let you down.

NEYLA
That's my boy. Now, don't fall behind... Well done, Gregory. And here is the secret door for the back.

GREGORY
Thanks, Neyla. I'd really like to work with you someday.

NEYLA
I hope that we can work together someday, too, Gregory. But for now we have to work alone. I'll see you around, Gregory.

GREGORY
Okay, see you around, Neyla. And thanks again.

SNEAKY HERMIT
There's the other half of the King Carrion heart, Gregory.

GREGORY
I see it, Sneaky Hermit. It looks like Neyla was right: I think I can get the King Carrion heart from here.

SNEAKY HERMIT
You can try to get the King Carrion heart all you want!

The thing that is holding it up there is kind of locked down good, and the guards around here are carrying the keys. You have to pickpocket their keys one by one.

GREGORY
I can pickpocket their keys one by one without making a sound. It shouldn't be a problem.

SNEAKY HERMIT
Good job, Gregory. Now get to that winch, unlock the locks, and grab that half of the King Carrion heart... Great work, Gregory. Now come back to the safe house, I'm ready to do my mission now.

GREGORY
I hear you, Sneaky Hermit... Okay, Sneaky Hermit, I'm back.

SNEAKY HERMIT
Okay, good, Gregory. I'm off to go do my mission now. I'll try to make it back in time, you guys.

ANTI GREGORY
Just be careful out there, Sneaky Hermit.

SNEAKY HERMIT
Don't worry, Anti Gregory, I'll be careful out there, buddy. If you want Gregory to look at some diapers with you, just ask him, okay?

ANTI GREGORY
Okay, Sneaky Hermit, I'll ask Gregory to look at some diapers with me. If he wants to.

GREGORY
Uh, no thanks, Anti Gregory. I need to tell Sneaky Hermit what to do in his mission. Then I'll look at some diapers with you, buddy.

ANTI GREGORY
Okay, Gregory. Just let me know when you are ready to
look at some diapers with me.

GREGORY
Okay, Anti Gregory, I'll let you know when I'm ready to
look at diapers with you, buddy.

CARMELITA
Do you want me to look at diapers with you, Anti
Gregory?

ANTI GREGORY
Uh, no thanks, Carmelita. I'm kind of good for now.
But thanks anyway.

CARMELITA
Okay, just let me know when you want me to look at
diapers with you.

ANTI GREGORY
Okay, Carmelita, I'll let you know when I want you to
look with me.

GREGORY
Roger is holding up in his temple, got any idea how to
get him out of hiding?

SNEAKY HERMIT
I heard from the radio that there is a jet inside this
truck that I can use to break that dam.

GREGORY
Awesome. Now be careful, Sneaky Hermit: Roger may
have other jets up there. They may stop you from
breaking that dam.

ROGER
[on intercom]
All jets, go stop that other jet from breaking the dam.

SNEAKY HERMIT
I'd better be careful, Roger just called those jets in to stop me.

GREGORY
Nice shooting, Sneaky Hermit. That dam is out of the picture.

SNEAKY HERMIT
Okay, I'm on my way back to the safe house now. Oh no, Gregory: one of the parts of the dam hit the jet! I'm going down! Ouch.

GREGORY
Sneaky Hermit, are you okay?

SNEAKY HERMIT
Yeah, I am, Gregory. I just had a little trouble climbing down. I'm on my way back right now.

GREGORY
Okay, Sneaky Hermit, just hurry back: Anti Gregory is happily getting ready to do his part.

SNEAKY HERMIT
Don't worry, Gregory, I'm on my way back right now. Just tell Anti Gregory that I will hurry back in time.

GREGORY
Okay, Sneaky Hermit, I will tell him that.

SNEAKY HERMIT
Okay, guys, I'm back.

ANTI GREGORY
Hey, you're back! Is it time to do my mission now?

SNEAKY HERMIT
Hold on, Anti Gregory. I have a mission for Gregory, and then I think I have something for you, buddy.

ANTI GREGORY
Come on, Sneaky Hermit, I really want to go out there right now.

GREGORY
Anti Gregory, calm down, buddy. Sneaky Hermit will come up with something. Just keep looking at diapers while I go out there.

ANTI GREGORY
Okay, fine. I'll keep on waiting.

GREGORY
Sneaky Hermit, I'm gonna go do my other mission now.

SNEAKY HERMIT
Okay, Gregory, I'm going to have Carmelita go with you just in case you go near the snakes.

GREGORY
Okay, Sneaky Hermit. Let's go, Carmelita.

CARMELITA
I'm coming, Gregory, just give me a second. Okay, let's get a move on.

GREGORY
Ah, snake! Carmelita, help.

CARMELITA
It's dead, Gregory.

GREGORY
Thanks, Carmelita. I don't like those snakes when they do that.

CARMELITA
It's okay, Gregory. Some kids are scared of snakes.

GREGORY
I know that, Carmelita, but it's different for me. I'm still scared of snakes a whole lot.

CARMELITA
Okay, now get up there. I'll meet you back at the safe house.

GREGORY
Okay, Carmelita, see you back at the safe house.

SNEAKY HERMIT
We have been looking at that ruby on top of Roger's temple. I think that ruby can be useful for the heist.

GREGORY
Okay, I think that might be a good thing for us to do, Sneaky Hermit. So how am I going to get that ruby down?

SNEAKY HERMIT
I think you can hit the ruby a few times to get it down.

GREGORY
Okay, Sneaky Hermit, I'll give it a try.

SNEAKY HERMIT
Okay, Anti Gregory, it is your turn, buddy! You have to go to that ruby and grab it. I will go out there and help you in this mission.

ANTI GREGORY
Okay, Sneaky Hermit. I'm going to get that ruby right now.

GREGORY
Anti Gregory, you can pick up that ruby with your hands. And you have to put the ruby on the mat that Sneaky Hermit put down for you: if you don't put it on the mats in this mission, then you have to start all over again! And stay away from the snake holes as well. I'm gonna see you guys back at the safe house.

WIZARD
THIS RUBY WILL BE PUT TO GOOD USE IN THIS OPERATION OF YOURS. I THINK YOU GUYS SHOULD KEEP ON GOING. YOU BETTER HURRY! I THINK THIS RUBY CAN BE USEFUL FOR BREAKING DOWN THE DOOR OF ROGER'S TEMPLE. KEEP WORKING ON IT, YOU LITTLE HEROES.

GREGORY
Good work, you guys, now come back to the safe house.

ANTI GREGORY
We're on our way back now, Gregory. Just hold on, buddy.

SNEAKY HERMIT
Okay, Gregory, we're back. When you do your mission, you have to be with Carmelita.

GREGORY
Okay, Sneaky Hermit. I don't mind being with Carmelita in my mission! Let's go, Carmelita.

CARMELITA
I'm on my way, Gregory.

SNEAKY HERMIT
Okay, Gregory, I need you to get down that hall and see

how much Spice is there.

GREGORY
I would like to get to the end of that hallway, Sneaky Hermit, but these lasers are in my way. How can I get through them?

SNEAKY HERMIT
There's a barrel with some dynamite inside. I think you can jump inside that barrel, walk over those lasers, then jump out of the barrel before it goes kaboom.

CARMELITA
Nice job, Gregory.

GREGORY
Thanks, Carmelita. Now let's get a move on... I'm in position in the Spice grinder. What's next?

SNEAKY HERMIT
Roger won't come out of hiding, so you can smash up all the Spice in there.

GREGORY
Okay, Sneaky Hermit, I think I can break the Spice in here with a little help from Carmelita. She is a great helper.

SNEAKY HERMIT
There is some TNT down there; when you are inside the barrel, the guards won't be able to see you if you are not moving. So try not to get caught in this mission.

GREGORY
Okay, Sneaky Hermit. I will try my best not to get caught by the guards.

ROGER
[on intercom]
Guards, what's going on down there? My Spice grinder
is broken. Now I need to get a new plan.

SNEAKY HERMIT
Good work, Gregory. Now come back to the safe house,
it's time for the operation.

GREGORY
I hear you, Sneaky Hermit. Let's go, Carmelita.

CARMELITA
I'm on my way, Gregory.

GREGORY
Okay, Sneaky Hermit, we're back.

SNEAKY HERMIT
Okay, Gregory. You did a good job out there with
Carmelita. I'm really happy that you two are working
together.

CARMELITA
Hey, Sneaky Hermit, I'm sorry, but I have to meet up
with Neyla and Cammy. I'll see you guys later on in the
operation.

SNEAKY HERMIT
Okay, Carmelita, see you later.

GREGORY
So, what is this operation, Sneaky Hermit?

SNEAKY HERMIT
I'm glad that you asked, Gregory: this is Operation Wet
Tiger! First, Anti Gregory will start the operation. Then
we'll both head to the chopper. Then Anti Gregory will
head to the elephant's mouth for Gregory. Gregory will

make his way to the elephant's mouth with Anti Gregory. Then Roger will come out from his temple: once he's out, Gregory will make his way to Roger, grab the other half of the King Carrion heart, and we're out of here.

ANTI GREGORY
Okay, I'm gonna go ahead and start the operation now, Sneaky Hermit.

SNEAKY HERMIT
Okay, Anti Gregory, I'll be out there in a minute... Let's head out for the chopper, Anti Gregory... Okay, I need you to open the elephant's mouth for Gregory, while I stay here and help you from the sky.

ANTI GREGORY
You got it, Sneaky Hermit.

ROGER
[on intercom]
All guards, drop the bombs now.

SNEAKY HERMIT
Uh oh, Roger just called for his guards to bomb Anti Gregory. I better help him out! Yes, the bombs are down! How are you doing, Anti Gregory?

ANTI GREGORY
I'm working on it.

SNEAKY HERMIT
Just lift the elephant's mouth faster.

ANTI GREGORY
Yes, I know I can do it... The elephant's mouth is open, Gregory! Bring the TNT in now.

ROGER
My temple is filling with water! Now I need to go on to
Plan B: come and face me, Bouthiette! I am so
powerful, I will beat you.

GREGORY
Boy, when we tick somebody off, we really get the job
done.

NEYLA
Yes, you guys can really make somebody mad.

GREGORY
Neyla, you're back for round two, I see.

NEYLA
That man is a bad Spice trader: he should be brought to
justice.

GREGORY
All I'm after is the King Carrion part: if you want me to
take him down, the bust is all yours.

NEYLA
Just try to keep up.

GREGORY
Neyla, now!

NEYLA
I'm sorry, Gregory, you need you to take Roger on your
own for a while. I'll be back.

GREGORY
Uh, okay, where are you going?

ANTI GREGORY
Uh, Gregory, I'm coming, buddy!

ROGER

This is it? This is the Bouthiette Gang I've heard so much about and feared these long hours?

ANTI GREGORY

Hey, Roger! My name is Anti Gregory, and I will renew your fear.

ROGER

Who is Anti Gregory? All I see is a blue kid who is so very weak.

ANTI GREGORY

I might be blue, and not as smart as the other guys, but one thing I'm not is weak.

ROGER

Defend your lord.

ANTI GREGORY

Victory belongs to me! Gregory is going to want this half of the King Carrion heart safe and sound.

NEYLA

Anti Gregory, up here, buddy.

ANTI GREGORY

What? Neyla! Throw down a ladder, Gregory is hurt real bad. Can you hear me? I said Gregory is hurt.

NEYLA

There he is, Cammy, just as I promised. Roger has already been incapacitated.

CAMMY

Excellent police work, Neyla. Carmelita has never been able to catch the Bouthiette Gang, yet you have captured them in just a few short weeks.

CARMELITA
Well, I never...

CAMMY
Really, Carmelita, accept your defeat gracefully.

NEYLA
Actually, Cammy, there is a good reason Inspector Box has never caught the Bouthiette Gang: she and I have been with them the whole time.

CARMELITA.
What? Wait, Neyla, what are you doing?

NEYLA
Cammy is really a member of the Bandit Thief Gang, Carmelita, and we have been working for her this whole time. I'm sorry, Carmelita, just play along.

CARMELITA
Okay, Neyla. I have always played along with you. And with Gregory, too.

CAMMY
You two really care about the Bouthiette Gang very much. Men, place these two under arrest.

CARMELITA
Neyla, I hope you know what you're doing. I don't think I like this.

CAMMY
I think I should put you two somewhere the Bouthiette Gang will be as well...

NEYLA
Just shut up, Cammy. We will get you, and don't think we won't.

SNEAKY HERMIT
I can't believe it, why would she do that? Ah man, I'm alone, my friends are going to jail, and I need Anti Gregory to drive the team car for me...

CAMMY
Come on, keep on moving, you fools.

CARMELITA
How could you join the Bandit Thief Gang, Cammy?

CAMMY
Because, Carmelita, with you guys out of the way, I can get half of the King Carrion heart for myself.

NEYLA
I can't believe you, Cammy. You played us like puppets.

CAMMY
And you are right about that, Neyla. Now that you two and the Bouthiette Gang are out of the picture, I can make my move.

GREGORY
But why would you want to take us, Cammy?

CAMMY
Just shut up, Bouthiette. There's no one that can save you now.

ANTI GREGORY
Um, excuse me, Cammy... You kind of forgot someone.

GREGORY
Anti Gregory, be quiet. She doesn't know that yet. Just keep it between us.

ANTI GREGORY
Okay, Gregory. I got it.

SNEAKY HERMIT

Don't worry, guys, I will find you soon. I just need to find a way to to save you guys... Yes, I made it to the team car, and it's covered in leaves. I just need to uncover it on my own... Oh man, I need to drive the team car on my own as well, but I don't know how to drive yet! Well, I think I can try to drive the team car... Whoa, tree! That was close. I need to be careful while I'm driving the team car. Watch out, you guards, before I run you guys over! Okay, thank you for getting out of the way... I am getting the hang of this driving thing, now I just need to follow Cammy to see where she's going...

***

SNEAKY HERMIT
There she is. Where are you going, Cammy? I better not get caught by Cammy or her guards... Okay, now I just need to get to this other road, just in case Cammy sees me. Okay, I think I'm safe for now... Where is she going now?

CAMMY
Get in there, you two.

NEYLA
Let them go, Cammy.

CAMMY
I don't think I will ever let them go, Neyla.

CARMELITA
You better let them go, Cammy. Or else.

CAMMY
Or else what, Carmelita? What are you going to do?

CARMELITA
I will take you down myself.

NEYLA
Carmelita, I don't think you are going to do anything to her, because she is going to do something to you.

CARMELITA
I was just helping out, Neyla.

NEYLA
I know that you were helping out, Carmelita, but just let me handle it for now.

CARMELITA
Okay, Neyla. I'll let you handle this for a while.

CAMMY

Okay, shut up, you two. I am going in there, Neyla, and
I'm taking Carmelita with me.

SNEAKY HERMIT

Oh man, Cammy just put Gregory, Anti Gregory, and
Neyla in her jail! If I don't bust them out soon, they will
be stuck working with some uncool shoes, and I'll be
out two best friends and one girl cop... Okay, now I
need to get in the safe house and figure out a way to
break Gregory and Anti Gregory out of prison... Okay, I
need to get to the tower and find out where Cammy put
Gregory and Anti Gregory in jail and try to find out
how to break them out. And I need to find a way to get
Neyla out, too... Ah hah! Cammy is out making her
rounds. Wait a second, if I can use my Hermit Nippers
to hit her and hear what she says... This is great! If I
can use my Hermit Nippers on her a few times, I will
be able to hear whatever she says, and I might be able
to hear where she locked up Gregory, Anti Gregory,
and Neyla.

CAMMY

The Bandit Thief Gang is falling apart, and there is no
Spice in my plans this time, because the Spice is out of
the picture. Oh well, at least the Bouthiette Gang and
Neyla are locked up good, and I can move on to
everything else, and I can do whatever I want now. Ah
well, they will get out of my way soon enough... Those
fools: they are still cops, they keep on sending me
criminals, and I keep on making money. How come no
one has ever thought of this before? Brainwash
criminals and they will tell me where they are hiding
their money! I'm very smart. If only I had Spice for the
job, but I can't use Spice. I'll have to use something else
for now... That no good Bouthiette Gang! That blue kid,
what's his name? Anti Gregory! Yes, Anti Gregory, he'll
be the first one pranked. I will brainwash him and he
will do whatever I tell him to do... That Gregory

Bouthiette thinks he is really good, but he has to think again because I am gonna be better than him. Maybe I should put him in the hole for a long time to make him go crazy.

SNEAKY HERMIT

Oh my goodness, that was the most evil thing I have ever heard in my life. She's not a good cop. Man, that was the most evil thing I have ever heard in my life: making people tell her where they put their money, so that she can tell them what to do. I should get to work on getting Gregory out of the hole... That computer can make the train go slow. If I can hack into that computer, I could make the train go even faster! Okay, I'm in the computer now. If I can get all the way down there, I should be able to make the train go a little faster... I need to be careful of red enemies that will try to stop me from getting to the end over there. I need to blast that wall away so that I can go through... That's one computer down, now the train should be moving a little faster... It looks like they are going to put up a little fight this time... Try and stop me, you fools! Two down, four more to go... Oh man, now it's faster... That's three computers down, the train should be moving even faster now... There are more fast ones again... You'll never take me alive! That's four computers down, now two more... Yes, the train is at full speed now. Now on to the last computer, and then I can save Gregory... Yes, the train is coming out of the tunnel! There it goes! That should make a good path for Gregory to come out... All the guards along the prison wall are out with a tracking GPS, there's no way for Gregory to escape. Unless I take those guys out with Hermit Nippers... That does it! The tracking GPS is offline. Gregory, can you read me?

GREGORY

How I missed that good voice of yours.

SNEAKY HERMIT
Save the love for later, buddy. Do you see that hook
above the train?

GREGORY
Yeah.

SNEAKY HERMIT
It's your only way to escape: just make your way up
there and get out. I already sent you the safe house's
coordinates. We will meet each other there.

GREGORY
Wow, you really thought of everything.

SNEAKY HERMIT
Don't I always?

GREGORY
Yeah, you do. Thanks for busting me out.

SNEAKY HERMIT
Oh, well, you know the old saying: if you can't count on
a friend to bust you out of jail, what kind of friend are
they?

GREGORY
Truer words were never said, buddy. It's good to see
you again.

SNEAKY HERMIT
Gregory, it's good to see you, too.

GREGORY
Thanks again for busting me out.

SNEAKY HERMIT
No problem, Gregory, but I've some bad news for you,
buddy.

GREGORY
What is it, Sneaky Hermit?

SNEAKY HERMIT
Anti Gregory is still in his cell.

GREGORY
Yes, I knew that, Sneaky Hermit. So what is the plan to get him and Neyla out of jail, Sneaky Hermit?

SNEAKY HERMIT
Well, I haven't thought that far yet, Gregory. But I'll need you to do some missions before we can free our friends. The first thing that I need you to do is to take some pictures of some codes.

GREGORY
Okay, got it. Wait, what?

SNEAKY HERMIT
Don't worry, I'll explain later. And then your second mission is to follow some guards and make them hit this giant attack robot. No, really! Gregory, I need to send these guards over to this giant attack robot.

GREGORY
I'm sorry, Sneaky Hermit, but that giant attack robot kind of looks like a water tower to me.

SNEAKY HERMIT
It does look like a water tower, Gregory, but it is a giant attack robot. And your third mission is to follow Cammy to steal two tank keys and a tank lock. Now, once you are done with all three jobs, we'll be ready to make a play for our little buddy Anti Gregory. And Neyla, too.

GREGORY
You got it, Sneaky Hermit. I'll go do one that is a little

hard for me.

SNEAKY HERMIT
It doesn't matter which job you do first, Gregory. I need you to do your missions quickly so that we can bust Anti Gregory and Neyla out of jail.

GREGORY
Don't worry, Sneaky Hermit, I'll try my best to be fast on my missions.

SNEAKY HERMIT
To get to Anti Gregory, I need you to pickpocket Cammy to get her keys and the tank lock.

GREGORY
Okay, Sneaky Hermit, but how do I get past her body guards?

SNEAKY HERMIT
I think you can take them on one by one, then you can get behind Cammy and pickpocket her.

GREGORY
That's a good idea, Sneaky Hermit. I think I'll give it a try right now.

CAMMY
Who goes there? Where... Where are my guards? Uh, they're gone again... What? Where are those lazy body guards? They're all fired.

SNEAKY HERMIT
Good work, now we're all set up to get a tank... Gregory, I need you to do another mission that has something to do with the guards.

GREGORY
I'd love to Sneaky Hermit, but I have no idea what you

are talking about.

SNEAKY
Okay, I'll explain it one piece at a time: do you see that
box?

GREGORY
Yes, I see the box, Sneaky Hermit.

SNEAKY HERMIT
And do you see that guard over there?

GREGORY
I can see the guard, Sneaky Hermit.

SNEAKY HERMIT
I need you to pickpocket that guard's pocket, walk over
to the box, and unlock it. Then punch in the code to set
off the alarm.

GREGORY
Hold up, Sneaky Hermit. You want me to set off the
alarm?

SNEAKY HERMIT
Don't get scared, Gregory. It's just another way to get
to Anti Gregory.

GREGORY
Right, sorry, Sneaky Hermit. So when I set off the
alarm, the guard will come running and type in the
code. And you want me to take a picture of the code.

SNEAKY HERMIT
That's the plan! When the guard puts in the code, you
have to take a picture of it. There are five codes that
you need to take a picture of.

GREGORY
Uh, okay. See, you lost me again.

SNEAKY HERMIT
Don't worry, Gregory, just do what you have to do now.

GREGORY
Okay, Sneaky Hermit. I'll get on it right now.

SNEAKY HERMIT
Good job, Gregory, now you've got four more to go... It looks you have to make this guy move. Try ringing that bell, and pick his pocket when he returns to his position... Nice work, Gregory. Now you just got three more to go... Great job, Gregory, you just have two more now... Nice one, just one more now... Great work, Gregory! Now we're all set to free Anti Gregory... Okay, Gregory, I'm in position to go to the bridge! Are you ready to do this, buddy?

GREGORY
Sorry, Sneaky Hermit, but if the guards come on the bridge, they will see us. Then we'll be dead.

SNEAKY HERMIT
Don't worry about it. There are some statues on the bridge: if you break them, you will be able to act like statue.

GREGORY
I look like a statue, the guards walk on by, and then pow! I hit them from behind. I like your idea, Sneaky Hermit.

SNEAKY HERMIT
Thanks, Gregory, I'm glad you like my ideas... I'm all done here, time to go up on the bridge... I'm done with this side of the bridge. Cover me, I'm on the move... I'm done with this side. I'm on the move again... I'm going

on to the other side now. I'm almost done... I just got one more to go, cover me... The last bomb is in place, let's get out of here! Okay, the bridge is out of the picture... Okay, Gregory, I need you to go find Anti Gregory in his cell. I think that pipe will lead you to him: just wait until the water goes off, then go find him.

GREGORY
Alright, I'm heading inside... Psst, Anti Gregory! Hey, Anti Gregory!

ANTI GREGORY
What? Gregory, where are you?

GREGORY
Over here, in the back wall.

ANTI GREGORY
Gregory! Oh, I'm so glad to see you. They've been forcing me to eat hot meals, and I'm feeling kind of weird. You gotta get me out of here.

GREGORY
No problem. Sneaky Hermit has found some kind of weakness in the other cell. If you and Neyla can get in a big fight, the guards will throw you guys in there.

ANTI GREGORY
Well, I think that me and Neyla can take thirty guards each, if we had to.

GREGORY
That's a good idea, Anti Gregory. If you and Neyla can each take out thirty guards, then Sneaky Hermit and I will take care of the rest.

ANTI GREGORY
Psst, Neyla! Are you in there?

GREGORY BOUTHIETTE

NEYLA
Yes, I am, Anti Gregory. What's up, buddy?

ANTI GREGORY
I just talked to Gregory, and he told me that you and I
have to fight thirty guards so we can get locked up in
the other cell.

NEYLA
You want me to help you fight thirty guards so that
they can lock us up in another cell together?

ANTI GREGORY
That's the plan, Neyla.

NEYLA
Okay, Anti Gregory, I'll help you by fighting thirty
guards. But I won't get locked up in the same cell as
you.

ANTI GREGORY
Okay, Neyla. It's a deal... Come and get it, punks! I'm
gonna destroy all thirty of you guys... Oh yeah, I got six
guards, Neyla.

NEYLA
Good job, Anti Gregory. I like working with you,
buddy... Oh hey, I got nine guards now.

ANTI GREGORY
That's good, Neyla. I'm just a little behind you.

NEYLA
Now I got thirteen guards.

ANTI GREGORY
Good job, Neyla. I got eleven guards now.

NEYLA
I'm happy for you, buddy.

ANTI GREGORY
I'm already up to twenty now, Neyla.

NEYLA
That's good, Anti Gregory. I'm up to nineteen now.

ANTI GREGORY
It looks like we're almost done with these guards,
Neyla.

NEYLA
It looks that way, Anti Gregory. Twenty-one going
down.

ANTI GREGORY
That kind of rhymed there, Neyla. Twenty-seven! I've
got twenty-seven down now.

NEYLA
I kind of got twenty-seven as well.

ANTI GREGORY
Thirty! Take that, you punks. Is that enough for you
guys? If you want to put me in another cell, bring it on.

NEYLA
I'm sorry, Anti Gregory, but I have to ditch you for a
while, buddy.

ANTI GREGORY
Okay, Neyla. I will see you again, won't I?

NEYLA
Yes, you will see me again soon, Anti Gregory.

SNEAKY HERMIT
Okay, Gregory, it's time for the operation that I like to call Operation Breakout. First, I will head out and break into the tank, then make a little room for you to crawl under it. Then we will go up to the gate to the prison, and I will break open the door. You and I will run inside and find Anti Gregory in the other cell the guards locked him in. Then we have to turn on the brainwash boxes to make Anti Gregory break stuffs. Once Anti Gregory is free, we will get the heck out of here... Okay, Gregory, I'm heading out to the tank... Okay, I made some room for you. Come under the tank quickly, and we will get a move on... I can't see you, just try to stay under there while I'm driving the tank so that the guards don't see you... Let's see if they fall for it... Suckers... I'm about to shoot down the door now. I would get out of the way, unless you want me to shoot you as well... Okay, now head inside, and I'll meet you in there... I'm kind of stuck in the tank, Gregory. I think you have to go on without me for a while. I'll find another way inside and we will find each other.

GREGORY
Okay, Sneaky Hermit, I'm in position.

SNEAKY HERMIT
Great, I'm right behind you already.

GREGORY
Good. Now, I think we have to split up from here, buddy.

SNEAKY HERMIT
I had a feeling that we'd have to split up here. Okay, then. I think I'll go this way, and you'll go that way!

GREGORY
Okay, I'll see you on the other side, buddy... Uh,

Sneaky Hermit, I think I just found the computer to open the gate.

SNEAKY HERMIT
Okay, good. I'll meet you back over there, Gregory. Make your way up there and open the gate.

GREGORY
You got it, Sneaky Hermit. You can count on me.

SNEAKY HERMIT
Thanks, Gregory. I'm heading to the other side where they're keeping Anti Gregory.

GREGORY
Okay, Sneaky Hermit, I'm on my way back right now. I'll see you on the other side.

SNEAKY HERMIT
Anti Gregory looks like he's in a bad dream.

GREGORY
He told me the guards were making him eat hot meals.

SNEAKY HERMIT
Did he say that he had to do some bad stuffs with the guards?

GREGORY
I don't know if he did say that. But he was really scared, and he said he wasn't feeling like himself.

SNEAKY HERMIT
Are you sure he really said that? He does get scared sometimes when we're out doing things.

GREGORY
He does get scared sometimes. When we free him, we will let him buy those diapers that he really wants.

SNEAKY HERMIT
Yes, we will let Anti Gregory buy the diapers he wants so bad. Now stop talking. Let's free him now.

GREGORY
You got it, Sneaky Hermit. Let's free our little friend.

SNEAKY HERMIT
There are some lasers in front of you: I need to turn them off from this computer here. Just walk up to them, and I will turn them off... Turning off the first lasers right now... Turning on the brainwash box...

ANTI GREGORY
Ow! What's that sound? It hurts my ears.

SNEAKY HERMIT
That one is down, now go find the other ones... Time for laser number two... It's all you, Gregory!

ANTI GREGORY
Ow, that sound is back again! Man, it really hurts my ears.

SNEAKY HERMIT
Just one more left. Look around for it, it should be around here somewhere.

GREGORY
I'm on it.

SNEAKY HERMIT
Turn it on now, Gregory!

ANTI GREGORY
Ow! The sound is back again! I can't help it! No! Leave me alone!

SNEAKY HERMIT
Great, now that Anti Gregory is brainwashed, I need
you to go down there and tell him what to do. You have
to tell him to break those brainwash boxes: when he
does that, he will go back to normal.

GREGORY
Anti Gregory, I need you to break all those brainwash
boxes for me.

ANTI GREGORY
Okay, I will break them all for you, sir... Ow, my head!
Who? What? Is this Heaven?

GREGORY
Sorry, buddy, you're no angel.

SNEAKY HERMIT
Just do your best thinking about what happened.

ANTI GREGORY
Okay, Sneaky Hermit, I will.

CAMMY
What the fart is going on in here? I should do it
quickly, before Anti Gregory has been freed. He's got
friends... Maybe I should get going before they catch
me.

ANTI GREGORY
Don't worry, guys, I still have Cammy's half of the King
Carrion heart safe with me. She'll never get away with
it... Oh no, Cammy! She's getting away!

GREGORY
Anti Gregory, lift those bars up so that we can chase
after her.

GREGORY BOUTHIETTE

ANTI GREGORY

I'm on it, Gregory... Let's go, guys... You are not a good
brainwasher.

CAMMY

Oh, come now, Anti Gregory. We were going to make
such good friends. We were going to do some stuffs
together, and I will be able to help you as well.

ANTI GREGORY

The only help that I need is to never remember you
again.

CAMMY

Oh, come on, don't be like that. You know you want to
be with me, and you want to do some fighting.

ANTI GREGORY

I'm done talking with my mouth. Now I talk with my
fist.

CAMMY

Sorry, Anti Gregory, but our time is done now.

ANTI GREGORY

Ah! She's getting away.

GREGORY

Don't worry, buddy, we'll find her. With the three of us
back together, she doesn't stand a chance.

SNEAKY HERMIT

It's good to have you back again, Anti Gregory.

ANTI GREGORY

I'm glad that I have good friends like you guys.

GREGORY

Thanks, Anti Gregory, and we are glad that we have a

good friend like you as well.

SNEAKY HERMIT
Yeah, we are really glad to have a good friend like you,
Anti Gregory.

ANTI GREGORY
Thanks, guys. I'm glad that you guys really like me so
much. So, now what, Sneaky Hermit? Are we going to
follow Cammy?

SNEAKY HERMIT
Nope, we are going to let you buy diapers, Anti
Gregory.

ANTI GREGORY
Oh yes, thanks, Sneaky Hermit! I really want to buy
diapers so badly.

GREGORY
And that is why we are going to let you buy a lot of
diapers, Anti Gregory. And we know that you might
hide inside your diapers when you see guards.

ANTI GREGORY
Oh yeah, I will be hiding inside my diaper a lot,
Gregory.

SNEAKY HERMIT
Okay, Anti Gregory, there's the store.

ANTI YOURSELF
Okay, Sneaky Hermit, I'll be right back. You guys will
be fine here by yourselves. Do you guys want anything
in the store?

SNEAKY HERMIT
Uh, no thanks, Anti Gregory. I'm kind of good for now.

GREGORY

Yeah, I'm kind of good as well, Anti Gregory. You just go buy your diapers, buddy.

ANTI GREGORY

Okay, Gregory. I'll be right back, you guys... Okay, guys, I'm back. I did buy myself four diapers, and a diaper bag as well. I am good for a while.

SNEAKY HERMIT

Okay, Anti Gregory. Let's get a move on, buddy.

ANTI GREGORY

You got it, Sneaky Hermit. Let's go find Cammy again so we can beat the crap out of her.

GREGORY

You said it, Anti Gregory. And we need to find Carmelita and Neyla as well.

SNEAKY HERMIT

I heard that Cammy has Carmelita, you guys. We need to save her.

ANTI GREGORY

How are we going to free Carmelita, Sneaky Hermit? We don't know where she is. And we don't even know where Neyla is either.

GREGORY

Anti Gregory is right, Sneaky Hermit. How are we going to find Carmelita and Neyla? We don't even know where they are in Cammy's hideout.

SNEAKY HERMIT

You guys do have a point, but I know where Carmelita is being brainwashed by Cammy. And Neyla has her own half of her hideout next to Cammy. We are going to walk into a war, you guys.

ANTI GREGORY
Uh oh, I don't like wars, Sneaky Hermit. How are we
going to get past it?

SNEAKY HERMIT
Don't worry, Anti Gregory, Neyla just sent me an email.
She told me that her tanks aren't going to kill us,
they're going to help us. But she also said that if she
doesn't know that it is us, then her tanks are going to
shoot us.

GREGORY
I bet Neyla's tanks are going to know it is us, Sneaky
Hermit, and they will help us take down Cammy's army
as well.

SNEAKY HERMIT
You do have a good point there, Gregory, but I don't
know if her tanks are going to know that it is us when
we get there. Hey, Anti Gregory, are we there yet,
buddy?

ANTI GREGORY
We are here, Sneaky Hermit. I see Neyla's army tanks,
and they are everywhere.

SNEAKY HERMIT
You are right, Anti Gregory. Don't worry, we will get to
the safe house. Let's go, you guys.

ANTI GREGORY
Whoa, we made it. That was close.

SNEAKY HERMIT
Okay, Gregory, I think I need you to go out there right
now, buddy.

GREGORY
You got it, Sneaky Hermit. And what do you want me

to do when I get out there?

SNEAKY HERMIT
I'll tell you when you get out there, Gregory.

ANTI GREGORY
Good luck out there, Gregory.

GREGORY
Uh, thanks, Anti Gregory. I'm just going to be out there for twenty hours, buddy.

SNEAKY HERMIT
Okay, Gregory, I need you to take some pictures of Neyla's hideout, Cammy's blimp, and one of her tanks.

GREGORY
Okay, Sneaky Hermit, and what do I need to do after that?

SNEAKY HERMIT
When you are done taking pictures, I need you to head up to that tower over there and find the King Carrion eyes.

GREGORY
Okay, Sneaky Hermit. I'll do that right now.

SNEAKY HERMIT
It looks like Neyla is using that bank as her own hideout. I might call her and tell her that we may need help taking Cammy down... That's the blimp that Cammy used to get away from the prison. I think we might use it to get to the tower... It's Cammy's boats! It looks like she's got them ready for the war... Looks like Cammy is ready for war now: she's got those tanks ready to go. I would stay away from them if I were you, Gregory... Okay, that should do it. I need you to head up to that tower now... The door is locked from the

inside. Try to find another way inside the tower.

GREGORY
Sneaky Hermit, there's more than just the King Carrion eyes up here.

CARMELITA
Why are you doing this? Neyla told me about your plan. I'm a good cop!

CAMMY
Oh yes, Carmelita, you are a good cop. And I will do what I have to do with you now. I know that you are a good cop.

CARMELITA
Then why are you doing this to me?

CAMMY
Because, Carmelita, you are a good cop. You see, while chasing Gregory Bouthiette, I was able to put you away in the jungle. I no longer need you and Neyla now that I am a part of the Bandit Thief Gang.

CARMELITA
Liar! You will never get away with this. I will try to find a way to stop you.

CAMMY
Yeah, I don't think you will be able to stop me for a while. And once I brainwash you, I will make your mind do whatever I tell it to do.

CARMELITA
I won't be brainwashed that easy.

CAMMY
You are right about that, Carmelita: it won't be easy. Now just go to your happy place, and stay there

forever.

SNEAKY HERMIT
I don't think they see you. Just take some pictures and head back to the safe house.

GREGORY
No, I've got to help Carmelita. She's in trouble.

SNEAKY HERMIT
There's nothing you can do to help her! Just take some pictures and come back to the safe house. I swear, we'll find a way to help her... I think that computer has Carmelita's mind in it. If I can find a way to turn it on, I might be able to free her mind from Cammy... Oh man, this is bad. Carmelita is being tangled around her arms and legs. Very bad, but we might be able to find a way to get her out of there... That's... That's a mind shuffler! I didn't think it was real! Those are Cammy's Shadow Guards: it might take some work to make them leave Cammy's side... The King Carrion eyes! It looks like Cammy is using them to brainwash Carmelita. I think we need to use some bad mojo stuffs to get the King Carrion eyes free... That's all the pictures I need. Now head back to the safe house. We need to come up with a big plan of attack.

GREGORY
Okay, Sneaky Hermit, I'm on my way back right now... Okay, guys, I'm back. So what are the plans for this place, Sneaky Hermit?

SNEAKY HERMIT
I'm glad you asked, Gregory. There's one mission for you to do in this place where they are holding some ghosts. If I can sound just like Neyla, I can tell all of her army tanks to go onto Cammy's side of the battle. Then I might go out there and collect some bad mojo power to free Carmelita and the King Carrion eyes. Then I

need Anti Gregory to kidnap this guy: his name is General Bandit Thief Foot. You need to bring him to the safe house. I may need to have some words with this guy. We all got our missions, good luck... I'm going to do my mission first, you guys. I will tell one of you guys when I'm there.

GREGORY

Okay, Sneaky Hermit, I think you might need to call for this guy right here, because he really wants to talk to you.

ANTI GREGORY

I hope you don't mind me telling you some stuffs to do, Sneaky Hermit.

SNEAKY HERMIT

Anti Gregory, you can always tell me what to do, whenever you want, buddy.

ANTI GREGORY

Thanks, Sneaky Hermit. I think I might need to use your computer when you are out there collecting some bad mojo power.

SNEAKY HERMIT

Don't worry, Anti Gregory, you can use my computer all you want.

GREGORY

I'm just going to watch you from here, Anti Gregory, and make sure you're okay with Sneaky Hermit's computer.

ANTI GREGORY

Don't worry, Gregory. I will do my best with Sneaky Hermit's computer.

SNEAKY HERMIT
That's my buddy, Anti Gregory. I'm counting on you,
buddy... That's it, I know that she has bad mojo
somewhere. I think I will carry it on my back the whole
time, and I will collect all of the red gas to free the King
Carrion eyes.

ANTI GREGORY
Huh?

SNEAKY HERMIT
It's simple, really. I'll take the bad mojo bomb with me,
and I will go to different places to collect all the red gas
to free the King Carrion eyes.

ANTI GREGORY
Wow, sounds easy.

SNEAKY HERMIT
Not really. I need to be careful while I'm carrying the
bad mojo bomb on my back: if I take any damage while
carrying the bad mojo bomb on my back, I'm done for.

ANTI GREGORY
Wow, sounds hard.

SNEAKY HERMIT
Yes, it is hard. There are going to be some guards
coming after me, and I need to use these switches to
help me collect the red gas.

ANTI GREGORY
What? No way that would work! I'd use that switch to
kill the guards before they ever got near me.

SNEAKY HERMIT
That's a good idea, I think I might do that. Thanks for
telling me what to do... Okay, the first place is done.
Now it's time for me to move on to level two.

ANTI GREGORY
Good job on level one. The level two place is
somewhere around here.

SNEAKY HERMIT
Awesome, now that level two is done, I can move on to
level three.

ANTI GREGORY
Now, the location of level three has got to be
somewhere around here.

SNEAKY HERMIT
Good, now level three is done. It's time for me to move
on to level four.

ANTI GREGORY
I know that level four is somewhere around here. I
know that you will find it!

SNEAKY HERMIT
Okay, now that level four is done, it's time for me to go
on to level five. Once I'm done with level five, I can
head back to the safe house.

ANTI GREGORY
I'm really getting the hang of this. Now you get to do
level five in the wishing well. Don't worry, you will find
a way down there.

SNEAKY HERMIT
Awesome, now level five is done. Now that I have
collected all the bad mojo gas, I will be able to free the
King Carrion eyes... Okay, guys, I'm back.

GREGORY
Good, Anti Gregory can go do his mission now.

ANTI GREGORY
Yes, that's right, Gregory. I'm out of here, guys.

SNEAKY HERMIT
Hey, Anti Gregory, can you see the general from there?

ANTI GREGORY
Nope, just an old man coming up the ramp.

SNEAKY HERMIT
Don't be fooled by him, that's General Bandit Thief
Foot: he is one of the toughest guys you've ever met,
and he knows the code to Cammy's castle.

ANTI GREGORY
But what if he doesn't want to come? I don't want to
hurt him.

SNEAKY HERMIT
Oh, don't worry about that, he's only afraid of two
things: fire and water. Other than that, you can hurt
him if want to; he might even come in handy as a
helper.

ANTI GREGORY
Wow, that is handy!

SNEAKY HERMIT
Good job, Anti Gregory, now bring him back to the safe
house. And be careful! Don't let the guards see you
with him... Well well, General Bandit Thief Foot, we
have a lot to talk about. You wouldn't mind telling us
the castle's codes, hmm? Don't feel like talking, huh?
How about a little of this?

GENERAL BANDIT THIEF FOOT
Hahahaha.

SNEAKY HERMIT
Talk, you little punk.

GENERAL BANDIT THIEF FOOT
Hahahahahahahaha.

SNEAKY HERMIT
Good job, Anti Gregory. Now let's head back inside,
buddy.

ANTI GREGORY
Okay, Sneaky Hermit. I'm right behind you, buddy.

GREGORY
Okay, guys, I'm out to do my mission now.

ANTI GREGORY
Oh, wait, Gregory: I just want to say good luck out
there.

GREGORY
Uh, thanks, Anti Gregory. I'll be back, buddy.

SNEAKY HERMIT
Okay, Gregory, that little house over there is a home for
ghosts.

GREGORY
Okay, so you want me to go in there and set them free.

SNEAKY HERMIT
Well, yes, I do need you to free the ghosts. But I need
you to head inside first. Then I will tell you what to do
from there.

GREGORY
Okay, Sneaky Hermit. I'll head inside right now.

GREGORY BOUTHIETTE

SNEAKY HERMIT
I'm glad you asked, Gregory. Our new missions for the war are thus: first, I need you to go out and get this voice box. I can use it to tell Neyla's tanks to go break into Cammy's half of the war. Then I need Anti Gregory to go out there, get into one of Cammy's tanks, and shoot all of Neyla's tanks. I did ask her if you can shoot all of them, and she said yes. Finally, I will head out and turn on the computer in the tower where Cammy has Carmelita's mind. Oh, and Gregory, I do know that you have flying powers: maybe you can use them to fly around the war when we do the operation. Now we have all of our missions. Good luck!

ANTI GREGORY
I'm gonna go out there and do my mission first, Sneaky Hermit.

SNEAKY HERMIT
Okay, Anti Gregory, I'll tell you what to do when you get there.

ANTI GREGORY
Okay, Sneaky Hermit, I'll be ready for you to tell me what to do.

GREGORY
Good luck out there, Anti Gregory. I'll be watching you from the safe house, buddy.

ANTI GREGORY
Thanks, Gregory. I'll be back soon.

SNEAKY HERMIT
Anti Gregory, just try your best to drive the tank while shooting all of Neyla's tanks. Once you are done with that, just come back to the safe house.

ANTI GREGORY
Ouch, that hurts! Oh man. Okay, this seat has to go back farther than this... Okay, guys, I'm in the tank.

SNEAKY HERMIT
Remember, just keep shooting all the tanks, then come back to the safe house when you are done.

ANTI GREGORY
See you later, sucker! Anti Gregory scores again! Stay down, you little punk... You are done for! Okay, guys, the tanks are done for.

SNEAKY HERMIT
Good job, Anti Gregory. Now that the tanks are done, we have clear skies for the war.

ANTI GREGORY
Okay, guys, I'm back. Sneaky Hermit, you can do your mission now.

SNEAKY HERMIT
Okay, thanks, Anti Gregory. I'll be back, you guys.

GREGORY
How are you going to hack the computers down there when they have no power?

SNEAKY HERMIT
It's simple, really: there's a little battery in this big, long hallway.

GREGORY
That hallway is one big death trap, but I think you can get through it.

SNEAKY HERMIT
You are right about that one. I will get through this big deadly hallway, and I will get the battery to turn on the

computer in the tower. Without that thing online, we won't be able to get the King Carrion eyes, or free Carmelita.

GREGORY
You are a good friend, Sneaky Hermit. Just make sure that those traps don't cut you into hundreds of hermit crab pieces.

SNEAKY HERMIT
Why did you have to say that? Yes! I got the battery. Now I just need to hack into that computer over there.

CARMELITA
I'll get you, Cammy!

CAMMY
Ah, how many times are you going to say that? It's not going to happen.

CARMELITA
I mean it, I'll get you.

CAMMY
I'll get you! I'll get you!

CARMELITA
I mean it, I'll get you.

CAMMY
Yes, yes, so I heard.

SNEAKY HERMIT
Okay, now I only got two more computers left. Just need to head back and hack them one at a time.

CAMMY
Hmm, maybe I should try and switch your brain another way... Okay, I have found a way to switch your

brain. Do you want me to do that to you right now?

CARMELITA
No, you butthead! No!

SNEAKY HERMIT
With that computer online, I can get the heck out of
here... Okay, guys, I'm back.

GREGORY
Okay, good. I'm gonna go and do my mission now. I'll
see you guys later.

ANTI GREGORY
Good luck out there, Gregory. I hope you get all those
keys.

GREGORY
Uh, thanks, Anti Gregory. I will get all the keys.

SNEAKY HERMIT
Cammy is planning on taking control of Neyla's army
tanks by fooling them with a prototype voice
modulation device. To get the thing working, she'll
have to jack it into the satellite underneath Neyla's
hideout.

GREGORY
So you want me to steal the device and hook it up on
our side, so that we have control of Neyla's army.

SNEAKY HERMIT
That's right. But I need you to steal some keys from
here and there to get access to the more secure areas of
the castle.

GREGORY
Okay, I'll get those keys right now.

SNEAKY HERMIT
You'll need those keys to steal a wiretap and the voice
modulator. Then head to the sewers beneath Neyla's
hideout.

GREGORY
Okay, Sneaky Hermit, I'm on it.

SNEAKY HERMIT
Good work, Gregory, now use those keys to get the
wiretap... The wiretap is at the far end of this room.
This is easy, buddy... Oh yeah, that wiretap is
awesome... The other set of key guards are somewhere
around here... Nice work, now the voice modulator has
to be around here somewhere... They have a lot of
guards around the voice modulator, this could be a
little hard... That's it! Now that you've got Cammy's
voice modulator, let's go put that thing to use... Cammy
has locked down the door to the sewers. Find the guys
in charge and steal their keys... Good work, Gregory.
Now head to the sewers... You need to crawl under one
of the tunnels and find the door to the sewers... I think
this sewer will take you to Neyla's hideout.

GREGORY
It looks like we got lucky: Cammy's men have already
placed Neyla's satellite cable. How should I hook these
up?

SNEAKY HERMIT
Splice in the wiretap, then attach the voice modulator.
I'll do the rest from here. This is going to be cool... Uh,
hello, mercenary tank forces! Would you mind
spinning your turrets for me? Wow, this is cool! Uh, I
mean, you are all very cool. Carry on... Okay, guys, we
are ready for the operation. I named it Operation High
Road. Here's the plan: first, Anti Gregory will head to
the castle and shut down the search lights with the
code that the general told us. Then Gregory and I will

go to the tower and make sure that Cammy's Shadow Guards are gone. I will hack into the computer and see if Carmelita's mind is in there, and I will set the bad mojo bomb on the mind shuffler. Gregory and I will grab the King Carrion eyes, and we will get the heck out of here.

ANTI GREGORY
Okay, guys, I'm gonna go start the operation now.

GREGORY
Okay, Anti Gregory, head to the castle and turn off the search lights. After you do that, Sneaky Hermit and I will head to Cammy's tower. Good luck.

ANTI GREGORY
I hope that General guy told the truth or this is gonna get ugly. Oh yeah, the lights are down! Sneaky Hermit, time to call in the cavalry. I'll see if I can find some extra firepower to help out.

SNEAKY HERMIT
Attention, bloodthirsty mercenary forces: the castle defenses are down. Seize this opportunity for aggressive military action by pressing an attack on the castle. Charge for victory! For glory! That should do it.

GREGORY
Now that you are done being the war guy, feel like flying to that blimp?

SNEAKY HERMIT
Just make sure you grab the rope hanging off that thing. I don't want to drown.

GREGORY
Hold on, buddy. This could get rough.

GREGORY BOUTHIETTE

SNEAKY HERMIT
Alright, let's head to the tower.

CAMMY
What? The mercenaries have reached the castle's defenses. All of you, go! Defend this tower to the last man... Don't worry, my dear, I still have time to finish with your mind.

CARMELITA
Let me out of here so I can kick your butt.

GREGORY
Okay, Sneaky Hermit, it looks like the Shadow Guards are out of the picture. Are you ready to free our violent little cop friend?

SNEAKY HERMIT
Yes, I am. This big old thing is a dinosaur, it might be hard for me to hack. But this computer must have Carmelita's mind somewhere... That should do it!

CAMMY
Aha! I've finally finished the work on your mind. You and I are about to become best friends.

CARMELITA
Okay, new best friend, hands up! And I mean all of them.

CAMMY
My dear, you really should... Huh? Shadow Guard? Shadow Guard!

CARMELITA
Come back here, you witch!

GREGORY
That Carmelita, always getting into trouble with her

gun.

SNEAKY HERMIT
She is really awesome. Stand clear, Gregory: this might
get bad.

GREGORY
Sneaky Hermit, are you okay?

SNEAKY HERMIT
This is no place to talk. I found one of the King Carrion
eyes, can you find the other one?

NEYLA
Don't worry, guys. It's safely in hand.

GREGORY
Neyla?

NEYLA
Nice job clearing out Cammy. I wouldn't have done
that to try getting the King Carrion eyes. Gregory, try to
keep up with me. I'll take you to your team car. And
hurry! We need to find Anti Gregory and Carmelita.

GREGORY
Sneaky Hermit, take the eye and escape on the blimp.
I'm gonna go with Neyla.

SNEAKY HERMIT
But the plan! This wasn't in the plan!

NEYLA
Attention, all bombers: focus your attacks on Cammy's
blimp... Gregory, take the eye and get out of here.
Hurry, Cammy is coming.

GREGORY
Okay, Neyla, I won't let you down. You did your best.

GREGORY BOUTHIETTE

NEYLA
Nice job, Gregory. Now get out of here with that eye.

CAMMY
Actually, Mr. Bouthiette, that eye belongs to me.

GREGORY
Heads up, Sneaky Hermit, you are about to be under
fire. Get to the blimp's turret and stay sharp.

SNEAKY HERMIT
Okay, I can do this. I can do this... That did it! The sky
is clear. Okay, guys, I'm heading out for our team car.

CARMELITA
Come back here, Cammy, that blimp won't save you!

SNEAKY HERMIT
Crap. Gregory, can you read me? Carmelita just shot
me, and the blimp is on fire. I'm going down! Down!
Down!

CAMMY
That eye belongs to me, and I want it back.

GREGORY
No way, do you think I'm crazy? You know what, on
second thought, don't answer that. I really don't need
you to tell me what you think.

CAMMY
Not crazy, just dumb. You are a little boy who is
playing dress-up in his parents' clothes. Oh, I know all
about you and the Bouthiette clan.

GREGORY
Then you understand why this eye needs to be
destroyed.

CAMMY

Oh, just shut up, Bouthiette. I already know why you want all the King Carrion parts, but I don't care. I am above good and evil.

GREGORY

And you think I would give the eye to someone who claims to be above good and evil?

CAMMY

Enough talk, Bouthiette. It won't take me long to take the eye away from you.

SNEAKY HERMIT

Hello? Is anyone there? Guys, I'm alive! I'm... What the?

CARMELITA

Oh no, Sneaky Hermit! Is that you, buddy? I am so sorry, I didn't know it was you. Here, take my hand, and I will get you out of here.

SNEAKY HERMIT

Okay, Carmelita, just let me get the eye first. Okay, let's get out of here.

CAMMY

Enough. You have shown me all of your moves.

GREGORY

I feel sorry for you. You don't even know what's right or wrong... Huh? Ow!

CAMMY

I know not to let my guard down right in front you. You should feel sorry for yourself.

GREGORY

She got the eye... She's got the eye!

GREGORY BOUTHIETTE

CARMELITA
How does this thing work? What's this do? And this?

SNEAKY HERMIT
Guys, are you there? I still got the eye. I am with Carmelita in one of Cammy's tanks. We are going to the team car.

ANTI GREGORY
Okay, Sneaky Hermit, I'm on my way, too. I'm in one of the tanks, too... Do what you can, Gregory!

GREGORY
There's nowhere left to run. We both know that I can beat you in a fight, so why don't you just hand over the eye?

CAMMY
You are right, Bouthiette. You've proven that you can beat me in a fight, but with this King Carrion eye, I can battle in your mind! You have a strong mind, Bouthiette, I never would have guessed.

GREGORY
I am out of here. You will be going to jail when my friend Neyla gets here. If you need me, I'll be in the team car with this King Carrion eye.

CARMELITA
Gregory, are you there? We are in the team car now. Where are you?

GREGORY
Don't worry, Carmelita, I'm on my way right now. How's Sneaky Hermit doing?

ANTI GREGORY
He's doing okay, Gregory. He just needs to rest for a while. Now hurry! We need to go.

GREGORY
I'm already here, buddy.

ANTI GREGORY
Oh my goodness, you scared me!

GREGORY
Sorry about that, Anti Gregory. Now let's get out of
here.

CARMELITA
Yes, I agree, let's get out of here right now. I want to
tell you guys something.

GREGORY
Okay, Carmelita, you can tell us something.

CARMELITA
Okay, good. But first, I just want to go somewhere to
get something to eat.

ANTI GREGORY
Yeah, me too. I'm getting hungry already. I know just
the place where we can eat.

GREGORY
Yeah, I'm getting hungry as well.

SNEAKY HERMIT
Guys, what happened?

GREGORY
Sneaky Hermit! Are you okay, buddy?

SNEAKY HERMIT
Yeah, I am, Gregory. Where are we now?

CARMELITA
We are going to get something to eat now, then we will

get back on the road.

SNEAKY HERMIT
Okay, good, because I'm getting hungry as well. Where
are we going to eat?

ANTI GREGORY
We are already here, guys.

SNEAKY HERMIT
Oh, sweet, I always like coming here.

GREGORY
Uh, Sneaky Hermit, Carmelita is going to tell us
something while we eat.

CARMELITA
Yeah, I do have something to say, Sneaky Hermit.

SNEAKY HERMIT
Oh, okay.

ANTI GREGORY
Hey, do any of you need to use the bathroom? Because
I'm gonna go right now if anyone wants to join me.

GREGORY
I'm coming with you, Anti Gregory, because I have to
use it as well.

SNEAKY HERMIT
While you guys use the bathroom, Carmelita and I will
get our food.

GREGORY
Okay, Sneaky Hermit, we will be back out when we are
done using the bathroom.

SNEAKY HERMIT
There's no need to rush.

CARMELITA
Man, those guys are really funny, Sneaky Hermit. You are very lucky to have friends like them.

SNEAKY HERMIT
Thanks, Carmelita. We are really lucky to have you as a friend as well.

CARMELITA
Hey, thanks. I'm glad to hear that from you, Sneaky Hermit.

GREGORY
Hey, Anti Gregory, are you almost done in there, buddy?

ANTI GREGORY
Yeah, I am, Gregory.

GREGORY
Okay, well, hurry up. We need to head to our table and listen to Carmelita, because she still has something to tell us.

ANTI GREGORY
Okay, Gregory, just go to the table without me. I'll be there soon.

GREGORY
Okay, Anti Gregory. Just come out when you are done, okay?

ANTI GREGORY
Okay, Gregory. I will see you at the table.

GREGORY BOUTHIETTE

SNEAKY HERMIT
Hey, Gregory, you're back. Where's Anti Gregory?

GREGORY
Anti Gregory is still using the bathroom, Sneaky
Hermit. He said he will come out soon.

SNEAKY HERMIT
Okay, I hope that he will come out, because Carmelita
still needs to tell us something.

ANTI GREGORY
Hey, guys, I'm out. Sorry about that, my zipper got
stuck again.

GREGORY
Oh, I didn't know that you had a zipper on your pants.

ANTI GREGORY
I always wear pants with zippers on them.

SNEAKY HERMIT
Huh, I didn't know you always wear those pants, Anti
Gregory. Why didn't you tell us about that?

ANTI GREGORY
Because I thought that you guys would be mad at me.

GREGORY
Why would we be mad at you, Anti Gregory? You know
when your zipper is stuck, you can always come to us
for help.

ANTI GREGORY
I'm sorry, guys. I just didn't have the time.

SNEAKY HERMIT
It's okay, Anti Gregory, you don't have to be sorry. Now
eat, buddy.

ANTI GREGORY
Okay, good, because I am really hungry now.

GREGORY
Okay, Carmelita, what is it you wanted to tell us?

CARMELITA
Okay, I was looking at the pictures from Roger's party, and the next Bandit Thief Gang member is Jean, and he has three King Carrion parts in Canada.

SNEAKY HERMIT
Wait, what? Jean has three King Carrion parts? And he's in Canada? But why?

CARMELITA
Because he wanted to be a hero a long time ago, but today he's evil, and he is taking over northern Canada.

GREGORY
I don't know why he wanted to be a hero a long time ago. Can't he just be a hero now?

CARMELITA
No, because he's evil now. In the north, there are trains and he has the King Carrion parts in his three trains. We need to find those trains and steal those King Carrion parts back.

ANTI GREGORY
And how are we going to get those King Carrion parts, Carmelita? I mean, why are we going to northern Canada anyway?

GREGORY
We just have to deal with it, Anti Gregory. And don't worry: we can steal those King Carrion parts back in no time.

SNEAKY HERMIT
Gregory is right, Anti Gregory. We can steal the King
Carrion parts back from Jean.

ANTI GREGORY
Okay, I'm in. I can't wait to steal them back as well, but
I can't go until I change myself first. I'll be right back.

GREGORY
We are gonna be in the team car, Anti Gregory.

ANTI GREGORY
Okay, I'll be there soon. It's a good thing I got some
extra diapers in my diaper bag. I'd never be able to
change myself with just one diaper left.

CARMELITA
Where's Anti Gregory? He's taking a long time to
change.

ANTI GREGORY
Okay, guys, I'm done. Sorry about that, I just needed to
change my diaper.

SNEAKY HERMIT
Okay, Anti Gregory. Just drive now, buddy.

ANTI GREGORY
Okay, Sneaky Hermit, I will. Canada, here we come!

***

GREGORY
Just let us know when we are in Canada, Anti Gregory.
We are going to play a little game in the back.

ANTI GREGORY
Okay, Gregory, I will let you know when we are in
Canada... Hey, guys, we are here in Canada now.

SNEAKY HERMIT
Oh, good, there's the safe house.

GREGORY
Okay, Sneaky Hermit, I'm gonna go out there and steal
Jean's train blueprints.

SNEAKY HERMIT
Okay, Gregory. I'll let you know when I find the trains
that have the King Carrion parts.

ANTI GREGORY
Good luck out there, Gregory. I hope that you come
back safe.

GREGORY
Thanks, Anti Gregory. I always do come back safe.

ANTI GREGORY
Uh oh, umm, Carmelita? Can you please help me out
here? I need some baby powder because I have a bad
itch in my diaper.

CARMELITA
Okay, Anti Gregory. I can help you, buddy,

ANTI GREGORY
Okay, good. Thanks, Carmelita. I don't like having bad
itches in my diaper.

CARMELITA
There you go, Anti Gregory.

ANTI GREGORY
Thanks, Carmelita. I feel much better now.

SNEAKY HERMIT
I got a lead on the King Carrion parts: in through town,
and out into the wilderness.

GREGORY
Hey, Sneaky Hermit, I'm gonna go hunting for bottles
again, if that's okay with you.

SNEAKY HERMIT
Okay, Gregory, you can go hunting for bottles out there
all you want. It might take me a while to get you a
mission anyway.

GREGORY
Okay, I got six so far... Oh man, this guy is not going to
move. I can just go over here... Oh, that guy up there
has something good! Hey, come back here, you! Give
me your coins and ruby... Hey, Sneaky Hermit, I think
one of the cabins has a vault in one of them. I might
find out when you tell me where to find the blueprints.

SNEAKY HERMIT
Okay, Gregory, I was thinking the same thing. Just
keep looking for bottles, Gregory. I still need to find
your mission.

GREGORY
Okay, Sneaky Hermit, I'll keep on looking for more
bottles. I'll talk to you later, buddy... Okay, I got nine
now... Hah! The duck with a shovel... Bye bye, ducks!
Okay, I got ten bottles so far. Hmm, I thought for sure
it would be up here... Or is it on the other side? I ain't
going down there, that's some cold water... Oh, hey,

there are trains in this place, just like Carmelita said. And I think that one might make a good getaway... Okay, now I can climb up... Oh, hey, I can get on a train. Now it can make a good getaway for my mission. Billy goat... Or mountain goat. Whatever goat... Duck found me! Bye bye, duck... Thirteen bottles so far. Still need to find them all before I can get to my mission... I got a topaz, whatever that is. There's another bottle over there. Sweet! That's fourteen already. Oh, sweet, I found another one there on the roof. Yes, I got fifteen bottles already. Now, there's still more bottles in the wilderness... So let's go into the wilderness!

ANTI GREGORY
Carmelita, can you put more baby powder in my diaper?

CARMELITA
Sure, Anti Gregory, I like helping you out a lot. There you go, buddy.

ANTI GREGORY
Thanks, Carmelita.

GREGORY
Oh, these bears will kill me... Oh fart, fart, fart, fart, I'm a dead boy! Oh, sweet: twenty bottles, as I'm running for my life from a bear that's gonna kill me... Twenty-one... I know that they can't go on the train tracks... And for the first time... Oh, wait, I thought there was bottle up here. Oh well. It looks like I can get this thing and run around, yes... Eagle attacks! Okay, let's mess around with a guard and the bear... Run for your life, dude! Oh, not me, dang it! Get the bear or the moose... While I run in terror... Okay, I only got twenty-nine bottles. I still need one more, and I know exactly where it is... Uh oh... Let's study the bear, since it just killed that moose and walked away... Okay, Sneaky Hermit, I found all the bottles.

GREGORY BOUTHIETTE

SNEAKY HERMIT
Okay, good. Your mission is set up now.

GREGORY
Okay, I see the spot.

SNEAKY HERMIT
That cabin is really old, but don't be fooled. It's where
Jean keeps the blueprints to his Iron Horse trains.
Sneak inside and find them: they will tell us where he
keeps his King Carrion parts.

GREGORY
Ransacking his files doesn't sound hard. Climbing on
rock walls? That will be a challenge.

SNEAKY HERMIT
You are in luck! Before Jean took over, this used to be a
good place for rock climbers. Some of their wall-hooks
are still around.

GREGORY
I think I just walk toward them and climb up.

SNEAKY HERMIT
That's right. Now, before you jump off the hook, you
have to lean back. It will give you more altitude.

GREGORY
Thanks for the tip. I'll give it a try.

SNEAKY HERMIT
Jackpot, Gregory! That's Jean.

GREGORY
Looks like he didn't notice me coming in.

SNEAKY HERMIT
Just stay out of sight and take pictures of his train

routes. They will tell us about his King Carrion parts.

GREGORY
Alright, I'm on it.

ANDY
Hello, Andy here.

JEAN
Nice to talk to you, Mr. Andy. Do you have time to feel
the wind?

ANDY
Yes, I do for you, old chum. I like to talk to you a lot.

JEAN
If you talk too much, it will hurt your brain.

ANDY
Yes, that's right. Must keep one's blood as one's brain...
Is there anything that you'd like to talk about?

JEAN
First off, are you still coming to pick up the Northern
Lights Battery?

ANDY
Yes, I am. But it might take me a while to get there. I
will try to get the Battery by the end of the week.

JEAN
Awesome. And second, when are you going to let me
take a look at that King Carrion brain of yours?

ANDY
Jean, you butthead, you already got your hands on the
choice King Carrion parts... Although, when I get there
to pick up the Northern Lights Battery, I can give you a
little peek at the King Carrion brain. And you might

show me your King Carrion parts...

JEAN
Easy there, partner. You are up in your head. I just got to place the parts I got.

SNEAKY HERMIT
Gregory, Jean hid the Iron Horse blueprints in his trophy bass: head to the fish above the fireplace, and steal those plans... Good job. Now get out of that cabin before you get caught.

ANDY
It sounds like you are already doing good work with your King Carrion parts. Since I see that you are doing so well, I will let you see the King Carrion brain.

JEAN
That will do fine. By the way, are you ready for the hoedown?

ANDY
Yes, I am. And I will be doing some bad stuffs in the places the other Bandit Thief Gang members were at. I headed to Cammy's place first, then to Demetrie's place. I know what he was doing with his King Carrion parts.

SNEAKY HERMIT
You already found the blueprints to one of the Iron Horse trains; I think you can find the others in the other two cabins... Yep, just like I said. Head on top of the fireplace and steal the Iron Horse blueprints... Jean will be in for a good surprise when he checks this vault: the code should be 1, 2, 9... You got the music box move! Two down, one more to go... The last trophy bass is above the fireplace. Be careful.

JEAN
[on intercom]
Attention, you cabin guards: I heard that someone has stolen all of my Iron Horse blueprints. Everyone, stay sharp. You all need to work together and look out for that thief.

SNEAKY HERMIT
Nice job, Gregory. That's the last of the blueprints... With all of the Iron Horse blueprints, we might be able to find the trains with that satellite dish.

GREGORY
Top of the mountain, huh? That shouldn't take long.

SNEAKY HERMIT
This is the only way up. Keep an eye out for those rock climber wall-hooks, they might be useful... This is great! We now have a satellite feed to the three Iron Horse trains on my computer. Head back to the safe house so I can give you, Anti Gregory, and Carmelita the run down.

GREGORY
Okay, Sneaky Hermit, I'm on my way back right now... I'm back. Okay, Sneaky Hermit, what's our mission?

SNEAKY HERMIT
I'm glad you asked, Gregory. Thanks to your work, we now know the three King Carrion parts: two lungs and the stomach. We won't be able to jump on board the trains while they are moving, but there are some Spice balloons: you guys need to work together to collect Spice, then jump on top of the train with a full Spice balloon. When you guys are done with that, I will jump on board and steal each of Jean's parts. We should have the first King Carrion lung in a few hours.

GREGORY
Okay, good. I'm gonna go and do one of my missions
now.

CARMELITA
Hey, Anti Gregory, do you want to do a little role-
playing with me?

ANTI GREGORY
Sure, Carmelita. I always like role-playing.

CARMELITA
Okay, good. Let's go.

SNEAKY HERMIT
Where are you guys going?

CARMELITA
I'm taking Anti Gregory with me to do some role-
playing. When Gregory gets to his first mission, Sneaky
Hermit, can you tell him that he will have a little role as
well?

SNEAKY HERMIT
Okay, Carmelita. I will tell him.

CARMELITA
Thanks, Sneaky Hermit. I will make sure that Anti
Gregory is safe.

SNEAKY HERMIT
I know you will, Carmelita. Now go do your little role-
play.

GREGORY
Okay, there's one of my missions. I wonder what kind
of mission it is.

SNEAKY HERMIT
Gregory, I have something to tell you, buddy.

GREGORY
What is it, Sneaky Hermit? What happened?

SNEAKY HERMIT
Carmelita is gonna be doing a little role-playing with
Anti Gregory, and she wants you to play as well.

GREGORY
Okay, what kind of role am I gonna have?

SNEAKY HERMIT
Carmelita just put Anti Gregory in a big cage, and she
just put three locks on it. She's right below you: you
just have to follow her the whole time.

GREGORY
Okay, Sneaky Hermit, I will follow her. Because she is
not like Cammy, and she will be checking Anti Gregory.

SNEAKY HERMIT
Okay, that's a good plan. Just don't let her see you: I
don't want to be alone again...

CARMELITA
Hey, Anti Gregory, are doing okay in there, buddy? I
know it's tight in there, but Gregory will let you out.

ANTI GREGORY
I'm okay, Carmelita. And thanks for the cookies.

CARMELITA
No problem, buddy. I know that you guys like cookies
so much. It's just to help you out.

ANTI GREGORY
Yeah, me and Gregory do like to have cookies together.

Sneaky Hermit doesn't mind... But why are we doing this again?

CARMELITA
I just wanted to have fun with my two friends. Neyla and I planned this role-play before we saw you guys again.

ANTI GREGORY
Do you think that Neyla is still our friend, Carmelita? I don't know about this. I think it is wrong to trust her now.

CARMELITA
It's okay, Anti Gregory, just stay put. You'll be safe in there. I'm gonna go walk around and kill some guards.

GREGORY
Anti Gregory, I came to break you out.

ANTI GREGORY
Fat chance. This thing is triple padlocked, and Carmelita is carrying all the keys.

GREGORY
Come on, buddy, you know I'm good at stealing keys.

ANTI GREGORY
She's tough, Gregory. If you try to get a key, you better run for it. Carmelita will chase after you.

GREGORY
Leave her to me.

CARMELITA
What? My keys? One slip up, and you are mine! What? Just... Bouthiette! You can't run forever, punk... You can't sneak up on me... I will find you, there's nowhere to hide...

ANTI GREGORY
Thanks, Gregory. I was getting a charley horse standing
in that box.

GREGORY
No problem, you know how I love to mess with
Carmelita.

ANTI GREGORY
Yeah, that's weird. See you back at the safe house.

SNEAKY HERMIT
Okay, Gregory, we need to break into the Iron Horse
trains. But the only way in is through the caboose,
which is locked. To blow the locks off, you need to
collect the Spice from those balloons.

GREGORY
How am I going to get up there and collect the Spice
gas?

SNEAKY HERMIT
Anti Gregory is already near an ice plane: jump on its
strut, and he will fly you up to those balloons. Once you
have enough gas, you have to land on the Iron Horse
train's caboose.

GREGORY
Why do I need to land on to the caboose?

SNEAKY HERMIT
The Spice is very unstable at low altitudes: unless you
land on the train's caboose, you won't have time to get
the gas tank to the lock before it blows up.

GREGORY
You are saying that I need to land on the caboose, or
get blown to bits.

GREGORY BOUTHIETTE

SNEAKY HERMIT
That's right. Just put on the vacuum backpack, then get
on the ice plane.

ANTI GREGORY
Hang on tight, we are going up... Just remember to
keep on flying up here...

SNEAKY HERMIT
The Spice gas is lighter than air, so jumping on the
balloon will help you... That did it! You got enough
Spice gas. Time to land on a caboose... Meet Anti
Gregory at the ice plane, there are still two more
cabooses to blow open.

ANTI GREGORY
Here we go again.

SNEAKY HERMIT
You got enough Spice gas. Target another caboose...
Meet Anti Gregory at the ice plane. You guys are doing
great. There's just one caboose left.

ANTI GREGORY
One more caboose! Try not to get blown up.

SNEAKY HERMIT
You are filled up on gas, target the last caboose... You
guys did it! All the Iron Horse trains are unlocked...
Come back to the safe house, I am ready to do a
mission now.

GREGORY
I hear you, Sneaky Hermit... Okay, Sneaky Hermit, I'm
back. You can go on your mission now.

SNEAKY HERMIT
Okay, Gregory. I'll be back, you guys.

JEAN
[on intercom]
Attention, guards: you boys did a good job last night.
Soon I will have enough Spice gas. Get ready, later we
are going to kill us some bears.

GREGORY
If I'm right on this, Iron Horse #1 is on it's way right
now.

SNEAKY HERMIT
I see it, and it's moving very fast.

GREGORY
Just jump onto the caboose, then head in through the
hatch. Piece of cake... Awesome work, Sneaky Hermit!
That's one weird King Carrion lung for us, and one less
Iron Horse train for Jean.

SNEAKY HERMIT
Okay, guys, I'm back. Things are looking great: we
already have our first King Carrion lung; however, Iron
Horse #2 and #3 are going to be really hard. Anti
Gregory, I need you to kidnap some bear cubs and put
them in this fence that is holding down a nearby hand
cart. We'll need it if we are going to catch up with Iron
Horse #3. But don't worry, the cubs won't get hurt!
Although I won't say that for the guards...

ANTI GREGORY
Awesome, I'm gonna go and kidnap some bear cubs.
Wish me luck, you guys.

SNEAKY HERMIT
We are going to need this hand cart to chase down Iron
Horse #3, but for the time being it's all fenced in.

ANTI GREGORY
No problem, I will be able to tear that fence apart.

SNEAKY HERMIT
That fence is too tough to break with my hermit claws
or your hands. No, the only way to break that fence is
with the love of a mother for her child.

ANTI GREGORY
Uh, you got something to tell me?

SNEAKY HERMIT
Yes, I found two bear cubs for you to put in that fence.
The noise from their crying will surely bring their
mother running.

ANTI GREGORY
I get you, that big mama bear will be able to break that
fence in no time to free her cubs.

SNEAKY HERMIT
That's correct.

ANTI GREGORY
Beware, cubs, for you are hunted by me, Anti Gregory!

SNEAKY HERMIT
Good work, Anti Gregory. I've found the last bear cub,
you just need to grab it... Sorry to say, but the other cub
is somewhere in this bear cave. Be careful, Anti
Gregory... That was fast, the mother is already on her
way... That was cool. It was just a natural thing, only
more deadly.

ANTI GREGORY
I'm on my way back to the safe house, Sneaky Hermit.

SNEAKY HERMIT
Okay, Anti Gregory. Just let me know when I can head
out there.

ANTI GREGORY
Okay, I will let you know... Okay, Sneaky Hermit, you
can do your mission now.

SNEAKY HERMIT
Okay. Thanks, Anti Gregory.

GREGORY
Heads up, Sneaky Hermit, here comes Iron Horse #2.
You and your RC chopper ready?

SNEAKY HERMIT
We will get the job done, provided I can catch up with
that train... This better work, Gregory, or we won't be
able to get to the second King Carrion lung. Okay, I can
shoot forward, and drop mine bombs as well... I should
take those guns out before things get ugly... This is it,
the final stage! I'm so close! Yes! Iron Horse #2 is all
clear. Now it's all up to Gregory to finish the job...
Okay, Gregory, you can go do your part now.

GREGORY
Okay, Sneaky Hermit. I'm gonna go and steal back the
second King Carrion lung from Iron Horse #2.

SNEAKY HERMIT
Gregory, Iron Horse #2 is still moving really fast. You
won't be able to make it on board.

GREGORY
Relax, Sneaky Hermit. There's more than one way get
inside Iron Horse #2.

SNEAKY HERMIT
The other King Carrion lung should be somewhere in
the front of the train. Be careful, Greginator... Gregory,
there were like, six guns on that train! I'm glad I'm not
doing this mission... Awesome work. We have two King
Carrion lungs. Now all we need to get is the stomach.

GREGORY BOUTHIETTE

GREGORY
Okay, Sneaky Hermit, I'm back! So what's the plan,
Sneaky Hermit?

SNEAKY HERMIT
This is a little operation I'd like to call Operation Choo
Choo: first, Anti Gregory will head out to the hand cart,
where we will meet him. Then you have to climb onto
Iron Horse #3 and get to the King Carrion stomach. I
will get ready with a little RC time. Once that's done,
you will grab the King Carrion stomach and we will all
get the heck out of here.

ANTI GREGORY
Okay, I get to start the operation. I'll let you guys know
when you can come out.

GREGORY
Okay, Anti Gregory. Just head to the hand cart, and we
will meet you there.

ANTI GREGORY
Hop aboard, guys, we got a train to catch!

GREGORY
Got it. Strong work, Anti Gregory.

ANTI GREGORY
Yeah, thanks. I always do my best for these missions.

SNEAKY HERMIT
Okay, Gregory, now it's your turn, buddy. You have to
get on that train.

GREGORY
That Jean is one strange guy. The other Bandit Thief
Gang members only got a single piece of the King
Carrion parts, and he walked away with two lungs and
a stomach. It still creeps me out.

SNEAKY HERMIT
Get creeped out later. You have to get onto that train.

GREGORY
You're right. It's time for a little train robbing.

JEAN
Those kids are taking the King Carrion parts from my Iron Horse trains and it's making me mad. But the King Carrion stomach is doing good so far. Ain't nobody gonna get past me. Yes, they won't...

NEYLA
Hey, Gregory, thought I might find you here. You just can't stay away from these King Carrion parts, can you?

GREGORY
Oh, I just do it to see fun ladies like yourself.

NEYLA
If you want some fun, why not climb on top of the train? I can even show you my new ride.

GREGORY
No thanks, Neyla. I'm kind of good for now.

NEYLA
Are you sure, Gregory? Hey, maybe you can call your little friend to have a fun fight with me.

GREGORY
Come in, little friend. Neyla wants to have a fun fight with you. Are you up to it?

SNEAKY HERMIT
I already launched the RC chopper, if she is ready for a fun fight.

GREGORY BOUTHIETTE

NEYLA

Come on, Gregory, let's play... What the heck? Alright, you little RC friend. This should be fun... Hey, Sneaky Hermit, I'll be back for round two, but I need to go for a little while.

GREGORY

That was some fast flying, little friend.

SNEAKY HERMIT

Whatever you say, Gregory.

ANTI GREGORY

Hey, Gregory, get to that King Carrion stomach fast. This old handcart is starting to fall apart... I never thought I'd see the day a stomach would be turned evil.

GREGORY

It looks like Jean's locked this thing down good. We need to set it free from its lock.

SNEAKY HERMIT

Then that's just what we will do. Just make sure you take some cover when it comes out.

NEYLA

Okay, Sneaky Hermit, I'm back for round two. I do hope that you can beat me, buddy... Okay, guys, I'm gonna see you guys somewhere else. I have to go, so I will see you guys later.

SNEAKY HERMIT

Stand clear, Gregory. This might get messy... Gregory? Gregory, are you okay?

GREGORY

I got an upset stomach, but other than that, I feel great... Alright, we got all three parts. Now let's get out of here.

SNEAKY HERMIT
Okay. You heard him, Anti Gregory. Let's get out of here.

ANTI GREGORY
You got it, Sneaky Hermit.

CARMELITA
I can see the team car, guys.

SNEAKY HERMIT
Hey, Carmelita, where is Jean going now? Is he still in Canada?

CARMELITA
Yes, he is, Sneaky Hermit. There are some Northern Lights elsewhere. One night they will be brighter than ever, and the next day they will be gone. He is going to a lumber camp, and we won't know if that place is real or not anymore.

GREGORY
Well, we just have to get there. Then we'll know it's still real. Does Jean have more King Carrion parts now, Carmelita?

CARMELITA
Gregory, Jean has the King Carrion talons. His friend Andy is on his way to pick up another Battery from him.

SNEAKY HERMIT
Okay. So where is the Battery, Carmelita? We need to sneak onto Andy's blimp and steal the King Carrion brain from him. Andy does have the King Carrion brain, right?

CARMELITA
He does have it, Sneaky Hermit. But it might take us

some time to steal the talons back from Jean.

ANTI GREGORY
Carmelita, I can see the lumber camp.

GREGORY
Oh my goodness, it is real! That's the place. Good job,
Anti Gregory.

ANTI GREGORY
Hey, thanks, Gregory. I always know where we go every
time.

SNEAKY HERMIT
Okay, Gregory, you have to go out there right now. We
don't have much time, because Andy is still on his way
to pick up another Battery from Jean.

GREGORY
You got it, Sneaky Hermit.

ANTI GREGORY
Good luck out there, Gregory.

GREGORY
Thanks, Anti Gregory. I will do my best out there. But I
will still find more bottles out there.

SNEAKY HERMIT
Okay, so here's what we know so far... One: Andy's
blimp is on its way to pick up another Battery from
Jean. And two: the only way we will have a crack at
Andy's King Carrion brain is finding a way to sneak
onto his blimp.

GREGORY
But before we do that, we need to steal back the King
Carrion talons from Jean. Time is short, and we need
to take some pictures.

SNEAKY HERMIT
True, true. But before we do that, this lumber camp is
not on my map: I need you to take a look around here.
I bet you can climb on ice now, you've learned a lot
about climbing on ice.

GREGORY
Awesome, I can climb ice now. I will take some
pictures. And I am going bottle hunting as well.

SNEAKY HERMIT
I could really use those pictures... Those sawblades
look very old. I think that this camp has been around
for a while... Jean's house, the lair of the beast, the den
of evil. A really bad place for people to be... Awesome, I
can sense a wifi link to that boat. I think I can hack into
its computer... This place is bear country alright.
Awesome... He's putting out a radio signal! Okay, that
should do it. Now for the real point of the whole thing:
head to that lighthouse and try to find a way to sneak
in... There's a Battery charger, but where's the Battery
Andy is coming to pick up? Just looking at that spinner
is makes me dizzy... I was right: the front door is locked
from the inside... Maybe you should get a shot of old
Jean... Oh Gregory, listen in! He's talking to himself.

JEAN
Come on, Jean, you got it in you. Those lumberjack
games need some more competition, eh? What would
you do to get some more people for the lumberjack
games? Bullseye! I will use the King Carrion talons as a
trophy. That should bring in the competition, haha!
Oh, it's tough being this tough. It sure is.

SNEAKY HERMIT
Head back to the safe house. We need to talk about
these lumberjack games.

GREGORY
Okay, guys, I'm back. Okay, Sneaky Hermit, what
missions do we need to do in this place?

SNEAKY HERMIT
I will tell you right now. As you know, Jean has put the
King Carrion talons up as a trophy, and we might need
to compete in these lumberjack games. First, I need
you to bug his house. To do that, you need to steal
some radios and place them everywhere around this
place. We all still know that Andy is on his way to pick
up another Battery from Jean, so I need you guys to
work together to find out where the Battery is. I need
you to head inside the bear cave to steal the radios
there to bug the place. We really need to do this in
time: that blimp is on its way. Let's get to work.

ANTI GREGORY
Hey, Gregory, just tell me when it is my turn to do my
mission.

GREGORY
Okay, Anti Gregory, I will let you know. But I am gonna
be doing some more bottle hunting.

SNEAKY HERMIT
The wild bears in this area have some radios, and I
need you to steal them. Then head back out and place
them everywhere around here.

GREGORY
I'm always up for bugging someone's home.

SNEAKY HERMIT
First, sneak inside the bear cave. I will tell you the rest
from there.

GREGORY
Alright, I'm on it.

SNEAKY HERMIT
The radio transmitters have all been tagged in their mouths. You are going have to sneak up and snatch them while they're yawning.

GREGORY
That sounds safe.

SNEAKY HERMIT
Oh, and steer clear from that thin ice: walking on it will surely wake the bears.

GREGORY
I'll keep that in mind.

SNEAKY HERMIT
Only you could have pulled that off. Head outside, and I will fill you in on the next step... To form a receiver array, you will have to place the radio transmitters in precise locations around Jean's base of operations.

GREGORY
Seems easy enough.

SNEAKY HERMIT
Once you are in position, just place the radio transmitters where they belong.

JEAN
[on intercom]
Hey, all of you guards: I'm gonna tell you about the events from last month. The blue lumberjacks have won their first events, and they got a first place trophy for their good luck. Now the blue lumberjack team are gonna be going to a different place for this month.

SNEAKY HERMIT
Nice work, the array is up and running... Gregory, I have found what appears to be an ancient log-chopping

book that might be helpful for the lumberjack games.
But the book is kind of frozen deep in an ice wall, and
you are the only one who can get it free.

GREGORY
How are we supposed to get to it, wait for global
warming?

SNEAKY HERMIT
That laser there is used to cut through petrified logs. If
it could be bounced out that window, we should be able
to aim it at the ice wall and free the book.

GREGORY
How do I aim the laser out the window?

SNEAKY HERMIT
There should be a switch on the other side of this wall:
throw it on, then head outside... If I did my math right,
and I always do my math right, then the code should be
3, 5, 8... Awesome, that is a nice move.

JEAN
[on intercom]
Attention, all you sawmill guards: just make sure you
all do your jobs. There is a hero somewhere in my
hideout, and I need you to keep an eye out for that little
butthead. Make sure you all kill him; if he escapes,
then you will all be fired.

SNEAKY HERMIT
Nice work, Gregory. You got the laser pointed out the
window... Now, to get the laser pointed at the ice wall,
you are going to have to alter the direction with the
crystals I put in your pocket.

GREGORY
I see. I just need to walk where the laser stops, place
the crystal, and then it will bounce the beam into a new

position. That log chopping guide is as good as ours.

SNEAKY HERMIT
Stand clear, Gregory: something else is coming out of
the deep freeze! I have never seen an animal so full of
life, so ready to live! So much for that: he's back in the
deep freeze.

GREGORY
Cheer up, Sneaky Hermit, we got the log chopping
guide... Anti Gregory, you are up, buddy.
ANTI GREGORY
Okay, I will see you guys later. I get to have a costume
in this place.

SNEAKY HERMIT
Rumor has it that several off-duty guards meet in that
cabin for an RC combat club.

ANTI GREGORY
This is going to be great, I haven't been in any RC
combats since I was five years old. This is going to be
fun.

SNEAKY HERMIT
Those guards will not let you in the combat club
without a costume... That old moose head should work,
but there's no way that you can get up there. Hide in
this barrel while I send in Gregory to get the head for
you... Gregory, can you can grab that moose head for
Anti Gregory?

GREGORY
Anti Gregory, heads up.

ANTI GREGORY
Hey fellas, I think you can beat me, if you want to bet
on it.

GUARD
Oh, I'm in. I ain't got money, but I ain't losing to a new
guy like you.

SNEAKY HERMIT
Okay, Anti Gregory, now I know this isn't your first
time doing RC combat, but just let me tell you what you
have to do: you just have to control the RC car, and you
can only shoot while you are stopped.

GUARD
You won, man, but I don't have a lot of money.

ANTI GREGORY
That might be okay. It all depends.

GUARD
Depends on what?

ANTI GREGORY
That you know where the Northern Light Battery is.

GUARD
Well, I guess I owe you...

SNEAKY HERMIT
Nice work, Anti Gregory. Now head back to the safe
house. I'm ready to tell you guys where the Northern
Light Battery is.

ANTI GREGORY
Okay, Sneaky Hermit, I'm on my way back right now...
Okay, I'm back. What is our new mission this time?

SNEAKY HERMIT
I was reading the log-chopping guide, and I know that
we are not going to be able to beat Jean at his own
game, so I think we have to cheat. Now, I came up with
a plan: we need to steal an eagle egg. First, Anti

Gregory has to lure a bear into breaking the oil mains. I know that you can fly over the eagle's nest, Gregory, but you need to avoid the eagles as they go towards you. Then you have to grab the eagle egg and come back to the safe house. Thanks to Anti Gregory's work in the combat club, we know that the Northern Light Battery is in a silo. We just need to work together so we can hide inside the Battery and be brought onto Andy's blimp. We all got our missions. Good luck.

GREGORY
If we can trust Anti Gregory's informants, that's the silo with the Battery inside it.

SNEAKY HERMIT
To prepare for travel, we have to drain the Northern Light's energy from the Battery.

GREGORY
Anti Gregory is in position to throw you onto the boat.

SNEAKY HERMIT
Once on board, I will hack into the computer, and I will throw the hook onto the silo.

GREGORY
Okay, and I'll climb on top of the silo to grab the hook. How many hooks are we going to use?

SNEAKY HERMIT
Three should be good. Once I'm done with the hook, Anti Gregory and I will go to another boat. You should stay in position.

GREGORY
Finally, I get the easy gig.

ANTI GREGORY
I'm all set to throw you over to that boat. My aim hasn't

been too good these days.

SNEAKY HERMIT
Now to hack into the computer...

GREGORY
Okay, I can see you coming. I'm already on top of the silo. Throw the hook up to me, and I will put it on the silo... The first hook is in place. You guys should go to another boat before someone picks you up... The second one is in place, one more hook to go. Then this thing will be on empty... I was wondering what happened to that guy. Guess he just wants to stay frozen.

SNEAKY HERMIT
That did it. With the Battery chamber empty, we will be all set to move in.

GREGORY
If we are going to get an eagle egg, you have to destroy all the local oil mains first.

ANTI GREGORY
It looks pretty sturdy. I am a little strong, Gregory, but my fists can't punch through metal.

GREGORY
No problem. See that old bear down there? His name is Grizzle Face. Guards ignore him because he's blind and practically nerve-dead, but if that guy smells fish, there's no stopping him. Use Grizzle Face to destroy all the local oil mains.

ANTI GREGORY
But I don't smell like fish, do I? How do I lure him around?

GREGORY

Sneaky Hermit is in position to use his Hermit Nippers
to shoot the fish up to you. It'll be plenty to lure Grizzle
Face to your position.

ANTI GREGORY

So you want me to throw the fish at the oil mains so
that old Grizzle Face can knock them apart?

GREGORY

That's the idea. You might even want to throw the fish
at the guards, might improve their odor... Nice work!
Draw old Grizzle Face to the next local oil main by
luring him with fish.

SNEAKY HERMIT

Well, it worked, Anti Gregory. Now that the oil lines
are all destroyed, Gregory is ready to fly off to the
lighthouse... That lighthouse is a conductor for
collecting the Northern Lights. We need to shut it
down before the silo fills with energy again, or else it
will be impossible for us to hide inside.

GREGORY

So you want me to go in there and bust the thing up?
That sounds like work for Anti Gregory.

SNEAKY HERMIT

Actually, this job will require all three of our skills. The
front door is locked, and you are the only one that can
climb up to the hatch on top. Once inside, sneak down
to the ground floor and let us in. We will help you
finish the job.

GREGORY

Alright, see you on the ground floor.

SNEAKY HERMIT

Nice climbing, Gregory. You made it up to the hatch.

JEAN
[on intercom]
Attention, all of you guards working at the lighthouse: I heard that the lumberjack games are still on tomorrow, and I got some judges who will give me all 10s tomorrow. I hope they don't give me the wrong numbers like they did last year. And make sure you all get ready for the log-chopping contest. And the ice wall climbing. And the spinning log-rolling event as well. And keep an eye out for that little kid who is a hero.

ANTI GREGORY
Thanks, Gregory. Just let me at that Northern Lights attractor: it will be slag in minutes.

SNEAKY HERMIT
Not quite that simple, Anti Gregory. I need to reverse the energy flow from the control computer while you lift the main circuit breaker; that should give Gregory a good opportunity to climb up the power lines and overload the system from the top.

GREGORY
Up, down, up, down. They should put an elevator in this place.

SNEAKY HERMIT
Get climbing, Gregory. We can't keep this thing reversed forever.

ANTI GREGORY
Yeah, this is heavier than it looks.

SNEAKY HERMIT
We did it, the Battery charger is overloading... In order to overcome Jean in the lumberjack games, we need a little help from the Canadian eagles. Their nest is out on that iceberg: steal one of the eggs, and then bring it back to the safe house. We will use the egg, then the

eagle will make Jean lose his score.

GREGORY
Sure, sounds easy enough. Except for the part where I have to swim to the nest through freezing water.

SNEAKY HERMIT
Why swim when you can fly? With the oil mains all destroyed, it makes a clear sky for you to fly to the eagle's nest.

GREGORY
I get it: I can just fly over the nest in that wind, and it will give me more air for me to fly to the eagle's nest.

SNEAKY HERMIT
Just make sure to stay out of the fire: get too close, and old Grizzle Face will be eating fried hero for dinner.

GREGORY
That's a nice tip, Sneaky Hermit.

SNEAKY HERMIT
Watch out for those eagles, they don't look friendly... Nice work. If you can get that eagle egg back to the safe house safe and sound, we will be all set for the lumberjack games... Great work, Gregory.

GREGORY
Okay, Sneaky Hermit, so is it time for the lumberjack games?

SNEAKY HERMIT
Yes, it is time, Gregory. The lumberjack games are on. We all know that we're not good enough to beat Jean at his own game, so it pains me to say... We have to cheat. Anti Gregory, you will compete in the log-chopping competition: give us a good score, then let Jean up for his turn. While he's chopping, I will sneak the eagle egg

onto his log; then the angry parent will make him lose his score. And Gregory, I know that you are a good climber, so I signed you up for the ice wall climb. When Jean is climbing, we will use these hooks to pull him off the wall so that he won't beat your score. And finally, I will compete in the log-spinning event, where Gregory will make sure he won't beat our score. If you guys are ready, I say we head out and show these lumberjack meatheads what we're made of... Okay, guys, let's head down and win those talons from Jean. Gregory, try to keep low when we get close. We don't want him to see you... Excuse me, sir, we humble lumberjacks would like to compete in your lumberjack games.

JEAN
Think you got what it takes to win the King Carrion talons, eh? Well, I'll sure let you play, as long you pay the entry fee.

SNEAKY HERMIT
Well, we will, sir. We will just take our positions for the competition.

JEAN
Enjoy the moment while you still have a chance: this is as close as you will ever get. This year's first event will be a power chopping contest. It's not like anyone is gonna beat my record, but I'll let him try... Not bad, blue boy, but watch and learn as I destroy that log without even breaking a sweat.

GREGORY
Okay, Sneaky Hermit, you are on. Plant the eagle egg on Jean, and the angry eagle parent should mess up his ax swinging.

JEAN
What? I think you better rethink those score, boys. You promised me that you'd give me perfect 10s, right? So

your blue friend knows how to handle an ax. Let's see how well you can handle a wall of ice... Pretty good for a little boy, but now watch how I climb an ice wall.

SNEAKY HERMIT
Anti Gregory, use those hooks to hook onto Jean. You will need to hook him up with all three hooks to pull him off the wall.

JEAN
It seems you have pulled the wrong cards again. Did I tell any of you the story about the last judges that gave me a score other than 10? I see we are tied with only one event to go. Lucky for me, I saved my best event for last: the log-spinning competition.

SNEAKY HERMIT
Okay, looks easy enough. I just need to stay out of the water.

JEAN
You are one lucky hermit crab, I'll give you that. Now watch how a steamroller does it.

ANTI GREGORY
This is crazy! Jean's got those judges scared so good, there's no way he could lose.

GREGORY
You are right, Anti Gregory. Those guys need to go. Okay, I'm just pulling this off on the fly, but what if I lure the judges one by one into that cave, and once inside, you can knock them out and take their clothes.

SNEAKY HERMIT
That is a good idea. With all three down and out, we will be able to take their places at the judges' table. Gregory, you can lure the judges into the cave with your alarm clock move.

GREGORY BOUTHIETTE

ANTI GREGORY
That's a great plan, Gregory, but you have to move fast:
once Jean finishes the log rolling event, the gig is up.

JEAN
What? I thought I warned you judges about the
consequences for incorrect scores... Wait a second, you
aren't the judges I hired. It's that Bouthiette kid and his
annoying friends! Well, if you want the talons, then
maybe you should just take them!

SNEAKY HERMIT
Ouch, my aching head! Those talons really pack a
punch. Gregory, Anti Gregory, wake up!

GREGORY
Yeah, I'm awake. But not so loud, I have a splitting
headache.

ANTI GREGORY
Huh? Where are we? What's going on?

SNEAKY HERMIT
This looks like the sawmill control room. Jean must
have put us in here to interrogate later. I, for one,
would like to escape before he returns.

GREGORY
It looks like we are sealed pretty tight in here. Unless...

SNEAKY HERMIT
Unless what?

GREGORY
Unless you can fit through that hole.

SNEAKY HERMIT
I think I can fit through there. I'll try to help you guys
from the outside. If there's any trouble, I'll call with

this walkie talkie: you might be able to help me out with these sawmill controls.

ANTI GREGORY
While you guys do that, I'll try to open that steel door. Given enough time, I might be able to make some progress.

GREGORY
Sounds like a plan. Good luck, Sneaky Hermit. And remember to shout if I can help you from up here... Sneaky Hermit, are you okay? I can't see you from here, but I heard the fall.

SNEAKY HERMIT
I'll be fine. Just give me a moment to catch my breath.

JEAN
Well now, you butthead, I see that you were able to find a rat hole to crawl through.

SNEAKY HERMIT
Well, I just dropped my glasses and had to come and pick them up.

JEAN
I ain't like you, boy, I ain't dumb. While you were all unconscious, I paid a visit to your little safe house and found all the King Carrion parts. Lucky thing, too, Andy was looking to plunk down a king's ransom for the whole lot. I even threw in the talons.

SNEAKY HERMIT
You sold all the King Carrion parts? Andy has them all?

JEAN
I wouldn't expect one of your kind to understand the finer points of commerce; you hermit crabs are too dumb to know a woodcutter from a woodchuck.

SNEAKY HERMIT
That's it, it's time I show you just how dumb we hermit
crabs really are. Gregory, on my command.

GREGORY
I hear you.

SNEAKY HERMIT
Prepare yourself, Jean. En garde!

JEAN
Okay, walnut, get ready for a beatdown.

GREGORY
Call out which lever I should pull.

SNEAKY HERMIT
Saws!

GREGORY
Got him.

SNEAKY HERMIT
Fire!

GREGORY
Bam.

SNEAKY HERMIT
Logs!

GREGORY
Okay.

SNEAKY HERMIT
Sawblades!

JEAN
Come in here, boys! Let's get this butthead.

SNEAKY HERMIT
Flames! Flames!

GREGORY
Ten-four.

SNEAKY HERMIT
Saws! Saws!

GREGORY
On it.

SNEAKY HERMIT
Cook him!

JEAN
Eat dynamite, hermit crab.

SNEAKY HERMIT
Saws!

GREGORY
Bam.

SNEAKY HERMIT
Fire up! Saws! Saws! Logs!

JEAN
Come out, boys. Let's get to killing.

SNEAKY HERMIT
Cook him! Log drop!

GREGORY
On it.

SNEAKY HERMIT
Fire up! Saws!

GREGORY
Done.

JEAN
Oh fart, I've been done in by some darn hermit crab.
Times are changing.

SNEAKY HERMIT
Once again, brains triumph over brawns.

GREGORY
Good job, Sneaky Hermit. That was some fast thinking.

ANTI GREGORY
Don't forget about me.

GREGORY
You did a great job opening that door, Anti Gregory.

ANDY
[on intercom]
Attention, uh, Jean: Andy's carrion blimp will arrive to
pick up the Northern Light Battery in exactly one
minute.

SNEAKY HERMIT
Okay, enough patting ourselves on the back. If we are
going to get the King Carrion parts back, we have to get
onto that blimp.

GREGORY
The Battery silo isn't far. If we run, we can make it.

ANTI GREGORY
Enough talk, let's move.

GREGORY
Shake a leg, that blimps on it's way... I'm so mad,
Sneaky Hermit.

SNEAKY HERMIT
Don't worry, Gregory. I'm making some plans for us to
do things on the blimp.

GREGORY
Okay, good. If I see Andy, I am going to kick his butt so
hard he won't be able to stand up again. It won't be
good for him, but it will be so good for me.

ANTI GREGORY
Uh, guys, the team car is floating away on an iceberg in
the ocean.

GREGORY
I'm sorry, buddy. I will make it up to you. I promise.

***

SNEAKY HERMIT
Okay, guys, I have made some plans for us to do on the
blimp.

GREGORY
What kind of things are we going to do, Sneaky
Hermit?

SNEAKY HERMIT
Okay, this is our target right here: his name is Andy,
and he can't fly because his wings aren't made for
flying. He couldn't keep up with the other boys when
he was younger, and now the Bandit Thief Gang make
fun of him because he can't fly. Now he is going to put
the King Carrion parts back together and if that
happens...

GREGORY
Oh, I'm not gonna let that happen. Not on my watch.

SNEAKY HERMIT
You said it, Gregory. You're going out there right now.

GREGORY
Okay, Sneaky Hermit. I'll be back, you guys.

SNEAKY HERMIT
My computer tells me that you will find the King
Carrion parts in that big part of the blimp. You have to
go in there and see what they are doing to build King
Carrion.
GREGORY
Sounds good. I'm on my way.

SNEAKY HERMIT
Don't waste any time here, Gregory. Just head over
there and take some pictures.

GREGORY
Relax, Sneaky Hermit. I got it under control.

SNEAKY BACK
Whoa! I had no idea that they could build King Carrion
so fast.

GREGORY
Calm down, Sneaky Hermit. He may be in one piece,
but he doesn't seem to be alive. Just stick to the plan.
What kind of pictures should I take?

SNEAKY HERMIT
You are right! To build a plan of action, try taking a
picture of King Carrion's head and a mech egg. And
one of those spinning magnetic inducers: they seem
important to the plan. But stay away from the guards.
If you get detected, we won't have time for a second
try... These magnetic inducers seem to be holding the
King Carrion parts together... I'm picking some sound
waves from inside those mech eggs, I wouldn't get too
close... King Carrion doesn't seem to be alive yet. We
still might have a chance... Gregory, I'm picking up
some voices from the front of the blimp. I think it's
Andy... Neyla! Neyla's here, too... There he is: the
mastermind of this operation, and the root of our
problems... I can't believe it, she must have been
working with Andy all along! I don't really need to see
the pictures on the wall to know the plan behind this
whole thing: clearly Neyla and Andy have been working
together to put King Carrion back together, and they
are starting to realize their goal.

GREGORY
Look, Sneaky Hermit, I know that you don't really like
it that much, but I need a quick plan of attack. Try to
think of a way, any way, to keep King Carrion from
coming to life.

SNEAKY HERMIT
Well, those magnetic inducers seem to be holding the King Carrion parts together... If you can reverse them, it should pull King Carrion apart. But the inducer speed control is locked down tight. If you can pickpocket the guards keys, you might be able to climb up and reverse each magnetic inducer deck at the top of their rotation.

GREGORY
Consider it done.

SNEAKY HERMIT
Now get to the speed control station and slow down those magnetic inducers... Now that the magnetic inducers are slowing down, get up there and reverse the polarity of each deck.

ANDY
What's all this, then? The magnets have been reversed, but by Jove! It seems to have locked the King Carrion parts into place. Awesome.

NEYLA
Gregory Bouthiette! Of course this would be your doing.

ANDY
Ah, Mr. Bouthiette, no doubt you believed a reversal would pull the old bird apart, eh? But it seems to have had quite the opposite effect. I'm truly grateful: when fully powered up, I'll join myself to it and be reborn.

GREGORY
All this because you can't fly? You are a butthead.

ANDY
No, I am not. But to you, I am. I have known you for a short time now, and now you will have to sit tight while

I join myself to the King Carrion frame. The other Bandit Thief Gang members did a good job with their King Carrion parts, but they were too concerned with doing their own thing with the separate pieces when they stole them. But not me, no: I have created this blimp, and I saw the parts for what they really are...
The keys to life everlasting!

GREGORY
So, what? You had Neyla play a trick on me back in India when I stole the other King Carrion parts from the other Bandit Thief Gang members? All this time, I was trying to find them for myself, but you were behind it all.

NEYLA
It's not what you think, Gregory! I didn't mean to play a trick on you and your friends. I only wanted to help you guys, and just wait until you guys got the rest of the King Carrion parts from the other Bandit Thief Gang members. And I know that you don't like it when people do this to you guys, but I did help you get the King Carrion eye... I liked helping you to find the parts.

ANDY
Ah, but the other half of the King Carrion parts were still with the other Bandit Thief Gang members. Think, Bouthiette! What kept King Carrion alive for thousands of years?

GREGORY
He had a strong hate for me and my family.

ANDY
Yes, that's right! Hatred for you and your family. And I know you want to take him down again, but this time is gonna be different. This time, Bouthiette, I will make people hate. Hate! All around the world! And I will become the most powerful bad guy in the whole world.

GREGORY BOUTHIETTE

GREGORY
You can't make people hate.

ANDY
Oh, but I can do it, Bouthiette. To make people hate, I will blow up their whole cities one at a time. And there is nothing that you can do to stop me. When you and your blue friend were locked up by Cammy, you guys had a little hate for every Bandit Thief Gang member that you had defeated. I will use Spice to create a cloud of hatred under the blimp, and I will power it with Northern Light energy.

GREGORY
The Northern Lights! You've been collecting the Northern Light energy so that you can control everyone under the blimp...

ANDY
Oh, my good friend, you think you know so much about everything I am going to do! Thank goodness for Demetrie: when you took him down, it made me so happy to see his nightclub shut down when Carmelita and Neyla put him in jail.

GREGORY
You are going to Paris to do a light show under your own blimp? That is so uncool.

ANDY
Uncool, is it? It's not uncool for me, I was the one who made the plan! Ah well, my new body awaits me. Be a dear, Neyla, and deal with this boy while I'm gone. Ta ta!

NEYLA
Dumb Andy, you know I would never turn my back on Gregory and his friends, and the cops, and Carmelita as well! But I can turn my back on you.

ANDY

How dare you turn your back on me. Fine! If you don't want me to go in the King Carrion frame, I can still bring him back to life without being inside!

NEYLA

If you bring him to life, Andy, you will make him go out of control.

ANDY

I don't care what you say, Neyla. I will bring him to life.

NEYLA

Step away from that control station, Andy, or I will beat you on my own.

ANDY

It's too late, Neyla! I have already turned King Carrion on! And now you will all die.

NEYLA

Gregory, get out of here! I'm gonna go and kill Andy. Just head back to the safe house. I'll meet you there soon.

GREGORY

Okay, Neyla. I'll see you around on the blimp.

KING CARRION

Behold, I am reborn! I'm coming for you, Bouthiette.

GREGORY

Sneaky Hermit, what do we do now?

SNEAKY HERMIT

I got some bad news, you guys: I just heard that Andy has already turned King Carrion back on. Now King Carrion is out and free. Neyla is going after Andy, but we are still on our way to Paris for a light-wave show.

But we still got a chance! We all know that Andy's blimp is still moving without him actually controlling it. We have to do some team-ups to take out all these engine rooms one at a time. We pulled off tough jobs in the past, but they were just a warm-up for what we are going through tonight.

GREGORY

Okay, I'm gonna go out there and do my missions first. And I'm still going to keep an eye out for those bottles.

SNEAKY HERMIT

Okay, Gregory. I'm gonna wait until you get to your first mission... This engine room is locked down tight. Since we can't get in it, we have to destroy it from the outside.

GREGORY

I hope you're carrying heavy bombs, Sneaky Hermit, because that is one tough engine to blow up.

SNEAKY HERMIT

It just so happens that there is some dynamite down there for you to use to destroy the engine room. But that dynamite is not tough enough to blow it up by itself: there are three dynamite sticks for you to put on that barrel... Just make sure you don't jump out of the barrel before you get to the engine room, or else you will get blown up.

GREGORY

Alright, let's blow stuff up.

SNEAKY HERMIT

Good work, Gregory. Now that you have enough dynamite sticks, you should be able to blow up the engine room.

GREGORY
That's one less engine room for King Carrion to use.

SNEAKY HERMIT
To do some damage in the next engine room, you and I
are gonna have to work together.

GREGORY
Happy to have you along, Sneaky Hermit. So what do
you want me to do?

SNEAKY HERMIT
Pickpocket keys to the engine room from the guards;
once you got the door open, I'll take over.

GREGORY
Okay, you should take your position now: it's not
gonna take me too long to convince those guards to
lend me their keys.

SNEAKY HERMIT
Okay, I'm waiting by the engine room door.

GREGORY
Okay, Sneaky Hermit, you're on!

ANTI GREGORY
I'm looking at these blueprints here, and you need to
use your Hermit Nippers to break every one of these
bulbs to get up to the second level. But here's the hard
part: if you miss or hit the wrong bulb, then this place
and everything in this engine room will go kaboom...
Okay, Sneaky Hermit, you are all set to head up to the
second level... If I'm reading this right, you are going to
have to use your Hermit Nippers again to break those
power nodes and get into that control room. Once
that's done, you should be able to shut down that
engine room... Make it all the way, Sneaky Hermit!
Once you hit the switch, that engine room is toast...

GREGORY BOUTHIETTE

That's one less engine room for King Carrion to take power from.

SNEAKY HERMIT
That's one of the engines that needs to be shut down. I won't lie to you, Anti Gregory, but this is going to be one tough job for both of our skills.

ANTI GREGORY
My skills? Okay, Sneaky Hermit, if you say so.

SNEAKY HERMIT
First, I need to hack into the computers in the engine room. Once that's done, you will need to finish the job from the inside

ANTI GREGORY
Anti Gregory will be ready to go.

SNEAKY HERMIT
Make way for Anti Gregory!

GREGORY
Okay, Anti Gregory, it looks like you have to lift those Batteries up, and when you are done with that, make your way up to the second level. Then jump on them... Heads up, Anti Gregory: you got company... Nice work. Head up to the second level and jump on those Batteries. That should finish them off... Awesome. Now head into the control room and pull the plug on this thing... Another engine bites the dust... Anti Gregory, it looks like I'm gonna need some help to get into that engine room.

ANTI GREGORY
Happy to help.

GREGORY
Sneaky Hermit tells me the door to that room is locked

down by wall-mounted power stations located throughout the blimp. I need you to take out all of the power stations! Then pry open the door to the engine room by hand.

ANTI GREGORY
No sweat, Gregory.

GREGORY
Okay, I'm at the engine room. Head on back and pry open the door for me.

ANTI GREGORY
Your turn, buddy.

SNEAKY HERMIT
Careful, Gregory! This place is packed with some bad stuffs! First, you need to make your way to the far end of the room and get up to the second level engine room system... Gregory, the control center is on the opposite side the room. You'll have to jump on the spinners to make your way to the control center... That Andy really knew his codes. I think the code to this vault is 7, 2, 5... You got Shadow Power! That's lights out for this engine... I just got word that Carmelita is flying her chopper and trying to find this blimp. She is looking forward to stopping King Carrion as much as we are. We must stop King Carrion before he becomes too powerful! She told me that she wants you to help her take down King Carrion, Gregory. But the problem is that she can't find the blimp herself. To help her find the blimp, we'll need to turn on these four radio towers. Once Carmelita has found the blimp, she will take one of us on board to team up and get in a fight with King Carrion. This is it! We don't have time for another plan. We're almost over Paris, and if that Hate Mind Control goes off, well... You know the story... Okay, Gregory. We need to send a signal to Carmelita so that she can find this blimp. To do that, I'll need you

to get on top of those very tall towers. They're too big to climb, and too tall to jump onto normally.

GREGORY
What's this all got to do with this thing you got me wearing?

SNEAKY HERMIT
It's an experimental mega jump-pack. You should be able to mega jump high enough to reach the towers. Be careful.

GREGORY
Alright, sounds like fun.

SNEAKY HERMIT
Aha! It looks like Carmelita has just picked up our signal. She is heading for us now.

CARMELITA
Look, Gregory, I don't have time to say hello. I need you to get onto my chopper and take the gun while I drive this. Now hurry, Gregory! We got a bird to take down.

GREGORY
Alright, Carmelita. Let's end this once and for all.

CARMELITA
You're doing it, Gregory... Keep it up... Nice shot! You got him, Gregory! Keep at it, we're winning! Yes! King Carrion is not gonna like that... You could have been a cop; that was some good shooting.

SNEAKY HERMIT
Gregory! Gregory! We got a problem here: King Carrion is looking very mad, and I think he's going to take it out on us!

GREGORY
I'm coming, guys. Hold on.

SNEAKY HERMIT
Hurry up, Gregory! We need your help.

ANTI GREGORY
Make it fast, Gregory. We don't want to die!

SNEAKY HERMIT
Help us, Gregory! We are gonna die!

KING CARRION
THERE'S PLENTY OF ME TO GO AROUND.

GREGORY
You may have come back to life, King Carrion, but you are still the same bird that we've taken down time and time again. This won't be any different.

KING CARRION
BE BRAVE WHILE YOU CAN, BOUTHIETTE. I WILL STILL KILL YOU. I WILL KILL YOU MYSELF! MY HATE WILL BE IN ME FOREVER.

GREGORY
We... We did it.

ANTI GREGORY
Right on!

SNEAKY HERMIT
It's a good moment.

NEYLA
Hey, guys, I finally got Andy! And I see that you guys took down King Carrion already.

GREGORY
Yes, we did, Neyla. Thank you for all your help.

KING CARRION

YOU ALL THINK YOU HAVE WON THE BATTLE. I WILL KILL ALL OF YOU. MY HATE WILL SMASH YOU.

GREGORY

Watch out, that thing is still kicking.

SNEAKY HERMIT

I think King Carrion just said something about a hate chip. I think it's the source of his power!

GREGORY

If we remove it, he might stop attacking.

ANTI GREGORY

Then let's do a little head opening. I'll lift open his head, and Sneaky Hermit can go to town with his Hermit Nippers.

KING CARRION

YOU WILL NEVER BEAT ME, BOUTHIETTE GANG. YOU WILL NEVER ESCAPE FROM MY WRATH. I AM KING CARRION. I WILL DESTROY. I STILL HAVE MY HATE. I WILL DESTROY YOU IN YOUR SLEEP.

SNEAKY HERMIT

Let's get out of here, he's about to explode... Ouch! My glasses! And my legs! I can't feel my legs!

ANTI GREGORY

What? Sneaky Hermit! I'll save you!

SNEAKY HERMIT

Thanks, Anti Gregory. You saved me.

ANTI GREGORY

No problem, Sneaky Hermit. Now let's get out of here.

NEYLA

Hey, guys! Wait for me! I'm coming with you.

GREGORY
Where have you been, Neyla?

NEYLA
I leaned Andy on King Carrion, and now he's dead.

GREGORY
That was nice of you to do, Neyla. I really thought you
died in that explosion back there.

NEYLA
No, I did not die.

SNEAKY HERMIT
Guys, look! The King Carrion parts are just lying there.

CARMELITA
Guys! You're okay! Hey, Neyla, you're back.

NEYLA
Yes, I'm back, Carmelita. And now King Carrion and
Andy are both dead.

GREGORY
Here, Carmelita. I want you to break the hate chip.

CARMELITA
Okay, thanks, Gregory. I will break it with my foot right
now.

GREGORY
Neyla, are you okay?

NEYLA
Yeah, I am. It's nothing.

CARMELITA
It doesn't look like nothing, Neyla. Are you sure that
you're okay?

NEYLA
I can't move on, Carmelita. I must die now.

CARMELITA
Wait, what? Neyla, you can't sacrifice yourself!

NEYLA
I'm sorry, guys... But I have to sacrifice myself now.

GREGORY
Neyla, wait! You don't have to do this.

CARMELITA
Just let her go, Gregory. It's her mission. Now I need to take you guys.

SNEAKY HERMIT
Umm, Carmelita, I need to get help. Anti Gregory has already left.

GREGORY
Okay, Sneaky Hermit, you guys can go now. I'll go with Carmelita.

CARMELITA
Come on, Gregory. Let's go.

NEYLA
Goodbye, guys. I'll miss you.

GREGORY
Neyla, no...

CARMELITA
It's too late, Gregory. She's dead now.

GREGORY
Okay, let's go. I can't stay and watch.

CARMELITA
Okay, Gregory. Let's go, buddy.

GREGORY
Carmelita, thanks for all your help during this whole
journey.

CARMELITA
It's always fun being with you guys on these journeys,
Gregory. But I think you need to go with your friends
now.

GREGORY
Are you sure, Carmelita? Do you really want me to
jump out of this chopper right now?

CARMELITA
Just do it, buddy. I won't mind.

GREGORY
Thanks, Carmelita. I'll see around.

CARMELITA
I'll find you, Greginator.

THE BOOK OF ADVENTURES 3: HONOR AMONG HEROES

SNEAKY HERMIT
This is it, Gregory! The gang is assembled and in
position to help you get up to that vault. For the rest of
the operation, you are The Ball.

GREGORY
Roger that, Sneaky Hermit. I'm starting my approach.
Getting over these fortress walls shouldn't be a
problem. Looks like we are running five by five here.
Make sure everyone is ready.

SNEAKY HERMIT
I hear that. Artillery, sure you can make that shot?

PANDA
I endeavor not to miss.

SNEAKY HERMIT
Excellent. Radio control?

PINKY
In position.

SNEAKY HERMIT
Random teammate?

ANTI GREGORY
I'm pumped.

SNEAKY HERMIT
Submersibles?

DEMETRIE
Show time, baby.

SNEAKY HERMIT
Telekinetics?

GAGE
I am on the job.

SNEAKY HERMIT
Alright, it's time to do this! The Ball is in motion...
Radio control, take up for position for a Yank-86, over.

PINKY
I got it under control.

SNEAKY HERMIT
The Ball has stopped rolling; we need to clear out
everything.

PINKY
I'm on it... First is away... Second guy is pulled... Third
is skyward. Roll on, Ball, over.

SNEAKY HERMIT
Telekinetics, request for timber.

GAGE
Got it. I am already in position.

SNEAKY HERMIT
Let it go, Telekinetics. The Ball's in position.

GAGE
Okay, the tower is down, and the path's clear now,
over.

SNEAKY HERMIT
Nice work. The Ball's back on track.

GREGORY
Ball to Artillery: requesting door, over.

PANDA
Launching. Stand clear.

SNEAKY HERMIT
I got word that the door has been blown open. Nice shooting... We got word that The Ball is almost near the lab. Submersibles, are you ready?

DEMETRIE
Spear gun loaded.

SNEAKY HERMIT
Submersibles, fire away.

DEMETRIE
First is down.

SNEAKY HERMIT
I'm reading that both lasers are down. Strong work, Submersibles.

DEMETRIE
Any time.

DREADED GREGORY
How's your wife doing, Craig?

CRAIG
Oh, very well, Dreaded Gregory. Thank you for asking. Very thoughtful.

DREADED GREGORY
And your son, ah, what's his name? Zack?

CRAIG
Jason, sir. He is well, too, sir.

DREADED GREGORY
It's a shame that you won't be able to see them again.

CRAIG
Uh, sir?

DREADED GREGORY
I'm afraid that I had to poison your drink and lunch.
Sorry, Craig, but I don't need anyone like you. You
should have changed the code from 1-2-3 after you
installed the system.

CRAIG
I did! I swear!

DREADED GREGORY
And now you're going to die any second now... Yes,
water leaking into the lab. I'm on my way down now.
Oh, and get a janitor for the lab elevator. Craig's spit on
it.

SNEAKY HERMIT
The Bouthiette vault is just across these hills. I'm on
my way to your position for the loot taking, over...
Power down the code to the vault.

DREADED GREGORY
Well well well, look who decided to pay me a visit at my
hideout. Gregory Bouthiette, what a surprise from my
old friend.

GREGORY
This vault belongs to the Bouthiette family. You are
trespassing.

DREADED GREGORY
No, Gregory, you are trespassing! Because you are in
my hideout, of course, and you are not supposed to
come anywhere near my hideout. Now you will lose the
key to the vault: hand over your glasses, Gregory
Bouthiette.

GREGORY
Sorry, Dreaded Gregory, you can't have these glasses!
Because I need these to see everything, and you can't

take everything away from me.

SNEAKY HERMIT
Quick, let's regroup with the others! Follow me...
Hurry!

DREADED GREGORY
You will never get away, Gregory.

SNEAKY HERMIT
Jump for it... This place is flooding, we don't have
much time... The tunnel is gonna go, hurry! We are
almost home free... The team car is just up ahead...
Whoa!

DREADED GREGORY
There's no escape, Gregory. I can't let you leave. You
don't have the guts to stop me, because you are weak,
Gregory.

SNEAKY HERMIT
It's not working, save yourself!

GREGORY
If you want to destroy someone, then destroy me
instead.

DREADED GREGORY
Okay, I will. I have never liked you, Sneaky Hermit.
You are lucky this time.

SNEAKY HERMIT
Gregory, no! Hold on, Gregory, hold on!

***

A flashback in my head...

SNEAKY HERMIT
Okay, Gregory, I have been looking for our friend Anti
Gregory, but I can't find him anywhere on my
computer!

GREGORY
Have you tried finding him in Venice, Sneaky Hermit?
I think his dream-time teacher sent him on a walk of
his own. I hope that he stays away from Dawn Owen
White.

SNEAKY HERMIT
Who's Dawn Owen White, Gregory? And how did you
hear about him?

GREGORY
I just got an email from a friend: he told me Dawn
Owen White got set free from jail, and he's in Venice
again. He is going to be an opera singer someday.

SNEAKY HERMIT
Okay, let's head to Venice... Given how Anti Gregory
walks, he's got to be somewhere around the city. If he's
not in jail, then that's where we'll find him... That glass
dome is too big for us to break. We need a way in...

GREGORY
Cops really like to keep a presence around here.

SNEAKY HERMIT
I'm afraid it's a losing battle. Dawn Owen White runs
the show in this neighborhood. His guards are running
the streets, not the cops.

GREGORY
Noted. Hmm, looks like I have found my way inside.

SNEAKY HERMIT
That dome is covered in glazed tile, there's no way to

climb up there.

GREGORY
Uh, come on, Sneaky Hermit. There's always a way.

SNEAKY HERMIT
Nice climbing, Gregory. I got the blueprint to the vent system in front of me! I shall guide you to the jail cell.

GREGORY
Hey, Anti Gregory, is that you?

DEMETRIE
Anti Gregory: that name is a stain on my pants, bro. What? Bouthiette, you got some nerve to come around here.

GREGORY
Demetrie, long time no punch. I see you're still in jail.

DEMETRIE
And you're still a crackerbox.

GREGORY
Let's get past the name-calling and get to business.

DEMETRIE
Looking for your main man Anti Gregory. Hey, sorry, but I'd rather see you get caught by the big time guard police.

GREGORY
Wait... If those cops get their hands on me, who's gonna break you out of jail?

DEMETRIE
You might get the cell door open, but you will get busted. And get thrown in here. And I will get the double sentence. Awesome.

GREGORY

How about I get the cops' attention? You will make a run for it. Once they are all outside shooting, you can slip out in no time.

DEMETRIE

Now that's a plan that I can get behind. Demetrie is free, and Bouthiette is cooked. Key for the cell is in the lady's office.

GREGORY

Okay, great. This other lock won't be a problem, I should be able to crack it by hand.

DEMETRIE

Get me out of here, and I'll find Anti Gregory, no sweat. Just keep on the down-low and out of sight near the coppers, bro. They are a bad bunch of bunnies.

CARMELITA

Your attention, police: thank you for your time. We are now ready to find out what Dawn Owen White is up to. As we all know, Venice's streets are being watched by White's guards, so we need to do this carefully if we are going to put Dawn Owen White away for good! But to do that, we may need some help from some friends of mine. I will contact Sneaky Hermit and tell him that we will help him out on his missions. And don't kill them, because those guys are my friends, and I told them to help us. We need to play along with them. Just try not to kill them, okay, men?

SNEAKY HERMIT

Nice work. Head back to Demetrie's cell and free him. If he's true to his word, we will be talking to Anti Gregory in no time.

CARMELITA

Let's get back to business, now where was I... Hold

tight, boys. The power is on the fritz again. It will come back in a few minutes.

SNEAKY HERMIT
Better make sure that you are under a desk when the lights come back on.

COPS
Let there be light... Ah, come on.... Better... On, off, on, off... This is shocking.

DEMETRIE
Can you really crack this coconut?

GREGORY
Sure, just takes a light touch.

DEMETRIE
Good. Let's get some shine, bro! I swear, you spring me, and I'll hook you up with your friend Anti Gregory. Dig?

SNEAKY HERMIT
This safe will be tough to crack, but I have seen you open harder locks.

GREGORY
I'll do what I promised: I'll have the cops shoot me so that you can make your escape.

DEMETRIE
Awesome. Don't worry no mind, I will let Anti Gregory know where to find you. Meet at Rialto Bridge. Big Italian landmark.

GREGORY
Okay, I guess it's show time... Hello, all you butthead cops. And lady. Anyone feel like some exercise?

CARMELITA

Gregory! Stay here, men! I'm gonna go and talk to my buddy. I'll be with him for a while.

GREGORY

And... I'm out.

CARMELITA

It's good to see you again, Gregory.

GREGORY

It's good to see you as well, Carmelita.

CARMELITA

But you must know I need to chase you again, buddy.

GREGORY

Yeah, I do know that you have to chase me. Hey, Carmelita: when we put Dawn Owen White in jail again, do you want to get some milkshakes with the three of us?

CARMELITA

Yes, I would love to do that, but I need to help you find your friend Anti Gregory again.

GREGORY

Okay, good, because we do need your help finding Anti Gregory. You are awesome for helping us out so much.

CARMELITA

Hey, thanks. And I think you are awesome as well, buddy... Just keep on going, Gregory! You're almost there.

ANTI GREGORY

Hey there, Gregory. I'm happy to see you. Wait, Carmelita? Is that you? It's good to see you as well, Carmelita.

GREGORY BOUTHIETTE

CARMELITA

Hey, Anti Gregory. It's good to see you, buddy.

GREGORY

Quick, Anti Gregory! We need to get out of here now.

CARMELITA

See you later, Gregory, and tell Sneaky Hermit that I said hi.

GREGORY

Thanks for the quick escape. I owe you one... Again.

ANTI GREGORY

No problem, Gregory. And it's good to help you out again.

GREGORY

You are really good at this whole dream-time stuff, huh?

ANTI GREGORY

It's a little hard, but I will get the hang of it.

GREGORY

Listen, Anti Gregory, we need you back on the team. That whole thing with Sneaky Hermit... It wasn't your fault. He doesn't blame you at all.

ANTI GREGORY

Sorry, Gregory, but I walk a different path. My dream-time master, Gage, has been training me, so I have to listen to him. He told me to not return to the team until the black water runs clear again. So here I stay.

GREGORY

Are you sure you want your master to be in charge of you?

ANTI GREGORY
Yes. He tells me everything to do, and I will do
everything that he says. So here I stay.

GREGORY
Sorry, sorry. Tell me everything. I've missed you,
buddy.

ANTI GREGORY
Well, it's a long and awesome story. Got any gum?

SNEAKY HERMIT
Anti Gregory cannot come back to the team until what
Gage said comes true: whether we like or not, we need
to deal with Venice's tar problem, or, as Anti Gregory
puts it, make the black water run clear. Thanks to
Carmelita's files, we now know what Dawn Owen
White is up to. We still need to get inside his opera
house: if he's hiding something, I will be able to hack
into his computer and find out what he's up to. We
should also keep an eye out for the singer himself. With
some luck, we might be able to pull this all together...
This opera house is Owen's base of operations.

GREGORY
Nice place. I'm sure there are some coins lying around
in there. What's the plan?

SNEAKY HERMIT
If you can get me inside to one of Owen's computers,
we are sure to find out what he's up to.

GREGORY
Okay. Got a plan for entering? I'm guessing the front
door is not the safest option.

SNEAKY HERMIT
That wooden hatch should be a good place to slip in
undetected. Head down there, and we'll meet up in a

few minutes... Owen is known to rely on 3D technology to secure his firewall: in order to search his computer, we'll need to use these 3D glasses.

GREGORY
Awesome. Nice touch, Sneaky Hermit.

SNEAKY HERMIT
To open this door, we'll need to press the 3D buttons at the same time, okay? On my three: one, two, three... Nice! Looks like Dawn Owen White is really bad with these 3D stuffs. Let's do it again: one, two, three... Alright... Darn it, I can't jump very far over this water. I am a good jumper, but nothing to help me to jump high enough for this water.

GREGORY
Don't worry about it, Sneaky Hermit. I'm sure there is something to help you across. There seems to be plenty of boats to make a nice bridge for you.

SNEAKY HERMIT
Okay, I'll wait for your signal.

DAWN OWEN WHITE
[on intercom]
Good evening to you, my fine, good guards: Owen here. I have some good news for all of you! I heard that everything in the opera house is good to go, and nothing can get into it. I would like to see Jake, Johnson, and Jason in the main vacuum room right now; I want to have a little chat with the three of you. And if any of you catch these boys trying to make a run for it, shoot them in the back.

SNEAKY HERMIT
That door ahead of you seems to be very hard to break down; I'll need to use my Hermit Nippers to break through it... Thanks for the path, Gregory. Maybe I

should return the favor with some good old Hermit
Nippers... Okay, stand clear.

GREGORY
Thanks, buddy.

SNEAKY HERMIT
Hmm. This door is made of very hard glass. My Hermit
Nippers won't break it down. See if you can try to find a
way around it through that air vent.

DAWN OWEN WHITE
Well, nice of you boys to stop by. But I've got some bad
news for you boys: Johnson has already made a run for
it. That's pretty bad, but I do still have you guys. Now
just let me think about this for a few minutes...

SNEAKY HERMIT
Thanks, Gregory. Judging from the amount of security,
we must be getting close... It's live! Make sure your
watch is on, and one, two, three... We're in! Yes, this
computer's very big; I can hack into it easily.

GREGORY
Just as long as you're enjoying yourself...

SNEAKY HERMIT
Aside from a few tense moments, this break-in is going
pretty well.

GREGORY
It's not over yet. Hack into the system so we can get out
of here.

SNEAKY HERMIT
Oh, it would be a snap to hack into Dawn Owen White's
operation from this old dinosaur... Huh, what? An
alarm? Sorry, Gregory, I guess this dinosaur has teeth.
I'll get into the system as fast as I can. Watch my back:

there are sure to be guards on the way.

GUARDS
Don't move! Don't move! Don't move!

SNEAKY HERMIT
Halfway there...

GUARDS
Don't move! Don't move!

SNEAKY HERMIT
I almost got it...

GUARD
Don't move!

SNEAKY HERMIT
So close... Download complete! Now we can find out
exactly what Dawn Owen White is up to... Heads up,
Gregory. I just heard a radio message from one of
Dawn Owen White's men: the boss is moving towards
your position.

GREGORY
Great, you want me to take him?

SNEAKY HERMIT
No, we need to find if he's behind the city's tar
epidemic. With a few photos, we should be able to help
the cops prosecute him and put an end to this
nonsense.

GREGORY
Never thought we'd be helping the cops.

SNEAKY HERMIT
Really? You always seem to aid Carmelita a lot.

GREGORY
Yeah, well, she's different. Your average law enforcer isn't that, I don't know, attractive? Hold up, here he comes... That's despicable!

SNEAKY HERMIT
Get a picture before he finishes. This is perfect... Awesome, a few more of these and the cops will bury this guy. Follow him, he might be heading for some more tar... He's at it again, get a picture! That poor bird bath. I guess more of a bird death trap now... He's on the move again. Keep it up, Gregory, this is great work... I can't tell about this! He's polluting a waterwheel with deadly, sticky tar! That is just some monstrous... Keep on him, we want to make sure the cops see just how bad this tar is...

DAWN OWEN WHITE
So far, so good. I have been doing tar, and no one has seen me.

SNEAKY HERMIT
He seems to be working on a switch but there's no tar anywhere... Yet. Get a photo anyway... He's doing something... But what? What? I can't believe it! He flooded that whole tank with tar, now all those poor dead fish... As much as I hate what this monster might do next, you should probably keep on his tail. Someday the people will learn the truth due to your pictures.

DAWN OWEN WHITE
Yes, it's me. Get the engineer on the phone.

SNEAKY HERMIT
Gregory, see if you can latch onto the car Dawn Owen White is riding in. We should be able to listen in on his phone conversation: from the look on his face, it seems important.

DAWN OWEN WHITE
Listen, Austin, this ferris wheel was a good idea: she's a pumping the tar fast. Nobody but nobody must know about this! Still, is it going to be enough for my opera recital? Bella! When the people come to see me sing, I want to make sure they keep coming, even if they don't feel like it! One way or another, there will be opera fans again, hehe! Okay, see you soon.

SNEAKY HERMIT
That monster! He's twisted a time-honored amusement park ride into a tool for wrongdoing! Break open that control panel, I'm on my way to do a little rewiring... Look away if you must, for you are about to witness the dark side of electrical engineering... Kill a bunch of poor innocent fish, will he! That will do it... Okay, Gregory. I'm going out there now.

GREGORY
Okay, Sneaky Hermit. Just be careful out there.

SNEAKY HERMIT
Don't worry, Gregory. I will be... Hey, Gregory, you better get over here. My sources tell me that Dawn Owen White has hired the Blue Vipers gondola gang to take out Carmelita.

GREGORY
The Blue Vipers? Those guys are bad news. We have to get them before they get to her.

SNEAKY HERMIT
She is off on her mission; the thugs can't be far behind.

GREGORY
On my way. Just make sure you have one of those police boats hot-wired by the time I get there.

SNEAKY HERMIT
Let's see... Just cross the blue wire with the red wire
and... Done.

GREGORY
Just in time: there go the Vipers.

SNEAKY HERMIT
I'll shoot, you drive... This river is packed with boxes,
make sure that you jump over them, or we are dead.
Let's take these guys out.

GREGORY
There goes one of the Blue Vipers. Nice shooting,
Sneaky Hermit... Awesome work, that's the end of the
Blue Vipers.

CARMELITA
Another mission complete. This city is beautiful, but a
bit quiet for my taste.

SNEAKY HERMIT
I hope you know that by saving Carmelita, we are only
making our operations harder for us.

GREGORY
Maybe so, but what's the fun if there's no one helping
you out? Besides, she's helped us out in the past.

SNEAKY HERMIT
That, and you got a thing for her.

GREGORY
And I got a thing for her. Look, I'll put this boat away!
It might be useful for later. Stay out of trouble.

SNEAKY HERMIT
Okay, Gregory, I heard from Dawn Owen White's
computer that his tar pumping is getting worse, and

that is a problem for us, so I made some more plans for us to do. The first problem is all the tar under these buildings here: it's there so that he can sink them one by one, which will make things even harder for us. We need to stop his plans to destroy all the buildings in Venice during his opera recital on the first day of Carnival. To stop people from seeing the recital, we'll need to destroy his balloons and sign. If no one shows up, he won't be able to sink anything. Next we'll steal the blueprints to his vacuum room which are located in three coffee shops owned by Dawn Owen White himself. The bad news is that the coffee houses are heavily guarded, so you'll need to use a costume and pretend to be a guard. Also, some Vincenetti goons have been called in to support Owen's guards, but I think we should leave them all for Carmelita to take care of. Finally, we'll have to ask Anti Gregory to join us out in the field: if he's already learned the ball move, he'll need to use that move to take out the tar drums.

GREGORY
Sneaky Hermit, looks like you found one of Dawn Owen White's Vincenetti goons. Are you on your way to the police station for the bait and switch?

SNEAKY HERMIT
Yeah, he's following me, too close for comfort. You gotta move.

GREGORY
Now to get one of those cops involved... Hey, all you fake cops! Go home, we don't need any more dumb thugs in Venice.

COP
I might not be a real cop, but I got feelings, pal. And you just hurt them.

GUARD
Are you talking to me, fruitcake? Because I don't need
a date.

COP
Eat missile, punk.

GREGORY
This was a great plan, Sneaky Hermit. Now we can just
sit back and watch the fireworks.

SNEAKY HERMIT
Thank you. I pride myself on my deviousness these
days. With her cop friends under fire, there's no doubt
Carmelita will come out and take out the entire
Vincenetti Gang herself.

GREGORY
Devious.

COP
Inspector Box, I'm glad to see you. This Vincenetti
puke is giving me all I can handle.

CARMELITA
Stand your ground, soldier. We'll take him together.

COP
He's hit... You almost got him... Keep at him, Inspector
Box... You got him good that time... He's about to come
down... You almost got him... These Vincenetti guys are
everywhere! I'm not going to last long without some
good old firepower... Keep at him Inspector Box... He's
about to come down... Yeah, he's hit... Trash this
punk... I am deep in trouble. I need backup, and I need
it now... Show him who is boss, boss... He is perfect for
you... Yeah, he's hit! All the Vincenetti goons have been
killed. Everything is clear out here.

CARMELITA
Good work, soldier. You fought well for once. You
fought for freedom. I'm proud of you.

SNEAKY HERMIT
Dawn Owen White keeps the blueprints to his main tar
pumping station in three parts. Each is hidden behind
one of the paintings in one of his coffee houses.

GREGORY
Not really easy, there is a guard in front of the coffee
house.

SNEAKY HERMIT
Since we destroyed his ferris wheel, Owen has gone all
out with guards. In fact, he's got all of his guards
checking up on each other. But if we can get inside, we
can show that he is behind the tar problem.

GREGORY
I'm with you. I'll pretend to be a guard while in
costume. When the coast is clear, you'll head inside
and steal the blueprints. With me standing up front, no
one will know something's up.

SNEAKY HERMIT
When you are approached by guards, they'll make you
give them a password. Take too long or mess it up, and
they will know that you are a fake.

GUARD
Hey, you! What's Dawn Owen White's house
password?

SNEAKY HERMIT
Sending password, Gregory.

GREGORY
Bass, bass, bass, opera.

GUARD
Okay, I guess you are the late shift. Thanks for coming,
I got big plans for tonight! Carnival is a good time,
huh?

SNEAKY HERMIT
I can't believe that worked! You got the worst Italian
accent I have ever heard. No offense.

GREGORY
Head inside and grab the blueprints. No telling how
long until another guard comes by... First coffee house
I've ever seen with a wall-to-wall laser boobytrap...
Dawn Owen White really is old school if he is using a
painting safe. I miss doing codes like these. The trick is
to find the safe's code somewhere in the painting! It
might take some searching, but it should to be there.
Just keep at it... Strong work! We're still clear out
front.

SNEAKY HERMIT
I'll meet you at the next coffee shop. Once you take the
guard's post, I'll move in.

GREGORY
Second verse, same as the first.

GUARD
You! Ferris wheel password, quickly!

SNEAKY HERMIT
Here's the password, Gregory.

GREGORY
Opera, bass, opera, opera.

GUARD
Sorry about that, but am I glad you're here! Mama's
making spaghetti tonight, and I'm starving. I'm gonna

GREGORY BOUTHIETTE

eat three, no, four plates worth!

GREGORY
I guess you really like her cooking.

GUARD
Mama Mia, I want to be buried in her sauce. It's
heaven.

SNEAKY HERMIT
Any problems with that guy?

GREGORY
Said he wanted to be buried in his mom's pasta sauce.

SNEAKY HERMIT
Yeah, that's, uh... That's strange.

GREGORY
You know, I just can't get it out of my head: have you
ever had pasta sauce that good? I don't want to make
you mad or anything, but I just don't think I ever had
cooking that good. Are we, like, missing out on a whole
universe of flavors here? Alright, two out of three.
Almost there, buddy... You know, maybe there's a good
Italian restaurant around here...

SNEAKY HERMIT
Enough with the sauce! Keep your focus, we're on a job
here. Thugs everywhere, death around every corner...

GREGORY
You're right. We have one more coffee house to head
to, then we're done.

SNEAKY HERMIT
Yes, now you're talking sense.

THE BOOK OF ADVENTURES

GREGORY
And then we eat.

TONY B
Hey, you! Tell me the daytime password.

SNEAKY HERMIT
Kid's stuff: here it is.

GREGORY
Opera, opera, opera, opera.

TONY B
Yeah, you know the code, but what's my nickname?
There's only one Tony B on the payroll, and I'm famous
in the family.

GREGORY
I'm new, just got called in from Rome.

TONY B
They know me in Rome! I am the most awesome player
in Rome. You're telling me you never heard my
nickname there?

GREGORY
Umm... My cell phone is going off, I should probably
take the call. Could be the boss.

TONY B
Yeah, okay.

SNEAKY HERMIT
Talk to some of the other guards in the area, and see if
any of them know Tony's nickname.

GUARD
You! What's Dawn Owen White's house password?

GREGORY BOUTHIETTE

GREGORY
Bass, bass, bass, opera.

GUARD
Okay, you're legit.

GREGORY
Hey, you know Tony B's nickname?

GUARD
Tony B, that butthead! He's, uh, what one calls an
egomaniac. I don't know nothing about him, and I
don't wanna know.

GREGORY
Alright.

GUARD
Hey, you. What's the daytime password?

Gregory.
Opera, opera, opera, opera.

GUARD
Yep, that's the password. Sometimes I forget them
myself, you know?

GREGORY
You and me both, pal. Hey, uh, do you know what Tony
B's nickname is?

GUARD
Hahaha, yeah, that fathead likes to call himself Tony
Da Destroya B. What a butthead.

GREGORY
I couldn't agree more.

SNEAKY HERMIT
Nice job getting the nickname. You're really fitting in with these monsters, Gregory. Maybe you should switch teams, get an apartment with Da Destroya.

TONY B
Hey, what's the midnight password?

SNEAKY HERMIT
Sending password, Gregory.

GREGORY
Bass, bass, bass, bass.

TONY B
So, babyshot, what's my nickname?

GREGORY
Come on, everyone's heard of Tony Da Destroya B! You're the terror of every playground from here to Sicily.

TONY B
Hahaha, real funny. Least I'm not on guard duty during Carnival! Who's got the last laugh now, tough guy? Me, that's who!

GREGORY
Don't take too long. If that guy comes back to chat, I'm out of here... You've got some real skill with these codes, Sneaky Hermit. It usually takes me twenty minutes to figure those things out. You are just flying through them... Get out of there! It must have been rigged to an alarm... We need to head out back to the safe house. That alarm is attracting all kinds of guards.

SNEAKY HERMIT
Agreed. We got the blueprints to the tar vacuum, so our work here is done.

GREGORY BOUTHIETTE

GREGORY
Let's go, Sneaky Hermit.

SNEAKY HERMIT
Ah, the sweet smell of the safe house.

GREGORY
Okay, Sneaky Hermit, I'm gonna go out there and do
my last mission.

SNEAKY HERMIT
Okay, Gregory. I'll meet you out there soon... I'm
taking over this Carnival fireworks stand as the base
for our next job. We need to take out the sign and
balloons advertising Dawn Owen White's big comeback
opera recital.

GREGORY
I hear ya. If no one shows up for him to extort with his
building-sinking scheme, then why would he bother
with the demonstration? Excavating all that tar seems
like a big operation, you'd think he'd hold off until he
has an audience.

SNEAKY HERMIT
Exactly. I cobbled together a few explosives powerful
enough to destroy those balloons, but I'm a little short
on fuses.

GREGORY
Then I'll be quick.

SNEAKY HERMIT
Place the bomb when you get near the anchor, or
kaboom! Bouthiette parts everywhere... Excellent, one
less ad polluting the Venetian skyline... Head on back
to the fireworks stand. I got another stick of TNT
ready, and the wind is facing the right direction for
stage two of our plan.

GREGORY
That explosive had some kick.

SNEAKY HERMIT
It was a child compared to this ferocious beast. Don't
dilly-dally with this one: it's got a longer fuse, but
you've got farther to run.

GREGORY
Ferocious beast.

SNEAKY HERMIT
Run, Gregory, run! Fear the beast! Hurry, before the
wind changes... Haha, stage two: the balloon carried by
the wind will impact on Dawn Owen White's sign... The
combustible gases in the balloon will ignite, and bam!
Hindenburg Part 2... Darn it, darn it! The wind died,
and the balloon's caught... Sorry, Gregory. See if you
can climb up and knock the balloon free. I'll start
putting together another stick of TNT for the sign. Such
a shame, I was really hoping to see that balloon burn.
But that's just how it happens sometimes... A quick
whack will free the balloon... Whoa, looks like we got a
new ferocious beast on this operation! Come on back
and... What? Sorry, sir we're kind of closed... Hey, let
go of me! Gregory, get back here! Quick! Help,
Gregory! This is crazy! I gotta lock up and... Oh no...
Gregory, he's breaking down the door! Where are you?
Please, help! Help...

DAWN OWEN WHITE
Ahh, Gregory Bouthiette. My boys and I picked up one
those pictures of me that you sent to the cops. Nice try,
but I own this town.

GREGORY
Put my friend down, or I'm gonna knock out all of your
teeth one by one and make you eat them.

DAWN OWEN WHITE
That's the toughest talk you got? You joke! You are a
butthead. Back in my day, we made people pee their
pants just by looking at them.

GREGORY
Believe me, old timer. I don't make jokes.

DAWN OWEN WHITE
Oh, I know all about you and your gang. You are
nothing without this guy's brain. I think I might scoop
him out of his shell real slow, and use it for my tomato
plants.

SNEAKY HERMIT
I don't really like tomatoes.... Gregory!

DAWN OWEN WHITE
Turn it on. Burn him up.

SNEAKY HERMIT
Let go of me, you butthead.

DAWN OWEN WHITE
Shut up and hold still. Shock him.

SNEAKY HERMIT
I swear, I'll get you for this.

DAWN OWEN WHITE
You'll get nothing but a grave, pal.

SNEAKY HERMIT
Gregory, hurry it up!

DAWN OWEN WHITE
Quiet down, lunch meat. Power up. You want this
butthead? Take him... I won't forget about this. You
guys are dead.

GREGORY
Are you okay, Sneaky Hermit?

SNEAKY HERMIT
I'm fine. My arm kind of hurts, but it will heal... Now I
need to go out there and find Anti Gregory.

GREGORY
Good luck out there, Sneaky Hermit. You're gonna
need it.

SNEAKY HERMIT
Thanks, Gregory. I will do my best to talk to him.

ANTI GREGORY
Gregory said you were looking for me.

SNEAKY HERMIT
We need your help to destroy some tar drums.

ANTI GREGORY
Sneaky Hermit, Gage told me not to help you until the
black water runs clear again.

SNEAKY HERMIT
Come on! What happened to the old Anti Gregory, the
guy who just sits around in the safe house and does
nothing until your mission is ready? The guy who
always wears diapers? The guy who doesn't even
bother asking questions later? Where's that guy?
Where's... Where's my old friend?

ANTI GREGORY
I... I'm sorry, Sneaky Hermit. I did try to save you
before it was too late, but I just want to be on my own
for while.

SNEAKY HERMIT
Get over it, Anti Gregory. I don't blame you and never

have. Who cares if I'm in a wheelchair? The only thing I feel bad about is losing my friend.

ANTI GREGORY
Look, I'd like to help you. You are like, my second bestest friend. It's just that I told Gage I would stay here and do my training until the black water runs clear again.

SNEAKY HERMIT
Well, maybe you can help. You wouldn't have to punch anyone...

ANTI GREGORY
I'm in! Keep it good for me, and I will mash up anything you like.

SNEAKY HERMIT
As a student of the dream-time, I imagine you've already learned how to do the ball form?

ANTI GREGORY
Yeah, sure, no problem. Though, this is my first time doing it.

SNEAKY HERMIT
Excellent. Go into ball form and clog up that pipe: the pressure built up should shoot you skyward. Maintain your ball form and smash into the tar drums around town.

ANTI GREGORY
Awesome. Yeah, that works for me. I'm sure Gage won't mind.

SNEAKY HERMIT
Just go into ball form, then clog up that pipe... Just keep on bouncing up and down so you can stay up... This is great, Anti Gregory. Those tar drums are part of

Dawn Owen White's plan; with them out of the picture, you are that much closer to seeing the black water run clear. I promise... Awesome bouncing, buddy... You are really getting the hang of this! That tar drum didn't know what hit it... Keep this up, and the tar drums will send a thank you card... That's the last of them! Really nice work, Anti Gregory. It's really good to see you back in action.

ANTI GREGORY
It feels good, Sneaky Hermit. I could never forget my friends, even if I'm a different person.

SNEAKY HERMIT
Okay, Gregory, I just talked to Anti Gregory, and now it's time for Operation Tar Be Gone. Here's the plan: we need to get Anti Gregory back on the team. Gregory, you'll need to put your costume on and head inside the opera house right through the front door. Make your way down to the pump room, then let me in through the side door. Thanks to the blueprints we stole, I now know just where to use my Hermit Nippers. Then we'll go for Dawn Owen White's demolition switch. We can't go anywhere with something that powerful, so I will do a little opera singing of my own. I'll snatch the demolition switch, and we will meet up with Anti Gregory. By then, the black water is sure to be clear, and he will be free to come with us... This is it! Dawn Owen White is due to arrive for the opera recital in just a few minutes.

GREGORY
We did a great job taking out the advertising. No one will show up to listen. No audience means no demolition demonstration.

SNEAKY HERMIT
True, but to finish the job we'll need to take out the main tar vacuum. Use your costume to gain entry to

the opera house. Then head down to the pump room,
and let me in through the side door.

GREGORY
No problem, signore.

GUARD
Hey, you, what's the midnight password?

GREGORY
Bass, bass, bass, bass.

GUARD
Okay. Don't be inside too long, the boss' opera recital is
about to start.

SNEAKY HERMIT
Stay in costume here, or the operation is done for...
Dang it, a double button door. Uh, I'll think of
something. Just give me time.

DAWN OWEN WHITE
You! I don't really know you. What's the secret opera
password?

SNEAKY HERMIT
Sending password, Gregory.

GREGORY
Bass, bass, opera, opera.

DAWN OWEN WHITE
Okay. Send word to the rest of the guards that under no
circumstance am I to be disturbed during my big opera
recital.

GREGORY
Yes sir. I'm certainly looking forward to the
performance, but only when I'm done in the pump

room will I be heading out to the stage. Umm, if it isn't too much trouble, would you like to help with this double button security door?

DAWN OWEN WHITE
But of course! For a fellow music lover, it would be a pleasure... On three: one, two, three... Be quick in there, you don't want to miss out.

SNEAKY HERMIT
Psst, Gregory. Gregory, over here.

GREGORY
Nice to see you, buddy.

SNEAKY HERMIT
Okay, we need to act quickly while the recital is getting underway.

GREGORY
Are you ready with your Hermit Nippers?

SNEAKY HERMIT
Once I destroy all six tar pipes, the vacuum should start to lose suction.

GREGORY
Look, if your Hermit Nippers attract any guards, let me do the fighting. You just keep on taking out the tar pipes. We need to stay on schedule... Looks tough, might take more than just Hermit Nippers... We got company. Just stay with the tar pipes... This is getting harder, better hurry up with those pipes...

SNEAKY HERMIT
Just one pipe left.

GREGORY
Nice work, buddy. Is there still time to catch Dawn

GREGORY BOUTHIETTE

Owen White's recital?

SNEAKY HERMIT
We're right on schedule. If I'm correct about this, he
should be about to perform an aria originally written as
a duet. That's when we strike.

GREGORY
Think he'll let you on stage with him?

SNEAKY HERMIT
Of course, he's a musician. He'll be overjoyed to have a
good counterpoint. Just be ready to drop the
chandelier when I lure him underneath it.

DAWN OWEN WHITE
Ah, Mr. Tomato Fertilizer. I see you've got a death
wish.

SNEAKY HERMIT
I couldn't resist showing you up at what you treasure
most: opera singing.

DAWN OWEN WHITE
You're a vocalist? Fine. A duet is coming up: we'll sing
first, and then I will gut you.

SNEAKY HERMIT
Bring it on, grandpa. I'll sing you under the table...
Now!

DAWN OWEN WHITE
What? No!

CARMELITA
Freeze, Dawn Owen White. You are going back to jail.

DAWN OWEN WHITE
This recital is over.

SNEAKY HERMIT
He's still got the demolition switch!

CARMELITA
Dawn Owen White never, ever freezes.

GREGORY
I'll drive, you shoot.

CARMELITA
I need immediate back up. Dawn Owen White is
heading east; all units converge.

COP
Roger.

CARMELITA
Sorry, Gregory, but I have to do my job, buddy.

SNEAKY HERMIT
Can you go any faster?

GREGORY
This is it. Shoot out his engine, and we'll have him.

SNEAKY HERMIT
The river is full of cops. We are in trouble here.

CARMELITA
Attention, Dawn Owen White: you are traveling in an
unsafe rage. I want you to stop your engine now, or I
will take you out. If you don't do what I say, Dawn
Owen White, then I will let my friends keep shooting
you. I repeat, stop your engines now, or I will have to
do this. You hear that, Gregory? Take Dawn Owen
White down.

GREGORY
That Carmelita is always a good talker.

GREGORY BOUTHIETTE

CARMELITA
Good luck, Gregory. I will be waiting for you guys to
take down Dawn Owen White.

DAWN OWEN WHITE
No, we can't go down like this! We are going down
soon... No!

GREGORY
Keep on shooting him, Sneaky Hermit.

SNEAKY HERMIT
Yes.

GREGORY
He's out of control. Get ready for a sudden stop.

DAWN OWEN WHITE
No! More to the left, you butthead! We are gonna
crash!

GREGORY
It's over, Dawn Owen White. You're beat. Give us the
demolition switch, and we will all try to escape these
cops.

DAWN OWEN WHITE
You chase me for this? Oh, what the heck. I will give
you guys this, but I do have more...

ANTI GREGORY
Did you guys see that boat go out of control, jump, and
smash into that thing? Destruction! So cool.

DAWN OWEN WHITE
You think that was cool, punk? Hahahaha.

SNEAKY HERMIT
You monster, stop it! Stop it!

DAWN OWEN WHITE
Hahahaha!

GREGORY
Anti Gregory, I need your help. I've never seen anyone move that fast. Dawn Owen White's old, but he's still got it. Let's take him together.

ANTI GREGORY
But... But... I did the ball form for Gage, and the water is still black...

GREGORY
It will be clear any minute. Now come on, let's take him.

DAWN OWEN WHITE
You're right to be scared, blue kid. Your hermit crab friend hasn't been so smart.

SNEAKY HERMIT
Anti Gregory, help!

ANTI GREGORY
That does it! I'll brush my teeth with your spine! Anti Gregory has returned!

GREGORY
He's too fast! Lure him into the tar pool: that should slow him down... This one's out, I'm moving to another valve... All set with the tar... The valve's empty, I'll crack another... Ready with the tar... Anti Gregory, these pumps are out of tar. I saw some more of them over by the cops' station. Follow me to a fresh supply.

DAWN OWEN WHITE
Without the tar, I'll crush you boys like bugs. You may have more tar, but I'll listen to the song of your death.

GREGORY BOUTHIETTE

ANTI GREGORY
Anti Gregory knows no song, but I will kick your butt
really hard now, Dawn Owen White.

DAWN OWEN WHITE
Quick talking, you butthead, and die.

GREGORY
Lure him in: I'll let loose with the tar.

DAWN OWEN WHITE
So that's it: the old guard's out, and a new generation
steps in.

ANTI GREGORY
That's right. Stepping in big time.

GREGORY
Come on, Anti Gregory, I got the demolition switch.
Let's get Sneaky Hermit and run for it. We got cops
closing in.

SNEAKY HERMIT
Hey, guys, what just happend?

GREGORY
You got beat up good, Sneaky Hermit. Now let's get out
of here, we got cops closing in.

ANTI GREGORY
Yeah, let's go. I don't want to be here when the cops
show up.

SNEAKY HERMIT
Okay, guys. Let's get out of here.

***

GREGORY
Hey, Anti Gregory, are you okay, buddy?

ANTI GREGORY
I'm okay, Gregory; I'm just thinking about Gage. I really want to talk him.

SNEAKY HERMIT
Don't worry, Anti Gregory. We will go and see Gage now.

ANTI GREGORY
Okay, Sneaky Hermit. Thanks for your help, buddy.

GREGORY
Let's got to Australia, guys. I really want to see Gage, too.

SNEAKY HERMIT
You do know that you need to take an airplane there, guys.

ANTI GREGORY
Oh yeah. I don't mind taking an airplane to Australia, Sneaky Hermit. And I get to tell you guys some cool stories about me and Gage.

SNEAKY HERMIT
I can't wait to hear the stories, Anti Gregory.

GREGORY
I hope your stories are cool, Anti Gregory, because I really want to hear everything about Gage. And speaking of Gage, how is he doing anyway?

ANTI GREGORY
Thanks for asking, Gregory. Gage is doing well, and he told me that your master is looking for you, too.

GREGORY
Wait, what? My master is looking for me as well? But why would my master would be looking for me, Anti Gregory?

SNEAKY HERMIT
Hey, guys, look! We're here.

ANTI GREGORY
Wow, we're here! Gregory, look down there: it's Australia.

GREGORY
I can see it, buddy.

SNEAKY HERMIT
Uh oh. Guys, look: Australia is being torn apart.

ANTI GREGORY
Oh no, Gage is gone! What have I done, guys?

GREGORY
It's okay, Anti Gregory. Gage is not gone, we just need to look for him. As a team.

SNEAKY HERMIT
Hurry, guys, we need to get to our safe house before we can find Gage.

GREGORY
Okay, Sneaky Hermit. Let's go, Anti Gregory.

ANTI GREGORY
Okay, Gregory, I'm right behind you.

SNEAKY HERMIT
Okay, good. We made it. Are you guys okay?

GREGORY
Yeah, I am, Sneaky Hermit.

ANTI GREGORY
I'm okay, too, Sneaky Hermit. I need to find Gage right now.

SNEAKY HERMIT
Whoa, hold on there, Anti Gregory! I need Gregory to go out there now to find out where Gage is hiding.

GREGORY
Okay, Sneaky Hermit. I'll go out there right now.

ANTI GREGORY
Gregory, be careful out there. I will talk to you when you get out there.

GREGORY
Okay. Thanks, Anti Gregory. I'll be waiting for you to call me.

SNEAKY HERMIT
Hey, Anti Gregory, we still have your diapers with us, buddy.

ANTI GREGORY
Oh, good. Thanks, Sneaky Hermit. I owe you so much. I'll be right back.

SNEAKY HERMIT
These miners are really drilling the whole place up. Watch yourself, Gregory, they are willing to defend this place with their lives. Watch your back, they might be looking for something out here.

ANTI GREGORY
Gage spends most of his time up there in that cave, overlooking the valley and contemplating the depths of

deepness. I'd really appreciate you breaking the news to him that I want to break off my training.

GREGORY
No problem, buddy. I'm looking forward to seeing him.

ANTI GREGORY
And he is awesome. He'll get inside your head, and he'll freak you out six days from Sunday.

GREGORY
Yes, I know he's awesome, Anti Gregory... Sorry, buddy, this cave's empty. Got any ideas where he might be?

ANTI GREGORY
Well, I can see his hut, but he doesn't really hang out there on account of the smell.

GREGORY
I know about the smell, Anti Gregory.

ANTI GREGORY
It's a long story. I... I had to apologize up and down for like, a month before he'd speak to me again.

GREGORY
What did you do?

ANTI GREGORY
The unspeakable, Gregory. The unspeakable.

GREGORY
Um, thanks for speaking of it. I'm heading for the hut.

SNEAKY HERMIT
This place is packed with wall hooks. The miners must use them to haul up their drills. Looks like you're gonna get some rock climbing practice.

GREGORY
Sorry, Anti Gregory, nobody's home. By the looks of it, I'd say that Gage was fighting someone or something here. I'm starting to think that the miners might have got to him.

ANTI GREGORY
You might be right. They come in and get all angry and yell, and he'll be all peaceful, and they just get ticked. Then he'll try to find the middle way, and then they just go crazy and smash everything up.

GREGORY
Where do you think they might have taken him?

ANTI GREGORY
If they got him, Gage is a goner.

GREGORY
Maybe we should get Sneaky Hermit on the line.

SNEAKY HERMIT
It's tough to say, but given the layout of the miners' camp, I venture to guess that they use that area with the high fence as a makeshift stockade.

GREGORY
Hmm, looks like there might be a way up using that cliff below. Shouldn't be a problem.

SNEAKY HERMIT
Just keep an eye out for that gyrocopter. I'm positive it's what gave away Gage's position.

GREGORY
Good tip. Thanks, Sneaky Hermit.

SNEAKY HERMIT
These miners have no respect for these sites. They are

drilling into everything here at Ayer's Rock: caves, canyons, wave rock... The whole thing is sinking me.

GREGORY
Hey there, Gage, it's good to see you. Anti Gregory has come to ask to be released from his training.

GAGE
Okay, Gregory, I will release him from his training. And I'm happy to see you as well, but I want to go see Anti Gregory myself.

GREGORY
Sure. I'll just bust you out of here, and we'll go talk to him.

GAGE
Okay, Gregory, but I can't leave without my gear.

GREGORY
You really can't leave without your gear?

GAGE
Yeah, that's right, Gregory. My gear was taken away from me by those miners.

GREGORY
Yeah, I see the miners really did a number on your land here. We'll get your walking staff and moonstone; my friends and I have quite the talent for taking back things that were wrongly taken.

GAGE
Okay, Gregory. I think I can trust you to get my gear back for me. It was nice talking to you, my friend.

GREGORY
Okay, Sneaky Hermit, I'm back. Gage told me that he can't leave without his gear, so what do we need to do?

SNEAKY HERMIT

I made some plans for us to do, and I made a robot suit
for you to wear. It's almost like this new movie that I
went to see with Anti Gregory.

GREGORY

Uh, thanks, Sneaky Hermit. I can finally use my cyborg
voice now. And I will be able to control it, Sneaky
Hermit?

SNEAKY HERMIT

Yes, you will, Gregory. Just put it on now.

GREGORY

Okay, I will right now.

SNEAKY HERMIT

Gage won't be able to leave the stockade until he has
his walking staff and moonstone. He also said that we
should clear out Ayer's Rock of all the miners. Only
then will the dream-time spirits be at peace, and Gage
will be free to use his powers. Gregory must have
impressed him with their talk, because he has
requested that Anti Gregory and I meet with him
individually. Something about judging our thoughts.
I've discovered a way to the miners' path that should
make it easier for us to get up to Gage. He also said the
miners have foolishly unearthed The Mask of Dark
Earth; I'm guessing that it was his job to guard the
thing. Now that it's out, bad things are sure to follow.
Sounds like bullcrap to me, but we've done more
ridiculous stuffs over the years. I'm not gonna back
down and let this thing do some bad things to our
operation.

ANTI GREGORY

Okay, guys, I'm gonna go out there and see Gage now.

GREGORY
Okay, Anti Gregory. Just try to be brave, buddy. He won't be mad at you.

ANTI GREGORY
You're right, Gregory... Here I come, Gage! I'm coming to see you now!

SNEAKY HERMIT
That was nice of you to say that, Gregory.

GREGORY
Thanks, Sneaky Hermit. It was the least I could do for him.

SNEAKY HERMIT
I know that you are a little nervous to see Gage again, but he has requested that you and I each pay him a visit.

ANTI GREGORY
If it wasn't for Gage, I wouldn't be the Anti Gregory you see before you today. I'm just not too sure he'll be pleased with my progress as a mystic.

SNEAKY HERMIT
What are you talking about? You used the ball form to bounce up and down Venice! He'll be proud of you.

ANTI GREGORY
Maybe. But I lost my anger, and I got in a fight with Dawn Owen White.

SNEAKY HERMIT
To help me! I'm sure Gage is happy to see friends sticking up for each other. Head into this cave, it will take you right up to him.

ANTI GREGORY
Okay, Sneaky Hermit. Cave ahoy!

SNEAKY HERMIT
Anti Gregory, use these rock to destroy those
stalagmites. Of course, uh, throwing guards will work,
too... According to the mine's hydraulic flow chart, the
door ahead appears to be sealed shut.

ANTI GREGORY
Then I'll just bash it in! What's the good in having fists
if you can't smash steel doors with them?

SNEAKY HERMIT
It's too thick even for you. No, to get through, we need
to overload the pressure in this piston.

ANTI GREGORY
You want me to punch it? I can do that!

SNEAKY HERMIT
Use your ball form on top of the piston. Build enough
height, and the door is sure to open.

ANTI GREGORY
Piston, beware! You're about to be bounced... Yes! Eat
it, piston sucka.

SNEAKY HERMIT
Another locked door! To open this one, you'll need to
open all three pistons at the same time.

ANTI GREGORI
I did it! Three against one, and I still took you piston
chumps to school... Whoa, look at the size of that guy!
He must be jacked up by The Mask of Dark Earth that
Gage was warning us about.

SNEAKY HERMIT
Curious. It seems to make the wearer much larger...
Probably more aggressive, too.

ANTI GREGORY
I can take him. My righteous quest to see Gage won't
be stopped by some dumb butthead in a Mask.

SNEAKY HERMIT
Even if you wanted to, you've got nowhere to go: the
door there has an a electronic deadbolt. This whole
area runs off the same circuit. Even the drills are linked
up.

ANTI GREGORY
Then I'll throw this clown into the drills.

SNEAKY HERMIT
That might break the circuit. Give it a try... Keep it up,
that did some damage... One drill down, two to go...
Just one left...

ANTI GREGORY
Holy cow, that Mask can run!

SNEAKY HERMIT
That might be some bad news. Press on to Gage, he'll
have some answers. The door should be unlocked now
that the drill circuit is broken.

ANTI GREGORY
Open up! I have returned, Gage. The black water now
runs clear, and I'd like to... I am asking... Oh man...

GAGE
You want to join with your friends again, Anti Gregory.

ANTI GREGORY
Yeah, I would like to go back with my friends, and, uh,

we're hoping you'll come along, too.

GAGE
I would love to join you guys, but I still can't leave
without my gear. I need you guys to deal with the
miners, gyrocopters, and The Mask of Dark Earth.

ANTI GREGORY
Miners, gyrocopters, and The Mask of Dark Earth.
Yeah, that's a lot to deal with, but we'll help. I promise.

GAGE
I really missed you.

ANTI GREGORY
Thanks, Gage. I'm happy to see you, too.

GREGORY
Anti Gregory, let's motor out to Ayer's Rock and scare
away those mining dingoes. Gage wants it purified.

ANTI GREGORY
Awesome! This is the biggest truck I have ever gotten
to drive. I can crush houses with this baby! Oh yeah!

SNEAKY HERMIT
I have an idea of how to drive the miners out of Ayer's
Rock, but for my plan to work, we'll need to force the
drill on this rig deeper into the ground.

GREGORY
Okay, Sneaky Hermit, you've got my interest. Though it
looks like I gotta take care of a few guards if I'm gonna
get at the drill controls.

SNEAKY HERMIT
Defeat the guards, start the drill, then Anti Gregory will
begin phase two of my plan... Nice work, Gregory. The
sonic vibrations caused by that drill should drive the

giant scorpions in the area to the surface. If we can capture a bunch of red soldier scorpions and release them into Ayer's Rock, it'll be sure to push out the miners.

ANTI GREGORY
Sounds like a job for Anti Gregory. One question, though: how do I capture scorpions with the truck?

SNEAKY HERMIT
The vehicle is equipped with a supercharged E-brake, which, if pulled when moving, will cause a forward flip. Time it correctly, and you'll trap the scorpion in the mining nets built into the bed of the truck.

ANTI GREGORY
Okay, Sneaky Hermit: bring on the scorpions!

SNEAKY HERMIT
Not so fast. The truck's tires will heat up quickly in this blazing hot sand, so you'll have to cool them down by driving into the water or running over scorpions. Watch your heat meter and make sure they don't melt. And remember, we are only interested in the red soldier scorpions: the blue worker scorpions won't help us scare the miners off... The trucks controls are straightforward... Nice work, looks like more are being driven to the surface.

ANTI GREGORY
Here we go... You're mine! Yeah! There's no escape from Anti Gregory! That's it... Oh yeah!

SNEAKY HERMIT
That's five reds in the bed, keep it up.

ANTI GREGORY
Oh boy! Whoa! Here we go...

SNEAKY HERMIT
Anti Gregory, hang tight for a minute. My sensors are showing a drop off in underground movement... We'll have to drill deeper to keep the scorpions coming out... Gregory, you'll have to climb to the top of the drill tower and override the depth control system.

GREGORY
Okay, Sneaky Hermit. I'm on my way.

SNEAKY HERMIT
It's working! Wait a minute... It's draining the water around the tower! Anti Gregory, you'll have to rely on squishing scorpions to keep your tires cool from here on out.

ANTI GREGORY
No problem, Sneaky Hermit, I totally got the hang of it now... Oh yeah, he's caught! Come on... There's no escape from Anti Gregory, yeah! Here we go... You're mine! Handstand! Whoa...

SNEAKY HERMIT
Nice. Just a few more, and we'll have enough to clear out Ayer's Rock.

ANTI GREGORY
Rolling... Tumble... Oh boy!

SNEAKY HERMIT
Great job, Anti Gregory. Now back that truck full of scorpions up to the miners' entrance and deliver that not-so-friendly payload.

GUARDS
Noooo! Giant scorpions! Run for it, mates! Uh oh...

SNEAKY HERMIT
Nice teamwork, guys. Ayer's Rock is cleansed of most

of the miners. Gage will be pleased.

ANTI GREGORY
Okay, guys, I'm back. Your turn, Gregory: I need you to
steal back Gage's walking staff and moonstone.

GREGORY
Don't worry about it, Anti Gregory. I will steal them
back for Gage, and he will be with us again.

SNEAKY HERMIT
Just make sure that you get there, Gregory, so that I
can tell you where his walking staff is.

GREGORY
Okay, Sneaky Hermit, I will get going.

SNEAKY HERMIT
After capturing Gage, the dingoes confiscated his magic
walking staff and moonstone. Without these objects,
Gage is powerless.

GREGORY
Given that we're dealing with miners, I bet they
stashed the goods in one of their caves around here. It's
probably a secure location with plenty of guys on duty
to provide protection.

SNEAKY HERMIT
I agree. The most likely candidate is this mine shaft: it
appears to have the highest number of workers coming
in and out.

GREGORY
Good place to start. I'm on it.

SNEAKY HERMIT
Those caves are gonna be dark: your 3D glasses will let
you see things easier... If they're here, Gage's items will

be at the far end of this cave.

GREGORY
Time to take you back to your rightful owner... These miners are smarter than they look: they boobytrapped the moonstone! It looks like a light-sensitive detonator... If I can get it outside and into the sunlight, it should power down.

SNEAKY HERMIT
Gage's walking staff must be hidden in their other cave complex. I marked the entrance in your tracker... These caves don't have any light whatsoever... Lucky for you, Gage's moonstone has enough light for you to see in this cave. Watch your step, this cave is really deep.

GREGORY
I wonder what's so special about this staff... Another boobytrap! These guys sure are paranoid about a dumb stick. And from the sound of it, they called in reinforcements. Nothing like a horde of angry dingoes to make things a bit more interesting! Okay, Sneaky Hermit, I'm back. It's your turn, buddy.

SNEAKY HERMIT
Okay, thanks, Gregory. Now I can go and bring Gage's gear to him... Hey there, Gage. It's good to see you again. Anti Gregory has cleared Ayer's Rock, and now I kindly give you back your walking stick and moonstone. The time for escape has come.

GAGE
Thanks for getting my gear back, Sneaky Hermit.

SNEAKY HERMIT
Thank you, you're too kind. But tell me, how do you plan to escape?

GAGE
My plan to escape is to transform myself.

SNEAKY HERMIT
That's right, Gage, you can transform yourself! Well,
once you change shape, a guard is sure to come inside
and look for you.

GAGE
Once the guard is looking for me, I will climb onto his
back and slam him into the cell door.

SNEAKY HERMIT
Too true. Wait, here comes a guard...

ANTI GREGORY
Gage, just swing your stick to transform.

GUARD
What? Where did he go?

ANTI GREGORY
Gage, you are awesome! Slam him into the cell door!
Awesome work, Gage. Let's show these miners who's
boss. Head for the drills: I guess Sneaky Hermit has
found a weak spot.

SNEAKY HERMIT
Your moves are really awesome, Gage.

GAGE
I can do some other stuffs as well, Sneaky Hermit.

SNEAKY HERMIT
Uh huh. Yeah.

GAGE
I can see that those drills are tearing up the landscape.

SNEAKY HERMIT
I hear you. Those drill are tearing up the landscape.
They appear to be fragile at the base... Ram a guard
into it, and the whole thing will fall apart.

GAGE
Some things just don't change, Sneaky Hermit.

SNEAKY HERMIT
Oh yeah.

ANTI GREGORY
Sweet moves, Gage... Down it goes! Oh yeah, these
guys are toast... Gage, you are king! Keep it up. Sneaky
Hermit, got another plan to stick it to these miners?
Head for that far rock.

SNEAKY HERMIT
That grinder is tearing up wave rock.

GAGE
It's awful, Sneaky Hermit.

SNEAKY HERMIT
I know it's awful. However, the linked generator is
weak and easily destroyed, provided you can jump a
few guards over there and ram it.

GAGE
Okay, Sneaky Hermit, I'll give it a try.

ANTI GREGORY
You're the master, Gage... That machine is crying hot
tears from your great blow... Gage, you've done it! The
miners' machines are silenced! The dream-time spirits
rejoice.

SNEAKY HERMIT
Gage has said yes to joining our team, provided we can

rid his homeland from the dingo miners and deal with The Mask of Dark Earth. A tall order, but we're up for it. First we'll enlist some local wildlife to help clear out the miners. Anti Gregory will feed our foes to a loco crocodile; with some luck, he'll take a liking to the taste of miners and chow down left and right. Second, we'll hit the guys where they live, or at least where they relax. If we can clear them out of this lemonade bar, it will be a bad blow to their morale. They will be begging to go home! And finally, Gregory will use some mining stuffs to drill for some oil deep beneath the dry lake land, which is the key to getting rid of The Mask of Dark Earth.

ANTI GREGORY
Okay, guys. I'm gonna go and do my mission first.

GREGORY
Okay, Anti Gregory. Go out there and knock those guards out.

ANTI GREGORY
Oh, don't worry, Gregory. I will knock them out.

SNEAKY HERMIT
It's about time we subtracted a few miners from the equation.

ANTI GREGORY
You know I don't understand that math talk.

SNEAKY HERMIT
Uh... We need to, uh, put the smackdown... On these, uh, bad dudes. For justice.

ANTI GREGORY
Righteous! I'm the man for the job.

SNEAKY HERMIT
Gage will start luring miners to a position near this giant crocodile. Your job is to throw the thugs into the mouth of the monster.

ANTI GREGORY
Teaching him to like eating miners, huh? That's a sinister plan, Sneaky Hermit. I approve.

SNEAKY HERMIT
With some luck, the oversized reptile will be an invaluable asset in our efforts to drive away the miners. He might even take care of our Mask of Dark Earth problems. I spotted it prowling near the safe house.

ANTI GREGORY
Roger that. It's feeding time!

GAGE
I got the guards, Anti Gregory. I'm on my way right now.

SNEAKY HERMIT
Nice. You need to give him a taste for both types of guards: more kangaroos and more dingoes should do it.

ANTI GREGORY
Later, sucker! Hungry little fellow... Chomp that clown in half! That's right, miners are food! You like eating miners! Snack time! Remember to chew...

SNEAKY HERMIT
Great job, Anti Gregory! Now feed the croc one last thing: a big, tasty flashlight guard. I located one and marked him for you. Remember, you'll need to sneak up on this guy in order to grab him... Take cover, Anti Gregory! Here comes the guard wearing The Mask of Dark Earth. Let's see if all of your hard work with this

croc pays off... Crap! That Mask keeps getting away. Since when do Masks get away?

ANTI GREGORY
Okay, guys, I'm done with my mission. Now it's up to Gregory to do his.

GREGORY
Okay, thanks, Anti Gregory... Alright, boys. Look tough and get angry. It's time to intimidate the locals.

SNEAKY HERMIT
I'm not sure I can do it. How do you guys get angry?

ANTI GREGORY
Find the match deep inside yourself... Light it, and let the fire burn up your guts and boil your blood!

GREGORY
Uh, yeah... I pretty much do the same thing. Look, our goal is to drive away these miners, and we'll do whatever it takes... Listen up, dirtbags: time to clear out! This bar is Bouthiette Gang turf now.

GUARD
Tough talk, butthead, but you guys got no business with us. We here are known around these parts for our drinking skills, and this just happens to be a lemonade bar.

SNEAKY HERMIT
Gregory, I'm not sure this is such a good idea...

GREGORY
If a lemonade drinking challenge is what you have in mind, then the three of us will take on the best three lemonade drinkers you got.

GUARD
Fair deal: losers have to clear out... Ready, steady, go!

ANTI GREGORY
Suck it down!

GUARD
Show him who's boss!

SNEAKY HERMIT
Do not let him beat you!

GUARD
Stay on him!

GREGORY
Don't slow down!

GUARD
Go, go, go!

SNEAKY HERMIT
Nice going! Nice going!

ANTI GREGORY
Come on, man!

GREGORY
Come on, man!

GUARD
Show him who's boss!

SNEAKY HERMIT
We win.

GUARD
That's cheating! Why, that hermit crab spilled more
than he drank! Around here, there's only one way to

deal with cheaters. Turn on the fence, Jason: it's time we gave these cheaters a beating.

ANTI GREGORY
Nice shot, Sneaky Hermit!

SNEAKY HERMIT
This is tense. Gregory, are you okay?

GREGORY
I'm as fast as before, Sneaky Hermit.

ANTI GREGORY
Gregory, you're on fire!

SNEAKY HERMIT
Awesome shot, Gregory.

ANTI GREGORY
Great, Gregory!

GREGORY
They just keep coming! You're holding up, Anti Gregory.

ANTI GREGORY
Feeling strong... Behold, my powers of awesomeness!

SNEAKY HERMIT
Awesome hit, Anti Gregory!

GREGORY
Nice work, Anti Gregory.

ANTI GREGORY
Yes! The Bouthiette Gang rules the roost! We are the kings of the hill, the totally maxed-out heavyweight champions.

GREGORY
Those guys won't be coming back here any time soon.

SNEAKY HERMIT
Uh, guys... Looks like they saved their biggest guy for last.

ANTI GREGORY
He's wearing the freaky bad spirit Mask! He must be so jacked.

SNEAKY HERMIT
We should work together to take this guy down; that Mask has a powerful force in it.

GUARD
I will crush you three like bugs. Bring it on.

SNEAKY HERMIT
Lure him over, and I'll use my Hermit Nippers! Get him while he's out...

ANTI GREGORY
I'll try to knock him out with this barrel.

SNEAKY HERMIT
My Hermit Nippers are ready!

ANTI GREGORY
Barrel!

GREGORY
Finally! That guy was... The Mask! It's getting away.

SNEAKY HERMIT
We may have cleared out this bar, but that Mask is sure to keep making trouble for us. We need to destroy it.

GREGORY
Anti Gregory, I'll meet you at my last mission, buddy.

ANTI GREGORY
Okay, Gregory. I'll see you there.

GREGORY
You ready to head out to the oil fields? Should be right
through this cave.

ANTI GREGORY
Oh yeah! Sneaky Hermit said there would be heavy
machinery and destruction going down.

GREGORY
Sounds like your thing.

ANTI GREGORY
Y-E-S! Yeah!

GREGORY
We're going after some radioactive oil, right?

ANTI GREGORY
I don't know. I can never pay attention during those
slideshows... Don't tell Sneaky Hermit!

GREGORY
Wouldn't dream of it.

SNEAKY HERMIT
Gregory, phase one is to protect those power stations
while Anti Gregory gets all six oil wells flowing. Use
this Super Claw 10,000 to deal with any last miners
that might show up. Just move the claw around if there
are miners anywhere around you. Another thing that I
need to tell you is that you can use the claws to pick up
or release items. Before you're spotted, practice by
picking up that rock and dropping it in the pit.

GREGORY
This is easy.

SNEAKY HERMIT
You do seem quite adept. The other important feature
on the 10,000 model is the throwing action: just pick
up an item and throw it to the other side of that fence.
You can throw things quite a ways: go ahead and hit
that electric fence way out there with one of those
rocks.

GREGORY
I think I got the hang of it.

SNEAKY HERMIT
Nice shot. Let's see you do it again.

GREGORY
Face it, Sneaky Hermit, I'm really good at this.

SNEAKY HERMIT
Hope you're right, because it looks like the miners are
onto us... Defend the power stations by using
everything and anything in the oil field! This electric
fence should be especially handy for dispatching
guards... Here they come!

ANTI GREGORY
Yeah, give him the fence! Rock to the head? That's so
choice! I got one well flowing! Two more to go... He's
on fire, but not in the good way... Two down, one to
go... Taste deadly fence, miner guy! All three of these
wells are puking up crude oil. Give me a lift to the next
set.

SNEAKY HERMIT
You better deal with the remaining guards... Hurry,
Gregory! Grab Anti Gregory and move before the
miners get ahead of you... Okay, Gregory, it's safe to let

Anti Gregory go now.

ANTI GREGORY
Check out these guns! That pumping has got me so pumped. Boom goes the dynamite! Oh, that's a headache... Got another one going. I wish I could have seen him land! That guy is toast! Man, this is tiring! Just one more to go. That's a long fall... He's not getting up... That's it! They're all gushing now.

SNEAKY HERMIT
Nice work, guys. Now that all of the oil wells are active, we can move onto phase two.

ANTI GREGORY
Yeah, let's head out to the next oil field.

SNEAKY HERMIT
Okay, Gregory, it's safe to let Anti Gregory go now... Let's get that oil well burning! Gregory, drop a rock on the end of that long plank. Anti Gregory, you'll then jump on the other end, which should catapult the rock to the oil wells. The sparks on impact should start a fire.

ANTI GREGORY
Let's fire it up. Eat rock, suckers! Flaming gnarly death from above, yeah! Smash him!

SNEAKY HERMIT
Now for phase three: with the oil wells alight, the pressure differential should draw the deep, uranium-enriched, glowing oil to the surface. We'll need to be extremely careful in retrieving a small sample.

ANTI GREGORY
Gregory! Gregory, look at me! I'm glowing! Woo!

GREGORY
Okay, Sneaky Hermit, we're back. Is the operation on
its way now?

SNEAKY HERMIT
Yes, it is. You can feel it in the air! The miners are
about to pack it in; in fact, they'll probably be long
gone during the operation. The bad news is that we still
have to deal with The Mask of Dark Earth: it's clear we
need to destroy it. Time for Operation Moon Crash: to
start things off, we'll need Gage to take out the
gyrocopter. With it gone, we'll have clear skies for
phase two. Now, according to the book, The Mask of
Dark Earth is the arch enemy of the Moon Spirit. So,
given Anti Gregory's moon shape, we'll cover him with
the glowing oil and have him act like the Moon Spirit.
We'll then have him hang from a crane. The Mask will
be sure to see his arch enemy and come running. That's
when we strike! Anti Gregory jumps off the crane and
attacks the guard that has the Mask on his face. With
the Mask destroyed and the miners ran off, Gage will
be free to join the team for the Bouthiette vault job.

GREGORY
I'm gonna go out there and let Gage know that he will
start the operation, Sneaky Hermit.

SNEAKY HERMIT
Just stay where you are. I will talk Gage out of his hut...
Gage, I know that you have yet to join the team, but we
need your help to destroy The Mask of Dark Earth.

GAGE
Okay, Sneaky Hermit. So what's my objective?

SNEAKY HERMIT
Your objective is to take out the gyrocopter while it is
refueling.

GREGORY BOUTHIETTE

GAGE
Oh, okay. I'm up for that, Sneaky Hermit.

SNEAKY HERMIT
Glad to hear you're up to it. The bad news is that the gyrocopter has a sensor that will detect your moonstone. I suspect that's how they found and trapped you earlier. Get too close, and they'll detect you and take off out of reach. For this job, you'll need to run guards towards it, then jump off early before it senses you. Ram a few guards into that thing and it's sure to fall apart... Aim that miner, then jump off... Way to go, Gage! A couple more hits like that, and that gyrocopter will be history... That thing is on its last legs. Ram one more guard into it, and it's finished.

ANTI GREGORY
Behold, the Moon Spirit rises! Woo! Woooooooo!

SNEAKY HERMIT
Everyone keep an eye out for the Mask: it's sure to take the bait.

GREGORY
We got a little problem here, fellows: looks like Carmelita has finally caught up.

SNEAKY HERMIT
Dang it, we can't stop the operation now. We'll just have to give her a wide berth.

GREGORY
Roger that. Applying wide berth.

SNEAKY HERMIT
Quit horsing around and look out for the Mask. It's close. I can feel it.

GAGE
Hey, guys, I need some help here.

ANTI GREGORY
Here I come, Gage!

SNEAKY HERMIT
Did you get it? Is the Mask gone? Gregory, can you see?

GREGORY
Can't tell from here. I'll move in.

CARMELITA
Gregory! Thought I might find you here, buddy.

GREGORY
Carmelita, you, ah, got a little something on your face...

CARMELITA
I'm sorry, Gregory, but I have to do this to you. I need
to smash you.

GREGORY
Now that's not good... Sneaky Hermit, I could use a
little help here! How about putting a few of your
Hermit Nippers on Carma Larga here? They will pry off
the mask.

SNEAKY HERMIT
Finally! My Hermit Nippers are starting to kick in... Or
not. The chemicals in my Hermit Nippers must
somehow be interacting with the Mask to make her
even bigger.

GREGORY
Whoa, you're not kidding, Sneaky Hermit. She's getting
gigantic. Everyone, head for the big truck! We gotta get
some distance between her and us. She might shrink
back down with time.

GREGORY BOUTHIETTE

SNEAKY HERMIT
This is bad... Looks like she has picked up a ring of dynamite! All power to the Super Claw 10,000! Use it to keep any explosives off our truck! Maybe you can throw it back at her. Might slow her down...

CARMELITA
Oh no, what now? Guys, help!

ANTI GREGORY
She's too huge! We can't outrun her in the truck.

GAGE
What do we do now?

SNEAKY HERMIT
Guys, this is really bad. We need to come up with a new plan fast.

GREGORY
Time to stop running and deal with the real problem: pry off that Mask of Dark Earth, then maybe we'll get back the Carmelita we all know and love.

ANTI GREGORY
I don't really love her that much.

GREGORY
Okay, that's not the point. It's all about that Mask. We gotta find a way up there.

SNEAKY HERMIT
You're the climber, and I'm sure you always wanted to get closer to her. Can't get too much closer than climbing up her boot laces.

GREGORY
That's not a crazy idea...

ANTI GREGORY
Oh yeah, it's crazy.

GREGORY
You got a better idea?

ANTI GREGORY
Yeah, but we'll need a giant fighting robot.

GREGORY
Sorry, we're gonna have to go with the boot lace plan.

SNEAKY HERMIT
Watch out, Carmelita's troops are en route! It looks like you're in luck: looks like each side of the Mask is latched on with only one hook. Maybe if you hung off it, she'll swat you away and knock it off... Great work, Gregory! One hook to go... And the Mask is off!

CARMELITA
Oh no, I'm going down now! What's happening to me?

GREGORY
Carmelita, are you okay?

CARMELITA
Yeah, I am. Thanks for the help, guys. I'm glad that I'm back to myself again. Hey, Gage, how are you doing?

GAGE
I'm doing well, Carmelita. I really missed you.

CARMELITA
I missed you, too, Gage. Now we need to go, guys.

SNEAKY HERMIT
You heard Carmelita, guys. Let's go.

CARMELITA
Just hang tight, guys. I might be going fast.

GREGORY
You heard her, guys. Hang on tight.

CARMELITA
Okay, guys. We're here.

GREGORY
Thanks for the ride, Carmelita.

CARMELITA
No problem, Gregory. I'll meet up with you guys later.

GREGORY
Okay. See you around, Carmelita.

***

ANTI GREGORY
Hey, Sneaky Hermit. What are you doing?

SNEAKY HERMIT
I'm just looking at the blueprints of how we're gonna get into the Bouthiette vault. I think I just found a way.

GREGORY
What else do we need to get inside the Bouthiette vault, Sneaky Hermit?

SNEAKY HERMIT
I think we may need someone who is good with an RC chopper. And I think I might know just the person that can help us.

GREGORY
What are you going to do?

SNEAKY HERMIT
I'm gonna chat with Bartley and ask him if we can borrow his girlfriend, Pinky.

ANTI GREGORY
Oh man, we are going to have Pinky with us, Gregory!

GREGORY
Easy, Anti Gregory. Pinky is still Bartley's girlfriend, and Sneaky Hermit is just going to ask him if we can borrow her for the Bouthiette vault job.

SNEAKY HERMIT
Yeah, that's right, Anti Gregory. And Bartley just said yes, that we can borrow her for the Bouthiette vault job, but he told us we need to stop Black Blake from taking over Holland first. Which means you need to join this year's ACES Competition, Gregory. While Anti Gregory and I make a plan, you'll need to steal a nametag.

GREGORY
I'm on it, Sneaky Hermit. See you guys later.

SNEAKY HERMIT
Okay, Gregory, are you back yet?

GREGORY
Yes, I am, Sneaky Hermit. I got my nametag right here.

SNEAKY HERMIT
Okay, let's get a move on.

GAGE
Wait for me, guys.

SNEAKY HERMIT
Okay, guys, let's head inside through the window.

GREGORY
Uh, Sneaky Hermit, I'm gonna go out there and figure
out what we need.

ANTI GREGORY
Good luck out there, Gregory. Just be careful.

GREGORY
I will, Anti Gregory. Don't worry about me.

SNEAKY HERMIT
If we're going to succeed in this year's ACES
Competition, we'll need to know who we're flying
against.

GREGORY
What, do they keep the flight roster a secret?

SNEAKY HERMIT
Correct. In years past, competitors would go out at
night and sabotage each other's planes in preparation

for the next day's dogfight.

GREGORY

I get it. So now they keep the line-up a secret, and no one knows who to mess with.

SNEAKY HERMIT

Precisely. Look, Gregory, you're a good pilot, but we only got one plane, and you'll be up there against dozens of bogeys.

GREGORY

You know, normally I'd make some sarcastic remark about how overwhelmed I am by your confidence in me, but those are some grim odds. And, well, you know I'm always up for some sabotage.

SNEAKY HERMIT

Glad to hear it. Now, the roster is kept secret from the pilots, but not from the event staff.

GREGORY

Do we have a mole on the inside?

SNEAKY HERMIT

Our friend Demetrie has been hired to give colorful commentary during the dogfights. He'll know where the roster's hidden. Scout him out somewhere in the hotel lobby, but be careful: if you start a fight with the other pilots, we'll be kicked out of the competition.

GREGORY

Sure, we all play nice until tomorrow. Then we blow each other up at 300 feet... Demetrie, funny seeing you here. Never pegged you as a flyboy.

DEMETRIE

Like a dance floor with many lights, I have many profiles, dig? Don't even try to understand the silky enigma of Demetrie.

GREGORY
Sneaky Hermit seems to think that you have a copy of
the ACES flight line-up. That true?

DEMETRIE
And why should I talk to a two-bit, rooty boot
crackerbox like you? Question mark in bold, why?

GREGORY
We both know you're gonna tell me. You wouldn't have
bothered showing up if you didn't wanna talk, so spill
it.

DEMETRIE
I know, but to talk is like sitting on the electric chair.
Blake has eyes, eyes and ears, ears and fists! Demetrie
will be discovered, and the jig will be pinched.

GREGORY
Come now, Demetrie. A man like you can deal with
Black Blake. You got the best fashion sense of anyone I
know.

DEMETRIE
The fashion, style! You're right. If I can out-dress him,
I can certainly outsmart him: all is told through
clothes. Okay, I'll talk about the flight line-up if you
agree to owe Demetrie a favor, which I'll collect in a
few months' time.

GREGORY
A favor...

DEMETRIE
This is no small time favor, like, will you water my fish
or feed my plant. No way, bro, this is old-school-mafia-
blood-pact favor, like the movies! Big time!

GREGORY
Okay, Demetrie. Hook me up with the flight roster, and
we'll owe you one.

DEMETRIE
Done! The bargain, she is struck! To find the flight
roster, look behind one of the tacky paintings in Blake's
air hangar. It's hidden in a secret safe.

GREGORY
Art decryption lock, huh? I know just the guy for the
job.

DEMETRIE
Stand cool, here comes the big cheese.

BLACK BLAKE
I bid you all a most flamboyant welcome. My esteemed
comrades of the skies, welcome! Welcome to another
year of the ACES Competition. We've got teams here
from across the globe: Canada, Belgium, Ecuador,
Iceland, Korea, and many, many more, not the least of
which is last year's deadly runner-up, Team Matthew.

MATTHEW
This time, we're gonna drill you jokers fulla holes!

BLACK BLAKE
Now we all know that in a years past, some teams have
engaged in a little good-natured, late night hijinks...

PILOTS
Like when Team Canada stole Ecuador's parachutes...
Or when Team Iceland sawed the landing gear off
Korea's planes... Or when Portugal put rat poison in
Team Matthew's coffee machine.

BLACK BLAKE
Yes, yes, that was all so very funny, but no more! You

know the rules: no one, absolutely no one, is to leave the hotel after sunset. If my guards catch you outside, you will be beaten within an inch of your life. No exceptions. This will be a fair competition.

PILOT
Same as last year, and the year before: I got the scars to prove it!

BLACK BLAKE
I bid you an exuberant and exaggerated farewell. Pilots: sleep like geese tonight, and tomorrow, soar like eagles high! What? What? Haha.

SNEAKY HERMIT
They don't lock the front door of the hotel. This isn't jail, but you heard Blake: once outside, things will get dangerous... Careful, buddy! Blake's got plenty of guards on duty, and it's a long way up to his castle on the hill... I won't be able get into Blake's hangar with the drawbridge up. There should be a release lever on top of the castle somewhere. Sorry, buddy, but you're the best climber we've got.

BLACK BLAKE
The competition starts tomorrow, where are my guards? Sleeping? Watching television? Or just doing something else like they always do? I tell you, Jacob, the ACES pilots get better and better. We've got some real competition on our hands this year... Oh, but I'm not saying that it's too much for Team Black Blake. No no no, we've done a fine job training.

SNEAKY HERMIT
Pssst, Gregory! Hey, Gregory? Gregory, you up there?

GREGORY
Nope, sorry. Just us Black Blake goons.

SNEAKY HERMIT
Throw the switch and lower the drawbridge so that I can get up there.

GREGORY
Sorry, buddy, I don't see any switch.

SNEAKY HERMIT
But... But there just has to be a switch! I can't get in Blake's hangar from down here.

GREGORY
Hold on, I've got an idea... It's gonna fall!

SNEAKY HERMIT
Medieval, but effective. Thanks, buddy.

GREGORY
Sure thing. See you back at the safe house... If Demetrie's intel is accurate, the flight roster should be locked behind one of the paintings in this hangar.

BLACK BLAKE
[on intercom]
Attention, attention, castle staff: we've got a big, big day tomorrow! The first round of the ACES Competition is just 12 hours away. You've done an awesome job for this event, and this year promises to have some of the greatest dogfight action you've ever seen. However, I cannot stress enough that I must win. You've all been hired to help me achieve victory. In fact, if the unthinkable happens... If Team Black Blake loses, I'm gonna dismiss you all and start hiring a new staff. Am I making myself clear? Leave nothing to chance: no outsider is to enter the castle, no buttheads near the planes. If we lose... No, if I lose, I am going to take it out on all of you. Begone! Have a good night, and let's have fun tomorrow.

SNEAKY HERMIT
Okay, fellows: according to the ACES flight line-up, we'll be flying against Team Iceland and Team Belgium in tomorrow's semifinals. As you all know, we've only got a single plane, while our opponents will be flying fifteen apiece. You got that, guys? That's thirty to one! In order to give us a fighting chance, we'll need to pin these two teams against each other. First, Anti Gregory and Gregory will paddle through the sewers beneath town to gain access to an air vent leading into Team Iceland's hotel room. Steal one of their trademark viking helmets, then head over to Team Belgium's hangar. Smash up their planes and plant the helmet on one of the planes in order to frame Team Iceland for the damage. Next, Anti Gregory and I will steal one of Team Belgium's monogrammed handkerchiefs. Meanwhile, Gage will break into the supply truck carrying Team Iceland's lucky ice sculpture. Gregory will steal the thing and place the handkerchief to frame Team Belgium for the crime. Get it? We frame both teams so they'll be gunning for each other and not Gregory in the semifinals. All the while, I'll be setting up some defense around the Team Bouthiette air hangar. You never know when one of the other teams might come looking to do us some harm.

GREGORY
Okay, let's all get ready to do some sneaking around one by one.

SNEAKY HERMIT
Okay, Gregory. Just make sure that you're in position when you get there.

GREGORY
You got it, Sneaky Hermit.

ANTI GREGORY
Hey, Gregory, I'll be waiting out there for when you're

done talking to Sneaky Hermit.

SNEAKY HERMIT
Alright, see that armored supply truck? It's en route to drop off Team Iceland's lucky ice sculpture for the semifinals tomorrow. I've given the driver some bad directions so they should be going in circles for hours. We need you to get inside that truck, steal the sculpture, and plant some evidence implicating Team Belgium.

GREGORY
Good thinking. Team Iceland won't be gunning for me if they think that Team Belgium stole their lucky hunk of ice.

SNEAKY HERMIT
That's the idea. Now the first thing to do is steal one of Team Belgium's official gold-laced monogrammed handkerchiefs. Anti Gregory will head inside and get one those stodgy Belgians laughing: they're notoriously stone-faced. Then I'll move in and steal the handkerchief.

GREGORY
Seems like getting inside that truck might be a good job for Gage. He could use some of the guards' heads to bash in the back doors.

SNEAKY HERMIT
Agreed. I'll make sure he's in position.

GREGORY
Okay, Anti Gregory: no pressure, but you've got to find a Team Belgium pilot and get him laughing so hard that Sneaky Hermit can make the pull. This is serious business, buddy: those guys are uptight.

ANTI GREGORY
Hello, Belgium flyer! Do you like comedy? I think it's time for Mr. Salty Pants to crack a smile. What do you say? Why did the chicken cross the road to France? Because it wasn't Turkey! And you see, a chicken's not a turkey or a Turk... It's a chicken! A French hen! I can't make heads or tails of this coin... Haha, get it? It's totally funny, because, like, when you flip a coin, it either comes out as heads or tails. Come on, that's comic gold! Ever seen someone put their fist down their throat? Tadah! Hey, fist stuck... Guys, I need help... Hey!

GREGORY
Okay, Sneaky Hermit, it's go time. Make the pull while the Belgian's laughing, or he'll be sure to feel you fishing for the handkerchief... Nice work, meet me outside with the goods. It's up to Gage now... Sneaky Hermit's en route to meet me with the monogrammed handkerchief, but we won't be able to swipe the ice sculpture unless we get into that armored truck.

GAGE
Maybe we could try to break down that back door. That should be its weak spot.

GREGORY
I agree.

GAGE
I can use the guards' heads to bash in the doors.

GREGORY
Yeah, I'm sure the guards around here won't mind too much if you break the door down with their heads.

GAGE
I will do my best to catch up with the truck: it's moving fast.

GREGORY
Sneaky Hermit's set up a tracking point on the truck.
Should be handy, that thing's moving pretty fast... It's a
good start, but the truck has already powered up its
defenses. You'll have to pay attention to your next hit.
It could get sticky.

SNEAKY HERMIT
Keep it up, that truck can't hold out for long... Nice
work, Gage. The back doors are still holding on tight,
but the top of the vehicle's been blown wide open!
Okay, Gregory, your turn. You'll have to sprint hard to
catch up, but jumping inside through the roof should
be easy... This is it! Crack the safe and make the swap!
No pressure, but I think that the driver has figured out
where to go. You don't have much time... Great work,
Team Iceland is sure to blame Team Belgium. They'll
be all over each other in tomorrow's dogfight.

GREGORY
Okay, Anti Gregory, you're up, buddy.

ANTI GREGORY
Okay, Gregory. Thanks for letting me know.

GREGORY
No problem, buddy.

SNEAKY HERMIT
Looks like hard-partying Team Iceland has already
gone to sleep. Time to borrow one of their viking
helmets.

ANTI GREGORY
Why do you need me? Just have Gregory pick the lock
to the door and steal the thing.

SNEAKY HERMIT
This is a delicate business. We're trying to frame Team

Iceland for a crime they haven't committed: if there's any evidence of their door being forced, people might believe that they're innocent.

ANTI GREGORY
Man, you got devious over the years. So, uh, how are we supposed to get inside?

SNEAKY HERMIT
There are some sewer pipes beneath town that should connect up with the ventilation system of the hotel. Gregory's scrounged up a raft for the trip, but be careful: other pilots have caused trouble down there in the past, and Blake is sure to have set up some security.

ANTI GREGORY
I get to row a boat? Nautical!

SNEAKY HERMIT
Anti Gregory, just get moving... This is it. Gregory, make your way to the hotel air vent. Anti Gregory, stay and guard the boat... Nice work, you're almost there. Be careful not to wake these guys up: they are a very good group and, uh, probably set up some burglar alarms.

MATTHEW
Hey, Jason, you got the keys to the room?

JASON
Yeah, hold... Umm, they're not there... Umm, do you have them?

SNEAKY HERMIT
Nice work. Head back to Anti Gregory and the raft.

MATTHEW
No, you're the responsible one here! Let's just bang on the door.

JASON
Uh, no! Everyone in there is asleep, I don't want to wake them all up! Those guys will shoot at us tomorrow if we do that.

MATTHEW
Fine, we'll just go down to the front desk and ask for a spare. And you can forget about me being your wingman in the finals tomorrow.

ANTI GREGORY
Sorry, buddy, the valve gates have changed position. We need to escape through another tunnel, but fear not! Anti Gregory has a good sense of direction... Land ho!

GREGORY
Nice job. You really showed some finesse with those oars.

ANTI GREGORY
I always am, and always have been, finesse.

GREGORY
Uh, yeah... You good to plant this helmet on Belgium's plane?

ANTI GREGORY
Can do, buddy. Can do with a vengeance.

SNEAKY HERMIT
That's Belgium's prized plane strung up from the ceiling. It's held in place by these anchors: destroy them, and the plane should come crashing down.

ANTI GREGORY
Seems like these lasers might burn my butt.

SNEAKY HERMIT
True. You'll have to compact yourself using your ball
form to travel safely beneath the laser grid.

ANTI GREGORY
Check.

SNEAKY HERMIT
Then you'll just use your ball form to charge up and
destroy the anchors... Excellent work. Plant the viking
helmet, and Team Belgium's sure to blame Team
Iceland... Uh, Anti Gregory, I have been working on
getting our hangar security devices online, and they're
almost operational. Unfortunately, our friend Pinky
heard a rumor that a rival air team might be stopping
by to do mischief to our plane.

ANTI GREGORY
Mischief-makers coming here?

SNEAKY HERMIT
If you could stand watch while I finish getting the
systems online, that would be great.

ANTI GREGORY
Fear not, little plane! You will be safe while my fists are
on duty.

MATTHEW
Greetings, you buttheads. Didn't think I forgot about
Mesa City, did you? You little punks let me smash up
your airplane, and we're even.

ANTI GREGORY
You and what army?

MATTHEW
Army? Oh yeah! Okay, boys, I paid you good enough,
time to crack some skulls!

SNEAKY HERMIT
Anti Gregory, you can't hurt Matthew with your fists.
Try using the switch in the middle of the hangar.

MATTHEW
Ouch! Get that blue punk, these doors ain't holding
themselves open... Keep it coming, I'm a brick wall... I
can take it all day, butthead... Take him down! Now!
Burn that meatball, this is killing me... Hahahaha...
Ouch! Oh, right in the private area... Don't think this is
over, you butthead. You're not very powerful. This is
just the beginning of a very bad day.

SNEAKY HERMIT
Matthew wasn't making idle threats: I'm reading a lot
of hostiles moving through the sewers toward our
position. Fortunately my security devices are almost
online, I'll have just enough time for a quick test... Let's
see, I can switch between two computers by moving
from one to the other... Looks like they're working
perfectly! And just in time, too. Anti Gregory, we've got
company coming! If one gets through my trap, you'll
have to take him out.

ANTI GREGORY
Got it! The Bouthiette plane is as safe as a baby in it's
aircraft hangar crib.

SNEAKY HERMIT
Now they're coming in from the right......We stopped
that group, Anti Gregory, but it looks like more are on
the way. And they're packing explosives... We're
halfway there, Anti Gregory. Stay sharp.

ANTI GREGORY
Hands off the plane, butthead.

SNEAKY HERMIT
It's the final push. Keep that plane safe... Just a few

guys left... Yes, we got them! Nice work, Anti Gregory.

ANTI GREGORY
Matthew will need a lot more than muscle to stop us.

SNEAKY HERMIT
Looks like he's got muscle and firepower. Maybe it's time I brought in some backup. I just hope she knows ham radio talk... Pinky, do you read me? Are you out there?

PINKY
I read you, Sneaky Hermit.

SNEAKY HERMIT
Umm, this is a good time for you to help us out here. We've got some trouble and need your help.

PINKY
Like the fact Matthew has just called in some guys to head to your hangar? Don't worry, I won't let those goons hurt your team's plane.

SNEAKY HERMIT
Is your RC chopper ready to pull the guards?

PINKY
Yes, it is, Sneaky Hermit.

SNEAKY HERMIT
You are a good friend, Pinky.

PINKY
Thanks, Sneaky Hermit. I'm happy to help you guys out no matter what... Oh, wait! I just got word from Bartley, and he told me to use my Yank-86, Sneaky Hermit! You don't mind me using it, do you?

SNEAKY HERMIT
Not at all, Pinky. Just bring the hook down and yank the guards away. Just make sure that you don't let go of them once you have a clear shot.

PINKY
Sweet. I'll teach those buttheads not to mess with the Bouthiette Gang.

SNEAKY HERMIT
Some enemies need to get a few yanks. Just move forward, then move the other way through them.

PINKY
Yeah, these guys are heavy.

SNEAKY HERMIT
Pinky, you've got a big tank coming. They can do some serious damage to our hangar.

PINKY
Copy that, Sneaky Hermit. I have found the tank... He wasn't so tough.

SNEAKY HERMIT
Great job, Pinky. You're the best RC pilot I have ever seen.

PINKY
No problem, Sneaky Hermit. Those thugs deserved it. No one sells out Black Blake and walks away scot-free.

SNEAKY HERMIT
Okay, team, we're all set up for the semifinals. Once Gregory arrives at the team hangar, we'll fly the plane and suit up for the competition.

ANTI GREGORY
Okay, Gregory, it's time for you to go to the team

hangar.

GREGORY
Oh yeah, I forgot. Thanks, Anti Gregory. I'll see you guys later. Is Sneaky Hermit still there?

ANTI GREGORY
Yes, he is. He's just waiting for you. Good luck, Gregory.

GREGORY
Thanks, Anti Gregory. I'll win this for you guys.

SNEAKY HERMIT
Suit up, buddy. Almost time for the semifinals... Stay sharp, Gregory. Iceland and Belgium will be at each other's throats up there, but you're still outnumbered.

GREGORY
Relax, mom, this is gonna be great.

DEMETRIE
[on intercom]
Eyes to the sky, peeps, the semifinal round between Team Iceland, Team Bouthiette, and Team Belgium is now underway. The fights are on, dogfight action-reaction.

SNEAKY HERMIT
Okay, Gregory. The winner here is the last man standing. It's going to be rough, and I know you're afraid of heights, but I think you can do it.

DEMETRIE
[on intercom]
Another falling star! Remember, there is some ice cream, and it's only for five dollars. If you go, just get me some ice cream please, the cookie dough kind... And that plane goes down! A little sneak attack! There

goes another plane! That move was really awesome; he should use it again.

SNEAKY HERMIT
Awesome flying, Gregory! You made it to the final ten! Keep it up.

DEMETRIE
[on intercom]
Another plane goes down!

SNEAKY HERMIT
Good job, Gregory. You've just got two more planes to go...

DEMETRIE
[on intercom]
Tip to outstanding, Team Bouthiette is going to the finals!

GREGORY
Guys, I'm back. Do we have more missions, Sneaky Hermit?

SNEAKY HERMIT
Thanks to Gregory's flying, we are now in the ACES finals. Our opponents are Team Matthew and Team Black Blake. The rules in the finals are a bit different than normal: who ever takes out the defending champ will take the title! You hear that, boys? It's all about taking down Blake. Our only real competition will be Matthew himself, so we need to remove him from the competition. Here's the plan: I'll challenge him to a fist fight out in the town square. Gregory, you'll go find Carmelita and tell her that she needs to take out Matthew for us. Just let her know about the plan, then she will follow you to the town square. When those two meet, sparks will fly! With some luck, the big guy will get carted off to jail, and we'll have clear skies for the

finals! However, Blake won't be so easy to deal with: he commands a big team of flyers and has been known to bring in a lot of big gunships if things get grim. The answer to our problem isn't good, it is bad: behold, a feral specimen of Biggest Baddest Giant Wolf! I'll drug the beast so that Gage will be able to ride it and take out some of the guards who also serve as Blake's pilots. The fewer enemy pilots Gregory has to deal with in the finals, the better. Next, I'll hack into the aircraft control tower. If successful, I'll be able to intercept any messages Blake might send his gunships. Alright, team, we've got all night to prepare. If we take this thing, it will be for more than a trophy: Pinky will be sure to join our gang! After her awesome work defending our hangar, I'm sure we'd all agree that she's a good friend.

ANTI GREGORY
Okay, so what's the first mission, Sneaky Hermit?

SNEAKY HERMIT
I'm gonna be working with Gregory to bring Carmelita into the town square. Just wait until I'm done with Matthew.

GREGORY
You got it, Sneaky Hermit.

SNEAKY HERMIT
It's time to deal with Matthew. We can't risk him taking out Blake before you win the finals.

GREGORY
Not to mention that we deserve a little payback for what he did to our aircraft hangar.

SNEAKY HERMIT
True, true. Since Matthew's assault, Blake has been keeping an eye on him. We can't fight him out in the open for risk of getting disqualified; thankfully,

Carmelita is out in the field looking for us.

GREGORY
I hear you: we'll set them against each other. Matthew is an international criminal after all: Carmelita won't be able to resist.

SNEAKY HERMIT
My only concern is Carmelita's safety.

GREGORY
Oh, don't worry about her. She's more than a match for a meathead like Matthew.

SNEAKY HERMIT
Okay, I'll pick a fight with Matthew and bait him into meeting in the town square for a rumble.

GREGORY
You do that, and I'll get Carmelita's attention and lead her to the same place.

SNEAKY HERMIT
Agreed.

GREGORY
I gotta hand it to you, Sneaky Hermit: this is, well, an awesome plan.

SNEAKY HERMIT
Thank you, I'm feeling pretty good about it.

MATTHEW
Oh, beat it, butthead! Black Blake's been giving me the grill since that event in your hangar.

SNEAKY HERMIT
Perhaps you'd like to take out some frustration by engaging in a physical battle with me outside in the

town square.

MATTHEW
No way! I'm being watched here. That, and it wouldn't
feel right pounding a four-eyed runt hermit crab.

SNEAKY HERMIT
I'm sure you wouldn't win in a fight anyway; you've got
such a long, sad history of losing to the Bouthiette
Gang.

MATTHEW
I could rip apart your whole gang with one arm if you
jerks would sit still! Look at these arms! I'm
unstoppable.

SNEAKY HERMIT
Do you even know what I'm saying to you, or are you
too dumb to understand the words coming in through
your earhole?

MATTHEW
What? What's an earhole? Talk sense, why don't you.

SNEAKY HERMIT
You know, I have been thinking about your
appearance.

MATTHEW
Look, if you don't got nothing nice to say, then don't
say nothing at all. Get it? What, ain't got no sassy
comment, smart guy? Oh, I get it. You got nothing nice
to say so you're keeping quiet. That's real cute... You
really got nothing nice to say? That's cold.

SNEAKY HERMIT
Your mother was a broken down tub of junk with more
gentlemen callers than the operator.

MATTHEW

Nobody talks that way about my mother! Nobody!
Okay, you little broken down runt, looks you're gonna
get broken down even more.

SNEAKY HERMIT

Town square. Five minutes. Please don't be late...
Okay, Gregory, Matthew is on his way outside. Go find
Carmelita and lead her back to the town square.

GREGORY

Hey, Carmelita, over here! I need to tell you something.

CARMELITA

What's up, Gregory? Is there something wrong?

GREGORY

Yes, there is. Matthew is out of jail, and I need to lure
you to the town square so that you can have a little
fight with him. And put him back in jail.

CARMELITA

Okay, Gregory. Just lure me into the town square
quickly, buddy, because Matthew is on his way right
now.

GREGORY

Okay, Carmelita, just chase me to the town square.

CARMELITA

I'm right behind you... Thanks, Gregory. I'll see you
back at the safe house after the fight. Now just keep on
running.

MATTHEW

Mess with me... That little punk is gonna eat dirt...
Hey! You're that cop hag that busted me back at Mesa
City.

CARMELITA
Matthew: the biggest, toughest guy in the world, and still on the most wanted list. Yes, I'm that cop hag that put you away back in Mesa.

MATTHEW
Well, wise guy, uh, lady, feel like going for another shot at the title?

CARMELITA
It's my duty to put you behind bars. That, and I enjoy making tough guys cry like the dumb babies they really are.

MATTHEW
I ain't no dumb baby... Chicks like you make me glad that I hate chicks like you. Say goodnight, cop hag... Mother, that you? I'm sorry, I didn't know they were yours...

CARMELITA
Booking this butthead will take all night. Ah well, I'm sure that Gregory will have another mission for me to do with him later.

SNEAKY HERMIT
Ah! A perfect Biggest Baddest Giant Wolf.

GREGORY
So, let me get this straight again: you plan on stalking that thing, drugging it, putting Gage onboard, and setting it free to smash up the guards?

SNEAKY HERMIT
An airtight plan, I agree. It's simplicity itself. By channeling the wild destruction housed in that bloodthirsty creature, we should be able to thin out Black Blake's ranks. Which, of course, means fewer enemies flying against you in the finals.

GREGORY
I'm all for evening the odds in our favor, but come on.
This seems a little risky.

SNEAKY HERMIT
Not at all! I modified my Hermit Nippers with heavy
doses of skunk balm. It should be enough to pacify the
beast, provided he doesn't catch wind of me first.

GREGORY
Alright, that sounds okay. You can hang back and shoot
him at a distance.

SNEAKY HERMIT
Ah, well, given the weight of my Hermit Nippers, I'll
need to sneak up behind him, and take a shot within a
few meters.

GREGORY
Meters...

SNEAKY HERMIT
Quit trying to freak me out! Put Gage on the line...
After I put the wolf to sleep, it will be up to you.

GAGE
Okay, Sneaky Hermit. I'll be ready when you're done.

SNEAKY HERMIT
Thanks, Gage. You always know just what to say.

GREGORY
Good shot... He's caught you're scent, get out of there!
Bullseye... Nice work, big game hunter. The skunk
balm is already kicking in; he's almost asleep... Gage,
you're up. You should be able to possess the giant wolf
now that he's out. Run down those guards! And...
That's ten fewer pilots in the final tomorrow. Excellent,
that should even the odds for the finals... How do you

plan to hack into the aircraft control tower?

SNEAKY HERMIT
It's simple, really: the whole system is linked through computer nodes which monitor the power generated by the nearby windmills.

GREGORY
Seriously, all the power around here comes from the local windmill? I thought that was just for looks.

SNEAKY HERMIT
The control nodes tell a different story.

GREGORY
How do you plan on getting up there? It's pretty high.

SNEAKY HERMIT
You forgot that we have flying powers. It won't be too hard for me... Prepare yourself, computer. I will show no fear... Ah, nothing like a little hack job... Excellent, now for the aircraft control tower. Once that's hacked, the system will be mine.

GREGORY
That looks like a long jump, but I think you can make it.

SNEAKY HERMIT
Aha! My final opponent... Looks like they saved the big code for last. Bring it on, you buttheads... Success! I've got total access. Wait... The code's unstable, everything is speeding up! Windmill throwing star, eh? This little system bug might come in handy... Okay, thanks to our combined powers, we're now ready for the final round of the ACES Dogfight Competition. Put on your helmets, because it's time for Operation Turbo Dominant Eagle. In just a few hours, Team Iceland and Team Belgium will begin fighting it out in the B-

champs round. This will provide the perfect cover for step one of my plan: Gregory, use the catapult and your flying to gain access to the local gunships. Plant some tracking devices, then head back to the team hangar and suit up for the finals. Anti Gregory, you'll be up next: use your rowboat to pull down the aircraft communication antenna. With it out of commission, Black Blake will have to use his radio to call in the gunships for backup. If that happens, I'll be ready with our secret weapon. And with the tracking devices installed, I tell you it will not miss. In the end, though, it will be up to Gregory: in the sudden death finals, the first team to take out last year's champ wins. That is, if Black Blake doesn't take out all of the competition first.

GREGORY

Okay, so I will start the operation. I should go out now.

SNEAKY HERMIT

Excellent. The B-champs dogfight is beginning... With these guys going at it, no one will notice you slipping onto the gunships and planting tracking devices.

GREGORY

Sounds straightforward enough. Where did you get these trackers? They look kind of funny.

SNEAKY HERMIT

Best I could do on short notice. They're sensitive to extreme changes in altitude: you'll have to pull this job off at high elevation, or it's a bust.

GREGORY

Shouldn't be a problem.

SNEAKY HERMIT

Excellent, the first tracker's in place. If I'm not mistaken, there should be a little trampoline for you to jump to the other gunship... Well done, two down...

Great! Just one more tracker, and we're in business... Nice work, flyboy. The gunships' GPS data is flowing in. Head back to the hangar and suit up... Alright, Anti Gregory, Black Blake's communication antenna is held up by three support beams. Pull them out of place, and the whole array will fall apart.

ANTI GREGORY
Don't worry, if there's one thing I'm good at, it's rowing. And breaking stuff.

SNEAKY HERMIT
Keep it up! The falling planes are dangerous, but they're perfect cover for this operation.

ANTI GREGORY
Anti Gregory has broken you, but let that be a lesson to all antennas: I will not be trifled with.

SNEAKY HERMIT
This is it, eye of the tiger, buddy. Look for Black Blake: take him out, and this competition is all over. And go easy on the throttle, it's been sticking lately.

GREGORY
Quit worrying. I'll see you in the winners' circle.

DEMETRIE
[on intercom]
Okay, it's big time final round! This is what you came for, people! The deaths are bad for everyone, and the skies are full with the danger. Black Blake is being shot at!

BLACK BLAKE
Drat, that little boy is good... Gunships, converge on my position and destroy the Bouthiette aircraft. Send in a spare plane as well.

GUARD
Roger, Blake. All units en route.

SNEAKY HERMIT
Sorry, Blake, but you'll have to fight fair this year.

BLACK BLAKE
What? Who is this, how did you find this frequency?
What? No! Desist! Halt, I command it! Gah, this plane
is coming unfixed. About time for an upgrade, I'd say.

GREGORY
Oh no you don't, you weasel.

BLACK BLAKE
Weasel, am I?

GREGORY
I beat you. Your biplane is in pieces.

BLACK BLAKE
Ah, but we're both still airborne, aren't we? The victor
has yet to be decided!

GREGORY
Then let's settle it.

BLACK BLAKE
Beware, my boy, I have trained ten years in fisticuffs:
pugilism is my passion!

GREGORY
If you fight as well as you fly, this shouldn't take long.

BLACK BLAKE
En garde! Uh, a little help here... Men, defend your
leader! No, this can't be happening!

PINKY
And stay down, Black Blake! Gregory, it's you! Good
job taking care of Black Blake for me.

GREGORY
Wait, Pinky! Where have you been this whole time?

PINKY
I have been inside this plane the whole time, taking
care of some Black Blake guards while you were out
here fighting Black Blake himself... Let's talk on the
ground where it's safe.

GREGORY
Sounds like a plan, Pinky. Let's go.

SNEAKY HERMIT
Anti Gregory, do you see Gregory anywhere?

ANTI GREGORY
Nope, not yet, Sneaky Hermit. He's not anywhere.

GREGORY
Guys, up here!

SNEAKY HERMIT
Gregory, you're back! Pinky, where did you come from?

PINKY
Sneaky Hermit, Anti Gregory and Gage! I missed you
guys. I was beating on Black Blake's guards the whole
time.

ANTI GREGORY
You could have just helped Gregory defeat the real
Black Blake.

PINKY
I'm sorry, Anti Gregory, I was kind of stuck. When I

looked out of the window, I saw Gregory fighting Black Blake.

GAGE
And are you gonna help us out with the Bouthiette vault job, Pinky?

PINKY
Of course, Gage, but Bartley wants to make sure I get some missions with you guys, too.

SNEAKY HERMIT
Don't worry, Pinky, you will help us in some of the missions. But for now, we should just talk for a while and see where we need to go next.

PINKY
You got it, Sneaky Hermit.

***

GREGORY BOUTHIETTE

GREGORY
Okay, so what else do we need to do, Sneaky Hermit?

SNEAKY HERMIT
I think we need to find out of how to get inside the
Bouthiette vault, since I have no idea yet.

ANTI GREGORY
Well, there's gotta be some way to get inside the vault.

GAGE
I agree. Maybe we just need a little firepower on our
side.

SNEAKY HERMIT
Wait, Gage, did you just say firepower?

GAGE
Yeah, why? Is that the answer that you were looking
for, Sneaky Hermit?

SNEAKY HERMIT
Yes, it was. I know how we're gonna get inside the
Bouthiette vault now: we need The Panda's help.

GREGORY
Wait, what? Are we really gonna have The Panda on
our side, Sneaky Hermit?

SNEAKY HERMIT
Yes, we are, Gregory. I know you don't really want him
on our team, but we need him.

PINKY
So, what are we waiting for, fellows? Let's go to the
airport and get to China.

GREGORY
You heard the lady. Let's go to China.

ANTI GREGORY
Oh yeah! We're going on an airplane again, Gage!

GAGE
Okay, Anti Gregory. I know that you're happy about it,
but can you just relax, please?

ANTI GREGORY
Oh. Sorry, Gage.

SNEAKY HERMIT
Everyone just sit tight and relax. We might be on the
plane for a while: it is a long ride to China.

GREGORY
Don't worry, Sneaky Hermit. I'm just gonna be
listening to my music.

SNEAKY HERMIT
Okay, good. Just keep your eyes out for China, Anti
Gregory.

ANTI GREGORY
You got it, Sneaky Hermit.

PINKY
Hey, Gage, is it okay if I sit next to you?

GAGE
Sure, Pinky. You can sit next to me.

ANTI GREGORY
Hey, guys, we're here. And I can see The Panda down
there.

SNEAKY HERMIT
Alright, guys, let's go and see The Panda now.

GREGORY
Okay, good. We can finally get off this thing.

PINKY
Hey, guys, wait up! We're coming, too.

GREGORY
Stay sharp, team: for all we know, The Panda is just as dangerous as ever.

SNEAKY HERMIT
How can you say that? Just look at him! Have you ever seen someone more at peace with the world?

GREGORY
I'll admit, he does look kind of zenned out.

SNEAKY HERMIT
Uh, Mr. Panda, honorable Panda, we humbly wish to speak with you.

GREGORY
I guess he doesn't wanna talk. Sorry, Sneaky Hermit, let's go.

SNEAKY HERMIT
Be realistic, Gregory. He's clearly in a deep meditative trance. Hmm... It will take some doing, but I think I see a way to get the team up to his shrine.

ANTI GREGORY
Good, the walk up here tired me out. I don't wanna turn around now. Man, I miss the car. We never had to walk anywhere back then.

GREGORY
Okay, okay. Let's just get this over with.

SNEAKY HERMIT
Anti Gregory, you're up first. If you can get to the top of
that pillar, you should be able to use your ball form to
bounce all the way up to The Panda.

ANTI GREGORY
Okay! Bouncing is a lot easier than more walking;
seriously, do you guys wanna see my blisters?

PINKY
No way! Is he serious?

GAGE
I've got an idea: maybe you should bounce to the
pillars.

ANTI GREGORY
Yeah, okay, Gage. Bouncing pillars. Peace of cake.

GAGE
Try being firm with him.

SNEAKY HERMIT
I hear that; sometimes you just gotta be firm.

PINKY
No, seriously, was he for real about the blisters?
Because, uh... I don't know, it's... Sheesh.

ANTI GREGORY
Okay, I'm in position.

SNEAKY HERMIT
Pinky, you're up next. I'm not sure if you're aware, but
Gregory can jump onto small points: those bamboo
shoots would be an ideal means of ascent if they
weren't spaced so far apart.

PINKY
Hold on, hold on. Let me see if I can figure it out for
myself.

SNEAKY HERMIT
It's, ah, got to do with the ice...

PINKY
Okay, so clearly we'll need more points in order for
Gregory to ascend. The problem is... Where are we
going to get them? The answer: split each shoot down
the middle, thereby doubling the points of ascension.
However, the ice down there appears to be too thin to
walk on, so there's no way of doing it by hand... So I
think I might use my lightweight remote control car to
split the trees for us.

SNEAKY HERMIT
Perfect! That's exactly it.

PINKY
Great! Anything for Gregory; I love to see him pull off
those athletic moves... Good, I put some turrets on this
little lady. Perfect for splitting logs... There you go,
Gregory. I hope it's everything that you could have
wished for.

GREGORY
Uh, thanks. It looks great.

PINKY
My pleasure, really. Any time.

SNEAKY HERMIT
Uh, Gregory, isn't it time you climb up there and join
Anti Gregory?

GREGORY
Yeah, sure...

SNEAKY HERMIT
Whack the supports up on those pinwheels.

GREGORY
Really?

SNEAKY HERMIT
The pinwheels are the most important part of this plan.

ANTI GREGORY
Jump into my hands, and I'll throw you up there.

GREGORY
I'm all done up here.

SNEAKY HERMIT
Excellent. Now that the pinwheels are unstable, I need
to shoot them with my Hermit Nippers. One shot
should do the trick... Those pinwheels are about to go!
Gage, feel up for a challenge?

GAGE
Challenge? What, you mean get to those rockets?

SNEAKY HERMIT
That's right. You should be able to persuade the guards
to help you get up to those rockets.

GAGE
No problem, Sneaky Hermit. I'll do that.

SNEAKY HERMIT
Strong work. That falling pinwheel should serve as an
excellent makeshift elevator.

GAGE
An elevator, you say? Man, he's in a meditative state.

GREGORY BOUTHIETTE

SNEAKY HERMIT
I agree, he's in a super meditative state.

GREGORY
Let's just shout in his ear.

SNEAKY HERMIT
No, to break him out of this trance, we'll need to delve
into his mind.

GREGORY
A hacksaw, then.

SNEAKY HERMIT
No! It'll require channeling.

GAGE
So what's the plan, Sneaky Hermit?

SNEAKY HERMIT
Gregory, sit beside The Panda. Gage will bridge your
minds.

PANDA
I see you with your powers from your Bouthiette
history. Have you come here for revenge? To steal back
the pages from your book?

GREGORY
Whoa, this is just like the time I was beating the
stuffing out of you.

PANDA
Why should you care if I bury a few towns in snow?
You are a hero, just like me.

GREGORY
Uh, yeah, are you even listening to what I'm saying?

PANDA
Oh really? Bouthiette, you shall pay for your
disrespect... Still, to honor your Bouthiette ancestry, I
will send you to your doom with the beauty of my new
firework move: Flame Fu.

GREGORY
Uh oh... Snap out of it, this is all in your head!

PANDA
My mind is clear... Focused on your destruction...

GREGORY
We both know why you're here: you're fixated on your
greatest defeat. I beat you, and forever after you
wondered how it all fell apart.

PANDA
I don't like you, Gregory Bouthiette. You ruined me,
ruined The Panda!

GREGORY
And I never liked you, but that doesn't make any of this
real. Years have passed, and we have both changed.
Come out of this trance. Let's meet each other as we are
today and let go of who we were when this fight
happened.

PANDA
You are correct. Forgive me, my mind is not always my
own... Hey, guys. It's been a long time since I've seen
you all.

GREGORY
It's good to see you again, too, Panda.

GAGE
Panda, are you okay, old friend? What's wrong?

GREGORY BOUTHIETTE

PANDA
I'm glad that you asked... My daughter has been taken
away from me again.

SNEAKY HERMIT
Who took your daughter, Panda? I think we might be
able to help you.

PANDA
It's General Tony. He's been set free from jail. Now he's
back, and he wants to marry my daughter again.

PINKY
Oh no, this is not good at all. Bartley and I stopped him
before, but now we need to stop him again...

SNEAKY HERMIT
You're right, Pinky. We must help The Panda get his
daughter back, and put General Tony back in jail.

ANTI GREGORY
I don't really know anything about this General Tony
guy, but we need to stop him again.

PANDA
Will you guys help me get my daughter back?

SNEAKY HERMIT
Yes, we will, Panda. We just need to find General Tony
first.

PANDA
Leave that to me, you guys. After we do this, I will be
another member for the Bouthiette vault job, and I will
help you on your journey.

SNEAKY HERMIT
Is there a safe house for us, Panda?

PANDA
Yes, there is a safe house for you guys. I will let you guys stay there for all of your missions.

GREGORY
Thanks, Panda. We can find it on our own.

SNEAKY HERMIT
I thought you might be happy to have The Panda on our side, Gregory.

GREGORY
Not yet, Sneaky Hermit. I just want to see him help us out before I can have him on our team.

SNEAKY HERMIT
Oh well. I hope that The Panda will help one of us out during our missions.

PANDA
Well, there's your safe house, guys.

SNEAKY HERMIT
Thanks, Panda. Hey, are you gonna help us out with one of the missions I'm planning?

PANDA
I don't know, Sneaky Hermit, but I think I might help you guys out if you want me to.

SNEAKY HERMIT
Okay, I was just asking. Thanks again.

PANDA
No problem, Sneaky Hermit. I'll see you guys later.

SNEAKY HERMIT
We all know that our plan is to free The Panda's daughter, Katty. She's being held prisoner by this man,

GREGORY BOUTHIETTE

General Tony. A real monster of a guy: during a walk around, I saw him kick a puppy two times! He plans on marrying Katty next Saturday. With time as one of our problems, here's the plan: first, I'll talk to General Tony in costume and try to get hired as his wedding planner. Hopefully, with a man on the inside, we'll get some news on Katty. Still, we'll need more information: two of us will need to work together to steal a pair of keys and break into Tony's house! Once inside, I'll need to use my Hermit Nippers to shut down the laser doors and other security. Finally, thanks to Pinky's air flying, we picked up a radio signature out in the water. Someone needs to go eyeballing and figure out what it is. We can't leave anything to chance here, or Katty will live unhappily ever after.

ANTI GREGORY
I think I might go and do my mission first, Sneaky Hermit, because I really want to do this differently for once.

SNEAKY HERMIT
Okay, Anti Gregory, you can go do your mission first.

ANTI GREGORY
Okay. Thanks, Sneaky Hermit.

GREGORY
Anti Gregory, just make sure that you really look out there.

ANTI GREGORY
Relax, Gregory. I can do this on my own.

PINKY
Just let me know when you get there, Anti Gregory.

ANTI GREGORY
Okay, Pinky, I will let you know when I get there.

PINKY
The mysterious signal I picked up was somewhere on
the water's surface...

ANTI GREGORY
I'm not seeing anything.

PINKY
Keep scanning. These readings are clear.

ANTI GREGORY
Great snakes on a stick, I don't believe it!

PINKY
What, you found the signal?

ANTI GREGORY
It's the team car! Last time I saw it, it was floating away
on a block of ice in Canada... And now it's here!

PINKY
Highly probable, given ocean currents.

ANTI GREGORY
I've got to go get it! Don't worry, baby, mama's coming!

PINKY
Don't even think about swimming, Anti Gregory! That
water's freezing: you wouldn't last a minute.

ANTI GREGORY
But... But my baby...

PINKY
Hold your position. I should be able to drag the car to
you using my RC chopper.

ANTI GREGORY
Thank you, Pinky! Thank you and your bag of remote

control RCs... Use that hook thing to pull the car over to me... Turn hard to take out those missiles! I saw it on tv... Oh, my sweet car! How I missed you! Don't worry, I'll break you outta your ice prison.

PINKY
Careful, Anti Gregory: the locals seem to be on to you... It's no use, Anti Gregory, this area's too dangerous. We have to recover the car later.

ANTI GREGORY
But... I can't lose him again!

PINKY
Forget the car! You'll never make it.

ANTI GREGORY
But... No. No, either help me or get out of my way. I'm bringing him home.

PINKY
Okay, Anti Gregory. I've got a little fuel left; keep pulling as hard as you can, I'll try to clear the way... Sorry, Anti Gregory, but I'm outta fuel. And I can't do anything with those spikes in your way.

ANTI GREGORY
But... We're so close!

PINKY
You did your best. We just ran out of options.

SNEAKY HERMIT
She's right, Anti Gregory. It's hopeless out of there. Save yourself.

ANTI GREGORY
I will not. I will never leave him behind again.

PANDA
Words to tear at a father's heart. Would that I had such passion when they came for my little Katty... Fear not, brave Anti Gregory, I will destroy the spikes blocking your path.

SNEAKY HERMIT
Be careful with those fireworks, Panda: one careless shot can hurt Anti Gregory.

PANDA
You buttheads will not hurt that kid. The Panda forbids it. Come, buttheads, rush to your doom. The Panda reigns again.

PINKY
Anti Gregory, you did it! You saved the car.

PANDA
Well done, brave Anti Gregory. You lit the flames in my soul; I feel truly awake for the first time in years.

ANTI GREGORY
No, thank you, Panda. You can ride in my car anytime, and you can even sit in front for like, a month.

PANDA
A great honor. I accept.

SNEAKY HERMIT
Good job, Anti Gregory. You got the car back safe and sound. Now it's Gregory's turn to do his mission.

GREGORY
You're right about that, Sneaky Hermit. I'll meet you there.

SNEAKY HERMIT
Okay, Gregory. I'll be waiting for you.

GREGORY BOUTHIETTE

ANTI GREGORY
Oh man, I need to have a little break.

SNEAKY HERMIT
You earned it, Anti Gregory.

ANTI GREGORY
Excuse me for minute, Sneaky Hermit. I need to
change my diaper.

SNEAKY HERMIT
You go do that, Anti Gregory.

ANTI GREGORY
This may take a while. Just keep on doing your mission
with Gregory.

SNEAKY HERMIT
Okay... Gregory, we know that little tower down there
is where Tony is planning to have his wedding. We
need to work together and steal some keys for the
locks.

GREGORY
Alright, so let's get to those keys, Sneaky Hermit.

SNEAKY HERMIT
Hold on a minute, Gregory. It sounds like this job
needs both of us to steal the keys at the same time.

GREGORY
I see: if we steal the key from the first guard, he'll
report it in.

SNEAKY HERMIT
That's right. Since you are so good at this, I think I
should go first.

GREGORY
Okay. I'll take my position behind these guys over here.
Call me when you get the key.

SNEAKY HERMIT
You got it, Gregory.

GREGORY
I'm in position for the pull. The second you get your
key, I'll go for this one.

SNEAKY HERMIT
Roger, I'm en route for key number one... I got the first
key, go for the second before the guard calls it in...
Excellent, you got the second. Let's meet in front of the
statue for the hand off... Now that I have both keys, it's
time for me to head into the tower.

GREGORY
Are you sure you won't need my help inside?

SNEAKY HERMIT
I'm afraid this is for me and my Hermit Nippers only.

GREGORY
Right. Have fun with your Hermit Nippers.

SNEAKY HERMIT
Don't wait up, this can go all night.

GREGORY
The only way to turn off those lasers there is to get a
guard onto that little plate there. You will have to use
your Hermit Nippers to move the guard... I see you
packed yourself some sleep darts. Now just use one of
them, then do it again to the other guards on the upper
level... Awesome work, Sneaky Hermit. Now you need
to use your Hermit Nippers again on the guard on the
upper level. Use your sleep darts to put him asleep...

Sleep dart him now while he's on the plate! Excellent.
Now make your way to the top level and hack the
computer. Then get out of there, because this place is
starting to scare me.

SNEAKY HERMIT
Don't be scared, little computer, this won't hurt a bit...
The wedding planning file should be around here
somewhere... Okay, I got the wedding planning data.
I'm on my way back right now.

GREGORY
This is it: General Tony's palace. If we're going to get to
The Panda's daughter, we need to get a full plan of the
wedding.

SNEAKY HERMIT
I'm ready with my costume. When I head inside, he will
give me a little job as wedding planner.

GREGORY
Great. If you get the chance, try to get the rest of us
some jobs as well. Doesn't hurt to have more than one
guy on the job.

GENERAL TONY
No, you can't come out yet, my wife.

KATTY
But please! My father will be so worried. Just let me
tell him I'm alright...

SNEAKY HERMIT
Greetings, General Tony! I have heard about your
wedding, and intend to be your wedding planner.

GENERAL TONY
How insulting. I need no help.

SNEAKY HERMIT
I am so sorry, sir. I meant no disrespect.

GENERAL TONY
Be silent, my man. I'm sure that I can still have you as a wedding planner. I also need a great photographer to take pictures of my wedding.

SNEAKY HERMIT
I have one of the best photographers on hand.

GENERAL TONY
Really? Well, if he is the best photographer around, I want you to bring him to me at once. I will need to see some of his work before I give him the job.

SNEAKY HERMIT
Of course, I'll have him come by right away.

GENERAL TONY
You better not waste my time, wedding planner. I get very angry when people waste my time.

SNEAKY HERMIT
Okay, Gregory, I have marked some points for you to go to: take some pictures of General Tony's stone, and some pictures of the guards. If you're in costume, they may even pose for you. Good luck, Gregory.

GUARD
Stop there! What's the temple password?

SNEAKY HERMIT
Here's the password, Gregory.

GREGORY
Day, sun, day, moon.

GREGORY BOUTHIETTE

GUARD
Sorry, just being careful...

GREGORY
Listen up, meatheads: General Tony wants some
pictures of his staff, so big smiles all around. Or else.

SNEAKY HERMIT
Great shot, but you'll need a few more before talking to
General Tony.

GUARD
Halt! Tell me the sunset password.

SNEAKY HERMIT
Can't stop, here it is.

GREGORY
Night, night, night, night,

GUARD
Yes, sir. My mistake.

GREGORY
Alright, you dumb guards, put on some smiles and get
in a nice pose! General Tony wants some happy photos,
got it?

SNEAKY HERMIT
That's a good picture, Gregory. One more should be
enough to impress the General.

GUARD
Stop there! What's the new year password?

SNEAKING HERMIT
Sending password, Gregory.

GREGORY
Sun, moon, sun, sun,

GUARD
Sorry, just being careful.

GREGORY
Okay, you two, look happy. The General would like a
nice couple's shot.

SNEAKY HERMIT
You need to get a shot of the couple, but that guy is
messing it up. Get rid of him... Really, Gregory, that's
some nice photo work. Show those shots to the
General, and I'm sure he'll be impressed... Hey,
Gregory, get a shot of General Tony while you're in
there. It's always a good idea to study your enemy.

GENERAL TONY
Ah, the photographer. Make sure that you get my good
side. It takes a good man to get my good side... Why is
that I am the only man to get attention? Oh, nice shot.
Here, check out this pose: impressive, I know.

SNEAKY HERMIT
That will do, Gregory. Talk to the General now while
you got him buttered up.

GREGORY
Greetings, General Tony. As you may know, I am the
greatest photographer to get shots of your wedding.

GENERAL TONY
Hmm, let me see a sample of your work. I have a king's
eye, and a good sense of how good your pictures are.

GREGORY
Why, of course, my good sir.

GENERAL TONY
Hmm... I must say, these pictures are really good. Fine, you may have the honor of photographing my wedding.

GREGORY
A thousand thank yous, my lord. It will be a wedding none of us will ever forget.

ANTI GREGORY
Sneaky Hermit, Gregory is back. What's next for this operation?

SNEAKY HERMIT
Well, Anti Gregory, the wedding plans say General Tony will be having his wedding on Saturday. Katty is still not happy about marrying him, but... Wait, what? General Tony! How did he got into the safe house? He stole our computer! This is bad, all of our plans are on that computer... Oh, this is really bad...

GREGORY
Sneaky Hermit, calm down. General Tony may have stolen the computer, but we will get it back. We already know that General Tony will be marrying Katty on Saturday, and that we need to free her from him before that. Let's just get the computer back first before Sneaky Hermit goes crazy about it.

ANTI GREGORY
You got it, Gregory... And how are we going to do that?

GREGORY
Sneaky Hermit will head inside General Tony's palace and hack into the computer that is in the corner.

SNEAKY HERMIT
Okay, you got it, Gregory. I'll do that right now.

ANTI GREGORY
Good luck out there, Sneaky Hermit.

SNEAKY HERMIT
Thanks, Anti Gregory. I will come back safe, buddy.

GREGORY
General Tony's computer is somewhere in here. No need to be sneaky, let's just get the job done.

SNEAKY HERMIT
Okay, Gregory, I have found the computer... This place is a little hard for me, but no problem...

GUARD
You shall not pass here! You must die now.

SNEAKY HERMIT
He's got a defense avatar! This could get bad... Aha! I think I found something: his diary says something about going under the bell, then walk across the heavens... Are you getting this, Gregory?

GREGORY
I'm en route to the bell right now.

SNEAKY HERMIT
Better bring along Gage, this sounds like his sort of mission... It saids to stand under the bell... I need to do some work from here...

GREGORY
Got any ideas of how to do that walk-across-the-heavens thing?

GAGE
Just let me do this, Gregory, my friend. I will help you with my dream-time powers.

GREGORY
That's amazing.

GAGE
I may need to ride on your back while I do this,
Gregory.

GREGORY
Of course. If you need to ride on my back to keep the
dream-time thing going, be my guest. I'm not a big fan
of falling to my death.

GAGE
Okay, that was close. I need to head back to the safe
house now.

GREGORY
No problem. Take a rest if you need it; I'll push on
ahead and look for Tony.

SNEAKY HERMIT
Getting some weird readings up ahead: you'll wanna
use your 3D glasses.

GENERAL TONY
Ah, the world famous Gregory Bouthiette. It must feel
amazing to have followed the trail that I left for you
and your gang, considering you still need them.

GREGORY
I'm not ashamed to rely on my friends.

GENERAL TONY
Who needs friends when you can be on your own? You
will see that you don't need them. Umm, why try to talk
when I can just prove my point by fighting you on my
own? No one can beat me while I'm in the air, and you
will be no different.

GREGORY
Sneaky Hermit, are you hearing this? What's he talking
about?

SNEAKY HERMIT
I've read about these types of battlegrounds before.
You should be able to jump and hit General Tony in the
air; plus, you can fly to different places.

GENERAL TONY
Enough talking, Bouthiette. Time to put you in your
place. Hahahahaha.

GREGORY
Come back and take it like a man.

GENERAL TONY
Well done, my greatest wedding photographer. Now
you are going down once and for all.

GREGORY
Stop this, Tony. Release Katty, and this fight can end.

GENERAL TONY
No, Katty is mine! She's is going to marry me, and she
will be happy with me forever. I will never let you take
her away from me.

GREGORY
But she doesn't wanna marry you.

GENERAL TONY
She's a woman. The Panda was good back in his day,
but then he retired. And then you brought him onto
your side. Now he is going to help you save his
daughter. That is just uncool.

GREGORY
I've fought a lot of bad men in my time, but you, sir, are

the worst.

GENERAL TONY
Oh, it gets worse, Bouthiette. Now prepare for the fight
of your lifetime... You may have won the battle, but the
war has just begun! Take your little, dumb computer, it
won't help you! Katty is mine.

GREGORY
Katty is a person, not a thing that you play with. Sorry,
Tony, we are finishing this right now.

GENERAL TONY
Beware, beware the Tony family...

ANTI GREGORY
Hey, Sneaky Hermit, Gregory is back. And he's got the
computer back as well.

GREGORY
So what's the plan now?

SNEAKY HERMIT
Thanks to your fighting with General Tony, Gregory,
we got the computer back! As for missions: first, Anti
Gregory will go out and open up this lockbox. Then
Pinky will make her way to his position and hack into
the wires so we can hear whatever General Tony says.
Second, Gregory will go out and break into the
fireworks safe for General Tony's wedding. Gregory
will need some help to carry the fireworks, and I think
The Panda will do the job. Once Gregory collects
enough fireworks, The Panda will blow the hopping
vampires' gravestone sky high. Then Gregory and I will
go out and find another battery for the team car, but I
think we might need some help... When we are done
with all of these jobs, we will be ready for the
operation. Good luck.

ANTI GREGORY
Okay, I'm gonna go do my mission first. I'll see you
guys later.

GREGORY
Just be careful out there, Anti Gregory. We don't want
any bad stuffs coming for you.

ANTI GREGORY
Relax, Gregory. I got this under control.

SNEAKY HERMIT
Just let him have his own fun, Gregory. He always
worries about us, so just let him do what he wants to
do.

GREGORY
You're right, Sneaky Hermit. We should let him do
what he wants.

SNEAKY HERMIT
That's what I like to hear, Gregory.

PINKY
Hey, Anti Gregory, check it out! That box is kind of like
a phone line.

ANTI GREGORY
Yeah, a hard phone line.

PINKY
You're the only one on the team that can open it. Just
open the box, and I'll be there with my tools.

ANTI GREGORY
Sure, Pinky. Just stand clear and let little, strong Anti
Gregory do some work... Oh man, that's one bad gas...

PINKY
Crap, this is all my fault. Hang in there, Anti Gregory,
I'm coming.

GENERAL TONY
Hurry up, take him to the top. Bring him to my family
temple and blow him up until he is as good as dead.

PINKY
I'm too late! He's as good as dead.

SNEAKY HERMIT
No, there's still a chance. You can use your RC car to
beat the fuse and cut it before it's too late. It's the only
chance that we've got to save Anti Gregory... Use your
RC car gun to shoot those barrels. You've got to drive
fast to save Anti Gregory!

PINKY
Hold on tight, Anti Gregory. This might be a little
close...

ANTI GREGORY
Yeah, I will live. Thanks for the help, RC car. We will be
friends forever. You can ride in my car.

SNEAKY HERMIT
Anti Gregory, are you okay? Did General Tony find out
that you were there?

ANTI GREGORY
I'm okay, Sneaky Hermit. And yeah, General Tony did
find out that I was there.

SNEAKY HERMIT
Thanks, Pinky. You are a good friend to have saved
him.

PINKY

No problem, Sneaky Hermit. I'm always there if you guys are in trouble. If there is anything else that you need me to do, just ask.

SNEAKY HERMIT

Don't worry, Pinky, we will ask you if we need any more help.

GREGORY

Well, I'm going out there to do my mission now, Sneaky Hermit.

SNEAKY HERMIT

Okay, Gregory. I will be seeing you at the safe when you get there.

GREGORY

Okay, you got it, Sneaky Hermit.

ANTI GREGORY

Are you going to talk to The Panda, Sneaky Hermit?

SNEAKY HERMIT

It's the only way to have The Panda on our side, Anti Gregory. He will help Gregory out.

ANTI GREGORY

I hope you know what you are doing, Sneaky Hermit.

PINKY

Don't worry, Anti Gregory, Sneaky Hermit knows what he's doing. Would you like to look at more diapers with me, Anti Gregory?

ANTI GREGORY

Sure, Pinky, I can look at some more diapers with you.

GREGORY BOUTHIETTE

SNEAKY HERMIT
That's one of General Tony's caches for the wedding.

GREGORY
This lock is heavy. I might need some help carrying the
goods.

SNEAKY HERMIT
The Panda is the only man for the job. He's strong,
good with explosives, and he can blow the hopping
vampires' gravestone sky high.

GREGORY
Awesome. So The Panda will be able to help me out
with the fireworks, and I get to work with the big guy
now! Thanks, Sneaky Hermit... Uh, can you go get him
for me?

SNEAKY HERMIT
No problem, Gregory. I know you will be happy
working with The Panda. I'll go get him right now and
send him your way... This is it, Panda! We need you for
a field mission. Gregory is trying to break into the
fireworks cache, and he needs help.

PANDA
Okay, Sneaky Hermit, I will be there soon. You may go.

SNEAKY HERMIT
Uh, no need to be mean or anything. I'm putting my
neck on the line here. We are all counting on you.

PANDA
I will mind your neck... Hello, old friend. I'm about to
walk on the side of Gregory Bouthiette, and I cannot
carry you with me on the journey.

PANDA'S INNER SELF
You fool, this is your chance for revenge! He made fun

of us. Beat us. Made us weak.

PANDA
That is in the past. Everything has changed now. You
need to be okay with that.

PANDA'S INNER SELF
I will be okay with you beating him when you get there
and saving your daughter yourself! Destroy Bouthiette
now.

PANDA
Gregory is a teacher. We need to join him on his
journey now.

PANDA'S INNER SELF
I have no plans to join with my weaker side. I hope you
will kill him soon, because I don't want you to be with
him.

PANDA
You are strong, and I am almost as strong, but we
would be the cause of General Tony marrying my
daughter.

PANDA'S INNER SELF
Oh yeah? And what do you mean by that?

PANDA
If that were to happen, if I were to kill Gregory, Tony
will be my son-in-law.

PANDA'S INNER SELF
Very well. Bouthiette shall live.

PANDA
Fear not, Gregory! I shall not kill you this day.

GREGORY
It's a deal, Panda. I look forward to working with you
on this mission.

SNEAKY HERMIT
I know that you have been out of the game for a while,
so maybe it's time to show you what you can do with
your old moves... Such power! It looks like you have
woken up some hopping vampires. Kill them all at once
with a full tank of fireworks! Great, now you're ready
for anything. Gregory must be done by now; he might
need some help carrying the goods.

GREGORY
Okay, I'm done with this one: you handle the stuff, I'll
head out for the next cache.

PANDA
Excellent work, Gregory. I will make good use of these
fireworks.

SNEAKY HERMIT
The undead foe is on to you... They're closing in!

GREGORY
One more cache to go. We're doing great.

SNEAKY HERMIT
More hopping vampires! This is not good, they're
everywhere!

GREGORY
Okay, that's all the caches. Now it's time to blow up the
hopping vampires' gravestone. Once you're there, take
aim with your fireworks, and kaboom! No more
hopping vampires.

PANDA
No problem. I will blow that gravestone into a load of

fangs.

GREGORY
There are going to be fangs everywhere... Right. I'll just head back to the safe house.

PANDA
Yes, do that.

SNEAKY HERMIT
Once that gravestone's blown up, there will be no more hopping vampires.

PANDA
The deed is done.

ANTI GREGORY
Uh, Sneaky Hermit, The Panda is coming to the safe house now.

PANDA
Hello, fellows. I'm done with the hopping vampires' gravestone.

SNEAKY HERMIT
That was some good work you did out there, Panda. Now I'm going out there.

ANTI GREGORY
Good luck, Sneaky Hermit.

SNEAKY HERMIT
Thanks, Anti Gregory. I will be back soon.

GREGORY
Hey, Sneaky Hermit, are you and Anti Gregory finished up with the car yet?

SNEAKY HERMIT
I'm afraid that we need to get a new power source: the old one kind of got lost when it was in that ice cube.

GREGORY
Okay. Is there one that I can steal for you?

SNEAKY HERMIT
Pinky did spot one while she was using her RC chopper. I think I should be the one to get it.

GREGORY
So... What can I help with out here? If anything at all.

SNEAKY HERMIT
Stay close. I will need you for charging the battery...
Hello, my pretty!

GREGORY
Is the battery complete?

SNEAKY HERMIT
Yes, it's all in one piece. It just needs to be recharged.

GREGORY
Sounds like really bad news in these parts.

SNEAKY HERMIT
Well, I do have an idea...

GREGORY
Whatever it is, my cop friend is in as well.

CARMELITA
Hey, Gregory, Sneaky Hermit. I want to help you guys out, just play along. Now don't move, or I'll zap you.

GREGORY
Sorry, Carmelita, gotta go.

CARMELITA
Attention, cops: I've got Gregory. I repeat, I've got Gregory. I am ready to bring him back with me, put him in jail, and lock him up for good.

SNEAKY HERMIT
Nice acting, Gregory. The battery is charged up.

CARMELITA
No, it was an easy capture. I don't want a gold medal, he was really... Gregory, come back here!

SNEAKY HERMIT
Bring the battery back to the team car, and we will be ready to make a getaway out of here... Nice work. The car is ready to go.

ANTI GREGORY
You rock, Gregory.

GREGORY
Nice acting, Carmelita. You did well.

CARMELITA
Thanks, Gregory. I'll be waiting for the operation when you guys are ready to start it.

GREGORY
Okay, Carmelita. See you later.

SNEAKY HERMIT
Okay, guys, we are all ready to free Katty from General Tony. I call this Operation Wedding Crashers: first, Gregory will make his way to General Tony's treasure temple and let Anti Gregory and Pinky in through the front door. Then Pinky will use her RC car to destroy the computer in the temple, and she and Anti Gregory will grab the treasure. The Panda and Gage will work together to make their way to Katty. Gregory will

already be inside the palace making sure that those vases don't tip over and break. Then I will lure Carmelita to the palace, and she will take her place as Katty. When Gregory leaves the treasure temple, General Tony will make his way there. Once Anti Gregory and Pinky have the treasure, and we have Katty, we will be getting out of here.

GREGORY
Alright, I'm going out there right now and starting the operation.

ANTI GREGORY
I'll be waiting at the front door, Gregory.

GREGORY
I know you will, Anti Gregory. I'll see you there soon… I'm in the green light position; let's get a move on.

SNEAKY HERMIT
Ready…

PINKY
In position…

ANTI GREGORY
I'm pumped!

GAGE
I'm on the job.

PANDA
I, too, stand ready. Even if we fail, it will be an honorable effort. Katty will not forget.

GREGORY
Alright, everyone: let's go.

SNEAKY HERMIT
Pinky and Anti Gregory are ready to be let in: they should be in position by the front door.

PINKY
Opening a door for a lady? They say you are quite the gentleman.

GREGORY
I try to be kind to Bartley's girlfriend. Are you guys going to be okay in here? The security is tight.

PINKY
Yeah, we're fine. You gotta get moving if you're meeting up with The Panda and Gage.

GREGORY
Always staying on track, that's me.

ANTI GREGORY
What's the plan?

PINKY
According to the blueprints, there's a security system at the end of this hallway. I should be able to destroy it with my RC car, provided I don't trip up any blue security beams along the way.

ANTI GREGORY
Blue security beams? Oh man, this is crazy!

PINKY
That should do it! The laser door should be going away...

ANTI GREGORY
They must have another computer or something.

PINKY
But there was only supposed to be one! If that second computer boots up, there's no way we're getting in.

ANTI GREGORY
Pinky, I have been doing this for a long time: if there's one thing I learned, it's if the plan gets bad, always fall back to a different plan.

PINKY
Yeah, what's that?

ANTI GREGORY
Break stuffs.

PINKY
You... You're right! If I can destroy all the security nodes, then that laser door should be able to open.

ANTI GREGORY
Less talk, and more breakery.

PINKY
I don't have much time... Yes!

ANTI GREGORY
Wow, you are really good at breaking stuffs. I can respect that.

PINKY
Thanks, Anti Gregory. Let's get that treasure... Looks like a double-locked door.

ANTI GREGORY
Call it out, I'm ready.

PINKY
On my three... One, two, three!

ANTI GREGORY
Dragons, I got them!

PINKY
Okay, let's try it again... One, two three... Yes! We're in!

ANTI GREGORY
What do you see? Is it awesome?

PINKY
There's plenty of loot, but it is heavily guarded. Totally
unstable.

SNEAKY HERMIT
The Panda and Gage have already taken their positions
under the palace. Once inside, they'll start blasting.

GREGORY
Might as well do it with style... Okay, guys, I'm topside.

PANDA
The vases around you are some kind of Chinese
security, and they are really bad news.

GREGORY
I get it: if any of the vases fall, it will set off an alarm.

PANDA
Correct. Don't allow them to fall. I am putting my trust
in you, Gregory Bouthiette.

GREGORY
We'll get Katty. I promise.

GAGE
Let's get this show on the road, Gregory.

GREGORY
Gage's right; let's get this show on the road.

PANDA
Yes. We are right beneath the chamber, just a few inches from Katty.

GREGORY
Hear that, Sneaky Hermit? You're up... Lure Carmelita to the palace. I left her a calling card, and I'm sure she will see it coming inside. Oh, and take your place once you are done: you're on point for the treasure drop.

CARMELITA
Hey, Sneaky Hermit is luring me to the palace! Gregory must already be inside... I should follow Sneaky Hermit's next move now... Hey, I was right! Gregory left a calling card for me...

KATTY
Oh, father, you have saved me from General Tony. I missed you so much.

PANDA
Yes, my daughter. You are safe.

SNEAKY HERMIT
Heads up, Gregory: you've got company.

GREGORY
Okay... Uh, Sneaky Hermit? You know that wedding thing that I told you before, when I dress myself as General Tony and steal the bride? Make sure that the whole gang's there. Okay, I'm heading for the getaway right now. Over and out.

CARMELITA
Gregory and his good plans... I think he wants to have a fake wedding for General Tony, and I will play as the bride. I will give him and his friends a wedding that they will never forget. I hope Sneaky Hermit won't mind if I do that...

GENERAL TONY
What strange rumbles have me coming out here to see
you? Do not worry, my bride. I will make sure that you
do not escape. Uh, well, maybe I should go to my
treasure temple and make sure there is nothing going
on there...

GREGORY
Carmelita took the bait. Where are you guys at with
Katty?

PANDA
We're in the car, waiting for the treasure. And the
escape.

GREGORY
Hey, Anti Gregory, Tony's on his way to your position.
How are you coming along with the treasure?

ANTI GREGORY
We're doing awesome! Stand aside, Pinky...
Cannonball!

PINKY
No, wait!

ANTI GREGORY
Uh oh...

SNEAKY HERMIT
Okay, guys, parachute the treasure down to me. I'm
ready... Anti Gregory?

GENERAL TONY
My family temple... Destroyed! Never have I felt such
an outrage! You shall pay.

ANTI GREGORY
Eat it, Tony. I broke your temple, and I'll break your

face for messing with the Bouthiette Gang.

GENERAL TONY
You can not hurt me.

ANTI GREGORY
Oh yeah... Heads up, Sneaky Hermit! Treasure chest
coming down.

GENERAL TONY
The outrage! Stone dragon of the temple, I call for you:
aid the Tony family in its hour of rage.

ANTI GREGORY
Sweet strawberry shortcake.

PINKY
No, let go of me!

GENERAL TONY
Haha, the Tony line is master in this place. Hear me,
Gregory Bouthiette, my lineage surpasses yours in
every way.

GREGORY
It's not about the family name, Tony. It's what you do
with it.

ANTI GREGORY
Gregory, I'm okay. I broke my fall on one of these
wedding fireworks.

PINKY
Gregory, help! Slap this guy around so he'll let go... Ow,
he's really squeezing me...

GREGORY
Feel like making an exit?

PINKY
My hero.

GENERAL TONY
I still win, Bouthiette! You may have destroyed my
temple and hurt my dragon, but I still got the bride!
Katty is mine!

ANTI GREGORY
Jump in, quick! We're out of here.

GREGORY
Good work, Panda and Gage. Now let's get out of here
before we are done for.

SNEAKY HERMIT
Yeah, but first, let's see General Tony getting married
to Carmelita.

ANTI GREGORY
You got it, Sneaky Hermit. I'm already on it.

PANDA
I hope that Carmelita will shoot him with her gun. I
would like that so much.

GREGORY
Hey, cool. Finally, we both agree on something, Panda.
Let's get there first.

CARMELITA
You are going to jail now, General Tony. I was playing
as Katty to fool you, butthead.

GAGE
It sounds like Carmelita just shot him, guys. And she is
going to put him in jail now.

GREGORY
Good. Maybe he can stay in jail forever and think about
what he has done to The Panda's daughter.

PANDA
Hey, Anti Gregory, can you drive to Katty's grandma's
house? I need to drop her off there because I can't let
her come with us.

ANTI GREGORY
You got it, Panda. I don't know where to go, but I think
I'll find it. Just leave it to me!

SNEAKY HERMIT
I think everyone should hold on tight, because Anti
Gregory will be driving fast to get us there.

PINKY
Gregory, thanks for saving me back there. I really liked
it.

GREGORY
No problem, Pinky. You know I'd never let anything
happen to Bartley's girlfriend, because Bartley is my
friend.

ANTI GREGORY
Okay, Panda. We're here.

PANDA
Okay, thanks, Anti Gregory. I'll be right back, you guys.
I need to bring Katty inside to her grandma's house.

SNEAKY HERMIT
Don't worry, Panda. We will be waiting for you in the
car.

GAGE
I think we might be going to see Demetrie now. Are we,

Sneaky Hermit?

SNEAKY HERMIT
Quiet, Gage, I'm trying to chat with Demetrie right now.

GREGORY
Hey, Gage, do you think my master will be happy to see me again? And does he still want to wear diapers?

GAGE
I think he does, Gregory. He will be happy to see you again. I promise.

PANDA
Okay, guys, I'm back now. Let's get out of here.

SNEAKY HERMIT
Anti Gregory, head to a safe place to hide.

ANTI GREGORY
You got it, Sneaky Hermit.

GREGORY
Are you talking to Demetrie, Sneaky Hermit?

SNEAKY HERMIT
Yes, I am, Gregory. He wants us to help him out for another mission, and it's in a bad place with pirates.

ANTI GREGORY
Uh, Sneaky Hermit, did you just say pirates? As in, real pirates?

SNEAKY HERMIT
Yes, Anti Gregory, I did say pirates. And they have their own island that is filled with pirates.

PANDA
And are pirates bad news, Sneaky Hermit?

SNEAKY HERMIT
They are bad news, Panda. The pirates are on this
island called Bad Blood Bay.

GAGE
And are you sure that's where the pirates are at, Sneaky
Hermit? I am hoping to kick some pirate butts.

GREGORY
Yes, Gage, the pirates do have their own island. That
must mean Demetrie wants us to help him out getting
something back from the pirates. What's he saying,
Sneaky Hermit?

SNEAKY HERMIT
He's not saying anything yet, Gregory, but we need to
go there right now. Anti Gregory, take us to that little
boat that Demetrie got us.

ANTI GREGORY
You got it, Sneaky Hermit. I'm already heading there
right now.

***

GREGORY
There's Demetrie, and that's the ship that he's on.
Head there, Anti Gregory.

ANTI GREGORY
You got it, Gregory.

DEMETRIE
Hello, you Bouthiette Gang. I'm stoked you came.

SNEAKY HERMIT
Well, thanks for inviting us, Demetrie. So what do you
need us for during this big huge operation?

DEMETRIE
I'm glad you asked, bro. Have I ever told you dollies
about my grandfather before?

GREGORY
No, you haven't, Demetrie. What about your
grandfather?

DEMETRIE
Well, my grandfather used to be a diver, and he'd
always go underwater and search for some mean, true
treasures.

ANTI GREGORY
Wow, it sounds like your grandfather used to be a great
diver, Demetrie. Did he bring some stuffs back for you?

DEMETRIE
No, Anti Gregory, because my grandfather's diving gear
got duped from him by this pirate crap cat named
Randy T. Parker. So my grandfather retired from
diving and had a devilishly good-looking family.

PANDA
So, what are we here for, Demetrie?

DEMETRIE
I want his gear back, dig?

GREGORY
Sneaky Hermit, should we help Demetrie get his
grandfather's diving gear back?

SNEAKY HERMIT
I don't see why not. And if we help him, he might help
us out with the Bouthiette vault job.

GREGORY
Okay, we can do it, Sneaky Hermit, because I want
Demetrie on our side.

SNEAKY HERMIT
I was hoping you'd say that, Gregory. Okay, Demetrie,
we'll help you get your grandfather's diving gear.

DEMETRIE
Yes, thank you, Bouthiette Gang! I knew that you guys
would help me out on this stunt. I will join you guys on
the Bouthiette vault job when we're done.

ANTI GREGORY
Uh, Demetrie, does Bad Blood Bay have pirate ships in
the ocean?

DEMETRIE
What sort of place would Bad Blood Bay be without
pirates? Of course there are pirates. Why do you ask?

ANTI GREGORY
Umm, no reason. There's just a lot of pirate boats
everywhere.

GREGORY
Don't worry, Anti Gregory. We will get past them in no
time.

GAGE
Hey, guys, look: I see the safe house over there.

SNEAKY HERMIT
Hey, look at that. You're right, Gage: that is our safe
house over there.

PINKY
Hey, Sneaky Hermit, are you guys coming or not?

SNEAKING HERMIT
Yeah, we are. Just wait for us, Pinky... Okay, guys,
we're here at our safe house now. And I think you
ought to get out there right now, Gregory.

GREGORY
You got it, Sneaky Hermit. I will go out there and look
for Randy T. Parker.

ANTI GREGORY
Good luck out there, Gregory.

GREGORY
Thanks, Anti Gregory. I will be coming back safe,
buddy.

SNEAKY HERMIT
Randy T. Parker has retired, and he's living here in
town. I've marked his place for you... There he is!
That's Randy T. Parker!

GREGORY
I didn't even think pirates could get that old. I thought
that was just a rumor.

SNEAKY HERMIT
Well, it's not a rumor. He really is that old, and we
need him to tell us where the treasure is. How is your
pirate talk coming along?

GREGORY
Arrr, I forgot me lucky number 2 pencil at the starting
line.

SNEAKY HERMIT
Joke all you want, but it's not going to help when you
talk to that guy. He won't go easy on you.

GREGORY
Randy T. Parker, I came to talk of treasure. I heard it's
something that you're into.

RANDY T. PARKER
Treasure, aye, but I won't chat with you, you little
butthead. Get out of my sight. I won't chat with you.
The only person I will talk of treasure with is with my
old partner, Tim C. West.

GREGORY
Maybe we can work out a bargain...

RANDY T. PARKER
Shut your mouth-hole, lubber. I won't be dealing with
your lot, I assure ye.

GREGORY
Salt of the earth, that Randy T. Parker.

SNEAKY HERMIT
It's really hard to get anywhere with the old guy, but for
this plan to work, we need to fool him into thinking
that you're Tim C. West.

GREGORY
What happened to Tim, anyway?

SNEAKY HERMIT
His lieutenants mutinied on the old guy and went on
their separate ways. They took every part of his

costume as well.

GREGORY
This is the only pirate town left; they have to be around here somewhere.

SNEAKY HERMIT
You're right. That's Stone Jake, the toughest man you'll ever meet: he took the eyepatch.

GREGORY
Hmm, maybe I can drop an anchor on his head.

SNEAKY HERMIT
Good plan. That will do the job, matey... Stone Jake has a thing for monkeys: if you whack the palm trees, he's sure to come running. Perfect to lure him under an anchor.

STONE JAKE
What, be that monkeys? Where are ya? Hahaha, I got ya now! Tricky monkeys...

SNEAKY HERMIT
Nice work. I've already marked another point for the next lieutenant. He's underneath the boat... There he is! You need to steal his peg leg.

GREGORY
Peg leg? Seriously? Isn't that kind of harsh?

SNEAKY HERMIT
You'll need it for the costume. It is very unique. Look, what you need to worry about is getting past his bodyguards.

GREGORY
I'll have to pick them off one by one. Shouldn't be a problem.

GREGORY BOUTHIETTE

SNEAKY HERMIT
Okay, sneak up behind him and pickpocket his peg leg... Excellent work. You've just got one lieutenant left: Ned. I'm afraid that word has gotten out that someone has been taking down lieutenants, and he's hiding up in a crow's nest.

NED
Oh man, they're everywhere! Stay awake, keep your eyes open, Ned. You can't let them get to you, they will never get to you, and... Ah! Oh no, it's true! The agents of Tim have come for revenge!

SNEAKY HERMIT
Chase him down, he's got Tim's hat!

NED
Take that, scallywag! Avast! You won't take me... Avast there, you have got me back to the sea! I yield.

GREGORY
I just wanted your hat.

NED
Me hat? That's what this be about? Take the dumb thing, and away with ye!

SNEAKY HERMIT
Excellent, you've got the full Tim C. West costume. Head on back to Randy T. Parker and pretend to be his old friend. And remember your pirate talk this time.

RANDY T. PARKER
What, Tim C. West? You're back? You two-faced scallywag!

GREGORY
Aye, matey, but not to be rude... Let's talk of treasure, arrr.

RANDY T. PARKER
How about a round of a name-calling first, you baboon-brained, little-faced toilet?

SNEAKY HERMIT
I read about this, Gregory: it's kind of a talk that pirates do with each other, almost like a game. Just make sure that you never repeat anything that has already been said...

RANDY T. PARKER
You take first round, my old shipmate.

GREGORY
You're a sheep-brained, knuckle-dragging anchorhead.

RANDY T. PARKER
That be true enough, but you're a dumb, cross-eyed piece of filth.

GREGORY
Oh yeah? You're a marooned, grog-abusing sack o' maggots.

RANDY T. PARKER
Ha! You swear like a child! You're a bleating, clam-tongued whale fart.

GREGORY
You are a brainless, seaweed slurping bag of vomit.

RANDY T. PARKER
Harharhar, but methinks you're a donkey-eared, yellow-bellied cow pie.

GREGORY
Oh really? You're an idiotic, toothless waste of skin.

RANDY T. PARKER
Arrr, true, but you're a pig-breathed, duck-billed cabin
boy.

GREGORY
You're a pin-headed, twisted swabber.

RANDY T. PARKER
Haha, Tim C. West, it must be you! Forgive this old sea
dog and his sunburnt eyes for not recognizing you
straight away. I've never met a man on land or sea that
could curse half as well. Tell me, shipmate, why has it
been all these years since I have seen you?

GREGORY
I came back for me share of the treasure that we stole
back from that Reme Lousteau fella.

RANDY T. PARKER
'Twas a good adventure that we had, and I speak of it
drunk often, you and I burying the loot in the belly of
Dagger Island... Aye, and many a year I kept the map of
the treasure hidden in a safe place.

GREGORY
Aye, then let's have it. High time for us to give up on
our retirement.

RANDY T. PARKER
But, me old shipmate, I'm afraid I got some bad news
for you: I lost the treasure map to this mean pirate
named Frank in a game of cards.

GREGORY
What? What... I'm sure that this mean pirate will give it
back to you if you play another game with him,
shipmate.

RANDY T. PARKER

This Frank is a no-good pirate. He will never give it back to me, and he will do anything to stop anyone who goes near him or tries to take the map back from him. If you go and get the map, go alone. My pirate days are far behind me now.

GREGORY

Thank you, Randy. You have been a good friend.

RANDY T. PARKER

Aye, and you are still a good friend to me, Tim C. West.

GREGORY

Okay, Sneaky Hermit, I'm back. So what are our missions in this place?

SNEAKY HERMIT

Thanks to your talk with Randy T. Parker, we now know where the treasure is: it's somewhere on Dagger Island. But we need to get the treasure map back first, and get Demetrie's diving gear back as well. First, Anti Gregory and Gregory will go out and shoot the other boats so that they don't follow us when we head to Dagger Island. Harbor patrol will also show up, so be prepared for a fight. Then Pinky and I will work together to try and find the treasure map to Dagger Island. Finally, we will steal a pirate ship and set sail for Dagger Island.

ANTI GREGORY

Yes! Me and Gregory can finally work together again! I'm gonna go out there now, Gregory. Just wait until I get there.

GREGORY

Okay, Anti Gregory, just go out there now. I'll be ready to head out there soon.

SNEAKY HERMIT
You know he really wants to work with you, Gregory, so just let him do what he wants out there.

GREGORY
I know, Sneaky Hermit. I will let him do what he wants while shooting those pirate ships out there.

SNEAKY HERMIT
Okay, Anti Gregory: I need you and Gregory to go out there to blast the runners off any pirate ships that might come after us when we set sail for Dagger Island.

ANTI GREGORY
What about those boats out there at anchor? They look ready for breaking.

SNEAKY HERMIT
Don't worry about it. The pirates won't have time to row out there and fix their runners. Once you guys are done shooting the runners off those boats, the harbor patrol will start coming to fight you guys.

ANTI GREGORY
That sounds like a job for me and my little sidekick.

SNEAKY HERMIT
You said it. Take out the harbor patrol and then, when there's no one left, we steal a pirate ship... It looks like Gregory is done unlocking the boat. Good luck, sailor... Okay, guys: Anti Gregory rows, and Gregory mans the cannon. Just aim at the runners and pull if you wanna fire.

SNEAKY HERMIT
Nice going, guys. You're doing well as a team... That boat is not setting sail anytime soon... The harbor patrol has arrived!

GREGORY
They look pretty well armored, is this cannon gotta cut it?

SNEAKY HERMIT
You're right, Gregory. Anti Gregory needs to ram into them to sink them.

ANTI GREGORY
Oh yeah! I'm tired of dodging cannonballs. Time to do my favorite thing: ramming into them jolly boat-style.

SNEAKY HERMIT
Once Anti Gregory has rammed into them, you guys need to sink them with a well-placed cannonball.

ANTI GREGORY
Run in fear, you little harbor patrol punks! I'm gonna ram you into next week, arrr!

GREGORY
This guy's clear.

ANTI GREGORY
Later, sucker!

GREGORY
Armor's gone.

ANTI GREGORY
Gregory, you're on fire!

GREGORY
He's clean, ready to shoot.

ANTI GREGORY
Avast that, sucker! Alright, the Team of Excellence, Anti Gregory and his awesome gunner Gregory, kicked butt yet again.

SNEAKY HERMIT
Uh, sorry, guys. I wasn't aware the harbor patrol had a
cutter; you're not done yet. Gosh, that thing is big.

GREGORY
Everything has a weak point. Just look at the mast:
they've been patching it up for a while now.

ANTI GREGORY
Gregory's right! That mast will fall right before your
very eyes. No matter how times they bring it to bear,
we will bear it.

GREGORY
Not to sound like a butthead or anything, but I vote to
dodge their cannonballs.

ANTI GREGORY
Or we can dodge. That works, too... Team Excellence
does it again! Nice shooting, sidekick.

GREGORY
Hey, we would have been sunk without your rowing.

SNEAKY HERMIT
When you guys are done making out, I'll see you back
at the safe house. Sheesh.

ANTI GREGORY
Okay, Sneaky Hermit, I'm back. You can do your
mission now.

SNEAKY HERMIT
Okay, thanks, Anti Gregory. Pinky, I'll call you when I
get there.

PINKY
Okay, Sneaky Hermit. I'll be out there soon.

ANTI GREGORY
Good luck out there, Sneaky Hermit.

SNEAKY HERMIT
Thanks, Anti Gregory. I'll be back, buddy.

GREGORY
Come on, Anti Gregory. Let's go look at some diapers.

ANTI GREGORY
Okay, Gregory. I'll be there soon.

SNEAKY HERMIT
Okay, Pinky, I'm near your disc. I'll push the button
and let it do its thing. I'll launch the disc, let it bring its
data in, and it will let us know where the treasure map
is hiding.

PINKY
Roger, Sneaky Hermit. Let's light this candle.

SNEAKY HERMIT
No, be still, my heart! Pinky is Bartley's girlfriend, and
I don't want Bartley to get mad at me if I steal his
girlfriend from him. I am a really good friend to
Bartley...

PINKY
What was that? I didn't read you.

SNEAKY HERMIT
Oh, nothing. I was just saying that we can fly it now.
Let's do it.

PINKY
The data is coming in... The treasure map has got to be
here somewhere...

GUARD
Huh? What kinda witchcraft is that? Oh well, I'll just shoot it, then let the boss know about it.

PINKY
No, we haven't downloaded it yet!

SNEAKY HERMIT
Don't worry, Pinky! The pieces are still intact. The disc is destroyed, but we can still get the data on it.

PINKY
But it's broken, and I set it up to self-destruct if anyone picks it up.

SNEAKY HERMIT
Hmm... The disc will destroy itself before anyone can pick it up... Aha! What if we try to read its data before touching it?

PINKY
Right! I can use my RC car to go out and collect the data. It's got the same technology as the disc, so it should be able to download its data.

SNEAKY HERMIT
That's it! Use the car to go out and collect all the data, and we'll know where to strike inside the Skull Keep... The pirates are kind of scared after seeing the disc. It seems that they are scared of technology; your RC car will surely get their attention... Nice driving, Pinky. I've already gotten the data from that part of the disc.

PINKY
That does it: we should have all the disc's data.

SNEAKY HERMIT
Hold on, hold on... I got it! There's a little walkway up to the Skull Keep for us. Let's go.

PINKY

This Frank guy is really on it: he must have seen the
disc and brought the bridges up to the Skull Keep.
There's no way in.

SNEAKY HERMIT

I've dealt with guys like this before. They can't seem to
trust their own men, so they always have some sort of
escape plan. You just have to look around a little.

PINKY

Wow, Gregory must have taught you a lot.

SNEAKY HERMIT

Gregory? We're a team, in case you haven't figured that
out yet. We always work together. I have always been
the brains guy, and he's just a field kid.

PINKY

Just a field kid? It sounds like you're not happy about
it.

SNEAKY HERMIT

Well, yeah, but it's okay. I don't mind being the brains
of these operations. It's fun being the brains, but I wish
I could do what Gregory can do. I wish I could walk on
tight ropes and climb on flag poles... But I can't.

PINKY

You can do other stuffs! Gregory can't rewire things or
type codes like you do.

SNEAKY HERMIT

Gregory can't really type any codes at all.

PINKY

Yeah, he's not the type of kid you are, Sneaky Hermit.
Now come, let's get a move on. We're not going to find
another way in by just standing around here... Oh,

um… Sorry about that standing thing…

SNEAKY HERMIT
Give me a break, Pinky. It's just a saying.

PINKY
The door here is locked, but you should be able to use
your Hermit Nippers on that upper walkway.

SNEAKY HERMIT
Shhh! That must be Frank. Let's head up so that no one
can spy us.

PINKY
Agreed.

FRANK
I tell you something, by thunder, that disc in the sky
was just only the beginning!

GUARD
But, sir, it's gone. All the bridges lifted clear up this
morning.

FRANK
Sure, sure, everyone is always right on their stuffs, but
I don't want to hear more of them! Second Mate Jones!

SECOND MATE JONES
Yes, sir?

FRANK
You are now the new captain of the guards.

SECOND MATE JONES
Ah, thank you, sir.

FRANK
Guard this place with your life. There's a storm coming... I'll be inside torturing the prisoners. Call out if you need any help.

SECOND MATE JONES
No, sir... Uh, I mean, aye aye, sir.

PINKY
We can't get inside with these pirates guarding the door... Time for a little pirate beat down! Not bad fighting, Sneaky Hermit, not bad at all... Hmm, looks like a double button door. On three... One, two, three!

SNEAKY HERMIT
This is it! That's the chest the map is in. I think this might be easy to crack open.

PINKY
I don't know, it looks a little hard to me... If I had my tools, I'm sure I'd be able to open it.

SNEAKY HERMIT
Really? Let's head back to the safe house and get your tools.

PINKY
I think I would like to stay here and study it some more.

SNEAKY HERMIT
Sure, I'll be back in a second... I got your tools with me, and I'm on my way back!

PINKY
Great, but I think I've already got it... This is it! The Dagger Island treasure map! Ah! My eyes! I can't see... It's some kind of blinding dust... Whoa! I'm okay, but I think I landed near the front door. I can't get back to

the safe house with the bridge still up.

SNEAKY HERMIT
I'll save you! I'll think of something... Perfect! I'll use
my Hermit Nippers from the safe house...

PINKY
Hurry, Sneaky Hermit, I'm getting kind of scared
here...

SNEAKY HERMIT
Hang tight! I'm going to fire my Hermit Nippers in the
air for you to follow back to the safe house.

PINKY
This dust is so strong... I can't see a thing.

SNEAKY HERMIT
Don't worry, Pinky! I've already set up all of my Hermit
Nippers for you to follow safely back to the safe house.
I'm going to fire at the wire that is holding up the
bridge.

PINKY
I heard the bridges fall, but I don't think I can get back
to the safe house while blinded like this...

SNEAKY HERMIT
I will be firing some more Hermit Nippers for you to
follow back to the safe house; you should be able to
hear them.

PINKY
Okay. Just don't shoot them too far away, or I won't
hear them.

SNEAKY HERMIT
Pinky!

PINKY
Sneaky Hermit, thank you! I was kind of scared there
for a bit.

SNEAKY HERMIT
There now... Let's get you inside and see if we can get
that dust out of your eyes.

GREGORY
Oh man. Pinky, are you okay?

PINKY
I'm okay, Gregory. Thanks for asking. I'll be fine.

ANTI GREGORY
Man, we were getting worried about you, Pinky! We
don't want anything happening to you. Bartley called to
see how you were doing.

PINKY
Did you tell him that I'm okay, Anti Gregory?

ANTI GREGORY
Yes, we did, Pinky. We told him that you're doing
alright with us, and Gregory told him that he saved you
from a dragon, and he was happy to hear that.

SNEAKY HERMIT
Okay, thanks, Anti Gregory. You can go back to looking
at diapers now. Alright, Gregory, you've been out of
this for a while now; you can do your mission.

GREGORY
Okay, thanks, Sneaky Hermit. I'll be going right now.

ANTI GREGORY
Good luck out there, Gregory.

GREGORY
Thanks, Anti Gregory. I'll be fine, buddy.

PINKY
I'm gonna get this dust out of my eyes now.

ANTI GREGORY
Do you need any help, Pinky?

PINKY
No thanks, Anti Gregory, I got it. Just keep on looking
at diapers.

ANTI GREGORY
Okay, I was just asking...

SNEAKY HERMIT
Okay, Gregory, time for the main event.

GREGORY
I have been looking forward to this. Every hero dreams
of one day stealing a pirate ship. I don't know what it
is, but it feels good to do it.

SNEAKY HERMIT
As you will be the first one onboard, you might want to
keep your attacks quiet; if the nightwatch catches you,
this whole place is going to fill with guards. The rest of
the team won't stand a chance.

GREGORY
Come on, Sneaky Hermit, this is me you're talking to.

SNEAKY HERMIT
Anti Gregory will meet you at the jolly boat, but
remember, keep it quiet.

GREGORY
Okay... Looks like they mined the harbor after our last

boat trip. Must have really scared these guys.

SNEAKY HERMIT
Take these guys out... And keep it quiet.

GREGORY
Okay, guys, the coast is clear. Come on up.

ANTI GREGORY
Roger, I'll start rowing people over... Okay, the rest of
the gang is below deck. Let's fire this puppy up.

SNEAKY HERMIT
Once we start getting the sails going, it won't be long
before someone sets off an alarm.

ANTI GREGORY
No problem, we wasted that harbor patrol. The coast is
clear.

SNEAKY HERMIT
You guys really did good in the water, but they still
have cannons up in the Skull Keep.

GREGORY
Then let's get everything ready to set sail. Every second
we dilly dally just puts us in more risk.

SNEAKY HERMIT
Agreed.

GREGORY
Anti Gregory, take up the anchor. Sneaky Hermit, get
down below deck and get everything to set sail. I'll start
with the sails and get this boat ready.

SNEAKY HERMIT
Okay, Gregory, you're the captain. Sailing is easy...
We're almost out of range... Excellent! We made it into

open water... Use your cannons to take this guy down, and he'll be sure to surrender... Their masts are down; you can attack this guy if you want to, or just sink him down to Davy Jones' Locker... We're close to Dagger Island, drop anchor near the beach... You've got the map, Gregory. Use it... Dang it, more pirates. Stay clear if you can, there's no telling how many are here... Gregory, if you can, just try to stay away from those big lizards, because they will chop you in half in one bite.

DEMETRIE
Grandpapa's treasure! I have come to help you dig, dig?

ANTI GREGORY
We're all coming, Gregory. This is awesome.

GREGORY
Well, Demetrie, it's your loot. I think you should have it.

DEMETRIE
Grandpapa's water gun! I can totally use this to shoot stuffs under water. Now I can dance and dive at the same time now.

PINKY
Wow, your grandfather was a great diver. I never knew there was a water gun...

GREGORY
What else is in this thing?

FRANK
Yes, what else is there to see? Avast there! You think you all can outsmart the smartest man on the seven seas? I might be too late to see the opening of the treasure, but I'm just in time to take the gold now!

GREGORY
Let Pinky go. We can work out a deal.

FRANK
Pinky will be the lass' name, now I think I might take
the gold with me. You all head back to the ship now,
har har!

ANTI GREGORY
Let's thump this chump.

SNEAKY HERMIT
No, he'll hurt her. This guy's a killer.

FRANK
Aye, you got me by that name: killer. I won't say it
again: I want you all to go back to your ship, or her
death is yours. Pick your choice.

GREGORY
Guys, we don't have any options here. Everyone, back
to the ship.

PINKY
You can't just abandon me! Help, please! I'm so
scared...

SNEAKY HERMIT
Pinky, do as he says. Stay alive. We will save you.

PINKY
I... I trust you.

FRANK
And I trust you all to go back to your ship. Away with
ye now!

GREGORY
Oh man, I feel like I'm in trouble right now, Sneaky

Hermit.

SNEAKY HERMIT
Don't worry, Gregory. We will save Pinky.

GREGORY
I know, Sneaky Hermit, but I think Bartley will be mad at me now since we just left Pinky with that Frank guy.

SNEAKY HERMIT
Don't worry about her. We will save her, Gregory. We just need to do some stuffs out here first before we can get back to Bad Blood Bay.

ANTI GREGORY
Okay, Sneaky Hermit. What's our plan this time?

SNEAKY HERMIT
Well, clearly the only goal right now is to save our teammate, and friend, Pinky. The death's head of Frank's ship was seen going back to Bad Blood Bay. We all know we are not tough enough to fight with that ship, but I've got some plans to help us become stronger. First we'll need Demetrie's help catching some of these cannon blast collars. We'll need them to take down Frank's pirate ship. Then we need to take out some of the pirate ships that work for Frank so there won't be anyone to chase us. Finally, we will need to head to the misty, foggy side of the ocean to deal with the sea monster named Crusher. Now that we all have our missions for the ocean, it's time to head out and take a stand. Good luck.

GREGORY
Okay, good. Anti Gregory, come with me. I need you to steer this ship again.

ANTI GREGORY
You got it, Gregory. I'm the greatest driver ever.

SNEAKY HERMIT
We're close to the landmark: drop anchor near the
beach... You're all set with your gear?

DEMETRIE
Got the gear, got the coolest swimsuit... The coolest
that you'll ever know, at least. I'm the greatest diver
ever with my water gun.

SNEAKY HERMIT
Cool, Daddy O, how about you take yourself down to
the H_2O and get us some secret stuffs, yo with wing.

DEMETRIE
Hey, man, you can try to do the cool talk, but you ain't
got it. Just stick to hermit crab talk, please.

SNEAKY HERMIT
Okay, Demetrie, your mission is to find more of these
cannon blast collars. They will help us deal more
damage to the other pirate ships.

DEMETRIE
Awesome. I will find more of those for my man, and I
will fill your basket up as fast as I can, bro.

SNEAKY HERMIT
Awesome... Hey, do you want some 3D glasses with
your scuba mask? Might help you spot sharks... We
breached the surface, and we are lowering the basket
for you to drop the blast collars into... Nice work,
Demetrie. We've got one blast collar in the basket
already... Great work, just three more. Just keep on
going, Demetrie... Excellent, Demetrie! Now it's time
for you to do another thing: to get these blast collars to
work, we need the help of some yellow fish. There will
be some hammerhead sharks looking for those fishes
as well, so get ready for some fast swimming. We need
you to grab two fish for us... Nice work, we just need

one more fish... Excellent work, Demetrie. Here come the hammerhead sharks. Now you can shoot them for us! Nice shooting. We need to get as many sharks out of the area as possible. You are an awesome underwater swimmer, Demetrie. You just need to take out one more hammerhead shark now... Nice! That's all the hammerhead sharks. With them out of the picture, we have enough cannon blast collars to attack all the pirates ships when we head back to Bad Blood Bay. You are almost a new member of the Bouthiette Gang. We'll see how smart that Frank is with a cannonball in his face.

GREGORY
Anti Gregory, let's set sail, buddy.

ANTI GREGORY
You got it, Captain Gregory.

PANDA
Anti Gregory, you know that he is not really the captain of this ship.

GAGE
Come on, Panda, just let Anti Gregory have a little fun. I always do.

PANDA
Okay, Gage, I'll let him have his fun as well. But why does he always do it while on his missions?

GREGORY
It's just how he is, Panda. And not to make you mad, but I don't think you know how to have a good time yourself.

PANDA
You know, Gregory, I think you are right. I can try to have fun... With your help.

GAGE
Don't worry, Panda. Once when we are done here, Anti Gregory might help you have fun.

PANDA
I think he can. I'm going below deck now.

GAGE
Hey, Panda, wait up. I'm coming with you.

SNEAKY HERMIT
We're closing in on one of the red sail's dog clan. Get ready for a fight... Excellent, we got one away from it's pack. Just fire at the ship, and be ready to go onboard... Their masts are down, ram him and jump onboard... Deal with this red sail captain, and his crew are sure to surrender... Nice fight, Gregory. We've got another spot for us to have another fight with the other red sail dog clans... Get ready, fellows, we're getting closer to the action... It's a three-on-one battle! You're up, Gregory! That's the last of the red sail dog clan. With them out of the picture, we won't have anyone else to stop us from getting to Bad Blood Bay... Anti Gregory, send us to Crusher now.

ANTI GREGORY
You got it, Sneaky Hermit. I'll take us to Crusher right now.

SNEAKY HERMIT
Anti Gregory, are we almost there, buddy?

ANTI GREGORY
Yes, Sneaky Hermit, we are almost there. I think The Panda wants to come up and be with us.

PANDA
And you are right, Anti Gregory. I think you guys might need my help out here with the sea monster. I've got

my fireworks ready.

GREGORY
That's good, Panda. We'll really need your help with
the sea monster.

ANTI GREGORY
Okay, guys, I'm going below deck now.

GREGORY
You do that, Anti Gregory. We'll be going down soon,
too.

SNEAKY HERMIT
These deep, misty waters are said to be home for the
monster. Keep a sharp eye out.

GREGORY
Sorry, Sneaky Hermit, but I can't see anything in this
fog. If the sea monster is here, there's no way we'll find
him.

SNEAKY HERMIT
Panda, do you have any fireworks that can light the
place up a little to make it easier to spot the creature?

PANDA
My fireworks are not flashlights. Once I light them,
they can never stay forever. They come, then
disappear... Like lightning.

GREGORY
We should really get out of here. With fog this bad, we
might sail into a rock! The boat might take some real
damage.

PANDA
The sea monster is under us. Go below deck and warn
the others. I will take this monster down with my

fireworks.

GREGORY
Give a shout if you need any backup. I'll stand ready.

PANDA
So, now you choose to face me. Behold: The Panda, your master! Hide underwater? Hide from your fight!

GREGORY
The ship's getting pulled under. If we get tipped over too far on any side, we're as good as dead... Things are looking pretty bad down here.

PANDA
Yes, rise and let me punish you! Gregory, you are being needed now.

GREGORY
I'm here. What's the score?

PANDA
Protect the ship while I go below deck and get some more fireworks.

GREGORY
Uh, sure thing... Sneaky Hermit, did you check out that fight? Crusher must be on his last legs or something. I mean, what could he have left?

SNEAKY HERMIT
I'd say about another 10,000 tentacles. Just a rough guess... I got an idea! Whack the tentacles so that they stick to the ship. Then he'll have to come and pull them off... You got him, keep it up!

PANDA
A great battle that was. The two winners' names are The Panda and Gregory Bouthiette.

GREGORY
You really softened him up for me.

DEMETRIE
That was a solid action battle, bros. You two stand tall.

SNEAKY HERMIT
Say, Gage, do you think that you can get into the
creature's mind?

GAGE
Yes, I can, Sneaky Hermit.

SNEAKY HERMIT
Perfect, let's get to a spot with clear water.

GAGE
Leave it to me, you guys. I will get into his mind in no
time.

SNEAKY HERMIT
Then let's do it. Let's try to get ourselves a sea monster
on our side.

GREGORY
What's he trying to do?

SNEAKY HERMIT
Giving us a new ally out here on the sea.

GAGE
Crusher, I want to control your mind for the pirates.

ANTI GREGORY
Gage, don't leave us!

SNEAKY HERMIT
Don't worry, Anti Gregory, we will see him again.

ANTI GREGORY
Okay. What are we going to do now?

SNEAKY HERMIT
We are ready for the operation. For this operation, we are going back to Bad Blood Bay to free our friend Pinky, because A) she could be on Frank's ship, or B) she could also be in the Skull Keep. These are the two spots we need to check to see where they're hiding Pinky. Once we get back to Bad Blood Bay, we will be up for a pirate ship battle with Frank's ship. Do not sink this one, because Pinky might be onboard. Gregory will check the ship and Skull Keep while I control the Bouthiette ship. Once Greginator finds Pinky, I can hop on and save her. We'll have Pinky back on our team, and Demetrie, too.

GREGORY
Okay, let's go, Anti Gregory. I need you to take the wheel back to Bad Blood Bay.

ANTI GREGORY
You got it, Gregory. I'll take the wheel on the ship.

SNEAKY HERMIT
I'll be staying down here and looking at our plans, guys.

PANDA
Oh, Sneaky Hermit, stop it. Please. Your jokes are just bad.

DEMETRIE
I have to agree with him, Sneaky Hermit, bro. Your jokes are just bad.

SNEAKY HERMIT
Don't you guys think I know that by now? I'm doing it because it makes me happy, so you guys can just shut

up and go away now.

GREGORY
Battle stations! We're heading into action.

ANTI GREGORY
It's gonna be tight sailing in here, Gregory. Keep an eye
out for rocks.

GREGORY
Frank's masts are down; ram him, then jump onboard.

FRANK
Really, Bouthiette? A bad choice jumping onboard with
a lot of pirates. You know that you will never take them
down.

GREGORY
I don't know about all of you, but I'm sure I can take
them.

FRANK
Yeah, but you'll never manage to stay alive with all of
these pirates everywhere. Take heart, boys! It's been a
long time since we seen a good plank-walking.

GREGORY
Making me walk the plank? You are bad at making
good ideas, Frank. How uncreative.

FRANK
Not creative? I'll show you who can create ideas, you
little butthead!

GREGORY
That's the best back talk that you can come up with?
Your trash talk is nothing.

FRANK
That was not trash talk, blubbering Bouthiette, because
soon enough the sharks will take a bite out of you.

GREGORY
You got a real knack for pirate talk: put two words
together, and pow, scary pirate name-calling.

FRANK
Now that is just wrong, Bouthiette. Besides, you know
that I still have the girl, and you will never find her.

GREGORY
I'm not worried about Pinky: a girl as tough as her can
free herself by tomorrow morning, then come and steal
your wallet.

FRANK
Yeah, but that chick will never escape from the Skull
Keep. She's locked up in there, and there she stays until
she agrees to love me... Now be the time the sharks
lunch on your parts.

GREGORY
You're the captain... Step on it, Anti Gregory! They got
Pinky locked up in the Skull Keep.

ANTI GREGORY
Check!

FRANK
What? The butthead is getting away! After him, boys!
No matter what happens. It's all-out war.

GREGORY
Heads up, Anti Gregory, the whole town is trying to
blast us... Drop me off at the dock... I'll make a run for
Pinky, you stay here and keep the boat safe. We're
going to need it for the escape.

GREGORY BOUTHIETTE

ANTI GREGORY
Safe as a baby. Now get moving.

SNEAKY HERMIT
Gregory, there's a back walkway behind the Skull Keep.
Jump on the floating boxes. Pinky and I made a
walkway all the way to the top.

GREGORY
Pinky, are you here? It is time for a rescue... Frank's
trick! He's good.

FRANK
Ha! The landlubber fell for it. I told him he can not
trick the smartest man on the seven seas. Right,
Second Mate Jones?

SECOND MATE JONES
Aye, sir.

FRANK
Make sure that the Bouthiette ship doesn't get away.

SECOND MATE JONES
Um, sir, I have something to tell...

FRANK
Don't push my buttons, Second Mate Jones, or I will
kill you.

SECOND MATE JONES
The Bouthiette ship is making for the open water, sir.

FRANK
Hmm. You're right, Second Mate Jones. I think you
know what we need to do.

SECOND MATE JONES
Aye, sir.

ANTI GREGORY
Sneaky Hermit, Gregory's all blown up, and Frank's
boat is gaining on you.

SNEAKY HERMIT
Keep it together. If I can try to get to the open water, I
might be able to give this guy the slip.

ANTI GREGORY
But Gregory...

SNEAKY HERMIT
Keep it together! We're not done yet.

FRANK
Crap, they will make it out in this wind. I think we need
to shoot their mast, Second Mate Jones.

SECOND MATE JONES
Aye, sir.

FRANK
Get the cannons ready, and aim at the Bouthiette
ship... Fire! Avast there, you thought you could fool the
smartest man of the seven seas, but you can't get to
open water now!

SNEAKY HERMIT
Sorry, Frank. But I think this water is deep enough.

FRANK
Deep enough to be your grave.

SNEAKY HERMIT
Gage! Crusher, now!

FRANK
Ah! By thunder!

GREGORY BOUTHIETTE

SECOND MATE JONES
Crusher! Crusher! We're doomed!

GAGE
Hey there, Sneaky Hermit. It's good to see you again.

SNEAKY HERMIT
Good to see you, too. I might need you to help me save
Pinky. Just make sure that you whack the guards when
they come onboard.

PINKY
Sneaky Hermit, is that you up there?

SNEAKY HERMIT
It's a rescue, Pinky, hold tight... Done.

PINKY
Sneaky Hermit, thank you. I owe you one.

FRANK
Call off your squid, or the girl gets it.

SNEAKY HERMIT
Back off, Gage. I'll deal with this guy.

FRANK
I am tired of you Bouthiettes pushing my buttons. It's
time for you all to pay. You will never fool the smartest
man of the seven seas.

SNEAKY HERMIT
You getting this, Gregory?

GREGORY
Yeah, I got a plan to help you out...

FRANK
Avast!

SNEAKY HERMIT
Gage, get Gregory! He can't swim.

FRANK
Aye, shipmate, but who will be saving you?

SNEAKY HERMIT
Dang it.

PINKY
Nobody touches that hermit crab but us.

FRANKY
Me pirate flower, I thought you would never turn your
back on me... But you did turn your back on me to save
this fool.

PINKY
I like another smart guy, and he will beat you at your
own game.

FRANK
Alright, I've had enough of you. It's time for a duel: the
last person still standing wins.

PINKY
Get back here! Stand and take it!

FRANK
Smartest man of the seven seas!

PINKY
Are you okay, Sneaky Hermit?

SNEAKY HERMIT
Yeah, I am, Pinky. Thanks for the help.

GREGORY
Pinky, are you guys okay?

PINKY
Yeah, we are, Gregory. I just beat Frank in a fight, and
he's getting eaten by sharks now.

ANTI GREGORY
I guess he's not the smartest man of the seven seas
anymore.

PANDA
Yeah, he's not. And we got our two team members
back, plus Demetrie.

DEMETRIE
I would like to join you guys for the Bouthiette vault
job, please.

SNEAKY HERMIT
We always have room for you, Demetrie. Besides, you
did help us out in one of our missions today, bro.

DEMETRIE
Thanks, Sneaky Hermit, bro. I will help you guys out.

SNEAKY HERMIT
Okay. Now that we have Demetrie, it's time to head to
Dreaded Gregory's hideout, guys.

ANTI GREGORY
And that's where we'll find the Bouthiette vault.

SNEAKY HERMIT
Yeah, that's right, Anti Gregory. Is everyone ready for
the Bouthiette vault job?

GAGE
We're all ready, Sneaky Hermit.

SNEAKY HERMIT
Okay, guys, let's get a move on now. It's time to finish

our adventure now.

ANTI GREGORY
Dreaded Gregory, you better get ready for us! We're coming for you, butthead.

***

And now...

420

GREGORY
Whoa, that was a long flashback...

DREADED GREGORY
Well, welcome back, Gregory. I hope you had a good
flashback. While you were gone, I took you and
strapped you down.

GREGORY
What are you gonna do to me, Dreaded Gregory?

DREADED GREGORY
Oh, Gregory... You just don't get it, do you? I will never
let you know what I'm gonna do because that will give
away my plans. And I don't want to do that.

GREGORY
You know I will beat you when I get out of here,
Dreaded Gregory.

DREADED GREGORY
Yes, I do know that, Gregory. But I'm gonna take you
with me just in case one of your friends try to come
save you.

CARMELITA
Lieutenant Drew, get your men together. We're about
to do battle with Dreaded Gregory.

LIEUTENANT DREW
Yes, Carmelita... Alright, men, get ready to fight. We're
going in.

DREADED GREGORY
Oh, great! We've got some cops coming to save you,
Gregory.

CARMELITA
Hold on, Gregory! Men, attack!

GREGORY BOUTHIETTE

LIEUTENANT DREW
Okay, Carmelita, we're moving in now.

GREGORY
Come on, Carmelita. You can do it. I believe in you.

DREADED GREGORY
[on intercom]
Attention, guards: we've got some cops that are trying
to save Gregory Bouthiette, and I'm going to need you
to stop them.

LIEUTENANT DREW
Hey, Carmelita: we need you to come and help us out
here, please. Dreaded Gregory just called in his guards
to stop us, and it looks like there's a lot of them.

CARMELITA
Hang on, men. I'm on my way right now.

DREADED GREGORY
Hey, Gregory, is that your little girlfriend coming to
save you?

GREGORY
Yes, Carmelita is coming to save me, and no, she is not
my girlfriend.

CARMELITA
So, you've got friends, and I've got a shock pistol: we're
even, Dreaded Gregory.

DREADED GREGORY
You are a butthead, Carmelita. Do me a favor and hold
still so that I can smack you around... Hey, Carmelita,
why are you invading my plans?

CARMELITA
I'm here to save my friend, Dreaded Gregory, and you

are gonna be going to jail when I'm done with you.

DREADED GREGORY
Come on, Carmelita! What did I do this time? This is Gregory's fault. He should be going to jail, not me.

CARMELITA
You will not blame this on Gregory, Dreaded Gregory. You can only blame yourself.

DREADED GREGORY
How many times do I have to tell you, Carmelita? Gregory is the one who should be blamed.

CARMELITA
First things first, Dreaded Gregory: put Gregory down, and we can finish this once and for all.

DREADED GREGORY
I'm sorry, Carmelita, but I don't trust you. I can throw you far away from here, and you will have to face my guards instead of saving Gregory Bouthiette... Now to find those glasses... Poor Gregory, he looks just like his family. And he'll be as dead as them soon enough.

SNEAKY HERMIT
Gregory! He's over here! He's still breathing! He's alive! Hang on, buddy, we'll get you back on the boat and patch you up... Gregory is going to be okay, but he hit his head hard, so he's gonna be out for a while. But I think he'd want us to get his glasses back for him.

DEMETRIE
Go grab the glasses, jump in, do the swim and take it. It's just that easy to do, bro.

PINKY
Won't be that simple: that pool will shock anyone who has any metal on them.

SNEAKY HERMIT
She's right; get too close, and your diving gear will get
shocked by it. No, to get Gregory's glasses back we
need help from friends without metal.

GAGE
I think I can do it, and I can even get help from the
sharks.

SNEAKY HERMIT
That's a good idea, Gage. Do you think you can really
do that?

GAGE
Yeah, Sneaky Hermit, I can do this for The Greginator.

SNEAKY HERMIT
Okay, I believe you. Just try your best to get his glasses
back... Jump on the sharks' backs to control them. You
need to jump from shark to shark and ride them to the
pool. The sharks should follow you wherever you go...
Watch out, I think Dreaded Gregory has set some
bombs in the water. Try not to hit them.

GAGE
Sneaky Hermit, I've got some bad news for you: I tried
to get the glasses back, but they kind of fell in the
water.

SNEAKY HERMIT
It's okay, the glasses are not really gone. And now that
they're out of the electrified pool, Pinky will help
Demetrie get his diving gear on.

GAGE
I'm such a butthead.

SNEAKY HERMIT
Don't talk like that, Gage. I know you tried your best.

Just leave your shark friends behind, they kind of scare
me. And Gage, Anti Gregory wants to look at some
diapers with you.

GAGE
Okay. I'll be there soon, Sneaky Hermit.

PINKY
Sneaky Hermit is checking on Gregory, and he wants
me to help you get ready for your diving job.

DEMETRIE
I'm all ready to go down in the water and fetch The
Greginator's specs back for him, what do you plan on
doing with all that extra time?

PINKY
My plan is to not be alone with you in a swimsuit.

DEMETRIE
Yeah, you know, I'll get The Greginator's glasses back,
and then we can...

PINKY
Okay, Demetrie, first, get over yourself. And second, I
mean it, get over yourself. Third, jump into that ocean
and get The Greginator's glasses back.

DEMETRIE
You got it, Pinky.

PINKY
Demetrie, you better move faster! I think Dreaded
Gregory is trying to get the glasses, too.

DREADED GREGORY
Well well, if it isn't Demetrie. Coming to get
Bouthiette's glasses back from me? Fine. If you want
these glasses, Demetrie, you're gonna have to fight me

first.

PINKY

Good idea… There's nowhere for you to run, Demetrie.
I'm afraid to say this, but you're gonna have to fight
Dreaded Gregory in order to get those glasses back
from him.

DREADED GREGORY

You may have beat me this time, Demetrie, but you will
not get these glasses back from me.

PINKY

He took the glasses! I'm sorry, Demetrie… I think we
should come up with another plan soon. Just come
back to the ship.

DEMETRIE

That Dreaded Gregory bro was easy to fight. I had him
alone, and then he ran, Pinky, ran! And now I'm flat
nowhere.

PINKY

You were awesome in that underwater cave, Demetrie.

DEMETRIE

I think I may deserve a kiss for my fighting skills.

PINKY

Slow down. Remember rules one and two.

DEMETRIE

I know rules one and two, Pinky. I'm just a little
tweaked now. Mad, you know?

PINKY

I'm going to check on Sneaky Hermit. You… Just have
fun being you.

DEMETRIE
I will be going below deck and thinking of another way
to get The Greginator's glasses back.

PINKY
Gregory, you're up!

SNEAKY HERMIT
He should be in bed after the attack he took. Another
hit like that and your brain could snap.

GREGORY
Quit your worrying, I feel fine. Did Demetrie find my
glasses?

PINKY
No, Dreaded Gregory managed to get away with them.

GREGORY
Then we gotta go.

SNEAKY HERMIT
You're going nowhere, buddy. With Dreaded Gregory
around the Bouthiette vault, we can't make a good
plan. And those radar towers... Wait, Pinky, have you
practiced the punching mechanic on your RC car?

PINKY
Yeah... Oh! I see where you're going! That will work!
Smash the drones from the radar towers.

SNEAKY HERMIT
Perfect. Let's get your RC car on the track.

GREGORY
Not to interrupt this little plan of yours, but, uh, what
in the world are you two talking about?

PINKY
Explaining it will take too much time with many long,
uncool words. I could just show you.

GREGORY
Bring on the demo.

PINKY
Panda, can you launch my RC car onto that track?

PANDA
No problem. With my fireworks, it will fly as if a bird...
Fly, bird, fly.

SNEAKY HERMIT
Alright, our awesome RC car driver, time to destroy
those radar towers. Just pick up those pink balls, and
you can use them to destroy the radar towers. Just use
your RC car's punchers to knock the other RC cars off
the track. Once you get enough of the little pink balls,
I'll open the gate to the radar tower.

PINKY
Make way for the lady... Sorry, but I'm not playing nice.

SNEAKY HERMIT
Alright, the first gate to the radar tower is open.

PINKY
Scratch one radar tower... Oh, hello. And goodbye. Out
of the way!

SNEAKY HERMIT
Alright, I've opened the second gate.

PINKY
There goes number two.

SNEAKY HERMIT
You are very awesome at destroying things, Pinky.

PINKY
Ladies first... Mama's angry at you, son! Later,
butthead!

SNEAKY HERMIT
The third jump gate is all yours, and... Yes! All three
radar towers are cooked. Pinky, you're awesome.

PINKY
Thanks, Sneaky Hermit. I'm gonna be going below
deck now.

SNEAKY HERMIT
Okay, Pinky. I'll be down there soon... With all three
radar towers destroyed, we should have clear sky for
you to fly the Bouthiette plane.

GREGORY
I'm ready. I rested long enough.

SNEAKY HERMIT
Are you sure that you want to do this?

GREGORY
Come on, Sneaky Hermit, I'm The Greginator here.
This is my destiny we're fighting for here.

SNEAKY HERMIT
I know, but it might be a little hard getting up there.

GREGORY
It's gonna be harder down here when I watch the
others fight my battles for me.

SNEAKY HERMIT
Well, I got some goggles for you to wear until we get

your glasses back from Dreaded Gregory.

GREGORY
Thanks, Sneaky Hermit. I will keep these goggles with
me forever.

SNEAKY HERMIT
To stop those guns from firing, you're gonna have to
shoot their little ammo boxes. Wait until they're done
shooting before you shoot... Nice shooting! Good thing
Pinky took out those radar towers, or else those guns
would be shooting their missiles at you instead... Looks
like there are some bats coming to try and stop you as
well... Those bats have shields around them! You have
to shoot down the shields first, then you can shoot the
bats... Quick, before its shield comes back up! Good
shooting, Gregory, but it looks like Dreaded Gregory is
coming for you now...

DREADED GREGORY
Well, it's good to see you back on your feet again,
Gregory. How about you land your Bouthiette plane
and then you can just use your flying powers?

SNEAKY HERMIT
That's a good idea. You should use your flying powers.
You'll be able to fight Dreaded Gregory in the air.

DREADED GREGORY
Uh, Gregory, I think I should destroy you now while
we're both flying.

GREGORY
Just shut up, Dreaded Gregory. I tried to beat you once
before, and I can try to do it again.

DREADED GREGORY
Oh Gregory, you just don't get it, do you? No matter
how many times you try, you will never defeat me.

GREGORY
Okay, you know what, Dreaded Gregory? How about I just fight you now?

DREADED GREGORY
Okay, fine! Whatever! Let's do this... You think you can catch me, but you can't follow me into a new part of the sky! Captain Jacob, bring in my blimp now. I'm gonna have a little fun with Gregory on top of the blimp... Thanks, Captain Jacob. Now Gregory will try and follow us again...

GREGORY
This isn't working, Sneaky Hermit. He's just playing with us.

SNEAKY HERMIT
I'm trying to think of something, Gregory. Just give me time...

GREGORY
I'm finishing this once and for all.

SNEAKY HERMIT
Flying to the top of that big blimp? You're out of your mind!

DREADED GREGORY
You know, Gregory, I'm really impressed with your moves, and your powers, too. But you'll never be good enough to beat me.

GREGORY
I don't get it, why are you trying to get into the Bouthiette vault, Dreaded Gregory? You know you're not a Bouthiette.

DREADED GREGORY
You think I don't know that, Gregory!

GREGORY
You might look like me, Dread Gregory, but I'm just trying to be a nice guy. And nice guys always win.

DREADED GREGORY
You always tell me the same story, Gregory, but who's winning now?

GREGORY
This is just a set-up to steal my glasses, and to get my friends to turn on me.

DREADED GREGORY
No, not really, Gregory. I know that you and Sneaky Hermit are really good friends, and you guys have been with each other for a long time.

GREGORY
Yeah, that's right, we have been together for a long time. And we're like a family, Dreaded Gregory. Equals.

DREADED GREGORY
Then why is it called the Bouthiette Gang?

GREGORY
That's enough, Dreaded Gregory. I've got the glasses now.

DREADED GREGORY
I'll see you later, Gregory Bouthiette.

GREGORY
Time to meet the past... Sneaky Hermit, are you there?

SNEAKY HERMIT
Yeah, buddy.

GREGORY
I'm about to head into the Bouthiette vault, and I want

you and Anti Gregory to come with me. We're a team,
and a family, too.

GREGORY

SNEAKY HERMIT
Okay. We'll be right up, Gregory.

ANTI GREGORY
Wow, this is so cool. I never thought I would be in the
Bouthiette vault.

SNEAKY HERMIT
You can say that again, Anti Gregory. This place is
really cool.

GREGORY
I'm glad that you guys are happy to be in here, but it
looks like I need to go on ahead alone.

SNEAKY HERMIT
Do it, Gregory. This place was built for you. We'll hold
down the fort here.

GREGORY
Hmm. It could be dark in there... My ancestors really
knew how to make this place: nothing but huge piles of
gold... My very first ancestor was Jackson Bouthiette:
he knew how to crawl under tight spaces to get to the
other side of fire walls... Alex J. Bouthiette was a very
tough hero back in 1945. He discovered how to get to
very high places, though I am very scared of heights...
Drew Bouthiette was a bad hero back in 1932. He kind
of stole some stuffs, but then he became a very good
hero when he found out how to jump very fast...
Sammy H. Bouthiette was a really good hero from Los
Angeles. He was the one who taught me how to pick
guys up and then slam them down hard... Drake
Bouthiette was the first one to discover how to climb
on ropes and ladders. He even looks like my favorite
rapper... Jake Bouthiette was a very strong hero, and

he knew how to take on a lot of guards alone... This looks like my father's work. I think it's easier to do because he knew I like easier things to do. Nice work, dad... This must be the main door to the secret place that I really want to be. I just wish Sneaky Hermit and Anti Gregory were here to see this...

SNEAKY HERMIT
Well, we're holding the fort out here.

ANTI GREGORY
This is going to be the awesomest day. I will never forget it in my life.

SNEAKY HERMIT
I know that you're enjoying yourself, Anti Gregory, but do you think that you're just playing as a third wheel for Gregory?

ANTI GREGORY
No way, Sneaky Hermit, Gregory is the most awesome friend ever! I really like working with you and Gregory.

SNEAKY HERMIT
Yeah, sure, we all got here together, but where are we now? Only Gregory is inside the vault.

ANTI GREGORY
Watch out!

SNEAKY HERMIT
Dreaded Gregory's goons! They must have gotten through the door before we closed it.

ANTI GREGORY
Think of it this way, Sneaky Hermit: if that were you in that vault, and Gregory and I were out here, what would Gregory do?

SNEAKY HERMIT
Stop these guards, and protect his friends.

ANTI GREGORY
Right, and that's what I'm gonna do. Just keep your head down. I'm about to start cracking skulls, and I don't want yours to be one of them... Come and get it, you buttheads! I'm gonna kick all of your butts, and I'm going to crack open your heads one by one, and you guys are gonna be going down. Time for a beat down.

DREADED GREGORY
Uh, Anti Gregory, I knew that you were very awesome for fighting all of my guards by yourself.

ANTI GREGORY
That's right, Dreaded Gregory, and I'm gonna take you down next.

DREADED GREGORY
I know that, and I think that you should just shut up for a while.

SNEAKY HERMIT
Hey, you don't tell Anti Gregory to shut up, Dreaded Gregory! How would you like it if somebody told you to shut up?

DREADED GREGORY
I really don't mind if somebody tells me to shut up, Sneaky Hermit. I'll tell Anti Gregory to shut up if I want to.

SNEAKY HERMIT
It doesn't matter what you say to me, but you're being mean to Anti Gregory, and Gregory as well. I'm going to stop you.

GREGORY BOUTHIETTE

ANTI GREGORY
Me too.

DREADED GREGORY
Fine, you Bouthiette Gang. I give up.

CARMELITA
Hold it right there, Dreaded Gregory. You're going to
jail now.

GREGORY
Nice to see you again, my pretty lady.

CARMELITA
You too, buddy.

DREADED GREGORY
I don't like friendships. I may be beaten, but I'll take
you down first, Carmelita.

GREGORY
Not her!

CARMELITA
No one hurts my best friends... Gregory! Can you hear
me, buddy?

GREGORY
Carmelita? Is that you?

CARMELITA
Yes, it's me, Gregory. Are you okay?

GREGORY
I don't think so, Carmelita. Dreaded Gregory tried to
end you for good, but I took the shot for you.

CARMELITA
You didn't have to do that for me, Gregory.

GREGORY
I know, Carmelita, and I'm sorry. I want you to take me
back to my place and tell Bartley to turn me into a
cyborg, please.

CARMELITA
You know I will tell him that for you, buddy.

SNEAKY HERMIT
Gregory! You in here, Gregory?

CARMELITA
Sneaky Hermit! Up here, buddy.

SNEAKY HERMIT
Carmelita, it's good to see you again. What are you
doing in here? And where's Gregory?

CARMELITA
I have him, Sneaky Hermit. And Dreaded Gregory is
over there. I need you to take Gregory back for me,
Sneaky Hermit. And hurry!

SNEAKY HERMIT
Why? What happened to Gregory?

CARMELITA
Dreaded Gregory tried to shoot me, but Gregory took
the shot for me. He wants us to take him back to his
place so that Bartley can turn him into a cyborg.

SNEAKY HERMIT
Okay, Carmelita, I will... But wait, what are you gonna
do to Dreaded Gregory?

GREGORY BOUTHIETTE

CARMELITA
I'm gonna put Dreaded Gregory in jail, Sneaky Hermit.
I'll see you guys later. Now go! This place is coming
down now.

SNEAKY HERMIT
Okay, you got it, Carmelita. I'll see you later. Gregory,
I'm sorry, buddy. This shouldn't have happened to you,
my friend. Anti Gregory and I tried to stop Dreaded
Gregory, but he still managed to shoot you.

ANTI GREGORY
Hurry, Sneaky Hermit! This place is about to go... And
what happened to Gregory?

SNEAKY HERMIT
I'll tell you later, Anti Gregory. Now drive faster! We
need to get out of here.

ANTI GREGORY
Okay, you got it, Sneaky Hermit. But first, we need to
pick up our friends as well.

SNEAKY HERMIT
Okay, but hurry, please. Gregory's not really moving at
all.

PANDA
Sneaky Hermit, it's The Panda. Are you guys coming
back now?

SNEAKY HERMIT
Yes, we are, Panda. Get the others and tell them that
we need to go to Gregory's place. We have a little
surprise for you guys.

PANDA
Okay, Sneaky Hermit. I will get the others right now.

GAGE
Sneaky Hermit, I'm already outside. I'll be waiting for you guys to pick me up at this spot.

SNEAKY HERMIT
Okay, Gage, we're on our way right now.

ANTI GREGORY
Sneaky Hermit, I see them! I'll bring out the wings right now.

SNEAKY HERMIT
Okay, Anti Gregory, let's pick up the others and get out of here.

ANTI GREGORY
You got it, Sneaky Hermit.

PINKY
Hey, guys, I see them! They're coming back now.

ANTI GREGORY
Hurry up, guys, get in fast! We're going back to Gregory's place.

GAGE
Okay. I'm coming to sit up front with you, Anti Gregory.

ANTI GREGORY
Okay, Gage, hurry up. Gregory's not moving.

GAGE
What happened to Gregory, Sneaky Hermit?

SNEAKY HERMIT
Dreaded Gregory tried to shoot at Carmelita, but Gregory took the shot for her, and he wants us to go back to his place and let Bartley turn him into a cyborg.

PANDA
Yeah, we should be going now. Step on it, Anti Gregory.

ANTI GREGORY
Okay, Panda. Now hold on tight, you guys, and shut up.
We're going to fly back home.

GAGE
You heard Anti Gregory, you buttheads: hold tight and
shut up.

CARMELITA
Good luck, you guys. I'll see you all later.

SNEAKY HERMIT
Okay, Carmelita, we'll see you later.

ANTI GREGORY
We're at Gregory's house now!

GAGE
And there's Bartley.

BARTLEY
Sneaky Hermit and Anti Gregory! Where is Gregory?
Oh, and Pinky! And Demetrie, Gage, Panda...

SNEAKY HERMIT
Gregory needs help, Bartley. He wants you to turn him
into a cyborg. Can you do that?

BARTLEY
Yeah, I can turn him into a cyborg, Sneaky Hermit. I
am going to need your help, Sneaky Hermit and Anti
Gregory.

***

CARMELITA
How are you feeling, Gregory?

GREGORY
Like I'm ready for another adventure.

CARMELITA
That's cool, buddy. I put Dreaded Gregory in jail, and
he sent this letter.

GREGORY
Thanks, Carmelita. You're a real friend.

Dear Gregory,

I hope you're happy that I am in jail now. But when I get out of here, I will be coming after you and your friends again. See you soon, Gregory Bouthiette.

From
Dreaded Gregory

I'LL GET YOU BOUTHIETTES IF IT'S THE LAST THING I DO
An Afterword by Josh Myers

When Joe and I first got the notion to actually take a proper crack at starting up a micropress and doing our own thing, it was hardly a few seconds in before the subject of Gregory's work came up. Joe had mentioned to me several times before that his brother enjoyed writing and that he had some fully-formed works at the ready, so it was only natural.

Still, if I'm being perfectly honest, I was quite leery. As with any manuscript, you never know what you're getting into. With all Joe had told me about the book (based on a video game, written completely in dialogue, etc.), I had no idea what to expect. And when I agreed, sight unseen, that we would release Gregory's first book through our fledgling press (as its second book, no less), I couldn't shake the feeling that we were potentially about to shoot ourselves in the foot. But I decided to at least wait until I had seen the work before voicing any concern to Joe.

When Joe sent me Gregory's book and I could finally judge it for myself, all that fear and trepidation vanished.

This was a book we should put out.

This was a book we *had* to put out.

Yes, it's a bit jarring at first.

Yes, it takes liberties with form and structure and damn near everything else.

But it's also creative. It's unique. It's written by someone who gave it his all, just because he enjoyed doing it. And that is what's so damn important about it.

Fiction, particularly in the small press world,

has become so cynical in the last few years. So many writers are trying to be cooler than the next guy, more clever than the next guy, more detached than the next guy. It's getting harder and harder to find someone who just writes what they want to, because they want to.

To my way of thinking, Gregory Bouthiette is a much needed breath of fresh air.

I feel that this book, particularly coupled with the first volume of the *555* project, perfectly cap-tures what Carrion Blue 555 is all about. This book is a mission statement. Make no mistake, it would have been quite difficult to find a home for Greg's first book elsewhere. It's an unfortunate fact that this isn't the sort of thing most small presses would take seriously. It would have been seen as a joke, or a gimmick, or simply too risky.

I understand that.

I also don't give one good goddamn about that.

We put it out because we feel it deserves to be read. We didn't solely put this book out because Gregory is Joe's brother. That's just how we discovered it. If I didn't think this book was worth putting out, I would have told Joe immediately after reading it. There is a talent and a true joy shining through this book that will only expand in the future.

But after it was agreed that we would put the book out, I began to see another reason why this project was so special. Joe took it upon himself to edit Gregory's manuscript, and worked closely with him to clean it up while always maintaining the original vision.

Know this: the voice of the writer is 100% Gregory Bouthiette. But Joseph's presence as a guiding hand, as a mentor, and as a brother, is felt through and through.

The book you've just read is only in your hands because of the creativity of one man, and the love and dedication of his brother. Going for-ward with Carrion

Blue 555, I expect we will always come back to *The Book of Adventures* as a guide.
Thank you for reading.

Josh Myers
Lambertville, NJ
04/10/15

ABOUT THE AUTHOR

Gregory Bouthiette lives with his family in Chicopee, MA. He enjoys playing video games, watching movies and wrestling, and listening to music. His favorite musical artists currently are Drake, Zedd, and Ariana Grande. He is actively working on his second collection, *The Book of Adventures 2: The Adventures of Jake and Mason*, also due to be released by Carrion Blue 555.

Pictured above (from left to right): Gregory Bouthiette, author of this book; Joseph Bouthiette Jr. and Josh Myers, co-editors of Carrion Blue 555; Kaylee Stebbins, #1 fan girl of Carrion Blue 555.

CATALOGUE BLUE 555

CB555-01: 555 Vol. 1: None So Worthy
CB555-02: The Book of Adventures